Dear R

A numerous requests for copies of my earlier novels, Warner has combined two out-of-print books into one edition. *Strange Possession* and *Marriage to a Stranger* are two of my very favorite stories. Both are set in Alaska, the last American frontier, an area that for a long time has held a fascination for me. I hope you will enjoy these two contemporary stories. And look for *Hidden Dreams* and *She Wanted Red Velvet*, to be published in a few months under the title *Wishmakers*.

Please let me know if you enjoy these earlier works. I love hearing from my readers. Drop me a note through my Web site, www.dorothygarlock.com.

Take care,

Dorothy Garlock

BOOKS BY DOROTHY GARLOCK

DOROTHY GARLOCK

Dreamkeepers

STRANGE POSSESSION

MARRIAGE TO A STRANGER

WARNER BOOKS

NEW YORK   BOSTON

Copyright © 1982 by Dorothy Garlock
Excerpt from *Train from Marietta* copyright © 2005 by Dorothy Garlock

This edition published by arrangement with Berkley/Jove.

Strange Possession originally published under the name Johanna Phillips
Marriage to a Stranger originally published under the name Dorothy Phillips

Cover design by Diane Luger
Cover photo by Kunst & Scheidulin/Alamy

Warner Books

Time Warner Book Group
1271 Avenue of the Americas, New York, NY 10020
Visit our Web site at www.twbookmark.com

Printed in the United States of America

First Mass Market Paperback Printing: October 2005

10 9 8 7 6 5 4 3 2 1

ATTENTION CORPORATIONS AND ORGANIZATIONS:
Most WARNER books are available at quantity discounts with bulk purchase for educational, business, or sales promotional use. For information, please call or write:

Special Markets Department, Warner Books, Inc.
1271 Avenue of the Americas, New York, NY. 10020.
Telephone: 1-800-222-6747 Fax: 1-800-477-5925

Table of Contents

Dreamkeepers

BOOK ONE

STRANGE POSSESSION

To Betty O'Haver
sister, friend . . . lovely lady

CHAPTER ONE

THE SMELL OF burning spruce aroused her.

She lay with her eyes closed, feigning sleep. A clatter of iron told her that Mike was satisfied with the blaze in the fireplace and had moved to the big cooking range that dominated the other end of the room. Kelly opened her eyes a crack. He was pouring water from a granite bucket into the reservoir on the side of the range.

The strangeness of it all hit her. Here she was, in this spruce log cabin, deep in the wilderness, two hundred miles north of Anchorage, and she had not felt even a scrap of fright when she was awakened out of a sound sleep by someone moving about the cabin.

How different from Boston and the security-patrolled building where she had lived for eight months. The elegant, marble-floored apartment, its furniture spotlessly maintained, the vases of fresh flowers, arranged and placed in just the right places—somehow it had all seemed unreal.

After the first two months in her Boston home, Kelly should have settled into her new life, but the tension grew daily until she and her husband Jack were living like two hostile strangers. They pretended conjugal bliss in public, but they barely spoke to each other in private.

Jack. Oh, how his sister hated to hear Jonathan Winslow Templeton the Third called . . . Jack! Kelly could see her now, sitting in regal splendor behind the silver coffee service, every hair in place, her critical eyes looking over Kelly's own unruly black hair. The long, slim fingers knew just the right touch on the ornate, silver bell to summon the maid, who would enter the room like a robot, the smooth, discreet carpeting silencing her steps, her black uniform and crisp apron making her a shadow to be ignored. According to Katherine Templeton Hathorn, one didn't smile at a maid or acknowledge her presence as a person.

Katherine had never made any secret of her feelings about the girl her brother had met in Anchorage and married shortly after. To her, Kelly simply did not measure up to the Templeton standards. Katherine was forty-eight, had been married briefly and acquired a stepdaughter, Nancy. Now widowed, her main goal in life was to unite her brother and her stepdaughter in marriage. Kelly had been quite a setback to those plans.

Lazily Kelly opened her eyes and found herself looking directly at a dark window. Night had come quickly. She turned on her back, stretching luxuriously, pleasantly tired and relaxed. She was home! Home, in the wilderness of Alaska, where she had lived since she was ten years old.

After her mother had died fourteen years ago, she and her father had come here. He had built the main room of this cabin with his own hands. Later he had added two bedrooms and built two other cabins to rent out to hunters, as well as the main lodge they used to house winter skiers or people who came to ride snowmobiles on the trails around Mount McKinley. The tourist business had been good since the Anchorage–Fairbanks highway had been completed. They even had electricity now, which made available conveniences they had gotten used to doing without.

Kelly switched on a lamp, and sat up, rubbing her stocking feet on the thick fur rug on the floor. She surveyed the room. Everything was dusty, mousey, and in disorder. Cobwebs swayed like darkened moss in the gentle draft created by the half-open fireplace chimney. Well, what did she expect? she scolded herself. The resort had been closed since her father had died two years ago. Mike had been living here alone since Marty, his twin sister, had taken a job in Fairbanks. No doubt his cabin was spotless. This one would have been, too, if she'd let him know she was coming.

Mike and Marty had lived here almost as long as Kelly. They had arrived with their mother in response to an advertisement for a cook that Kelly's father had placed in the paper. Aunt Mary had been the nearest thing to a mother Kelly had ever known, as her own mother had been ill for many years before she died. Kelly had often wondered why her father never married Aunt Mary. She was sure he loved her. Only after her death did she discover why: Aunt Mary had a husband. A worthless man, who had never contributed to the support of his family, but, nevertheless, a husband. Kelly's father was as fond of Mike and Marty as if they were his own children, and when he died he left half of his estate to them and the other half to Kelly.

Five years ago Kelly had gone to Anchorage to work. Her father approved of her reason for getting away from the resort. Mike was in love with her. Kelly knew she would never feel anything more for him than sisterly love and it hurt her unbearably to see the look of longing in Mike's eyes when she turned suddenly to see him watching her. The whole situation made her want to weep. But out of sight, out of mind, she reasoned. Her job with the newspaper was interesting and on long weekends she could catch the train and be home in less than six hours. She made friends in Anchorage, but none as close as Mike and Marty. When her father died suddenly, it was a shock to them all. Mike had been working as a lineman for the utility company and they decided to close down the resort for the time being.

Four months after her father's funeral, Kelly met Jack. She literally ran him down as she made a dash to the office with her advertising copy. They collided with such force that she was almost flung to the sidewalk. Jack grabbed her and held her until she regained her balance. Then he helped her pick up the scattered pages of copy that had flown from her hand. After that, they stood looking at each other.

He stared at a tall, slim, sparklingly alive person with black hair in a flyaway tangle that stood out around her high-cheekboned face. Black lashes fringed the bluest eyes he had ever seen, but it was the smiling mouth that he couldn't seem to look away from. The upper lip was short, the lower one full and sensuous, and they were parted and tilted at the corners, showing small, perfect teeth.

Meeting the long stare from his deep-set brown eyes,

Kelly felt a curious spark leap between them, although she knew instinctively they came from different worlds. Though she was a tall girl, she still had to tilt back her head to look at him. His crisp brown hair and calm face, uncompromising jawline, hard mouth, and expensive business suit told her he was a man of wealth and position.

She murmured the proper apologies and hurried through the heavy glass door of her office building. It was distinctly untypical of Jonathan Winslow Templeton the Third to pursue a chance meeting, but there he was when she paused to wait for the elevator. He asked her out and she accepted. He was Jack Templeton, from Boston, in Alaska on business, If, during that first evening, he told her what kind of business, it passed her by, for she was in a glorious state of enchantment. He amused her with his wit and clever conversation. He charmed her with bits of flattery, and surprised her with carefully chosen questions about herself. She found herself pouring out her life story and he listened, watching her expressive face, his eyes moving from her blue eyes to the unruly curls and often resting on her sweetly curved mouth.

When he walked her to the door of her apartment that first night, he kissed her. It was by no means Kelly's first kiss, but it shook her to her roots, and she trembled like a leaf. Jack, too, seemed shaken and Kelly remembered him looking down at her in a strange, almost angry way. When her eyes met his, her lips were trembling and he kissed her again, wildly, hungrily. Her arms went around his neck and desire flamed between them.

They spent every possible moment together and within a week Kelly went to bed with him and no words of common sense would have kept her from his arms. She had been out with men before, infatuated with some, half in love with others, but after that first evening with Jack, she was consumed by passion. When he made love to her she was incapable of thought, lost in a sensuous mist, totally responsive to his strong, slender hands and his hard, possessive lips. Jack made no secret of his desire for her, and after that first week, his need deepened into a naked hunger to which she reacted wildly.

After a session of wild lovemaking, he proposed. He whispered hoarsely in her ear that he had to have her—he wanted to marry her. Kelly accepted without hesitation. He drew a deep breath and pulled her against him and held her fiercely, kissing her in a strange, tender, possessive way.

At the quiet wedding in City Hall, with one of Jack's business associates and his wife as witnesses, Kelly still felt that possessive attitude and it thrilled her. Kelly had called Marty and Mike. Marty had not been able to come on such short notice and Mike said a flat "no" to the invitation, but nothing mattered to Kelly as she waited for the moment she and Jack would be alone.

When they returned to Kelly's apartment after the wedding, there was a single yellow rose and a card from Mike that read: "It makes no difference. Love, Mike." Jack arched his brows when he read the message, and asked who it was from. Kelly found it difficult to explain her relationship with Mike—though she tried. Later she realized that marked the beginning of her husband's strange possessiveness.

Jack took her to Boston. Kelly was awed by the splendor of his home, the evidence of wealth and position, and most of all by his sister, Katherine. Two months later she knew she would never fit into his life. She had fallen in love, immediately and wildly. She had childishly married her Prince Charming, without a single thought to the consequences, the repercussions, the kind of life she would be expected to live. Now, with little to do because they had a daily cleaning woman and a cook, Kelly wandered aimlessly around the apartment, like a bird in a gilded cage. Her husband flatly refused to allow her to get a job. She remained isolated in the apartment to await his homecomings.

Jack had become Jonathan. She could not think of him as Jack in their home. An abyss lay between them, bridged only at night, when he came to her in the darkened room. He merely had to lay down beside her and she could feel his pulse accelerate. She accepted his passion and returned it. She was most vulnerable at night and he simply had to kiss her and they would come together with a strange, hot need for each other that consumed Kelly. Afterward she would lie awake hour after hour, until finally, exhausted sleep claimed her. She awoke to reach out for him and find he was gone. What terror and what ecstasy the night held for her!

One day she came downstairs and heard Katherine and Jonathan—that's the way she thought of him now—in the den. Katherine had come to discuss the dinner party they were to give for an important business associate.

"Well, talk to her, Jonathan. If you don't approve of her behavior tell her so." The clear, assured voice came distinctly into the hall and Kelly paused beside the door.

"There are times when I think I shouldn't have married her," Jonathan said tiredly and then angrily slammed his hand down on the desk. "Damn, damn her!" he exploded.

"I knew the instant I set eyes on her that you had made a ghastly mistake," Katherine said drily.

"That's enough, Katherine!" His voice was bitter, harsh.

"Well, it's your problem. The sooner you get out of it the better."

"She's like a ghost wandering around here. I thought maybe if we had a child . . ."

"Heaven forbid! You would be out of your mind to consider having a child by that woman. She's unhappy because she is out of her element. She simply does *not* fit into a cultured world."

"I'm going out of my mind, anyway. I can't concentrate on this deal with Waterman Electronics. I don't know how she'll act this evening. She may move about like a robot, or hide in the kitchen. Something has got to give soon. I can't take much more of this."

"Don't worry about tonight. I've talked to the cook about the menu and ordered fresh flowers. I'll even send over a dress for her to wear. Don't worry, Jonathan. I'll take care of things. I always have."

"Thank you, Katherine. Will Nancy be here?"

"Of course. Nancy will keep the conversation flowing among the women. She will . . ."

Kelly walked stiffly down the hall and into the kitchen, where she leaned against the wall. What had she become? What kind of a fool was she to hover outside a door and listen to her husband discussing her so coldly? It seemed she had lost everything—pride, self-respect, husband.

"Coffee, Mrs. Templeton?" The cook was looking at her strangely. "It's in the dining room."

"Thank you," she murmured, but stood there for a moment before she was able to push herself away from the wall.

She met Jonathan and Katherine in the hallway. Katherine nodded coolly and went out the door. Jonathan stood inspecting her, his mouth compressed, a line etched between his dark brows. Almost guiltily she removed her fingers from the polished surface of the hall table. She had to fight the urge to lift the hem of her skirt and wipe away the offending prints.

"Why don't you go shopping today or get your hair done for tonight?"

"All right." Her voice was expressionless and she looked down at the fingerprints marring the polished wood.

"It's merely a suggestion, not an order," he snapped. "Most women would jump at the chance to have unlimited credit at the shops. You wander around this place like a ghost and dress to fit the part. Look at yourself. You wear things that make you melt into the woodwork." His lips held a slight sneer.

The pain that pierced her heart whitened her face. She looked away from him. Her gaze fell on the door at the top of the stairs, the sweet haven of her bedroom, and she longed to be there out from under the gaze of this stranger she had married. She hurt so much that it seemed a flood of tears was trapped inside her body, yet she could not cry. It was as if her pride had closed the valve on her emotions so tightly that there was no way to release them.

"For heaven's sake!" His harsh voice shattered the silence and he stared at her angrily, for a time saying nothing more.

Kelly couldn't bring herself to look at him. Finally she heard the click of his heels on the marble floor and the slam of the front door. She closed her eyes, wincing.

Somewhere along the way they had lost each other.

Kelly sincerely believed she had tried to find a place for herself among the wives of his friends. The cool reception she received on each overture of friendship was due, she was sure, to the influence of Katherine and Nancy. The men had seemed to enjoy her company, but after one informal party, when in desperation to keep from standing alone she had lingered among them to exchange bits of chitchat and laugh at their light flattery, she had felt Jonathan's piercing eyes from across the room, and Katherine's disapproval.

Cheap and vulgar flirting was the way Jonathan had put it that night when he lost his temper and lectured her with a cruel, icy tongue. He had marched her upstairs to their bedroom and made love to her as if she was a woman he'd paid for. After that, she realized, she had grown frightened of him and began shrinking from him, retreating farther and farther within herself in order not to risk his disapproval.

They had done each other great damage by getting married. She could never be anything except what she was. He could never take her lively, outgoing personality and reshape it to fit into his world. In the process of trying to do so he was destroying everything that was unique and alive about her that had attracted him to her in the first place. She had become quiet and withdrawn, a person she scarcely knew herself. If she had hurt Jonathan, she bitterly regretted it. She only knew he was not the man she had met in Anchorage and she could not continue living with him. There was only one thing to do.

Once she'd decided, Kelly's mind clicked into gear. While she packed, tears trickled down her face and ran into her mouth. She wiped her eyes and pushed damp fingers through her hair. Where had their love gone? It was dead! You couldn't take warm, sweet love and put it in an atmosphere like this and expect it to survive. Divorce was easy these days. Jonathan would find a way to get it over with quickly—and without publicity. With her gone, the blame could be laid at her feet and he could save face.

She began to regain her self-respect. With it came anger like acid in her stomach. She thought about the reception she had received from his sister, about the cold, icy treatment her husband had given her, about the times he had spoken to her as if she tried to seduce every man she talked with. She remembered many times he had brought up Mike's name as if he were a stupid laborer with nothing on his mind but getting her to bed.

She had been the stupid one! She had no one to blame but herself, and it was up to her to get herself out of this impossible situation.

Kelly packed one large suitcase with the things she had brought with her, plus a few things Jonathan—when he was Jack—had bought for her in Anchorage. She placed the large sapphire and diamond ring on top of the note she left on the bedside table. On second thought, she placed her credit cards beside the note, which simply said that they both knew their marriage was a mistake and for him not to worry. She didn't want any kind of settlement—

only her freedom. She regretted that she had been an embarrassment to him and to his sister.

Kelly walked out of the apartment building feeling like a new person. About the time Jonathan, Katherine, and Nancy were greeting their dinner guests, she was stepping off the plane in Portland, Oregon.

The trip had given Kelly time to organize her thoughts. On the way to the airport she had stopped at the bank and withdrawn the money her father had left her. She'd recounted it on the plane. Even after paying for her ticket, she had enough to tide her over until she could find a job.

She had learned advertising layout at the newspaper in Anchorage. Her ads were good and original, and the salesmen who took them to the advertiser had little trouble selling them.

In Portland, Kelly found an efficiency apartment in a moderately priced building. After putting in a supply of food, she went to bed and stayed there for almost two days. She slept, got up and fixed herself a meal, then went back to sleep again. Not until she was in the quiet of her own place with no one to criticize her every move, did she realize how exhausted she was or how her nerves had stretched to almost the breaking point.

The first place she applied for a job hired her. The big, pleasant man who interviewed her was impressed with her knowledge of layout. There was one catch, however. She had to sell her own ideas to the advertisers. She would have a list of potential customers, no other salesman would infringe on her territory, and she would receive a commission, plus salary.

The first month she was astounded at the size of her commission check. She enjoyed her job, and being her own person once again. If she thought about Jack—she was back to thinking of him as Jack—he seemed a person she had met in a very nice dream. She never allowed herself to think about Boston. The months that had seemed so endless became blurred together in her head like a television show she had watched and half-forgotten.

Kelly had been in Portland for four months when she called Marty in Fairbanks and learned that Jonathan was looking for her. Marty giggled when Kelly told her about coming to Portland because that was the only connection she could make when her plane from Boston had reached Chicago. Marty explained that Mike had been especially worried about her after Jonathan, himself, had come out to the resort looking for her. They promised to keep in touch and Kelly swore Marty to secrecy.

That Jonathan was looking for her didn't bother Kelly at all. Let him wait to get his divorce papers signed, she thought bitterly. The wait would pay him back, in some small way, for the miserable time she had spent with him.

The months turned into a year and Kelly began to get homesick for the cozy cabin deep in the Alaskan bush. Soon the autumn snows would fall, and the clouds would scutter before the frigid winds. The days would become short, the nights long. Inside the cabin, warmed by a roaring wood fire, she would feel secure and at peace. She had saved more money than she had dreamed of saving in so short a time. Her little nest egg would go a long way toward putting the resort into operation again.

Kelly worked extra hard for another month, picked up her commission check, suffered through a farewell party given by fellow staff members, and caught a plane to Anchorage.

It was October. The Alaskan days were already short. Kelly sent word to Mike that she'd arrive on the afternoon train, and he was there waiting for her in the utility truck. He didn't ask any questions and she didn't offer any explanations.

The semi-darkened cabin was warm from the fire Mike had built in the fireplace before he came to meet her. He set her suitcases inside the door and went out to put the utility truck in the shed. She wished she didn't know how he felt about her. But it *was* good to be home and that thought crowded all others from her mind for the moment. She sighed heavily and sank down on the worn couch, pulled Aunt Mary's afghan over her, and went back to sleep.

CHAPTER TWO

EVERYTHING WAS AT peace in Kelly's world except her stomach, which was protesting loudly from lack of food. She dipped warm water from the reservoir and washed her face and hands. That would have to do for now. Tomorrow she would turn on the electric water heater and take a long, leisurely bath. As she stood there, Kelly's gaze was caught by her reflection in the small oak-framed mirror over the sink. At twenty five she was hardly over the hill, yet she was disturbingly aware that she was no longer the young, starry-eyed creature who'd left the bush five years ago.

She still remembered what it was like those first few years. As she walked down the street, she positively beamed with the pleasure of living. People turned to stare at her, not because she was so outstandingly beautiful, but because her face glowed with health and animation. Her walk, her whole being was suffused with robust enthusiasm that captured their attention.

Nothing brought a girl down to earth faster than a bad marriage, she thought, hanging up the towel. The sentimental dream-bubble of everlasting love with one man had burst, leaving her achingly empty.

The door opened and Mike's voice filled the cabin.

"Behold! Food cometh!" He kicked the door closed behind him and brought a small iron dutch oven to the cooking range. He lifted the lid and a delicious aroma wreathed up and filled the room.

"Chili! Smells great and I'm starved."

"Me, too. Get the bowls and we'll dig in." Mike hung his jacket on a peg beside the door.

"Not until I wash off two years growth of dust and mouse droppings." Kelly lifted the lid on the reservoir again and ladled hot water into a dish pan.

"A few mouse droppings won't hurt you." Mike grinned.

"Ugh! Don't talk about it!"

Kelly washed the bowls and the silverware, glancing occasionally at Mike's reflection in the mirror. He had turned a chair around and was straddling it. She could almost hear Aunt Mary say, "Michael, turn around and sit properly, for Pete's sake." Mike was looking older, too, Kelly thought, although they were both twenty-five. His hair was not quite as flaxen as it used to be, but it was still thick. He wasn't a handsome man; his face was too irregular for that. She could remember when she had been taller than Mike. Oh, how that used to bug him! Finally when they were about eighteen he had caught up with her, and now there wasn't a half-inch difference in their heights.

She felt guilty because she couldn't love him the way he wanted to be loved. Sometimes she wished desperately that she could feel a soul-stirring pleasure in his arms, feel electrified by his touch. He was so comfortable, so dear. He deserved much more than she could give him.

"You're going to rub holes in those bowls," Mike said softly.

The silence was charged with expectancy. Their relationship from now on would depend on this evening. Oh, God! Kelly thought, she'd need help. She didn't want to hurt him.

"Maybe so, but they're clean. Fill them up and let's eat. My stomach thinks I've deserted it."

"That's not all you deserted," Mike said with his back to her. "Why in the hell did you marry him, Kelly?"

"Love. A vastly overrated emotion, as I soon discovered."

He set the bowls on the table and rested a hand on the top of her head. "I've missed you."

She nodded, not answering, not disputing. She had missed him too . . . and Marty. They had been a part of each other for most of their lives and her marriage had cut her off from them.

"What happened when Jonathan came here?"

Mike's wide mouth hardened. "Not much."

"But what?"

"He looked around the place like he was a king inspecting the hovels where the peasants live. I should have punched him in the nose." Mike got up, opened a cabinet door, and slammed it shut. "I wish I'd brought some coffee."

"Go get it and I'll make a pot later," Kelly said absently.

Mike refilled his chili bowl. "What happened to the

marriage?" he asked when he was sitting across from her again.

"I don't want to talk about it." Pain made her voice harsh.

"From what I saw of him, he's a stiff-necked, arrogant, smart-ass!"

"I don't want to talk about it, Mike. The marriage is over!"

"Not according to him. He said, and I quote, 'She is not getting a divorce. She will be my wife until the day she dies.'"

Kelly's eyes flicked up to meet his and she saw the anger there. Her face flushed under his probing stare.

She shrugged. "He'll get sick of that after a while. His sister will be on his tail to divorce me and eventually he will. In the meanwhile, I couldn't care less about what he does. I never intend to marry again, so he has more to lose than I do." She looked up to see what effect her words had on Mike, but his face was bent over his bowl and his spoon paused only momentarily on its way to his mouth.

He shot her a closed look. "How long are you going to stick around here?"

She laughed. "Trying to get rid of me already? Think I might interfere with your weekend orgies?"

He grinned, relaxing. "You've got to realize, wooden-head," he said, using his old pet name for her, "that I'm a man with all the normal urges and won't wait forever."

"I know, Mike. We're too much like brother and sister to ever be anything more. Remember, Mike, Mike, go fly a kite? And Kelly, Kelly, with a big, fat belly?"

"Yeah," he admitted. "It was fun growing up here. I

wonder what would have happened to us if Uncle Henry hadn't taken us in."

"He never took you in, Mike. Aunt Mary worked hard and made the lodge pay off. My only regret is that she and Dad never married. I know they loved each other."

"Oh, I don't think they missed out on much," he said, with a satisfied smile. "I used to catch them kissing in the kitchen and every once in a while I'd see Uncle Henry pinch her on the bottom."

"You didn't! Why didn't you tell Marty and me?"

"Lots of things happened around here that I didn't tell you and Marty," he said insolently.

"That was stinking of you!"

"Yeah, wasn't it?"

"What other goodies didn't you tell us?" Kelly asked in an exasperated tone. This was a game Mike played very well. In the old days he used to torment her and Marty with his "I know something you don't know" attitude and they would follow him for days trying to wheedle information out of him. "You haven't changed a bit!"

"You have." He leered, his eyes lingering on her soft, rounded breasts beneath the pullover knit shirt. He made a lecherous face. "Time has improved you! You used to be a skinny monstrosity with legs that came almost to your neck!"

"Well, thank you, vile creature! I can remember when your front teeth looked like Peter Rabbit's and your ears like Dumbo's, the elephant. I suppose, now that you've grown so handsome, you have to carry a stick to keep the girls away."

"Let's just say I don't miss any opportunities," he said wickedly.

It was easy for them to fall back into the light banter. It was as if they had never been apart. The only thing missing was Marty.

"Marty said she might come back if we open the resort," Kelly said suddenly, with a fierce longing to have the three of them together again.

"She mentioned it. I don't want to give up my job with the utility company just yet. It'll take a bit of money to put the old place back together again." Mike got up and reached for his coat. "Wash out the pot, woodenhead, and I'll fetch some coffee. Tomorrow I'll run down to Talkeetna so you can stock up. That is if you're sure you're going to stay."

"I was never so sure of anything in my life. I don't think I ever want to leave this place again." She looked away, veiling her expression.

"Five years," he said softly. "You may be addicted to city life and don't know it."

"Go get the coffee, mister know-it-all. I'm a big girl, now, and I know my own mind, at last!"

"I hope so." He grinned. "It's taken you long enough." To emphasize the point, he slammed the door unnecessarily hard when he went out.

Kelly found the old blackened coffee pot, scrubbed it out, and filled it with water. She lifted a lid on the range and set the pot in the round hole so the flames lapped at its bottom.

It was good to be home. Although it was dark, she could see in her mind's eye the peaks of Mount McKinley dominating the skyline. Soon the snows would come . . . that breath of cold air Mike let in when he went out the door told her it could be any day now. The dark, drooping evergreens that shadowed the small settlement of three log cabins and a lodge seemed dreary and mysterious in the summer. But in the winter they appeared graceful and soft, skirted by snow.

There was a lot of work to be done, more than Kelly could possibly do alone, before the lodge would be ready to receive guests. The scrubbing alone would take ages. Another time-consuming chore would be cutting wood for the mammoth fireplace and for heat for her own cabin. That's about all she could depend on Mike doing. She had noticed the neat cords of wood beside his own cabin, probably not a winter's supply, but a good start. Maybe she could hire someone in Talkeetna to help.

Now that she was thinking about it, there were a million things to do and not much time to do them if they wanted to open when the season started. People liked a place to leave their snowmobiles before the highway got snowbound, because many of them would come up on the train, or by skiplane. They'd need a mountain of supplies, and a cook. A cook! That was one job she wouldn't do. She could cook up a meal for herself, but she couldn't on a large scale.

Ideas for advertising began to flick through her mind. They could place ads in the Anchorage and Fairbanks papers. There had been a big change in the economy ever since the oil companies had descended on the state. New corporations had sprung up and young executives had moved up from the States to run them. The country's huge size wouldn't stop them from taking a weekend in the bush. Skiplanes shuttled constantly back and forth between the resorts and the cities. Later, she mused, they could tap the vast resources of Seattle, Portland, and Vancouver for guests. For now, they would concentrate on getting them from closer to home.

Ever since the influx of "foreigners," as Alaskan natives called them, a powerful tide of newfound pride and racial identity had swept the state. Signs saying "Alaska For Alaskans," "Yankee Go Home," and "Happiness Is An Oklahoman Going Home With A Texan Under Each Arm," covered car bumpers. Kelly agreed to a certain extent. This was where she wanted to be, where she wanted to make something good and enduring; here, the only place in the world where she had roots, she didn't want the land spoiled with hamburger stands and neon lights.

Mike came in the door.

"Did you go all the way to Talkeetna to get that coffee?" Kelly teased.

"Had to see about my dogs." He handed her the coffee can and took off his coat.

"Dogs? You've got more than one?"

"I've got a sled team. They're half wild, so be careful."

"Are you going to race them at the Fur Rendezvous?"

"Not in the Anchorage to Nome race, but maybe in one of the shorter ones. I've only had them hitched together a few times. They're wilder than hell." He grinned.

"I want a dog. I can't remember a time when I didn't have one here."

"What kind do you want?"

"I don't care. Just a dog."

Mike went to the door, opened it, and yelled, "Charlie!"

A large, white, shaggy dog came bounding in with a frisbee in his mouth. He looked up at Mike expectantly and wagged his tail. Mike reached down and took the battered, chewed plastic disc. The tail stopped wagging and Charlie's eyes riveted to the frisbee.

"Not in the house, Charlie," Mike said sternly and the tail made a half wag. "Worthless piece of dog meat," he said affectionately and scratched the big head. "You got a two track mind. The frisbee and the . . . ball." Charlie jerked to attention on hearing the magic word. Mike laughed.

"Shame on you for teasing him," Kelly chided. "Come here, Charlie. What kind of a dog is he?"

"Part shepherd, part husky, I think. He's got to be part of something else with the disposition he's got. You can have him if you want him. He doesn't fit in with my sled team at all."

Charlie ambled over to Kelly and sniffed. She scratched his head and he leaned against her.

"How old is he?"

"Two years, I thought he'd outgrow playing with the frisbee and the ball, but it doesn't look like he's going to." Charlie peaked his ears on hearing the magic words again, and Kelly laughed, hugged his furry neck, and received a wet lick across her face for the trouble.

"Shall we team up, Charlie? I'll take care of you if you'll take care of me. What do you say?"

"I'll end up by taking care of both of you," Mike said drily. "Come on, Charlie, take this tooth punctured thing and get out of here." He held out the frisbee and Charlie clamped his teeth on it and bounded out the door. Mike shut it behind him.

Kelly washed mugs and filled them with coffee. "Is

there an extra Citizen's Band radio around, Mike? We used to have one here and in the lodge."

"There's a good base station in the lodge. I'll fix it up and we'll run a couple of substations. Marty's talking about coming back and . . . she might want to open the other cabin."

"She wouldn't have to do that. She could move in here with me."

"I don't think she'd want to do that." Mike grinned knowingly.

"Well, are you going to tell me, or do I have to start wheedling?"

"Start wheedling."

"Oh, come on!"

"All right. If you're going to be that way about it, I'll tell you. It wouldn't surprise me if Marty brought a man back with her."

"Man? You mean she's going to get married?"

"You make it sound so . . . obscene."

"I didn't mean it that way. I'm surprised, that's all. She didn't say anything about having anyone special."

Mike shrugged. "I don't know how special he is."

"Mike!"

He was watching her intently. "Don't get in a sweat. Marty's got a right to make her own mistakes."

"Then you don't like him?"

"Not especially, but that's not what's important, is it?" He got up and put on his coat. "I didn't like Jonathan Templeton, either." He was watching her, trying to read her face, and she looked up at him, her features torn by confused emotions.

"I can't imagine life without you and Marty." For the first time in months she felt weepy.

Mike's face had a strange, hard look on it, but it softened as he came toward her. He bent and kissed her cheek.

"See you in the morning. I've got the day off. We'll take a run up to Talkeetna and pick up a few things."

"I'm too tired to make out a list."

"Don't try. Bed down on the couch. Tomorrow we'll dig into the stuff up at the lodge and make this place livable."

"You're too good to me. What's the catch?"

"I've got designs on your body." He leered and his eyes raked her suggestively.

"Oh, get out of here, you . . . you . . . turkey! Now I know you're nuts!"

Kelly expected to fall asleep at once, but her mind refused to rest. Plans for the lodge, the comfortable relationship she had established with Mike, the prospect of Marty getting married, all blurred together in a swirl of thoughts. She tried to make her mind go blank but Jonathan's words sprang before her. "She will be my wife until the day she dies." Why would he say a thing like that unless he wanted to make Mike angry? But . . . Jonathan wasn't petty. He was probably frustrated because he couldn't get the divorce papers signed. She admitted, reluctantly, that *she* had been petty in making Katherine and Nancy wait for Jonathan's freedom. The marriage had, obviously, hurt him.

"I must divorce him," she said aloud, and the sound of her voice in the silent room startled her. She closed her eyes, feeling drained. Slowly sleep came to ease her troubled mind.

She woke once in the night with tears in her eyes and knew she'd been dreaming about Jack. Under the spell of her passion for him, the dreams they'd shared haunted her like an unforgotten melody. She could see his face, tender with love, bending to hers on their wedding night. "God, but you're beautiful, and you're mine. Say you love me. Say you love . . . only me." Jack faded away and Jonathan was shouting, "I never should have married her . . . damn her!" In the next breath, he muttered agonizingly, "Something's got to give. I can't take much more of this."

Kelly sank into an exhausted sleep and awoke only when she felt something rough and wet on her face. She opened one eye. Charlie was staring at her. She opened the other eye and saw the outside door open. Seconds later, Mike's square body filled it, and he kicked it shut after him. He brought in an armload of wood and knelt beside the fireplace.

"Are you going to lay on your butt all day? Get up, we've got things to do."

CHAPTER THREE

THE FIRST WEEK flew by. The second week ended and Kelly looked back with amazement at what she and Mike had accomplished. First, and most important, they had found Clyde and Bonnie Fisher, a middle-aged couple from Ardmore, Oklahoma. The Fishers had come to Alaska for better pay and found making a living just wasn't all that easy. But they loved the country and wanted to stay. Bonnie cooked fabulous, home-style meals, according to Clyde, and Clyde was about as handy as the pocket on a shirt, according to Bonnie. They both proved to be right.

"Think of the ads I can run in the papers! 'Come to Mountain View Lodge and meet Bonnie and Clyde.' " From the very first Kelly felt as if she had known them forever.

"That's the only reason I married that ugly ol' boy," Bonnie said with spirit, her twinkling eyes seeking out Clyde. "I looked all over the country for a man named Clyde. I swore I was goin' to get me one. We was goin' to be Bonnie and Clyde. Well, this ugly ol' cowboy was the only thing I could find, so I took 'im.'"

"And I let 'er catch me 'cause she's fat and soft and keeps me warm on cold nights."

They were a perfectly matched couple and Kelly loved the good-natured banter that passed between them. They would live in the lodge in the room behind the kitchen, and be more or less responsible for it. Salary didn't matter too much, as long as they had a place to live and food to eat.

The first snow began falling one night and by morning it was a foot deep. Kelly looked out the window at the strange, haunting beauty of a monochromatic landscape, set against the deep blue of the winter sky. She put the copper teakettle on the cookstove and went back to the window to watch Charlie dig his nose deep in the snow and come up with his battered frisbee. He came to the window and stood looking at her, tail wagging. Kelly couldn't resist his silent plea.

The instant she opened the door he was there, frisky and playful. Shivering in the cold, she took the frisbee and sailed it far out into the air. Charlie bounded after it, leaped, and caught it in his mouth. He stood looking at the closed door, then with a toss of his head, he threw his toy up in the air, then pounced on it when it landed.

Kelly continued to play with Charlie on her way to the lodge. "You're just an overgrown pup, Charlie!" Kelly had put on her old red down-filled jacket and her yellow wool toboggan cap. Her makeup-free face was sparklingly alive. "I've more important things to do than play. One of these days you're going to work, too. I'm going to hitch you up to my old sled. But not today . . . so have fun while you can."

Kelly left her boots on the mat inside the door of the lodge and let her gaze wander around the cozy room. A fire was roaring in the massive stone fireplace that held an eight-foot log. The room was not large, but uncurtained, double-paned windows gave it an appearance of spaciousness. The "family room," as they called it, shone with new pride. Even the potbellied stove at the far end of the room had a new coat of stove blacking to cover the few rust spots the idle years had given it. In this cold climate heating was a main concern and each of the three private bedrooms, as well as the dormitory room that held eight bunk beds, had wood-burning stoves. Guests would eat their meals at the long trestle tables set up in the cozy lodge kitchen. In the bush they didn't expect all the modern conveniences.

Comfortable couches against the walls sported bright new slipcovers that matched the indoor-outdoor carpeting put down for extra warmth, and soft bearskin rugs added a native touch. Several beautiful fur pelts were stretched and nailed to the walls, as were Kelly's father's collection of primitive Alaskan tools. Sets of fur-lined chairs stood adjacent to the windows so guests could enjoy the view of Mount McKinley on clear days.

Kelly was excited to see that everything was ready to receive the guests who would be arriving the next day. Two couples were coming up on the train from Anchorage and Clyde would meet them in the four-wheel drive carry-all. Mike was on emergency-call for the utility company and had to remain near the Citizen's Band radio.

Marty was coming home to stay at the end of the week. She had made one quick trip to the resort before resigning from her job in Fairbanks and had brought her fiancé with her. Kelly had decided she liked him even if Mike didn't. She suspected Mike secretly thought no man was good enough for his twin.

Marty had introduced her fiancé as Trampel P. Thornburg, and Kelly had thought, good grief why would anyone name a child Trampel? But Marty called him Tram, which wasn't so bad. He was a ski instructor and a wildlife photographer. He and Marty would occupy the third cabin and together they would arrange cross-country ski tours or overnight camping expeditions for the extra hardy wildlife enthusiasts. Many tourists loved winter safaris, especially those that offered excellent opportunities to observe caribou, moose, and wolf.

"Are you goin' to stand there admirin' or are you comin' to eat these flapjacks?" Bonnie called from the kitchen door.

"Flapjacks, again? I'll be so fat I won't be able to reach the table!"

"Well, land sakes! You're so skinny a good Oklahoma norther would blow you clear down to Texas. Get yourself on in here, now. You need somethin' that'll stick to your backbone with all the work you've been doin'."

Bonnie's square body was bundled up in a bright blue jogging suit complete with turtleneck sweater topped with a bibbed apron. She waddled around in fur-lined moccasins.

"Bonnie! What are you going to wear when it really gets cold?" Kelly's eyes had a vivid sparkle. "All you need is earmuffs and you'll be ready to trek to the top of the mountain!"

"If there's anything this Oklahoma girl hates more than Texas football, it's cold! I'm here to tell you I'm not pokin' my head out of this here lodge till spring!"

"You're priceless! Where's Clyde?"

"He's out on the end of that chain saw again. Give that man anything with a motor and movin' parts and he's as happy as if he had good sense."

In the late afternoon Kelly stuck her head out the door of her own cabin and called to invite Mike in for coffee. Closing the door, she viewed the room proudly. She loved the cozy, neat home she had shared with her father during her growing-up years. She remembered the winter they made the braided rug that covered the floor. He had braided the wool strips and she had sewn them together with nylon fishing line. It was as bright and as durable now as when new. A pillow-lined couch with a freshly washed slipcover stood on one side of the fireplace and a rocking chair on the other. A floor-to-ceiling bookcase which also housed the stereo set she had sent down from Anchorage when she gave up her apartment, and a winter's supply of reading material, helped to turn the cabin into a home. Although not fancy by city standards, it gave Kelly a feeling of permanence and security.

She set two mugs and a plate of Bonnie's freshly baked chocolate chip cookies on the trestle table that divided the kitchen from the rest of the room and smiled at Mike when he came in. He pulled off his boots and hung his coat on a peg.

"Sit down and ruin your appetite for supper." Kelly lifted the graniteware coffee pot from the stove.

"It would take more than what you're offering to do that," Mike said, reaching for a cookie. "Now if I could find me a woman who could cook like Bonnie, I might even marry her."

Kelly poured the coffee, then paused to listen before she returned the pot to the stove. "Do you hear a chopper?"

"Yeah, guess I do. The rangers up in the park have one, but they seldom come down this far."

The sound of the helicopter came closer and Kelly went to the window to peer out.

"You don't suppose our guests decided to fly in tonight instead of taking the train tomorrow?" she asked with a worried frown.

"So what? We'll get one more night's lodging out of them. Sit down and drink your coffee. Clyde's already on his way out to meet the helicopter. I can hear him grinding on the starter."

Kelly turned on another lamp and sat down across from Mike. Soon they heard the helicopter take off again and then the sound of a car returning from the clearing where it had landed.

"I should go up to the lodge and meet the guests."

"Let Bonnie handle it," Mike said, reaching for another cookie. "She's already got enough stuff baked to feed an army."

Kelly laughed. "If I don't knock off eating so much, I'll have to spend my vacations at a fat farm."

"You look a sight better than when you first came home. You looked like a starved alley cat." Mike's strong mouth deepened into a genuine grin.

"That's what I like about you. You say such nice things."

The car stopped in front of the cabin. Kelly saw the lights shining on the snow through the window. Then a car door slammed shut and someone hammered on the door.

"Who was the wiseguy who said Bonnie could handle it?" she said as she got up.

She flung open the door and a man's frame filled the doorway, his bare, snow-dusted head almost touching the top. Jonathan! He was wearing a sheepskin coat and carried a large suitcase in each hand. The chill that struck Kelly had nothing to do with the wind coming in.

Jonathan's dark eyes took in every detail of her appearance—her worn jeans and a faded flannel shirt that revealed her white throat and the tops of her unencumbered breasts. His bitter stare made the color rise to flood her face, all except her white lips, which parted and whispered a silent "No!"

His face was harsh and powerful, the jaw jutted in angry determination, the mouth straight and very hard. Kelly looked around, as if for someplace to go. In her dazed state, she realized Mike was on his feet. She turned slowly to meet piercing brown eyes. At once her mind jerked awake.

"What are you doing here?"

Mike moved up beside her and Jonathan stood silently, dwarfing them, his broad shoulders tense. He moved into the room and dropped his suitcases. Kelly closed the door and stood with her back to it.

"I asked what you're doing here!" Her voice echoed

shrilly. She drew in her lower lip, her face stiff with brittle cynicism.

"I came to see my wife. What do you think?" His mouth twisted caustically.

Her body tensed as she tried to stop trembling. Her blue eyes flickered restlessly, not touching on her husband, whose presence seemed to fill every corner of her mind. Damn it! Here she was quaking like a timid rabbit, just as she had done in Boston.

"I don't want you here!" Her voice had savage, raw feeling in it. "I'll sign your papers. You can stay at the lodge tonight, but I want you out of here in the morning."

Jonathan's features hardened even more. He glanced at Mike, who was watching him with a taut expression.

"I'm staying and the sooner you realize it the better." The icy eyes dared Mike to interfere.

"If Kelly doesn't want you here," Mike said through tight lips, "you're going, and that's all there is to it."

Jonathan hit him. One moment the two men were glaring at each other and the next Mike was flying across the room and landing with a thud against the trestle table. It was over before Kelly could intervene.

She ran over to him. "Mike? Mike? Are you hurt?"

He sat up, rubbing the back of his head. "What do you think? I don't bang my head on the table every day."

Kelly stood up and turned on Jonathan. "What's gotten into you? You had no reason to hit Mike," she said furiously.

Jonathan's hard-boned face was taut with rage. His hands clenched and unclenched. He looked as if he wanted to strangle the two of them.

"No reason? You better get him out of here or I'll kill him."

For a moment Kelly was lost for words. In the eight months she had lived with this man, he had never shown this kind of violence.

"You'd better go, Mike. I'll talk to him," she said quietly, her eyes begging him to obey.

"You're sure?" He darted a look of pure hatred at the man standing in a pool of water that dripped from his snow-covered boots.

"Yes, I'm sure." She reached behind Jonathan and plucked Mike's coat from the peg. Mike shrugged into it and put his stocking feet into his boots. As if to assert his authority over the situation, Jonathan stepped over, opened the door, and slammed it shut after Mike passed through. Immediately, he turned on Kelly and the look of fury on his face made her shake with a totally new fear.

"You adulterous witch!"

In the months before she'd left him she had seen him angry, but nothing like this. During the more than a year since they had seen each other, he had changed, aged, grown more bitter. Now, anger raged between them like a forest fire, scorching everything in its path. He jerked off his coat and hung it up, his powerful body tense with suppressed emotion.

"I could kill you for what you've done to me," he said when he turned to face her.

Silence stretched between them like a taut rubber band. Kelly walked on unsure legs to the cookstove and picked up the graniteware pot. Automatically she took a clean mug from the hook and poured coffee into it as well as into her own.

"How did you know I was here?"

"I've known every move you've made since a month before you left Portland." He sat down at the table.

The smell of the coffee made Kelly feel sick but she sipped it anyway. "It's nice to know I've been spied on," she said coolly.

"It took a while, but I found you," he said without looking at her.

"What took you so long? I've been here almost three weeks."

He drew in a harsh breath and moved restlessly, his dark eyes probing hers. "I had plans to make. Company responsibilities to delegate to others."

Kelly looked up, startled. She had no idea what to say to him. She looked down at his hands cradling his cup. They were pale and cold.

"Say something," he ordered. "Why do you think I left my business, Boston, my family and friends? Because . . . if you can't live in my world, I'll live in yours!"

Kelly stared at him without understanding, her lashes flickering up and down over her blue eyes. "You're not staying here! I don't want you here!" she blurted out.

He set his cup down and reached across the table to grab her wrist. "Why did you walk out on me without a word?" Kelly tried to pull her wrist free, but his fingers tightened. "Answer me!" he roared.

"I left you a note. It was more than you deserved."

"Katherine found your rings and credit cards in your room just before I was expecting an important guest. Why did you do it?" She could feel the tremor in the fingers that gripped her wrist.

"I explained in the note."

"Note? What note? I haven't heard one word from you in fourteen months and two days! Don't you think you owed it to me to tell me you were leaving?"

Kelly's temper flared. "I said I left you a note! Your sister, the keeper of the family's snobbish honor, probably snatched it to keep it from contaminating her precious brother. Don't you dare call me a liar, Jonathan Winslow Templeton the Third!" she said with a sneer. "I've got the starch back in my backbone and I'll never cower under anyone's glare again!"

Jonathan drew in a deep breath. "I never intended to make you cower. I hated it when you moved around the house like a ghost. Why didn't you talk to me, tell me what was wrong?"

Kelly looked up at him in disbelief. They hadn't talked during those last few months they'd lived together. They had spoken the same language, but they'd never communicated, except in bed. He wouldn't have understood how she felt, wouldn't understand now. She'd been his toy, a possession to set in the corner and take out and play with when the mood struck. From the day she walked into that luxurious nightmare she had not been allowed to be herself, only a shell of what the Templetons wanted her to be. Well, thank God, she'd gotten out of it. She would never go back!

"You could have called and told me where you were," he insisted after a moment, releasing her arm.

"There was nothing to say. I didn't need you. I can take care of myself."

"Nothing to say?" He leaned toward her, suppressed rage expressed in the flare of his nostrils and the tightness of his mouth. "You're my wife!"

"You should have thought of that before you allowed your sister to relegate me to the position of live-in whore."

"What do you mean by that?"

"I was never your wife. I never measured up to the Templetons," Kelly flared. "Why did you marry me?" she demanded.

Silence fell between them while his eyes moved from her face to the open neck of her shirt and down over the curves of her breasts. He bent over the table and stared deliberately before bringing his eyes up to hers.

"I think you know why." His voice was slurred, charged with emotion. "Don't tell me you didn't enjoy our sex life, because I know you did."

"So that's why!" She shuddered and looked away. "Sex! You should have propositioned me. You might have gotten what you wanted without marrying me."

"Shut up! I won't stand for that kind of talk from you." His head jerked up in pain and rage and his dark eyes blazed with anger.

"You won't stand for . . ." Kelly choked on her anger. "The biggest mistake of my life was marrying you, Jonathan Winslow Templeton the Third!"

"Damn it! Stop calling me that!" he thundered and banged his fist down on the table.

Kelly bit back her intended reply and fought down the impulse to slap him. Not trusting herself to sit opposite him, she got up and went to lean against the fireplace mantel. Absently she opened the door of the clock case and started the pendulum of the clock swinging.

Jonathan sat at the end of the table and surveyed the room. It was impossible to tell what he was thinking as he regarded the worn couch, the blue and black cookstove, the metal, mail-order kitchen cabinets.

"Why did you stop calling me Jack?" He asked the question quietly. For a fleeting moment Kelly thought she heard pain in his voice, but she dismissed the thought.

"You were no longer Jack when we got to Boston," she said flatly.

"What do you mean? I was the same person."

"You were not!" Anger and resentment flared again.

"I'm tired of arguing," he said. "I'm hungry. What's there to eat?"

"You can eat at the lodge where you'll sleep," she snapped.

Jonathan's answer was to take off his boots. For the first time he seemed to notice the water created by the melted snow he had tracked in. He set the boots against the wall, beneath his coat, and went to the cabinet to un-roll a length of paper toweling. He squatted down, blot-ted away the puddles, and threw the damp toweling into the fire.

Kelly gazed into the blaze, her head resting on her arm on the mantel. His arm went about her waist and he pulled her back against him. She stood rigid as she felt his hot lips against the cool skin on the back of her neck. The swift, panic-beat of her heart echoed the deep thud of his.

"Go away!" The gasping sound came from her as if she were suffocating. "I don't want you!" She waited tensely for him to release her.

She cried out in pain as he took hold of the hair at the back of her head and jerked her around to face him. She tried to move her head in protest, but couldn't avoid the lips that swooped down on hers. His kiss was an outright act of possession, a blistering insult. He ground her mouth beneath his own in reckless disregard, his teeth crushing her lips. She wanted to fight him off, hit him with her fists, scratch him with her nails, but some instinct warned her that to react in such a way would only arouse his temper more. Instead she kept perfectly still, her lips compressed. Slowly his lips softened. When she didn't respond, he lifted his head.

"Open your mouth!" he said harshly, his eyes blazing with anger. She froze, recoiling from his violence.

She was so close she could see the changes the last year had made in his face. There was an extra leanness in the planes of his cheeks, and new lines about his eyes. The bitterness reflected there struck her so forceably that she flinched.

"Is he a good lover?" he said through clenched teeth. "Does he satisfy you?" His hands moved to her shoulders and gripped them tightly.

Incredulous, she stared at him. "You . . . ! Mike isn't my lover!"

"I'm not a fool. I saw the way he looked at you!" His face contorted savagely, his jaw held in a vise. "Do you think I've forgotten the note he sent you on our wedding day, or the number of times you've mentioned his name?" He was shaking her shoulders, his fingers hurting.

Kelly stared at him, eyes wide in her flushed face. "I hardly mentioned him or Marty to you after . . . those first few weeks."

"I should have counted the number of times I heard you say . . . Mike did this . . . or that. We did this . . . or that, meaning you and him! You even talked about this place in your sleep."

She was taken aback, and lowered her lashes, trying to think. "What if I did? This is my home. Look around, Jonathan. It may not have marble floors and crystal chandeliers, but it's home and it's mine!"

"Ours!" he corrected.

"Mine!" she said stubbornly. "And I don't want you here."

"Ours!" he said again.

"Go away!" she hissed and tried to jerk away, but he held her immobile. "You've no right to come here."

His lips curled back from his straight white teeth in a hard sneer. "That's where you're wrong. I have three rights. One, my wife is here and I'm going to live with her. Two, when we were married you signed your portion of this property over to me to handle for you. And three . . . I have paid six years of back taxes on this property and that gives me the right to live here. It also gives me the right to say who will live here with me!"

"I don't believe you!" she gasped. "You wouldn't . . ."

"It depends on you, little wife. It depends on you."

CHAPTER FOUR

FOR A MOMENT Kelly couldn't move. She felt his eyes probe fiercely all the way down to her legs that were suddenly cold and shaking, although her face burned as though with a fever. He released her shoulders and she turned and walked slowly into her bedroom, closing the door behind her.

She stared at the stranger looking back at her from the mirror over her dressing table. She stood there for a moment, trembling, accepting that Jonathan was here and that he intended to stay. He was the Jonathan of Boston dressed differently.

"Oh, help," she muttered and looked away from the pale face and vacant eyes. What did he mean about her signing the property over to him? She had signed papers so he could handle the probate of her father's will, the clearing of the title, and the paying of the inheritance tax. Could he force Mike and Marty from the only home they had ever known? He couldn't! The three of them had put all the money they could scrape together into fixing up this place. By working hard, they could make a living here. "No!" she said aloud and wished she had the courage to pick up the chair and smash something! What was she going to do? They'd worked so hard! Tears sprang into her eyes and she blinked them away. She felt so . . . betrayed!

She was standing in the middle of the room, seeing nothing, her mind whirling in an eddy of bewilderment, when the door opened behind her.

"No," she said hoarsely before she turned to face him. "No," she said again. Her blue eyes were strained and over-bright. "You're not staying here, Jonathan. Go up to the lodge. One of us will be leaving in the morning."

He came into the room carrying the two heavy suitcases and stood looking around. The door to the small bathroom was open and he headed for it. He had to angle the bags through the narrow door to reach the other bedroom.

Kelly followed him through the bathroom and stood in the doorway. "You don't take *no* for an answer, do you, Jonathan? I said I don't want you here."

"I don't think you've given this much thought, Kelly. I didn't want to tell you I have the controlling interest here. I was perfectly willing to let things stand as they were, but you forced me to use that lever. Now you can either tell your friends that they have thirty days to clear out of here, and I'll give them that long, or you can face the fact that I'm here to live with you as your husband and make the best of the situation."

"You're inhuman! You don't care about anything except what you want. You think you can come here and order me to accept you in my home and make you welcome. I was never made to feel welcome in *your* home!

Do you have any idea how I felt after the first few weeks? Like a nonentity, an invisible person."

His dark brows drew a heavy line over his eyes. "There was no reason for you to feel that way. I gave you everything I could think of that—"

"Gave! Gave! You gave me everything except yourself, your time!" she shouted.

"You're hysterical. You didn't like my way of life and made no effort to fit into it. I'm here to show you that I can fit into your way of life."

"Then what?"

"Then we'll pick up where we left off."

"You're out of your mind! I'll never go back there! Never! You're not a human being. You're a computer, programmed to give orders and take what you want without regard to ordinary people like me and Marty and Mike. You've no feelings as simple as love, fear, longing for something, working for it. Everything you have has been served up to you on a silver platter. What do you know about people like me?" She clung to the door frame, rage making her weak. "You don't understand me. You never understood why I married you!"

"I understood a lot more than you realize." Jonathan's eyes had not left her face. "I understand you were unhappy in Boston and you're happy here. I understand that's why you left me, and not because you didn't love me."

"You've got to be the most conceited man alive!" She laughed in hollow irony. "You don't love a man who hides you away and takes you out occasionally, and watches you like a hawk to see you don't disgrace him. You don't love a man who barks at you and keeps you running to do his bidding like a nervous dog. Most of all, you don't love a man who keeps you in his home where the only communication you have is in the night . . . in the dark . . . when he isn't reminded that you're a simple girl with red blood . . . and not . . . blue!"

During this outpouring of harsh words Jonathan stood quietly. Only his eyes moved, becoming bright with inner rage. His face remained shuttered.

"Why didn't you tell me this before?" She could tell he was angry, but his voice remained calm.

"So you could discuss what was to be done about me with your sister? So you could take all my feelings out and hold them up for ridicule? Give me credit for a little more brains than that."

"Now you're being stupid," he said without looking at her. He lifted one of his suitcases up onto the bed, opened it, and began laying out stacks of socks and underwear. "Couldn't you have let me know you were safe?" He turned abruptly to look at her. "Do you have any idea of the anguish you put me through when you just disappeared? I had detectives searching everywhere I could think of."

"How did you find me?"

"I resorted to bribery. I corrupted an employee of the Social Security Department and, when your employer paid your tax into the treasury, I got his name."

"That's against the law!"

"I didn't give it a thought." He was staring at her pale, subdued profile. "You look older."

"I am older. A hundred years older."

"And you're different."

"After what I've been through, how could I possibly remain the same?" she flung at him bitterly.

Rage flashed in his eyes, darkened his face, and hardened the lines of his mouth. He moved so fast she had no time to slip back through the doorway. His hands gripped her shoulders.

"Do you think you're the only one who suffered? You've driven me crazy, wondering where you were, who you were with, and what was happening to you."

She tried to strike his hands away. "Don't touch me."

"I don't care what you want! I want to touch you. I want to feel every inch of you against me and I will! Do you understand, Kelly? We're man and wife for as long as we live. The only thing that will change that fact is . . . death! And I'm mighty tempted to kill you for what you've put me through."

She believed him and was terrified, but determined not to show it. "Have you worked out your method, or just dreamed about it?"

"When I get my hands on you, murder is the last thing I'm thinking of," he said harshly and crushed her to him.

She pushed at his chest as he drew her closer. "Let me go! I said I don't want you to touch me. I hate it!"

"Then you'll learn to love it again, because I'll touch you when and where I want to!"

Instinctively, she felt he was about to lose control, but desperately and recklessly she goaded him. Words fell out of her in a torrent, blatant lies, out of place, wrong, jarring.

"Mike is my lover! I want him, not you. I'm divorcing you and going to him. I'm crazy about him and I sleep with him every night and I'll sleep with him . . . tonight and tomorrow night. Find yourself another woman, Jonathan. I don't want you!"

"Damn you!" he muttered. His hands encircled her upper arms and her eyes darkened as they hardened into bands. His face was like carved granite, hard and bitter. Kelly closed her eyes, sure he was going to hit her. Instead his hands slipped up around her neck and closed about her throat. She gasped, trying to pull away, but his mouth came down on hers, savagely, relentlessly, prying her lips apart, grinding his teeth against her mouth. The thumbs beneath her chin and the fingers behind her head kept her immobile beneath his consuming mouth. She moaned at the pain he was inflicting on her and struggled so violently that their bodies swayed and crashed against the wall.

He moved too fast for her. He dragged her to the bed, pushed her down, and fell on her. Winded, they lay there, breathing hard. His dark head shut out the overhead light and his mouth burned, delved, bruised her own, forcing her to surrender her lips. His hands moved possessively over her. During the struggle, her shirt had become unbuttoned and his fingers slid inside to find the high, warm swell of her breast.

He raised his head and stared at the white skin laid bare by the open shirt. His fingers loosened and moved slowly, gently, in a caressing motion. The smooth, warm fingers softly caressed her trembling body. Her heart beat so hard she was deaf. She couldn't think. She couldn't speak.

Jonathan's eyes flickered to her face and she shook her head in silent protest. She couldn't bear the thought of submitting to him with this terrible chasm between them.

"Let me have you, darling," he whispered, and she heard the words through the singing of her blood and couldn't answer. Desperately she fought down the desire that spiralled crazily inside her.

"To hold you, touch you like this drives me crazy," he said in a strange, thickened voice, his mouth at her throat, then sliding up to close over her mouth, gently now. Her mouth quivered weakly under the persuasion of his kiss. The searching movement parted her lips and he began sensuously exploring the inside of her mouth with his tongue.

A strange, melting heat began inside her. The hungry, coaxing movements of his mouth were awakening the first, tentative response in her. One of his hands slid back and forth across her breast in a soft, possessive caress and her nipple, loving the feel of his palm, reacted automatically. Oh, the weight of him felt so good! She had missed the way he made her feel, the way he could force her to relinquish control, and fly away with him into the sensuous world where there were only his lips, his hands, the hard strength of his male body. Her lips began moving under his, clinging, returning the pressure of his mouth. She wanted him. She ached with the slow burning fire he was awakening in her body.

"I mean to have you," he groaned into her mouth and his body moved on hers urgently.

Abruptly, as though he had lifted her out of the well of sexual chaos, she went cold and stiff. "No," she said tightly. "No!"

"Oh, Kelly!" His voice was like a sound from the past, but she refused to be softened by the memory of the husky cry wrung from him at the peak of overwhelming pleasure.

She twisted out from under him and he let her go. He lay where she left him, breathing hard. At the door she turned back. He was sitting on the edge of the bed watching her.

"We were never suited. This was all we ever shared. It isn't enough. We must face it. Our marriage was a mistake." She saw him flinch as though she had struck him. "I didn't fit into your life and you won't fit into mine. It's best you forget I ever existed."

As she turned away, he said quickly, "I haven't totally disrupted my life to be put off so easily, Kelly. I'm staying. Forever, if necessary."

"I can't believe you want me when I despise everything you are, everything you stand for!" she cried.

His dark eyes mocked her. "What a liar you've turned out to be, Kelly," he drawled. "That isn't true and you know it. You can say all the words you want about hating me, but we both know differently, don't we?"

She wanted to slap him so badly her palm burnt. Self-respect made her resist with all her willpower and she clamped her lips down on the denial that bubbled up within her. She walked in silence through the bathroom, into her own darkened bedroom, and to the front door, where she began to jerk on her boots.

"You're not leaving here, Kelly." Jonathan stood in the doorway of her father's room.

"I'm going to the lodge and you can't stop me."

"Yes, I can stop you," he said calmly, "but don't force me. Get on that radio and ask Clyde to bring us something to eat. I haven't had a thing all day."

"I won't treat Clyde like a busboy! He isn't paid to bring me my meals," she replied coolly.

"He won't mind doing it this once. After this we'll either go to the lodge for our meals or you can fix them here. Tonight we're going to be here, alone. You can get on that radio or I will, and you know how snobbish a Bostonian can be when demanding service." He waited for her to speak. "Clyde will understand. I told him I was your husband and we'd been apart for a while, but that we're back together again."

Kelly felt suddenly sick, filled with humiliation and self-contempt for what happened in the bedroom. "Stay away from me," she snapped as he moved toward her. The burning temptation to give in to him was too new. The inevitability of her own submission was not the worst thing preying on her mind. It was the shameful truth that Jack wouldn't need to force her. He could take her whenever he chose. Already she was thinking of him as Jack again. There was nowhere to run. She was imprisoned, with snow and ice all around her and no choice but to submit to whatever he demanded. Of course she could defy him, but could she do that to Marty and Mike? There wasn't the slightest doubt in her mind that he would carry out his threat to put them out of their home. Maybe if she played along until she could see a lawyer in Anchorage . . .

Jonathan watched her closely, his own face expressionless. Kelly felt a shiver run down her spine.

"Don't . . . do this to me, Jonathan." The soft plea was out before she could bite it back.

"Poor Kelly. What a predicament!"

His mockery stiffened her spine. "I'm glad you think

it's so funny!" She glared at him, her eyes alive with angry tears. "It's a game with you. You don't care who you hurt."

"I care, Kelly," he insisted flatly. "I'm fighting for what I want the only way I know how."

Kelly took off her boots. Her head ached and her dry throat hurt when she swallowed. She sat down beside the Citizen's Band radio and pressed the key on the desk microphone.

"Break . . . Mountain View base station. Are you on the channel, Bonnie?" Jonathan stood watching her and she gave him a withering look.

"Yes-sir-ee, I'm here. Ain't ya comin' up to eat, Kelly?"

Kelly closed her eyes and gritted her teeth before pressing the key to answer. "Not tonight, Bonnie. I was wondering if Clyde would mind bringing something down for us."

"Course he will, honey. Land sakes, I don't blame you none for wanting to be alone with that husband of yours. Why, you just stay right there and I'll send Clyde down with a dish of that chicken casserole you like and a fresh-baked blueberry pie. You got coffee, ain't ya?"

"Yes, I have coffee."

"Ten four, Kelly. Say, honey, ya got the cookstove going, don't ya?"

"Ten-four."

"You might have to heat the casserole up a bit. Mike ain't been up for supper. Is he down there?"

"Negative. Mike, if you're on the channel, let Bonnie know if you're going up for supper."

There was a pause, then Mike's voice came in. "I'll be coming up in a few minutes, Bonnie. You okay, Kelly?"

"Sure. See you tomorrow. Thanks, Bonnie. Tell Clyde this won't be a regular thing."

"You get the coffee goin' and I'll send down everything but the candles and champagne. I'll be clear with ya, honey. You all enjoy yourself, now."

When Kelly looked at the doorway where Jonathan had stood, it was empty. She sat for a moment and tried to calm down. If he had been standing there with a mocking, "I told you so" look on his face, she might have hit him. She ran her tongue around the velvety innerside of her lips, which were still sore from his brutal kisses. Defiance and consternation swept through her, and she thought again what a naive idiot she had been to actually believe a man like Jonathan Winslow Templeton could love a girl like her. He was just frustrated now because she had left him. A man like Jonathan couldn't accept rejection.

The dryness in her throat reminded her of the bottle of Scotch in the cupboard. On her way to get it, she looked at herself in the mirror over the kitchen sink. You're a romantic, Kelly, she thought. She stared into serious eyes, dark circled and bright from tears she was too stubborn to shed. She'd read too many novels where the poor girl married her prince and they lived happily ever after. It was not a romantic world anymore and marriage was not a singular state. It was more of a stage in people's lives, different partners for different periods. Few stayed married forever and no one lived happily ever after.

She took the bottle from the cupboard, poured herself a stiff drink, and drank it in one gulp. She gasped. The fiery liquid burned all the way to her stomach. She leaned against the cabinet and coughed, tears blurring her eyes. Through her misery she felt a hand on her back and jerked away.

"Take your hands off me!" She struggled, flailing her arms.

"How much of that did you drink?"

"None of your business," she snapped, and pushed away from him. She opened the front of the firebox on the cookrange, uncaring that ashes drifted to the floor, and poked several small pieces of firewood into the opening before kicking it shut. Holding the coffee pot in front of her like a shield, she went to the sink. Jonathan stepped out of her way and she dumped the used grounds and refilled the pot with water. She heard the motor of the pickup as it approached the cabin, then the sound of the car door banging shut.

Jonathan held the door open for Clyde, who had a large covered tray in his hands. He stood just inside the doorway.

"I ain't supposed to track snow all over your clean floor," he said and grinned. "Bonnie done gave me strict orders."

"I'll take it then, Clyde. Don't want you to get into trouble with the wife." Jonathan took the tray. "Don't run off, though. Kelly and I were just having a drink and would like you to join us. Wouldn't we, darling?"

Kelly turned her back to him and forced a civil reply. "Of course."

"No, don't bother, Mr. Templeton. Bonnie told me to shake a leg on back."

"Jack. My name's Jack," Jonathan said easily. "I'm

afraid all we've got is water to go in the Scotch unless you'd rather have a straight shot."

"Straight will be fine."

Jonathan searched the cupboard and brought out a small wine glass. He poured from the bottle and carried the drink to Clyde still standing on the mat beside the door.

"I hear you're from Oklahoma, my favorite state. I spent a year at Tinker Airforce Base in Oklahoma City and got addicted to the place. How do the Cowboys look this year? Think they've got a chance to stomp O.U. again?"

"They got a damn good chance. They got a running fullback from a little town called Bowlegs, Oklahoma. That kid stands six foot four, if he's an inch. He weighs two hundred and forty pounds and can run and root like a razorback hog. He's the prettiest sight you ever did see, Jack. I'd love to see him against those pretty boys down at Norman."

"I went to Stillwater for a game while I was in Oklahoma. That little town comes alive when the college plays the university."

"It shore does," Clyde agreed. "Not even a good rodeo can stir the people up like that game."

"Do you think we could pull in an Oklahoma station if we put up a pretty good sized antenna? I doubt any of the games will be broadcast over the Anchorage station."

"I don't know, Jack. They've a powerful station in Tulsa. It'd be worth a try."

"We'll have to see what we can do about it, Clyde. And thanks for bringing down our dinner. Tell Bonnie thanks, too."

"Hey, now. That's okay, Jack. Glad to do it. It'll be great having another man around. Mike gets calls and is away a lot. I know ya'all ain't wantin' this old cowboy a hanging around so I'll just vamoose. Night, Jack. Thanks for the drink. Night, Kelly."

Kelly, who had kept herself busy at the stove so she wouldn't have to look at him, called out, "Night, Clyde." She didn't speak again until she heard the car door slam and the motor start. Finally, she turned to see Jonathan looking at her.

"I suppose you're pretty pleased with yourself," she sneered. "Clyde wasn't any challenge, at all. You charm men like him every day back in Boston!"

"Don't be nasty, Kelly."

"Poor Clyde was just an obstacle to overcome in your own cold-blooded, calculated way." She laughed sardonically.

A faint red stain ran along his hard cheekbones. "Think what you like," he said, and poured himself a drink from the bottle of Scotch.

CHAPTER FIVE

THE MEAL TASTED like ashes in Kelly's mouth. She sat across the table from Jonathan and never once let her gaze rest on his face. Her depression deepened.

"You look worn out. You've been working too hard."

Kelly flushed and ignored him.

"You've lost weight."

"Well, what did you expect? I'm hardly the Boston debutante," she snapped.

She could feel his eyes on her. "Thank God, you're not. But you could try to be cordial, at least. You look as if you expect to be executed," he said through his teeth.

She gave him a false, over-bright smile. "You want me to look like this? I'll smile like a lighthouse, if that's what you want. You're the man in charge. You command, I obey."

His eyes flashed angrily. "One of these days you're going to push me too far."

"And you'll get nasty? You mean nastier than usual?"

Jonathan laid down his fork very carefully and the

anger in his eyes intensified. "Stop the sarcasm, Kelly. You and I will be living here together and I've no intention of spending the winter sparring with you."

"You know the alternative."

Without answering, he began eating again—several helpings of the casserole and a large piece of pie. Kelly pushed her food around on her plate, knowing she should eat but not liking the feel of the food in her mouth. Instead, she drank several cups of coffee and rested her elbows on the table.

When Jonathan finished, he took his plate to the sink. Kelly scraped hers into a pan for Charlie, added the leftover casserole to it, and went to the door. Charlie bounded in the moment she opened it. He stood looking at Jonathan, then finally dropped the battered frisbee and, with a wag of his tail, began to gulp down the food. As he licked the pan clean, he moved it farther and farther into the room until it came up against Jonathan's foot. Charlie looked up at him and gave a low growl. Surprised, Kelly burst into peals of laughter.

"Charlie! You uncouth dog! You're not supposed to growl at Jonathan Winslow Templeton the Third. You're supposed to grovel at his feet." Kelly knew it was the Scotch talking, but she didn't care. "Be nice to him, Charlie, and he'll have a nice, big bone flown in from Boston." She poured another drink.

While she was washing the dishes, she had two more drinks and only vaguely heard Jonathan talking to Charlie and shutting the door after letting him out. She saw the hand reach out and take the bottle of Scotch and set it on the top shelf in the cabinet. She wanted to giggle. Did he think she wouldn't reach up and get it if she wanted more? She left the dishes on the drainboard and walked on unsteady legs to the door of her bedroom. With one hand on the doorframe to steady herself, she turned and tried to focus her eyes on Jonathan's face.

"I'm going to bed," she enunciated very clearly. "You can do as you please. Sleep on the couch or in my father's bed, if you can find blankets." She giggled and put her hand to her mouth. "Or sleep out in the snow with Charlie." Waving her hand carelessly, she swayed, then turned to go, but her feet wouldn't move. Jonathan caught her as she fell forward, his hands under her armpits. "I'm not sleeping with you. Do you hear? I hate the sight of you. Stay, if you've no more pride than to stay where you're not wanted, but you'll not get any pleasure out of my company!" The words had been burning in her head all evening and now they shot out at a frantic rate, clear and unwavering. She tried to stand up straight and push his hands away from her.

"You've had too much to drink," he said, apparently amused.

"Which is no business of yours." Her head was whirling and she found herself leaning against him for support. She closed her eyes. "Oh, my head!" she groaned.

He lifted her as if she weighed no more than a feather. Her head was swimming dizzily and she couldn't focus her eyes. She was only half aware that he was carrying her, then he lowered her to something soft and comfortable. She wanted to sleep, but his movements irritated her. Dimly she felt her shoes being removed and then her jeans. She tried to push him away when he lifted her to slip the shirt off her back. At last she was allowed to lay back and he covered her with something soft and warm. Almost instantly she was asleep.

During the night she began to dream lovely, wonderful, intensely exciting dreams. She was back with Jack in the king-sized bed at Captain Cook's Hotel in Anchorage, where they had spent the first two days after their marriage. She was submitting to his lovemaking, burning pleasurably under the smooth caress of his hands. The warmth of his body seemed to melt hers so that it molded to his shape. The dream was so deeply real she could feel his fingers on her bare skin searching for all the sensitive places and finding them.

She moaned aloud as his lips explored the warm curve of her throat and descended to the rounded flesh of her breast, fondling the stiff peaks until she turned her face into his neck and kissed his damp skin.

"Kiss me, darling," he breathed in her ear. "Kiss me and love me."

"Yes! Oh, yes!" Her lips, warm and eager, sought his that were firm, yet gentle, hardening with passion only at her insistence. Her hand stroked his wide chest, dark with rough hairs, and moved down to the flat, smooth-skinned stomach. Sensuous, languid, she took her time and explored his body boldly, giving herself up to this wonderful dream. "Jack . . . Jack . . ."

His mouth silenced hers and his palms moved down over her body and curved against her hips. He whispered love words in her ear and she felt his cheek against her breast. And then his mouth slid gently over the white skin until it enclosed her nipple. He repeated the caress, his mouth seductive, lazy, setting her ablaze with hunger. He was invading every inch of her now, exploring her body boldly, making her give herself up to him. He began to kiss her mouth deeply and Kelly slid her arms around his neck and pulled on the hair on the back of his head. His breath came fast and thick, hers light and gasping.

"Say you love me." The husky whisper in her ear was insistent. "Say it, darling."

"I love you, Jack. Jack, love me. Love me."

The laugh was low and tender as he covered her face with feverish kisses. "Oh, Kelly," he said thickly. "You've been under my skin for so long, tormenting me, driving me crazy. I've missed you so and I've wanted to make love to you for so long . . ." He pulled her head back and their mouths clung. He held her body between his roving hands and she made no effort to stop him. The pleasure rose to intolerable heights and she lost consciousness of everything but the powerful body that was driving her toward weightlessness. Now she was floating down from a great height and her stomach clenched in fierce panic. She dropped sharply, and cried out wildly, her hands clinging frantically to the only solid thing in her tilting world.

Soothing words calmed and reassured her. Hands gently stroked her taut body. Her heart settled in to a quieter pace as the tension and panic left her. Did he know he had taken her heart? She began to cry. Jack had taken her heart, but Jonathan had taken and crushed her bubbly spirit, her romantic illusions. She had fought to hold Jack, but in the end he had flown from her grasp. Now, like the princess in the fairy tale, she was under the spell of the wicked prince, Jonathan, who would destroy her. Finally her sleep deepened and the nightmare left her.

The sensation of something against her mouth woke her abruptly. Her eyes flew open and stared into amused brown eyes. She was lying naked in Jonathan's arms, her legs imprisoned between his. He had been kissing her. He laughed at the expression on her face. There was a relaxed charm about him that maddened her. His hand was on her breast, fingering her nipple!

Her face burned scarlet. She hadn't been dreaming! She had made love with him. "Oh! You're even lower than I thought!" She tried to push him away, but her strength was as nothing against his. "You . . . you took my clothes off!"

"You didn't object at the time," he pointed out with a grin that further infuriated her.

"I didn't know . . . You took advantage . . ."

"You were plastered," he interrupted, grinning.

"You had no right. You knew I didn't want you," she snapped.

"I had every right . . . and you did want me."

She shook her head like an enraged child, her face livid. "I did not want you, Jonathan!" She began to struggle.

He clamped his arms and legs around her and lowered his lips to her cheek. "You wanted Jack. It was just like those two days we spent in bed after we got married . . . only better."

Her eyes burned up at him resentfully. "Enjoy your little triumph. It won't happen again."

"Be honest. Your appetite for me is as great as mine is for you." His hands moved possessively over her, his fingers trembling. "You can feel how I want you. Admit you want me, too."

"I admit I enjoy being with a man. Any man," she taunted.

His hand moved to her hair and jerked her head around to face him. "That's a lie!" he said harshly. He looked at her mouth, that trembling mouth that had always fascinated him. "Your mouth is too beautiful to spit such lies." He kissed it gently before his lips hovered over hers so that his tongue could trace its way into the corners. "You're a lovely liar," he said, his eyes soft, his hands gentle in her hair. "Don't be embarrassed for wanting me, darling."

She felt as though he had penetrated her subconscious and raped her mind as well as her body. She must have been conscious at some level to remember what he had done to her and how his stroking hands had fired her desire for him. But she feared her blind, desperate need for love. It was too dangerous to care for anyone.

"Sex!" The word exploded from her and her eyes filled with tears. "That's all it is, Jonathan. Let me go, please. I want to get up," she said tiredly.

"Maybe it is just sex, but it's a start," he said patiently and moved away from her.

Kelly threw back the covers and walked naked into the bathroom. She could feel his eyes on her, but didn't care. She remembered the long nights during the first weeks of their marriage when Jack's passion, the force of which carried her over the first few times when she bared her body to him, made her feel as if it was natural and beautiful for him to view her from every angle.

She took her robe from the hook behind the door, slipped her feet into warm scuffs, and passed through her father's room to come out into the living area. It was warm. A big log blazed in the fireplace and the cook-stove was roaring pleasantly. She glanced toward the door. The floor and doormat were dry. Since no one had come in from outside, Jonathan must have built up the fire. She was surprised he knew how. She filled the coffee pot and set it on the stove. During the few short weeks she had been home, she had fallen into a routine: get up, stoke up the fires, put on the coffee pot, wind the clock, turn on the electric hot water tank. She did these things, now, automatically, and went to stand beside the window.

It was going to be a clear day with a blue sky. Soon the sun would be up, its low rays bathing the landscape in a warm, winter-rose color.

She loved this land of the very old and the very new. Ancient Eskimo and Indian cultures lived side by side with modern pulp mills, fisheries, and giant oil companies. Where else in the world were there glaciers and strawberries, dog teams and airplanes, skin boats (the design of which had not changed for a thousand years) and late model outboard motors? It seemed ironic that she and Jonathan should come together in this land of extremes.

The day promised to be clear enough to allow the first guests to view Mount McKinley from the lodge windows. Kelly thought of the poster she had painstakingly printed and framed to hang beside the window. "Mount McKinley, called *Denali*, meaning 'home of the sun,' by the Indians, is one of the most dramatic sights in Alaska. The light tan granite mass, crown of the Alaska Range, climbs upward to a height of almost four miles. No other mountain rises so far above its own base. The upper two-thirds of the peak is permanently snow-covered, and often takes on a pinkish glow at sunrise and sunset."

Thinking about the mighty mountain, this place her father had built, this home she loved, stiffened her resolve to stay here. She would not let Jonathan evict her and Mike and Marty from their home! They belonged here, he didn't.

Kelly turned from the window to see him taking coffee cups from the drain-basket beside the sink. She looked at him with new eyes. He wore a flannel shirt, obviously new, jeans, and wool socks on his feet. Dressed like this, he seemed more Jack than Jonathan, but he *was* Jonathan, and he could take all this away from her. She picked up her purse from the couch and took out her cigarettes and lighter.

"When did you start smoking?" He had poured two cups of coffee and set them on the table.

"I don't smoke much. Only when I'm nervous," she retorted.

"You're nervous now?"

"Wouldn't you be if everything you loved could be taken from you on a whim?"

He stood looking at her. He seemed taller in the jeans, tall and tough, a bargaining Bostonian with an eye to the main chance, even willing to dress the part in order to fit into the scheme of things.

His darkened eyes flickered with annoyance, but he

spoke calmly. "I haven't threatened to take your home away from you."

She shrugged. "Same thing. I either suffer your presence or Marty and Mike and I get out."

"I doubt if you suffer, Kelly," he said drily. "Come drink your coffee."

"Thank you, no. I'll take my bath now. I only run the electric heater long enough to get water for a bath. Electricity is expensive here. Of course, you'd know nothing about that." She flicked the end of her cigarette into the fireplace and glanced at him. He sat at the table, stirring his coffee.

The C.B. radio came on with an emergency call for Mike. Kelly waited until she heard Mike answer, then went into the bathroom and filled the small tub with warm water.

When she came out of the warm, steamy bathroom, her bedroom seemed cold, but she shut the door connecting it to the kitchen and took out flannel-lined jeans and a shirt. Then she noticed her bed had been neatly made and the clothes she had worn the day before folded and laid out on the end. She dressed, ran a comb through her hair, and went in her stocking feet to the kitchen. She was pouring coffee when Jonathan came to the door of her father's room.

"Are you feeling better . . . besides being nervous?" he asked drily.

"Much better." There was almost a pleasant tone to her voice. "You'll find sheets and blankets in the chest at the end of the bed."

"I saw them there," he said, and turned back into the room.

Kelly carried her coffee to the kitchen window and looked out at the large temperature gauge attached to a post just outside the window. It was eighteen degrees, about average for this time of year. There was no wind and the snow was fresh and beautiful. It was a perfect day for their guests to arrive. She hurriedly finished her coffee and put on her boots, coat, and yellow cap.

Charlie greeted her the moment she stepped outside. He had made crazy patterns in the snow and now leaped joyously. Kelly took the frisbee from him and sailed it into the air. The soft snow floated around him like a cloud as he dashed and leaped to catch it. She couldn't hold back her laughter.

"Charlie, you crazy dog! Come on, bring it here."

Shaking his head, as if the frisbee in his mouth was a live thing, he trotted back to Kelly. She knelt in the snow and put her arms about his neck, then took the frisbee from him and ran. Charlie was surprised at first then leaped after her, jumping high in the air when she held his toy over her head.

"No, you don't!" Kelly laughed, and tried to hit him on the nose. Charlie snapped at the battered plastic, braced his legs and pulled. Kelly went tumbling down into the snow, where she lay laughing, holding onto the frisbee with both hands. Charlie pulled and shook his head, deep growls coming from his powerful throat.

"Looks like a standoff to me."

Kelly looked up to see Jonathan standing over her, his hands deep in the pockets of his jacket. His gaze was so quiet and so penetrating that it seemed to reach down inside her. She felt something twist in her body and bit down on her lower lip. She let go of the frisbee and a surprised Charlie sat down in the snow.

Kelly got to her feet and brushed the snow from her jacket and jeans.

"I didn't mean to spoil your fun," Jonathan said from behind her.

"You didn't." The lie came easily to her lips. She headed toward the lodge. The light snow made walking easy, now; later it would be hard and crusty, then solid enough to walk on.

Jonathan followed beside her. As they neared the lodge, he took hold of her arm and held tightly when she tried to shrug it off.

"Let go of my arm," she said tensely, glancing up at him.

"No." He held her gaze as firmly as her arm. "Behave yourself, Kelly. I won't be snubbed by my wife in front of anyone. Do you understand?" He took a deep breath, his nostrils flaring. "What we say and do is one thing in private and another in public."

Tormented, she tried without success to break free of his hold. "I have my pride, too," she retorted. "I won't play the loving wife!"

"If you don't, you'll only make matters worse for yourself."

"Worse! How can matters be worse than they are?" she hissed.

"Believe me, they could be much worse."

They had reached the door and Jonathan held it open for her. Needing a chance to pull herself back together after their verbal combat, she took an unusually long time pulling off her boots and leaving them on the mat. She allowed him to help her with her jacket, then went toward the swinging doors leading to the kitchen. Half of her wanted to watch his reaction to the lodge; the other half wanted him to think she didn't care a fig.

"There you are! I swear to goodness, I told Clyde we just might not see you all day. I know how it was when me and Clyde got together after we was apart." Bonnie wiped her hands on her apron and held one of them out to Jonathan. "Now ain't you a handsome feller? You rascal," she said to Kelly. "You never told me nothin' about a husband. If mine was as handsome as yours, I'd a been braggin' all over the place."

Jonathan laughed. "Kelly didn't think I'd be able to get away so soon, Bonnie. That's why she didn't tell you about me."

"I know she's tickled you're here now. Married folks was meant to be together. I ain't for this woman libbers stuff. I want my man to lean on. Ain't that right, Kelly?"

Kelly found her voice. "Oh, yes. Jonathan's a pillar of strength."

"Jonathan? Clyde said your name was Jack." Bonnie looked up from her scant five feet to the man towering over her.

"That's right. My name's Jack. Only Kelly calls me Jonathan and that's only part of the time." His brown eyes glinted into her stormy blue ones. The look passed over Bonnie, who was waddling back to the stove in her fur-lined moccasins.

"I just fed Mike and sent him on his way." Bonnie moved the big iron skillet onto the hot part of the range. "I swear if that kid's legs ain't holler. Ain't one blessed thing wrong with his appetite. He ate three eggs, sausage, and hash browns, then topped it off with the last of the pie. What you gonna have, Jack?"

"I'll take the same, Bonnie, but make it two eggs."

"Over easy or wide awake?"

"If wide awake means sunny side up, that's how I'll take them."

"Well, get on over here and get you some coffee. Get some for Kelly, too. She looks all tuckered out. Skinny as a rail, that girl. Now that you're here, Jack, maybe we can fatten her up a little." Bonnie dropped big pats of sausage into the hot skillet. "She's worn herself out working around here. My land, you should've seen the mess this place was in. There wasn't anything too heavy for her to lift, and nothing too hard for her to do. She just flew right in there and did it and wouldn't wait one minute for the men. Mike takes things slow an' easy. That boy don't get in no hurry. He . . . Put the bread in the toaster, Jack."

Kelly closed her eyes in frustration. "Mike works hard," she said.

"I didn't say he didn't work, Kelly. I just said he was slow. Swear, if you ain't somethin' when it comes to stickin' up for that boy!"

"I'd hardly call him a boy, Bonnie," Kelly said drily and raised her eyes to see Jonathan watching her, the smile he had worn for Bonnie's benefit gone. "Mike has done a lot of work around here," she said, holding Jonathan's eyes. "He's never had anything given to him. He earned his share of this place."

"I'm sure he did. Now that I'm here, I can take some of the workload off his shoulders." Jonathan's voice was kind, but his face was not. Kelly knew he was furious and was glad.

The plate of food Bonnie set in front of her caused Kelly's stomach to lurch with hunger. She glanced up to see Jonathan's brows rise questioningly. She could tell he was enjoying her discomfort.

"Not hungry this morning, darling?" he asked silkily.

Her eyes, filled with rage, flashed to his face. He returned the look with taunting amusement. The battle lines were drawn, she thought bitterly. She was bound to lose some of the encounters, but she was determined to win the war.

CHAPTER SIX

I am the captain of my fate. The thought pounded in Kelly's head while she went through the motions of checking the guest rooms to make sure everything was ready. In the middle of counting the number of extra blankets neatly stacked on a closet shelf, she stopped, put her clenched fists to her temples, and closed her eyes.

It was ridiculous to think she was captain of anything, least of all her own fate! She was being swept along on the tide of Jonathan's overpowering personality. Already Bonnie and Clyde thought he was the greatest thing since fire. He was out there now, on one end of the big, two-man crosscut saw, helping Clyde cut the big logs into lengths to be further chopped into firewood. Kelly hoped Clyde worked him to death. She knew Jonathan would be too proud to stop even if he was about to drop in his tracks.

Kelly stayed at the lodge until the guests arrived, leaving only long enough to go to her own house and change into azure blue cord slacks and a matching turtleneck sweater that hid some of the gauntness of her slim hips.

Clyde left in plenty of time to meet the train and Jonathan, taking his cue from Kelly, came up to the lodge after changing out of the sawdust-covered jeans and sweaty flannel shirt. He had bathed, and Kelly wondered if he had used cold water, or if he had carried it from the reservoir beside the cookstove. He had put on tan trousers and a brown loose-knit shirt with cream ribbing at the neck and cuffs.

He came to where Kelly was standing beside the window looking out toward the faint peak of Mount McKinley. She could smell the familiar aroma of his aftershave lotion. He didn't speak and she moved away to turn on the lamps. It was three o'clock in the afternoon and already beginning to get dark. Soon they would be using electricity all day and the bills would pile up.

The guests were young, rowdy, and there were five of them instead of four. The girls had frizzed hair, thinly plucked eyebrows, and willowy figures once they removed their bulky snowmobile wear. The men had fashionably styled haircuts and expensive Nordic ski sweaters. Clyde set their suitcases inside the door, but when he started to remove his boots to carry the luggage to the rooms, Jonathan stopped him.

"I'll take care of that, Clyde, if you want to put the car away."

It was easy to tell what girl went with what man. One of the couples was rather short, the other of medium height. The odd man was taller and older than the others. He leaned on the small bar that served as a counter and eyed Kelly.

"Hello, snow-nymph. I don't have a reservation. Are

you going to throw me out?" His eyes ran over her like summer rain.

"That depends." Kelly saw Jonathan edge closer to the desk.

"Yeah? On what?" He looked intrigued.

"On whether or not you behave yourself." Her eyes glinted mischievously. He wasn't the enemy, just a harmless man who liked to flirt. He looked like a nice guy.

"May I ask you a crazy question?" He grinned broadly.

"Sure. What's the crazy question?"

"What's a classy looking dame like you doing out here in the boonies?"

Kelly laughed. "That line went out with hula-hoops and mini-skirts." She pushed the register toward him. "Sign your name and next of kin in case I decide to feed you to the bears."

Doctor Andrew T. Mullins, Seattle, Washington. Without allowing a flicker of surprise to show on her face, she moved the book toward the other guests.

"We have three private rooms and a dormitory," Kelly explained, looking at the tall doctor.

"We'll take the three privates," he said and threw a credit card down on the counter.

"You don't need to pay now." Kelly handed the card back to him and he squeezed her fingers.

"Going to run up the bill on me?" he teased.

"Hope so," she retorted, and glanced at Jonathan.

He stood behind the other couples, his eyes riveted to her, his face a frowning mask. There was no doubt he was angry. He watched her with barely controlled impatience, his body shifting restlessly.

"Dinner's at seven, but the coffee pot is always on.

The swinging doors lead to the dining area, which is also the kitchen. This is a very informal lodge so make yourselves at home."

Kelly almost broke into a grin when she saw Jonathan carrying the luggage down the hall. If only Katherine were here to see it! As the tall doctor turned to go, he winked at her and, feeling Jonathan's eyes on her, she winked back.

In moments Jonathan returned from the bedrooms. "Pull another stunt like that," he warned her, "and I'll break your neck!"

"What are you talking about?" Kelly demanded, goading him.

He slammed his hand down on the desk. "You know very well what I'm talking about. That was a come-on if I ever saw one." His hand snaked out and grabbed her wrist.

Her face turned pale and their eyes locked in silent battle. Damn him! He was going to push, push, push, until he drove her out of her mind!

"Give up, Jonathan. Go back to your tinfoil world, your elegant papier-mâché friends and their lifeless parties, where they cut each other's throats so politely. I don't need you here." She was surprised she could speak so calmly. Suddenly pale and haggard, he stared back as if he wasn't seeing her at all. She jerked her hand free and headed for the kitchen.

"We have an extra guest, Bonnie," she announced, taking a mug from the rack and pouring coffee as Jonathan followed through the swinging doors.

"Ain't that great? I peeked when I heard 'em come in. Tonight we're goin' to have chicken fricassee and dumplins. Don't that sound fancy? Kelly, get Jack a cup of coffee. That boy worked like a mule this mornin'."

"Keep your seat, I'll get it." He laid his hand on her shoulder as he passed and Kelly steeled herself to keep from flinching.

"If you're hungry, Jack, get yourself a piece of that carrot cake," Bonnie ordered. "We're goin' to have baked custard tonight along with the French rolls, peas and onions in cream, and tossed salad."

"Sounds good, Bonnie. Do you ever make Boston baked beans?" Jack glanced at Kelly and grinned. "My wife never learned to like them."

"I make Oklahoma beans and they'd put them Boston beans to shame, Jack. I don't blame Kelly none for not likin' 'em." Bonnie waddled between the stove and the counter, never glancing at the two seated at the trestle table. "One of these days I'll cook up a batch of pinto beans, tomatoes, and *jalapeño* peppers. Top that off with a pan of good, old yellow cornbread and you never had anything so good in all your life." Bonnie went into the pantry.

"We know what's on the menu. What's on the program for tonight?" Jonathan asked.

Kelly let out a deep sigh. It was so exhausting to be always sparring with him. As he turned to see if Bonnie was coming back into the room, she regarded him openly. His sharply etched profile seemed to be carved from granite. He was handsome, strong, and ruthless. Here, in the Alaskan wilderness, he seemed to take on a ruggedly masculine appearance totally different from the suave, socially prominent man of Boston. There was no doubt he stirred her physically. But did she feel love or hate?

His brown eyes held a question when he swung around to her, and she gave an involuntary shiver. What did he want from her? He had no need for a woman's enduring love. With that arrogant face, imperious head, and cultured background, he could get any woman he wanted. She put her hand to her breast as if to press her heart into obedience. She didn't want to love him. She wanted to be her own woman, not chained to him by the strength of her feelings.

Now his fingers locked about her wrist, making a double shackle. "Kelly, what's wrong?"

She flinched as if his words were razor sharp. "What could possibly be wrong?" she asked flippantly. "I've got the world by the tail going downhill backwards!" She felt as brittle as breaking glass. She wanted to cry for all those lovely nights so long ago when she'd been young and in love.

"Break . . . break. . . . Mobile one calling Mountain View base station." Mike's voice came in on the radio and Jonathan gave a muffled curse.

Kelly pressed the button on the microphone. "Mountain View, go ahead."

"Is that you, Ramblin' Rose?"

"Ten-four. You got the Ramblin' Rose."

"You got the Barefoot Renegade on this end."

"No kidding! I thought I had the president of Mobile Oil. What's your ten-twenty, Barefoot?"

"I'm out here on this ice-covered drag-strip heading for Hurricane. I've got a call to make there and may not make it back to the lodge tonight. I didn't want you to worry about me."

Kelly darted a glance at Jonathan, whose sharp eyes watched every move she made. She knew Mike wanted to spite Jonathan. She felt like a bone between two dogs.

"Ten-four, good buddy. Keep the rubber side down and I'll catch you on the flip-flop. This Ramblin' Rose will be clear."

"Bye, Rose. This Barefoot Renegade is . . . ga—on!"

Kelly looked up to see Jonathan raise his eyes to the ceiling in disgust. Her own eyes lit up and a giggle escaped her lips.

"What's the matter, Jonathan? Too much corn? We'll have to find a C.B. handle for you. Let's see, you could be the Boston Bean!" She felt deliciously wicked. Her blue eyes danced and her delicate mouth smiled mischievously. "Break . . . break for the Boston Bean. Are you on the channel, Bean?"

She didn't know what to expect from her teasing but didn't care. Under her gaze his hard features softened and his lips turned up. Finally he broke into a wide grin. They sat looking into each other's eyes and Kelly's thoughts were blown from her like leaves before a wind.

"Ten-four, Ramblin' Rose, you got the Bean." Had he really said that?

Kelly burst out laughing. Jack watched her in silence, a gentle smile flitting across his lips.

"Can you imagine Katherine's reaction to that?" She leaned forward, her eyes glinting between dark lashes. "She'd insist on Boston Bean, Esquire!" She propped her elbow on the table and cupped her chin in her hand, trying to suppress her giggles.

"Jack!" Bonnie's voice came from deep within the pantry. "Would ya help me get this box off the shelf? When God passed out arms, he gave me the leftovers!"

Reluctantly, Jonathan got to his feet, his eyes still on Kelly. There was nothing arrogant or frightening about him now.

"Jack!"

Jonathan muttered an oath. Then, "Kelly?"

"What do you want?"

He leaned over and kissed her on the cheek. "Thank you."

"What for?"

"For letting me have a glimpse of the Kelly I fell in love with two years ago."

Her face paled. Fear closed like a cold hand around her heart. She was furious with herself for letting down the barrier. All he needed was one little crack in the armor she had built around herself and he would work his way into her heart again.

"No! That Kelly is dead. I'm no longer the stupid, naive person you met in Anchorage."

"Jack!"

"Damn!" he muttered and turned toward the pantry.

"Watch it . . . Jack." Her taunting words dripped with sarcasm. "Your image is slipping."

His face was unreadable, and she wondered if her jeeringly spoken words had upset him. She felt uneasy beneath his stare and hurriedly looked away when she saw his face harden and a muscle jerk beside his mouth.

*   *   *

Dinner that evening was lively and amusing. Bonnie had covered the long trestle table with a blue denim cloth and served the food on heavy, white plates. An oil lamp, its glass chimney sparkling, stood in the middle of the table surrounded by bowls of deliciously cooked food. The guests, enjoying the homey atmosphere, kept up a lively conversation while Bonnie, dressed all in red with her bleached hair piled haphazardly on top of her head, kept the table supplied with hot rolls straight from the oven.

Kelly noted that the silence between her and Jonathan seemed to pass more or less unnoticed. She watched the pretty blonde with large breasts flirt openly with him, her heavily coated lashes brushing against her cheeks. The girl was blatantly eager but her companion merely transferred his attention to the other woman of the party. The two remaining males concentrated on Kelly, giving her little time to analyze her feelings when the blonde looped her arm through Jonathan's. They all passed through the swinging doors into the main room, where Clyde had built up a cheerful fire and Lawrence Welk music was coming from the stereo.

"My favorite music!" The tall doctor slipped his arm around Kelly and began to dance.

"Liar. You don't look like the Lawrence Welk type to me." Kelly followed his lead around the room, her hand on his broad shoulder.

"No? What type am I? Willie Nelson?" He held her away and smiled.

"I'd say you're more the Beach Boys type."

"How did you know?" He began to sing and whirled her around the room.

She laughed. "Stop it, you're making me dizzy!" Out of the corner of her eye she noticed two other couples dancing. Jonathan was standing with his back to the fireplace watching them.

"Your husband is watching us. Do you mind?"

"How did you know he's my husband?"

"He told me when he brought in the luggage." He held her away again to look down into her face. "Something tells me your marriage is on the rocks."

She looked up at him in surprise, then stiffened. "Something tells me it's none of your business!" Pain made her voice harsh.

"Oops! I put my foot in, didn't I? You're not quite over him, yet. Breaking up is hard to do, but you'll survive. Take it from me. It'll be easier if you send him packing, or else split from this place."

"I don't recall asking your advice," Kelly said coolly. "Now if you'll excuse me, I'll see about setting up a game table for my other guests."

"Games? Great idea. How about spin the bottle, or button, button who's got the button, or . . . strip poker?" He grinned and she had to laugh. It was impossible to be angry at him for long.

"Come help me set up the table. Do you play Scrabble?"

"If you let me use dirty words."

"Are you ever serious? What kind of a doctor are you?"

"I specialize in female sexual problems."

"Are you kidding?"

"Yes. I'm a foot doctor."

Later, Kelly learned Andy was a general practitioner

and had given up a lucrative practice in Seattle to become resident doctor on an Indian reservation in Washington. This was his first vacation in two years, and he had come to Anchorage to attend a seminar and to visit his sister.

As the evening wore on, Kelly found herself becoming tense at the realization that she would have to go back to the cabin with Jonathan. Even as she was trying to think of a reason not to leave, Jonathan was explaining that Bonnie and Clyde were in the room off the kitchen. If they wanted anything, they need only ring the bell on the desk.

"Breakfast will be served anytime before noon," he concluded, holding Kelly's jacket for her to slip into.

"We'll see you in the morning." He ushered her out the door before she could say goodnight.

The night seemed bitterly cold after the warmth of the lodge. Kelly eased down the icy steps, shrugging off the hand Jonathan offered. She refused to admire the beauty of the moonlight on the fresh snow or the dark, drooping evergreens that stood like proud sentinels around the resort buildings. She walked ahead of him toward her home, lost in disturbing thoughts. They reached the cabin and Jonathan opened the door and switched on the light before moving aside for Kelly to enter.

"I won't be so optimistic as to expect a few quiet moments with my wife before our own hearth." He helped her with her coat and removed his own.

She prickled with annoyance at his tone. "I'm having a cup of hot chocolate."

"Sounds good. I haven't had a cup of chocolate in years."

"Why not? Too busy drinking tea?" Even as she said it, she wanted to take it back. She glanced at him. He had settled down on the couch and extended his stocking feet toward the blaze.

"The boarding school where I lived didn't offer chocolate, so I never acquired a taste for it."

"How long did you live at the boarding school?" Kelly asked, pouring milk into a pan on the stove.

"Until I went to college."

Kelly was about to ask, what college, but she knew it would be Harvard, Princeton, or Yale, so she didn't bother. She lapsed into silence, thinking how little she knew about this man she had married. She stirred cocoa and sugar into the hot milk and poured the steaming liquid into mugs, then carried one to Jonathan and seated herself in the rocker, nursing her own mug in both hands.

"Isn't it time we started to get to know each other? It seems absurd that we've been married for two years without knowing the first thing about what makes each other tick," he said softly. "Of course we've been together only a third of that time."

"I think you know everything there is to know about me." She wished he wouldn't keep looking at her.

"That's where you're wrong. I saw a completely different side of you today."

"So?" She shrugged and lapsed into silence.

"Talk to me, Kelly." The force of his voice betrayed his irritation.

"What about? You never told me much about yourself, either." She tried to make her voice casual, uncaring.

"It didn't seem relevant. I think you can sum up my life in two words . . . work and work. I've spent far too many hours working, or flying around the world working. When I wasn't working, I didn't know what to do with myself."

"Oh, I'm sure Katherine and Nancy could have thought of something."

He threw her a piercing look. "What do you mean by that?"

"Don't be stupid. I'm sure you know Nancy would have loved to help you relax." She got to her feet.

"A remark like that almost makes me think you're jealous."

She stared in blank bewilderment, then jerked the empty mug from his hand. "Fun—ny!" She set the mugs on the table and opened the glass door of the mantel clock and began to wind the spring.

"Getting late, is it?" Jonathan asked in a sardonic tone.

"Yes, and I want to get to bed," she snapped.

"So do I," he said softly, and her face burned.

To cover her confusion, she tried to lift a large chunk of wood and put it on the fireplace grate. It slipped in her hands, the rough wood tearing at her palms and ripping a fingernail. She could have bitten her tongue for allowing the small cry to escape her lips. Jonathan was by her side instantly, taking the heavy log from her hands. He threw it on the grate and shoved it in place with the firetongs. By the time he turned, Kelly was halfway to the bedroom door.

"Kelly, wait. Let me see your hand."

"It's only a scratch," she said over her shoulder.

"I want to see for myself. I think it's more than a mere scratch."

She turned on him like a spitting cat. "Bug off, Jonathan. I've about had all of you I can take. Leave me alone!" In her anguish she felt herself losing control.

He searched her features intently. "All right, Kelly. I won't bother you if you'd rather be alone. I was concerned for you and wanted to help if I could."

Tears filled Kelly's eyes. She'd been prepared for bitterness but not kindness. She fled to her room before the tears could fall.

CHAPTER SEVEN

KELLY COULDN'T HELP SHIVERING. The look in Jonathan's eyes as she turned away from him made her afraid—not of him, but of herself. She hated him, hated her own weakness for him. Her head started whirling dizzily. Her breathing quickened and a longing almost like a pain washed over her—a longing for that time long ago when she and Mike and Marty had been young and silly. When the only problems they'd had were getting the latest Beatles record or enough gas in the truck to go to Talkeetna.

She walked slowly into the bathroom, catching a glimpse of herself in the mirror. She paused. It was like seeing someone else. Her body looked the same, but her face was empty. She felt as if she didn't belong to herself. She wanted to laugh, she wanted to cry. Tears won.

"You're dumb, Kelly!" she muttered. "You're dumb and stupid. You've not only screwed up your own life, you've ruined things for Mike and Marty as well."

The palm of her hand had begun to sting so she went to the bathroom in search of medication. She felt so lonely, so lost, so frantic.

She heard Jonathan moving about in the other bedroom and her heart gave a sudden sickening leap. She dabbed unnecessarily hard at the scratches on her palm where the red blood beaded. She knew and understood the bond that existed between her and Jonathan, just as she knew that the almost unbearable longing that swept her at times was more than a mere physical longing, but a yearning to belong, to have someone of her very own. She shook her head, trying to force herself to remember her true motive for leaving him, to steel herself against the dangerous knowledge that he was scarcely twenty feet away and his lips, his arms, his masculinity, could engulf her and carry her away to forgetfulness. To give way to the treachery of such thoughts could only lead to more heartbreak. A shudder ran through her. With trembling fingers she replaced the bottle in the medicine cabinet. Jonathan was a taker. He would take all she had to give and her own need, her pride, would be wiped away like so many snowflakes on a hot stove.

She cleaned her face, brushed her teeth, and glanced about to make sure the bathroom was tidy before she left it. In her bedroom she put on her warm flannel nightgown and put away her slacks and sweater. After turning down her bed, she switched off the lamp and went to open the door leading into the living room.

She wasn't ready to confront him again so soon, but there he was, framed in the doorway. The light was behind him and she couldn't see the expression on his face. But she could feel his eyes, so disturbingly intent, on her.

"It isn't going to work, you know!" she flung at him belligerently.

"Is your hand all right?"

"Yes!" Kelly was irritated that he could stand there so calmly while she felt as if she would fly into a million pieces.

"Get into bed and I'll bring you a hot drink." He spoke as if to a rebellious child.

"I don't believe you! You can't be real!" she wailed. "Can't you see I don't want you here? You have absolutely no right to interfere in my life. You really are something else, Jonathan. I can't find a word to describe you . . ." She was ashamed of the silly, childish words that tumbled from her mouth.

She began to shake uncontrollably and wasn't sure if it was from the cold or because her nerves were so strung out. She flung herself back into the darkened room with head bowed, slid into bed, and tried to tuck her cold feet up into the warm folds of her nightgown. She was paying the price for those few blissful weeks when her love for him had consumed her and she had allowed him to take over her life.

Jonathan came to stand beside the bed but she ignored him.

"Turn over, Kelly. I've brought you a hot drink." When she refused to move, he placed his hand on her shoulder. "You're shaking like a leaf. Turn over and drink this. It's only whiskey and a little sugar and hot water. It'll warm you up."

Kelly turned over, sat up, and almost snatched the mug from his hand. Anything to get rid of him, she told herself.

"Is there something that needs to be done aside from banking the fires?"

"No, but leave the doors open so the pipes don't freeze," she answered grudgingly.

"I'll take care of it." He took the empty cup from her hand, pushed her gently down into the bed and tucked the covers about her shoulders.

Her body was as taut as a bow-string and her limbs icy cold, but already warmth from the drink was beginning to penetrate her chilled body. She kept her eyes tightly closed, wishing desperately for sleep.

Cold air hit her in the back. The mattress sagged as Jonathan lowered his weight onto the bed. Her eyes flew open and she gave a high wail. Panic stricken, she flopped over to face him, then tried to back away.

"No! No, Jonathan. I won't sleep with you!" Her hands went to his chest to push him away from her. His skin was bare and warm and his masculine scent was so familiar! She smelled the mint of toothpaste on his breath when he leaned over her. Her heart beat with sheer horror. He was forging chains that were binding her to him. "Please! Please, don't." Her control broke and she begged pitilessly.

He ignored her pleas and pulled her to him, his muscled body free and unconfined. He searched and found her lips, opening them with the urgent pressure of his own. Her senses swam beneath his eager conquest. Pride forced her to continue to struggle in his arms and the gown worked up and over her thighs. Panic flared as he swung his bare leg over hers and held her softness pinned to the yielding mattress.

"You want me, darling!" he said slowly, his voice husky against her mouth. She tried to shake her head in silent denial, but he had locked it between his hands.

"You want me as much as I want you." His tongue played with her lips.

"Wanting and loving are not the same," she gasped in a breathless whisper.

"Think of the wanting. The other can come later."

"No! I can't do it, Jonathan," she mumbled frantically.

"Jack. Think of me as the Jack you loved during those few wonderful weeks," he insisted.

"It makes no difference!"

"It does to me," he returned in that soft, seductive voice.

"No!" Even while she was protesting, her blood ran like liquid fire through her veins. His hand caressed her back, stroking away the flannel gown and running urgently over her smooth skin, caressing her into surrender. She tried to protest, "No . . ." but the word was muffled by the drugging seduction of his mouth against her own.

Again she tried to push him away, but he tilted her to him, making her helpless, while his lips deepened their kiss. Her hands moved to his smooth, thick hair and fondled his neck and the strong line of his shoulders and back, then came up to stroke his cheeks and caress his ears.

Jonathan let his mouth wander over her face. "Say it, Kelly. Say you want me, that you like the feel of my body against yours."

Refusing to answer, she struggled with the weakness that swept over her. The sensual need she had been fighting was taking complete control of her. The power of the sexual drive she had suppressed and stifled for months swamped her, driving away all coherent thought except the one that told her she was doomed if she surrendered completely.

"Say it," he whispered in her ear.

"I can't! I can't!"

"Yes, you can. I'm not asking for your heart, but for the possession of your body. I won't force anything from you that you're not willing to give. I want to make love to you, and I know you want me too. There's no commitment, darling," he said in tense deliberation.

"No commitment? No! You want a woman and any woman will do! I won't be used!" She tried to scramble away from him.

"Darling," he groaned in protest, lifting his head and moving his body over hers to hold her, "that wasn't what I meant. You crazy girl . . . be still and let me love you."

Only later did Kelly pause to ask herself wildly what she was doing. She should be fighting him. Instead she wanted to feel his skin against hers. Obediently she raised her arms and allowed him to slip the nightgown over her head. Then she was in his embrace, his arms and legs locked around her and her breasts crushed against the fine cloud of hair on his chest.

"Sweetheart, you're so beautiful," he groaned in a husky voice. "Forget everything, but you and me and how I want to love you. You want me. . . . You do want me?" The muttered words were barely coherent, thickly groaned into her ear as he kissed the warm curve of her neck.

The deeply buried heat in her own body seemed to flare out of control, and she sought his mouth hungrily. Her hands moved to his back, digging into the smooth muscles. She felt the powerful tug of her own desire for him and admitted what her subconscious mind had known since the moment he came to the cabin. She wanted him.

He began to stroke her, whispering words, their meaning muffled for her as he kissed her soft, rounded breasts, nibbling with his teeth, nuzzling with his lips. He was totally absorbed in giving her pleasure and at the same time pleasing himself. She twisted and turned beneath him, bringing a groan of satisfaction to his lips. She was hungry for him, and returned his caresses with all the instinctive sexuality of her young body. Only Jack made love to her like this and he had been an expert teacher.

"Jack! Oh, Jack!" She arched her back, her senses surging to limitless peaks of pleasure. She was being carried on a tidal wave of desire.

"Darling, beautiful, Kelly," he breathed, his hands sliding down her spine to the provocative curve of her hips.

Their lovemaking was a devastating experience, and when it was over, he didn't move away from her. Instead, he cupped her face with his hands and sought her mouth with his.

"That was good, wasn't it?" he said huskily, running his mouth over her face. His lips paused to tease her lashes. "Kelly, Kelly. . . . How did I survive without you all those months? I love the feel of your breasts against me and the taste of your mouth. You're so soft, so feminine, so incredibly beautiful!"

Kelly lay tightly against his body, her head resting on his chest. She couldn't move. She was in an untenable predicament. He was an expert lover—gentle, sensitive to her desires. Their bodies came together perfectly. But there should be more. It was useless to deny that his hands, his lips, his husky voice, sent her into a mindless whirl of pleasure. She shivered, his arms tightened, and she wept silently.

"I can't get enough of you," he whispered as his lips traced a path across her forehead. He grasped her hand and held it palm down against the flat plain of his stomach. Her whole body went rigid as she fought the tremors of longing that were already shaking her control. She stifled the sob that rose in her throat and resisted surrender when his mouth came to rest on hers. His probing tongue encountered sealed lips where minutes ago it had found eager admittance. His hands became more demanding, his lips more persuasive, and she parted her own lips to object, to protest that she didn't want him again. He used that instant to find what he was seeking, and the touch of his tongue on her threatened to rob her of the ability to think, to remember the cold-eyed man who had treated her scornfully in Boston.

No! her pride screamed. He didn't love her. He was using her to satisfy his sexual lust. Her body shook with a different kind of tremor that Jonathan responded to immediately. He lifted his mouth and she buried her face against the damp, matted hair on his chest. Tenderly his fingers raised her face and moved over her cheeks, wet with tears.

"Don't make love to me again. Please . . . I don't want you to," she stammered.

"All right, sweetheart. But were my caresses so terrible?" His voice was soft and persuasive. "You enjoyed it, didn't you?" His lips were moving over her face, absorbing her tears. "I know I did."

"I don't want to get pregnant," she blurted out. "I would hate it!"

He remained still for a long while, raining gentle kisses on her face and holding her very tightly.

"Are you sure, Kelly? Are you sure you don't want us to have a child?" he whispered in her ear, and kissed her so gently that her whole body cried out for him.

She raised tear-drenched lashes that fluttered against his cheek. A wave of helplessness came over her, and she whimpered. As if in torment, she tightened her arms about his neck and hungrily sought his lips, wanting to escape her anguished thoughts. He remained perfectly still as her mouth moved over his.

"This is all we have," she sobbed helplessly. "I despise your snobbish way of life and you'll hate mine after you've tried it. It would be criminal for us to have a child. No! I never want to have a child by you, Jonathan!"

Her words made him go rigid. "If you're sure, Kelly," he said slowly. "If you're very sure you never want to have my child, I'll go to Anchorage and have a vasectomy."

His words stunned her. Had he really said them? He would give up, forever, the chance to have a child of his own?

"No!" Her arms clutched him frantically and her hands moved over his powerful body. "No! I couldn't let you do that. Oh, Jonathan, what are we going to do?"

His arms pulled her closer as her tears wet his chest. He rained kisses on her brow, cheeks, and throat. Her own mouth blindly sought comfort, tasting her salty tears on his lips, and the tang of his skin. The driving force of her passion was taking her beyond reason, beyond fear.

"Don't think about it, darling. If you don't want a baby, we'll do something about it. But for now . . . we'll have to take the risk, because I can't stop. . . ."

She sighed deeply and then blocked out everything but this moment . . . this night. She heard his ragged breathing as if from far away, and then she pulled him to her. Gradually the storm of passion overpowered them and they made wild, uninhibited love.

Afterward she lay quietly beside him. He buried his face in the curve of her neck, like a child seeking comfort. She held him and stroked him without speaking. But she couldn't dismiss a feeling of impending doom. Her need for him was making her a prisoner and inwardly she rebelled.

"I could have you again," he whispered hoarsely against her breast.

Kelly's mouth went dry. "Again?"

He laughed and nibbled her skin. "It's been a long, dry spell."

"Am I supposed to believe that?" she asked quietly.

"Absolutely," he said firmly and caught the lobe of her ear with his teeth and nipped it before burying his face in the hollow between her breasts. "Has there ever been another man?" he muttered. "Don't lie to me. Just tell me if you've slept with another man."

"There's been no other man."

He lifted his head and covered her mouth with his, and for a long time there was only the sound of their shaken breathing and the thump of his heart pounding against hers.

"Thank you, darling," he said in a voice trembling

with emotion. "I had to hear you say you've been only mine."

Something hurt inside her. She swallowed convulsively. He wanted to own her, possess her for his pleasure alone. What happened tonight would happen again and again. What had she expected? a small voice cried inside her. She and Jonathan couldn't live in the same house, much less sleep in the same bed without sex. It all boiled down to one thing: an arrangement. She would give Jonathan the sex he wanted and he, in turn, would let Mike and Marty keep the resort. It was as cold-blooded as that.

She had to sort out her emotions, untangle the confused motivations, and decide what she really wanted out of life. The image of Jack she had carried in her heart for so long had surfaced. The cold, possessive Jonathan of Boston had faded to nothingness when Jack held her in his arms. She needed time to think. She had rushed into marriage without any real idea of the kind of man she was marrying or the kind of lifestyle she would be expected to live. She couldn't afford to make that mistake again. If her home in Alaska was a prison, at least it wasn't the kind of prison Boston had been, where everything pressed down on her, chilling her, crushing her spirit.

Jonathan's hand slowly stroked her back. "What are you thinking about?"

"Our Boston apartment and what a beautiful prison it was."

He drew in a long, shaken breath and stroked the hair from her temples, his fingers touching her cheeks.

"And I was the warden? What do you feel for me, Kelly?" he asked wearily.

She moved her hand to his chest and felt his heart leaping under it. The rest of him was still, with a peculiar, silent waiting between them.

"Feelings shouldn't be involved where business is concerned, Jonathan," she whispered in husky tones.

He turned on his back and drew her to him. She settled her head on his body and heard the slow, regular rhythm of his breathing. His hands touched her gently, without pressure, as though reassuring himself she was here.

"Are you warm?" he asked and tucked the blankets close behind her.

"Uh-huh."

Finally she fell asleep.

CHAPTER EIGHT

SHE REFUSED TO open her eyes. She wanted to fall asleep again, because in sleep there was no regret, no incrimination.

"Kelly!" Her name was a soft whisper wooing her from the land of Nod. She turned her face into the pillow and the insistent voice grew crisper. "Kelly!"

"What do you want?" she said crossly into the pillow.

"It's nine o'clock."

"Nine o'clock?" Her eyes flew open and she turned to glance up at Jonathan standing beside the bed with a mug in his hand. "Nine o'clock? I don't believe it!"

"You've been sleeping like a baby for hours." He sat down on the bed. He had shaved, his hair was damp from the shower, and he was fully dressed in clean denims and a soft flannel shirt. "Drink your coffee and come alive, woman."

Kelly freed her arms from the confines of the soft, fleecy blanket and pushed her tangled hair back from her sleep-flushed face. She looked into teasing, brown eyes and was flooded with the sudden memory of the ecstasy she had shared with him just hours before. Shame and humiliation made her voice sharp.

"Nothing is changed!"

"What do you mean?" He handed her the mug which she was forced to take.

"You know what I mean. You seduced me, wore me down. I'll never forgive you!"

"Kelly, Kelly . . . I'm not asking for your forgiveness. All I did was make love to my wife, a normal, healthy expression of emotion."

The calm inflection in his quiet voice grated on her nerves and resentment burned in her eyes.

"Expression of emotion? Lust, you mean!"

"Lust or a biological urge. I prefer to think of it as making love." He smiled at her warmly.

"Love had nothing to do with it!" She spat the words at him and jerked the blanket up to her chin.

He laughed and she wanted to hit him. "Okay. Call it anything you want . . . but I liked doing it!"

"I don't give a damn what you call it! It won't happen again. I won't be a . . . vehicle for your lust!" The words exploded from her tense lips.

"My lust? Our lust, dear wife. Or is lust too masculine a word to describe a woman's sexual desires?" Amusement glinted in his dark eyes.

"Sex? Lust? Is that all you can talk about?"

Heavy lids hid his eyes and a secretive smile curved his mouth. Bending forward, he brushed his lips tantalizingly across hers. "Let's not fight, Kelly. Let's make love."

With a groan of irritation, she turned away from him. "I wish you hadn't come here!" she said viciously.

"You'll get over it. After I've been here a few weeks, you'll wonder how you ever lived without me." He took the mug from her hand and set it on the bedside table, then rubbed his fingers back and forth across her cheek. "We'll discuss this tonight while we're lying together in this bed, our arms around each other. It's good, isn't it? This touching and feeling every part of each other? We make love well, darling."

Kelly wanted to jerk away, but pride forced her to pretend his touch didn't bother her. She remained perfectly still, although her heart pounded like a scared rabbit's, and she kept her eyes averted. With a quick movement he flicked aside the blanket to reveal her long, slender, naked figure.

"Stop that!" She grabbed for the blanket.

He laughed and went around the end of the bed toward the door. "I'm expecting a chopper in about fifteen minutes. One of my men is bringing in some paperwork. I thought I would do the work in the chopper. Do you think you can get along without me for an hour or so?"

"Try me."

He grinned broadly. "I'll send the chopper away if you think you'll die of lust before I can get back." The amusement on his face enraged her. She clamped her lips together and refused to speak the words that boiled up in her. "The water is hot for your shower. Leave the water tank turned on. We can afford to have hot water all day."

"Sure. Now that Mountain View is part of a big conglomerate, we're merely a tax write-off." The reminder that her home was no longer hers tore at her heart.

"Think what you like, Kelly." He drawled her name.

"There are times when you tempt me to swat your behind."

Across the room her eyes challenged him and her thoughts whirled. If she stayed another night with him . . . if she slept another night in his arms. . . . Oh, she had to hold out against him!

"You're not staying here!" she almost shouted at him, but he had already left the room.

On her way to the lodge, Kelly paused to play with Charlie for a few minutes. Mike's utility truck was parked in the shed and a plume of smoke came from his cabin chimney. For one wild instant Kelly was tempted to go there and tell him what Jonathan had done. There was no doubt in her mind that Mike would agree to go away with her and leave the property to Jonathan. But she couldn't do that to Mike. He would expect her to divorce Jonathan and marry him. Head down and hands buried deep in the pockets of her coat, she headed toward the lodge, her mind so busy she failed to see the tall doctor waiting beside the steps.

"You look as gorgeous today as you did yesterday."

Kelly looked up into his smiling eyes. "Hi, Andy. Bye, Andy. I'm headed for the kitchen and gallons of coffee."

He slipped his hand beneath her elbow and they went up the steps together. "I had breakfast with your husband. He said you were tired and sleeping in."

The statement required no answer and Kelly shrugged out of her jacket and slipped off her boots. She could like Andy, if only Jonathan hadn't come to the resort and stirred up all the emotions she had thought dead. If only Jonathan was more like Andy . . . Kelly put a brake on her thoughts. She could *if only* until doomsday and it wouldn't change a thing.

"Come out, come out, from wherever you are!" Andy bent down and grinned into her face. "Back among the living? Do you suppose that husband of yours would let you take a snowmobile ride with me?"

"What's it got to do with him? How about askin' me, buster?" Although Kelly's tone was teasing, she held an underlying note of seriousness.

"Okay." He placed his hand over his heart. "Andy Mullins respectfully requests the honor of your presence . . ."

"Oh, stop!" Kelly laughed. "I'd love to go, but first I need to fortify myself with some of Bonnie's toast and coffee." She led the way into the kitchen. "What about your friends? Would they like to go, too? We can carry four."

"They're busy resting, sleeping in. I wouldn't be surprised if it took all day for them to rest up." His eyes twinkled down at her. She ignored the implication.

"If you say so. Morning, Bonnie." She took a cup from the rack. "Coffee, Andy?"

"Sure. A roll, too. I've already asked Bonnie to divorce Clyde and marry me. She's not only beautiful, she's also got the fastest cookstove in the West!"

"You ain't gonna eat again!" Bonnie put her hands on her ample hips, tried to look disgusted, and failed completely.

"Now, darlin', you said, and I quote: 'Ain't nothin' does my heart so good as to see a man what likes his vittles.' You said that not an hour ago." Andy took the cup

Kelly handed him and sat down at the table. "All I want is one little ol' roll."

"You don't have to pay no attention to everything I say! You'll spoil your dinner, that's what you'll do," Bonnie scolded. "I'm having Irish stew for dinner and barbecue ribs for supper. Clyde's already got them in the smoker."

"I promise to eat my share. Now hand over that roll before I shoot up the place." He shaped his hand like a six-gun and pointed it at her.

"I swear to goodness, Kelly," Bonnie complained. "I thought Jack could eat a lot, but this kid can outdo even him. I think we ought to add another twenty bucks to his bill."

"Good idea." Kelly lifted the bread from the toaster and sat down across from Andy. "Some kid!" she said softly for his ears alone.

"Jack had a stack of hot cakes and three pats of sausage this morning," Bonnie volunteered. She set down in front of Andy a roll as big as a saucer, dripping with melted butter, and glazed with icing. "He said a friend was coming in a helicopter to bring him some things and to make a list if I wanted anything. I said, well, we sure could use a new washer and dryer 'cause the ones we got must have come with the gold-rushers." Kelly looked up sharply and Bonnie, catching the disapproval on her face, added quickly, "I was just a teasin'. I didn't put nothing like that on the list. I wrote down some things like spices and a couple cases of tomatoes and a new broom. I wanted to add towels, but thought that better wait till one of us can go to the discount store. Men ain't got no sense a'tall when it comes to a buyin' something like that." She went back to the stove and lifted the lid on a large cooking pot. The grin she shot over her shoulder held just a dash of superiority. "Smell that, Andy? That stew's goin' to be just right!"

Kelly drove the snowmobile and Andy sat in the seat behind her. Her spirits picked up when they headed for open country. The snow was light and the churning lugs of the machine left a soft, fine cloud behind them. They followed animal tracks just to see where they were going and once Kelly stopped the machine when she saw a small herd of moose move out of the timber.

"You can never tell what a moose will do," she explained to Andy. "If pointed in your direction, they might run right over you. They get confused and sometimes jump out in front of cars. It happened to Mike and me once. We saw the moose coming and there was nothing we could do. Mike shoved me down on the seat and boom! We had a moose draped over the hood. The windshield popped out and we almost froze, driving in below-zero weather without a windshield."

Andy was a pleasant companion. Kelly showed him wolf tracks and told him that the legend about the wolf being a vicious killer was a myth.

"My father always thought the wolf was a very misunderstood animal. He kills only to eat, and rarely attacks man. He is a lonely animal. Occasionally, on a clear night we can hear his mournful howl. A wolverine is an altogether different and much more dangerous animal." Kelly shuddered.

As they drove back to the lodge, the breeze rushing

against Kelly's face and the snow whipping about her cleared her head and soothed her taut nerves. She had deliberately stayed away from the helicopter, which sat like a large insect on the white snow.

In the deserted family room of the lodge they sank down onto the couch and Andy told her about his job on the reservation. A soft light came into his eyes as he talked. He was dedicated to his work among the Indians. He told her of their pride, their dignity, and their great need. Andy was a fine man, she decided.

"Have you ever been married?" she asked suddenly.

"Sure," he laughed. "Hasn't everyone?"

"Divorced?" She didn't know why she persisted.

"Ages ago. She's married to a banker now. Couldn't stand my lifestyle. Nothing prestigious about living in a five room bungalow on an Indian reservation." All traces of merriment were gone from his face.

"She and Jonathan would have been great together." The words came before Kelly realized she was saying them.

"Now, now," Andy chided gently. "Methinks you . . ."

Kelly was saved from hearing more by Bonnie entering through the swinging doors.

"Dinner is ready anytime anybody wants to eat it."

Kelly's laughing eyes caught Andy's. "We're very informal here, or hadn't you noticed?"

"Is that what it is?" Andy asked innocently. "I like it. Reserve me a room for the last weekend of the month. I'm attending a seminar in Anchorage or I wouldn't leave here at all."

"Landsakes! I'll start a cookin' on a Thursday if I know he's comin' on the weekend. I'll have to get me a runnin' start to fill him up!" Bonnie's face was a wreath of smiles even as she complained.

"Marty and Tram will be here by then. Maybe we can plan an overnight ski-tour."

"Overnight?" Andy frowned, then grinned. "Dibs on sharing my sleeping bag with you."

"You're nuts! Do you know that?"

"Jack would have something to say about that," Bonnie said. She cocked her head and listened. "That's the chopper leavin'. Jack ought to be up here in a few minutes."

He was.

The instant he stepped inside the door, his eyes locked with Kelly's and she felt a pain deep inside her. Their hours of making love had pried open the dark door between them and brought her face to face with the Jack behind the sophisticated facade of Jonathan Templeton the Third.

Jonathan left his coat and boots beside the door and went directly to Kelly, pulling her up from the couch.

"Enjoy your ride, darling?" His arm went possessively across her shoulders.

"How did you know?"

He chuckled and his arm tightened. "How could I miss that yellow cap of yours?"

"True," she murmured drily.

"What we need is a good bit of that stew." Bonnie seemed to sense the tension and burst into speech. "I'll just step out on the back step and holler to that ugly old Clyde. He's out there a tinkerin' with that old motor again. Yaw'll go on in . . . everything's ready. I'll be right along and dip up the stew."

They had scarcely reached the kitchen when they heard Bonnie scream.

Kelly dashed for the back door, but Jonathan was there ahead of her. Bonnie lay in a heap at the foot of the steps, her leg twisted under her and her back against the rise of the stairs. They could see the path her feet had made when she slipped on the loose snow covering the icy platform at the top of the steps.

Andy was beside her in an instant. "Don't move. Lie still, Bonnie. Let me see what you've done to yourself."

Clyde came running from the shed. "What did you do, honeybunch? I told ya to be careful on that ice. Are ya hurt?"

Bonnie looked dazed. Her face and hair were wet with snow. "Clyde! Clyde, honey, I hurt my back . . . and my leg . . . 'n', oh, hell, I hurt all over!" Her face twisted with pain and her lips quivered.

Andy's experienced hands were traveling over her leg. "Get a blanket, Kelly," he said without looking up. Gentle fingers lifted Bonnie's chin. "For one thing, you've gone and busted yore leg and I'll have to shoot ya!" he said in a perfect imitation of her Oklahoma twang. To Clyde he said, "We need a flat board. She may have injured her back."

"There's a piece of plywood in the shed." Clyde began to rise to his feet, but Jonathan put his hand on his shoulder.

"I'll get it. Stay with Bonnie."

Kelly held the door open while the men carried Bonnie into the kitchen. She was obviously in great pain and tears seeped from her eyes, leaving dark streaks of mascara on her cheeks.

"I've really gone and done it, ain't I, Clyde? We had a good place here . . . oh, I'm so sorry, honey. I ruined everything!"

"Now you quit frettin'. You didn't do it on purpose. We'll get by. Ain't we always managed?"

Clyde tried to calm Bonnie while Kelly went for more blankets and Andy got his medical kit.

"How are we going to pay for this, Clyde? We ain't got no insurance." Bonnie began to cry in earnest.

"The lodge will pay the bills, Bonnie," Jonathan reassured her. "Don't worry. All you've got to do is lie still until we can get you out of here." Jonathan stood beside the table where they had set the board with Bonnie still on it.

"They can't, Jack! Them kids scraped up every penny they could. They worked so hard to get this place going. They was so good to me and Clyde. It'll break 'em if they got big bills and . . ."

"Insurance will pay it. Stop worrying."

"They ain't got no insurance. Kelly told us . . ."

"They have. I took care of it. Now, Clyde, see if you can get Mike up here so he can get on that radio. I'm sure he knows more about reaching the helicopter that just left here than I do."

Kelly helped Andy prepare Bonnie for the trip and Jonathan sat down at the table and quickly filled a sheet of paper with his strong handwriting. With the use of an emergency relay system, Mike was able to get a message to the helicopter pilot with orders to turn back to the resort.

An hour later they carried a sedated Bonnie, bundled in wool blankets, out to the clearing. Jonathan spoke to the pilot while Mike, Andy, and Clyde maneuvered the stretcher into place.

The three men stood back, as the powerful blades whipped the soft snow into a cloud, and waited for the helicopter to lift off. Afterward, they crowded into the cab of the truck and, with Mike driving, went back to the lodge.

CHAPTER NINE

"YOU'LL DO NO such thing!" Kelly's hands were deep in sudsy dishwater and she flung the words over her shoulder. They'd just served late lunch and she was in the midst of cleaning up. "Bring a chef out here! What do you think this is, the Mountain View Hilton?"

"You can't do all your usual work and the cooking, too, Kelly." Jonathan's calm voice grated on her already taut nerves.

"What makes you think I can't? I'm no delicate social butterfly, Jonathan. Butt out, will you? Marty will be here next week and we'll manage just fine."

He took a deep breath. His face was a dark mask and his voice was harsh.

"One of these days you're going to push me too far and I'm going to take a strap to your butt!"

She turned in surprise to see his eyes flickering over her face and his nostrils flaring.

"Ha!" she exploded. "I can see the headlines . . . 'Member Of Boston's Social Register Turns Wife Beater.'"

Jonathan suddenly looked so furious that all the strength drained out of her, leaving her limp in the grip of the hands that shook her.

"I'm tired of your ridicule! If you make one more derogatory reference to my background, I'm going to shake you until your teeth rattle!"

Kelly gazed into his eyes, so astonishingly bright with anger. "And what would that prove?" she demanded. "That you're bigger and stronger than I am? You want to hurt me, so go ahead!"

"You're damn right I want to hurt you! Don't you know you hurt me by walking out on me and letting me worry half to death over you?"

"The only thing I ever hurt was your pride. My rejection was a blow to your ego." She spit the words out recklessly and trembled with unspent emotion. "I was doing very well until you came. This is my home, where I belong. You'll never get me away from here, Jonathan, even if our property is in your name. You still don't own the business, so don't tell me how to run it."

His gaze was locked with hers, as her voice lashed him with bitter, unguarded words. "Don't make me lose my temper, Kelly," he said softly.

"You can't take my life over and dictate what I'll do."

"I'm not trying to take over your life. I'm trying to share it."

"Then let me go so I can wipe the dishes."

His hand slid along her spine, pulling her close to him. His eyes teased her. "Ask me nicely and I will."

"You're the most changeable, obstinate man I've ever known."

"Determined," he corrected softly.

"Obstinate, stubborn, mulish, pigheaded . . . stiff-necked!"

"At least you'll never be bored with me." He brushed her mouth with his lips.

"And I'll never have a moment of peace, either,"

He lifted her chin, tilting her head up to stare down into her eyes. She tried to pull away, and her hair brushed his face. His eyes narrowed with desire.

The intensity of his gaze made her uncomfortable but she returned his look coolly. "What you see is what you get." She regretted the words immediately.

His grin spread a terrible charm over his face and she felt a smile touch her own. She tried to banish it.

"Is that a promise?" He placed a feathery kiss on her nose.

"You're maddening!" She snapped her teeth at him.

"And you're not?" He took her hand and she felt something hard against her fingers. Looking down, she saw the blue flash of a sapphire. He slipped the plain wedding band onto her finger and then the sapphire and diamond ring. He folded her fingers into her palm and held them there. "It's time these were back where they belong."

She sucked in her breath, dismayed. Before she could say a word he bent his head and kissed her gently. Tides of overwhelming warmth washed over her.

"I've got to get these dishes done." She had to get away from him. The ache in her body was too much to bear. She had to keep busy.

"And I'd better fill the woodbox. That was one of Clyde's jobs, wasn't it?"

"That and keeping the fires going, the ashes hauled out, the wood cut, etc., etc. etc. . . ."

"Keeping the heat tapes on the pipes, checking the well pump, keeping the motors going, necking with the cook, etc., etc., etc. . . ." He grinned. "You think I can't manage a few simple chores?"

"Seein' is believin'." She turned her back to him and plunged her hands into the dishwater.

"Some of those chores can wait until I wipe a few dishes."

They worked silently side by side. Kelly's hands moved automatically while her mind strived to sort out Jonathan's confusing behavior. It would be wishful thinking to believe he felt more than pure desire for her. His determination to stay with her arose from simple frustration. A spoiled little boy had grown into a hard, sophisticated man who had been denied something he wanted very badly.

Once she had given him her love, and he had dropped it carelessly. Now, he wanted back the toy that had been snatched away from him. In his determination to possess her, he was robbing her of any chance to forget him, any chance for finding happiness with someone new.

She finished the last dish and straightened her aching back. "You're tired, you silly girl. Sit down and have a cup of coffee." Jonathan pushed her gently into a chair. "I'll see about the ribs in the smoker and fill the cookstove before I check the fireplace and take a run down to our house to be sure it's warm enough there."

"All right, Dangerous Dan McGrew," she said without humor.

"If I'm Dan McGrew, you're the lady that's known as Lou," he said softly.

"Don't tell me Yukon poetry was included in the curriculum at your fancy boarding school."

Jonathan stood before her, his expression serious, and began reciting:

"There are strange things done in the midnight sun
     By men who moil for gold;
The Arctic trails have their secret tales
     That would make your blood run cold;
The Northern Lights have seen queer sights,
     But the queerest they ever did see
Was the night on the marge of Lake Lebarge
     I cremated Sam McGee.

That, my darling wife, is from a poem by Robert Service, poet of the Yukon, who worked in a Whitehorse bank that's still doing business."

"Hear! Hear!" Kelly cheered, a big grin on her face. She loved poetry, especially ballads. "We'll work up a floor show and let you entertain the guests," she teased.

"And run the risk of losing me to Las Vegas?"

"I wouldn't be so lucky." There was no sting in her tone; her eyes were still warm with laughter.

"No appreciation. That's what's wrong with you, my girl." She watched him put his coat on and thought how easy it would be to fall back into the trap of blind adoration, accepting the desire he offered as a substitute for the love she craved. "Don't go away," he said lightly.

Preparations for the evening meal went smoothly. The food Bonnie had cooked that morning helped ease the workload, and Jonathan proved to be far more capable than Kelly had imagined. He scrubbed and oiled the potatoes, while she prepared greens for the salad. Finally, she couldn't suppress a giggle.

"What's funny?" he asked.

"You'd know if you could see yourself. I never expected to see the perfectly groomed, cool, no-nonsense Jonathan Templeton with soot on his face." She began to laugh. "You don't look very elegant,"

He laughed too. "*You* look elegant!" He grabbed a stack of plates. "What's the program? Do we all eat together?"

"I'll be waitress. Set places for the five guests and yourself."

"I'll be waiter. We can eat together afterward. How about Mike?"

"He said he'd be up later."

"When did he say that?"

"While we were waiting for the helicopter to come for Bonnie." She glanced around the kitchen and dining area. It looked neat and cozy. With the exception of the potatoes baking in the oven, the meal was ready to be served. She whipped off her apron, and took a large tray from the shelf.

"Now what?" Jonathan asked.

"Drinks. I think we should serve before-dinner drinks."

"Good idea. That's my department. Move aside and let the bartender take over." He loaded the tray with glasses, mix, whiskey, and rum. Kelly filled a bowl with ice cubes and reached for cocktail napkins. Jonathan looked over the tray with a critical eye then, with a conspiratorial wink, he headed for the swinging doors.

He was a perfect host. Why not, Kelly thought. He'd

certainly had enough practice. As the murmur of amused chatter flowed over her, Kelly experienced a feeling of unreality. It was almost as if she and Jonathan were entertaining guests in their own home.

While she served the meal, Jonathan set two places at a small table at the far end of the room. He smiled a lot in a slow, endearing way that lifted his mouth at the corners and spread a warm light into his eyes. She hadn't seen him smile like that since . . . Anchorage.

Kelly bantered pleasantly with Andy. The girl who had been so attentive to Jonathan the night before seemed to have transferred her attention to Andy tonight. Her nonstop chatter didn't leave room for much other conversation.

Jonathan and Kelly were silent during their own meal. When they'd finished, Jonathan carried their empty plates to the sink.

"Charlie will love the rib bones," he said, returning with the coffee pot. It was cozy and quiet and music from the stereo drifted softly into the room. "It went off without a hitch, didn't it?" He had a satisfied smile on his face.

"Yes, it did," she admitted.

The back door opened and Mike entered. "Smells good," he said. "Anything left?"

"Sure. Help yourself." Suddenly the room felt cold. Jonathan leaned back in his chair, maddeningly in command of himself. A look flashed between them. Don't freeze Mike out of my life! Kelly's mind shrieked. Her eyes shifted to Mike and she smiled. "Fill a plate and join us."

Jonathan was watching her shrewdly, eyes narrowed,

as he sipped his coffee. Kelly didn't know what to expect
next.

"Bring a cup, Mike. The coffee pot is here," he said,
his eyes still on Kelly.

"The potatoes are in the warming oven," she added.

"All this and potatoes, too? I'm hungry as a bear."

They spoke polite words, but might as well have
snarled at each other. Kelly was surprised at how confi-
dently Mike approached them, and felt a flash of pride.
He was family and she loved him. She was sure that one
day soon he would realize he loved her like family, too.
Her eyes softened when she looked at him.

"You'll have to clue me in on what's to be done around
here while Clyde's away, Mike," Jonathan said easily.

"Think you can handle Clyde's chores? I can always
get a few no-good loafers to come out for a while. I
would have done that before, but I wouldn't leave Kelly
out here alone with most of them."

Kelly met Jonathan's eyes with a pretense of calm.
Mike was handling himself just fine.

"I appreciate that."

Kelly flushed. Those three words set his seal of possession on her.

"If you think you can manage it, we'd better get on the
ends of that crosscut in the morning. I cut enough wood
this fall for my own use, but I didn't know Kelly was
coming back or that she'd want to open the lodge. Heat is
top priority in this country."

"Have you looked into propane gas for heating?"
Jonathan asked.

"Can't afford it. It would cost an arm and a leg to heat

this place with gas. Maybe later when we get the business going."

Here it comes, Kelly thought. Jonathan would reveal that he owned the lodge and Mike would be furious! She felt caught between two hungry dogs.

"I've been thinking," she interrupted anxiously. "Now that hunting season is on and the moose are coming down out of the timber, we could hire someone to butcher the animals our guests shoot. It might be an added incentive to bring hunters to the lodge. They could take the meat home in neat packages instead of draped over the top of the car."

"You should be banned from thinking, woodenhead," Mike said affectionately. "How many hunters would drive out here? If they come at all, it will be by train. Besides, they'll want to take their prize back and show it off before it's butchered. We've got the truck to haul it to the station. Anyway, if we set up that kind of operation, we'd have a hundred inspectors out here with a thousand different regulations."

"He's right, sweetheart," Jonathan said. "It's out of the question."

Jonathan and Mike were agreeing on something—and against her! She wanted to be angry, but instead felt relief. "Well, if that's the way you feel about it . . ." She gave them both a mocking smile and got up from the table. "I'll take my ideas to the dishpan. That's one idea you'll both approve of, I'm sure." Both men laughed and suddenly Kelly was almost happy.

"I'll help you." Jonathan began to clear the table. "About tonight, Mike. What do you suggest we do about . . ."

"I'll stay in the lodge tonight," he said quickly. "I can't do much to fill in for Clyde, but I can stay up here nights."

"Do we have to socialize with the guests?" Jonathan asked when he brought a load of dishes to the sink.

"I can do that, too," Mike said with a grin. "There's a cute little blonde in there who's been giving me the eye."

Kelly could scarcely believe the evening had ended so pleasantly. The weather was cold, hovering around the zero mark, when she and Jonathan walked down the snow-packed path to her cabin. Charlie came bounding out to meet them, the ever present, battered frisbee in his mouth. He headed straight for Jonathan.

Later, when Jonathan lifted the blankets, slid into bed beside her, and took her flannel-gowned body in his arms, she made no protest. She was so tired. She snuggled against his warm body and was asleep almost instantly.

CHAPTER TEN

MARTY AND TRAM arrived with the announcement that they had been married the day before in Fairbanks.

"We decided we didn't need that little piece of paper to stay together," Marty explained. "Then as long as we didn't need it, we thought we might as well get it."

Mike glowered at his sister, yanked a box out of the utility truck, and carried it to the cabin where she and her new husband would live. Tram had already disappeared inside and Jonathan was at the lodge.

"It's a shock to Mike that you're all grown up," Kelly explained with a laugh.

"Gripes! I don't know why it should be. We're the same age. All three of us, as a matter of fact. The best thing for him would be to find himself a woman!" Marty picked up one of the suitcases and reached for a smaller one. "Let's leave the rest of this for Tram and get in out of the cold."

Tram was a tall, thin man of thirty. His hair was thick and curly, a warm, golden toffee color. He was attractive in an unconventional way. The sudden smile that came over his face when he looked at Marty plainly said he adored her, which endeared him to Kelly immediately.

"Mike said your husband is here. Is he going to stay?" Marty shrugged out of her coat and dumped it on a chair. She was a slender girl with full breasts and narrow hips. She raised her straight brows and her wide mouth tilted into a grin. "I'm anxious to meet the fabulous Jonathan Templeton. I saw his picture in *Newsweek* a couple of months ago."

"What was that all about?" Kelly asked quietly.

"He resigned as chairman of the board of some big company and turned over the management of several other companies. I don't know anything about business, but it was something like that. The stock market did something or other when that happened." She looked closely at Kelly. "What's a man like him doing here? Are you going back to him?"

"I'm not going back *with* him, if that's what you mean. And as to what he's doing here, he says he's going to stay and help us run the resort." Kelly's voice dropped on the last word and Marty shook her head sadly.

"Are you still in love with him?" When Kelly didn't answer, she said, "You are! Well then, what's the problem?"

"I don't know if I love him or not. Sometimes I think I do and other times I know I don't. We don't fit, that's the crux of the whole thing. I was out of my depth, Marty. The months I spent in Boston were the most miserable of my life. I can't explain it. I was a different person there and so was the man I married. I was afraid to move in case I did something wrong. His friends made it clear I was an intruder. His sister despised me. And he became cold and remote. It was awful!"

"How is he now?"

"At first he was belligerent. Now he seems more relaxed and at times I think he enjoys himself."

"Do you sleep with him?" Marty asked bluntly.

Kelly's tongue moistened her lips. "Yes, I do."

Marty's blue eyes grew warm. "You crazy girl! I know you wouldn't sleep with him unless you cared for him!"

"Jonathan isn't an easy man to refuse." Kelly lifted stricken eyes.

Marty whistled. "Hell's bells!"

"Did you whistle for me, lover?" Tram came in and planted a kiss on Marty's mouth.

"Would you come running if I did?"

"Try me," he said, and pinched her bottom.

"Did Mike leave?" Kelly asked.

"Just a minute ago." Tram sat down to take off his boots and Marty hung up his coat.

"The blockhead! Now I'll have to walk up to the lodge. You two come on up around six-thirty and we'll have a before-dinner drink. I made a special dinner for your homecoming, if Jonathan hasn't let the fire go out in the cookstove." Kelly pulled her yellow wool hat down over her ears and wound her red scarf about her neck. "I'll leave you lovebirds alone."

Out in the crisp cold she walked with head down toward the lodge. She felt rather depressed about her own situation, but happy for Marty. Marty deserved to be happy. If only she and Tram and Mike could stay here. If only Jonathan hadn't paid those taxes . . . There she went again, she chided herself. Instead of worrying about the *if onlys,* she should be concerned about the *what ifs.* What if Jonathan told them he was the man in charge here? What if he made Marty feel unwelcome?

Jonathan did neither. He was relaxed, friendly, charming, helpful, and made it blatantly clear that he and Kelly were a team.

"I like him," Marty said while she and Kelly were cleaning the kitchen. "I can see him as the big business executive, though. He's very possessive of you, isn't he? He could scarcely keep his hands off you. I think he's head over heels in love with you."

"You're right about everything up to that point." Kelly lifted a big bone out of the roasting pan for Charlie. "It wounded his pride when I left him, but love me? . . . He doesn't! He hasn't mentioned a word about love. It's want, want, want, and you're mine. I won't be used that way!"

Marty looked at her for a long time before she said, "I wish I had some earth-shaking words of wisdom for you. The only thing I can say is to hang in there. He may change, but I wouldn't count on it."

"Count on what?" Her twin came up behind her.

"None of your business, brother. If you're going to butt in, grab a towel."

"That's woman's work!" He put an arm around each girl. "Never thought I'd get both of my girls back to take care of me. I've got the biggest washing, and . . ."

"Chauvinist! Get your own woman!" Marty kissed him on the cheek.

"Good idea. This one's spoken for," Jonathan said from behind Kelly. His arm went about her waist and he pulled her back against him.

"Ah . . . ha!" Marty cried. "You've lost out again, brother. You should have let me fix you up with Geraldine Jenkins. She can cook fabulous meals, sew, make jerky, tan hides . . ."

"But she's fat!"

"So? She can go on a diet come spring."

"By spring she couldn't get through that door!"

"Complain, complain, complain! Never satisfied, is he, Kelly? Tram! Tram, darling. Come take this brother away and tell him about the birds and the bees so Kelly and I can get this mess cleared away."

Pulled tightly back against Jonathan, Kelly listened to the light banter between these two people she loved so much. Her husband's warm breath tickled her ear and his heart thudded against her back. If only he could see Mike and Marty as she did. Why did she have to feel so pulled between him and them?

"Do you want help?" Jonathan asked against her ear. She turned her head slightly and warm lips found the corner of her mouth.

"There isn't that much to do. Marty and I'll do it."

Jonathan removed his arm after a brief squeeze. "Come on, Mike. I know it's a mind-blowing thought, but I don't think they appreciate us."

"Before you go, take this pan out for Charlie." Kelly held out the deep pan filled with table scraps.

His smile was charming, endearing, and Kelly's heart did a flip. Jack! Damn . . . she had to stop thinking about Jack.

"Charlie will appreciate me," Jonathan grumbled and headed for the door.

Minutes later, Kelly and Marty joined the men before

a huge fire in the family room. Jonathan was reclining on a bearskin rug with his back to an ottoman and pulled Kelly down beside him. She curled her feet up under her.

"Feet cold? Hold them close to the fire. It's below zero out there." His arm tightened around her. *Just another way to let everyone else know I belong to him*, Kelly thought drily.

"What do you think, Mike?" Tram took up the conversation. "Do we have a level enough space over in that clearing to launch a glider?"

"A glider?" Marty echoed. "You don't know anything about gliding."

"That's what you think, oh sweet one. I've had an ache to try my hand at gliding for a long time. Jack's got a motorized glider."

"Sounds dangerous," Marty protested.

"It really isn't, Marty," Jonathan said "When I was in Iowa last summer I tried it and got hooked. The young fellow who builds them taught me how to fly in just a few days. You sit under the wing in a harness suspended from the frame. A control bar in front of the harness connects to the rudder with control lines. The pilot controls the glider by shifting his weight. Lean back and it climbs; lean forward and it dives; move to the right, the glider turns right."

"Still sounds dangerous. How high up do you go? Tram, I'd die of fright if you flew in such a thing!"

Jonathan laughed, and tightened his arm around Kelly. "How about you, honey? Would it frighten you?"

"Depends. It sounds fragile."

"It is. It's only a hundred and fifty pounds of Dacron and aluminum powered by a fifteen-horse, two-cylinder motor. I figure we could put skis on it and pull it with the snowmobile to get it started. Think that would work, Mike?"

"It will if twenty-five miles an hour will get you airborne." Mike's eyes shone with interest.

"That should do it. The contraption is still packed in crates. You fellows will have to help me assemble it." Jonathan laughed. "Mechanics is not my long suit."

"We can put it together if we have the instructions." Mike's blue eyes were now dancing with enthusiasm.

"I still think you're crazy," Marty said. "It'll be too damn cold to work on the thing until spring."

"We can work in the shed," Mike said. "We've got an old potbellied wood stove I can set up. It will be warm enough for us to work."

"I knew it," Marty groaned. "Just mention putting a model together and he's off like a shot. Remember, Kelly, when he spent hours and hours on his darned old models and wouldn't play with us?" She put her hand on the top of Tram's head. "Darling, I don't want you to fall out of that thing and land on this."

Tram laughed and grabbed her hand. "I promise I'll fall in a snowbank. How's that?"

"Kelly and I will be going to Anchorage in a few days," Jonathan said in the lull that followed. "While we're there, I'll have the glider kit sent out. We should see about bringing Bonnie back, too. Her leg is in a cast, but she'll be able to get around. What do you think, sweetheart? Can they manage without us for a few days?"

"I guess they'll have to," Kelly said drily. He'd done it again, she thought bitterly. He'd won over Tram and

Mike with the glider and then mentioned the trip to Anchorage in a way that made it impossible for her to refuse.

They walked silently down the snow-packed path to their cabin and Kelly went to take a shower as soon as she hung up her coat. She had to admit it was nice to have hot water any time she wanted it. She stood beneath the warm stream and let the tension wash out of her. Later in bed she listened to the hiss of the water as Jonathan took his own shower. How could he possibly be content to stay in this primitive place? Why was he doing it?

She was still wondering about it when Jonathan got into bed and pulled her against his naked chest.

"Did the shower warm you up?" he asked, nuzzling her face with his lips. "Come on now. Admit it's nice to take a hot shower after coming in out of the cold."

"I never said it wasn't nice. I said we couldn't afford to run the electric tank all day. When you don't have much money, you have to be careful how you spend it."

"You don't have to be careful, darling. How can I make you understand that?"

"You can't." Her voice came out in a shaken whisper because his lips were tormenting the hollow at the base of her throat. The old familiar excitement was beginning to throb through her blood. Holding her breath so that she couldn't smell the scents of his hair and skin, she willed herself to lie perfectly still and not respond.

"You didn't have much to say about the trip to Anchorage." His lips had moved on to tantalize the tender swell of her exposed breast.

"You didn't give me any choice."

"Don't you want to see a doctor about birth control?"

His thumb stroked her nipple, sending a shiver of fierce pleasure through her body.

"Yes!" she said fiercely. "But I wouldn't need to see a doctor if you . . ."

He cut off her words with his lips. "Hush! I can't do that. Don't ask me to do the impossible." He made a hoarse sound and rolled on top of her, pushing her slender body into the softness of the bed.

Kelly couldn't hold back a groan of satisfaction that seemed to come from the pit of her stomach. Her heart was racing, her blood thundering in her ears. Her body was so taut she felt she would explode with the agony of wanting him.

Hungrily his mouth explored her parted lips, making them quiver in eager response until her own mouth opened to the sweet taste of his kisses. She touched his bare chest, his back, her hands possessive, stroking the tense muscles, hearing the blood pound in her ears, deafening her. Their kisses became harder as their naked bodies strained against each other. Kelly was terrified of the fire burning deep inside her. For a fleeting moment she considered pushing him away from her. But his body had hardened in intolerable desire, forcing her to feel the urgency of his need against her lower limbs. His hands moved down to cup her buttocks and she lost the power to resist him.

"Darling," he whispered, his voice shaking, "Kelly, Kelly, darling." His face was buried in her throat. "I've got to have . . . You'll hate me if I get you pregnant, but I've got to . . ." His mouth sought hers.

She broke off the kiss to take a shuddering breath. "I won't hate you, Jack." She enfolded him tenderly in her arms, luxuriating in the feel of his hard shoulders against her palms.

The heat of their passion overwhelmed her. As it spread through her limbs, all the pressures that had built up within her were released. For timeless moments the love she had felt two years before broke through the barriers she had erected and surged free in a burst of uncontrollable elation. Then he was sighing and sagging against her and the tears she had held in check for so long squeezed between her tightly closed lids, wetting his chest. He rolled onto his back, taking her with him, not saying a word, just stroking her hair, her cheeks and her throat until, soothed and comforted, she drifted off to sleep.

She woke in the night to find herself alone. Deprived of that warm male body she had become accustomed to having beside her, she felt bereft. The light was on in the other room so she left her warm bed and paused in the doorway. Jonathan was standing beside the fireplace, where a fresh log lay on the grate. He stood there, a solitary, lonely figure in pajama bottoms, his feet bare, his arm resting on the mantel. As she watched, he raked a hand through his hair, tousling it, then rubbed it wearily across his forehead. He reached over and turned off the lamp, then stood staring down into the flames, the red glow flickering on his bare chest.

"Jonathan . . ."

He turned and stared at her for a long time, his eyes roaming over her face as though trying to read her thoughts. Then, as if suddenly coming to life, he moved the screen back in front of the blaze and came toward her.

"It's cold, honey. Get back in bed." In the firelight his

eyes flickered over the white gleam of her body. "I got up to put on another log and discovered I had left the damper open. You're shivering."

He led her back to the bedroom, lifted the blankets, and she slid into bed. She could see her breath, it was so cold. He got in beside her and she went willingly into his arms.

"What were you thinking about standing there beside the fire?" she whispered against his skin. "Were you thinking how nice it would be in a centrally heated apartment with a cook in the kitchen to fix your breakfast and bring it to you on a tray?"

"No. Central heat and breakfast were the farthest things from my mind. But speaking of breakfast, I'd like some blueberry pancakes."

"Tough. I'm the cook and I want French toast."

"Blueberry pancakes." He poked her in the ribs and she wiggled and hid her face against his neck.

"I'd argue, but I'm too comfy. How about you?"

Jonathan smiled and held her very close. "Me, too," he whispered into her hair.

CHAPTER ELEVEN

IT SEEMED STRANGE to be sitting in the plane beside Jonathan. Kelly stole a look at him. His dark hair had grown long in the weeks he had been at the resort. Then the dark eyes that could sparkle with bitterness or amusement returned her look and he smiled, his staid features boyishly handsome. He confused her, excited her, angered her. They had little in common, except for a powerful physical bond, and here they were in his plane on their way to Anchorage just like a normal married couple.

"The trip shouldn't take over an hour," Jonathan was saying. His eyes flicked over her face, framed by the fur collar of her coat. Wisps of hair lay around her face and her eyes were large and faintly apprehensive.

Kelly looked down at the white and green landscape of forest and plains. This was rugged country, beautiful country, her country.

"Look! There's a herd of caribou." Her eyes, bright with excitement one moment turned sad the next. "They didn't even run. They've become so used to planes and helicopters they'll just stand and be slaughtered by so-called sportsmen who hunt by plane." Her voice was bitter.

"Isn't there a law against that kind of hunting?"

"Yes, but how can they enforce it in this vast country?" She looked out the window at the patches of pine dotting the white landscape. Alaska, as she had known it, was fast disappearing, becoming a "get-rich, oil-boom" state. Soon the image of Alaska—huskies trotting across the icy tundra, Eskimos bundled up in fur parkas, trail-weary trappers, and frosty-bearded old sourdoughs—would be just a memory.

"Why does it have to be this way?" She brought her concerned eyes back to Jonathan. "Why does everything have to change? There's no sameness to anything anymore. The country changes, relationships change, people don't bother to get married unless they're having a child, don't work if they can get a handout from the government. They scar the earth, destroy the wildlife, disrupt nature's cycle, contaminate . . ."

"Hush, sweetheart. There isn't a thing we can do about most of those things. At least we're not guilty of one of them. We got married."

"Yes. We got married," she echoed, but there was no joy in her words and she turned back to the window so he wouldn't see the pain in her eyes.

The plane landed and was towed to a private hangar. A blond man with a blond mustache waited at the bottom of the steps. He and the other men working around the plane remained silent as they observed Kelly coming down the steps, Jonathan behind her, his hand tucked beneath her elbow.

"Hello, Mark. How are you standing this cold weather?"

"Not bad, sir. I don't find all that much difference between the weather here and in Boston."

"This is my wife, Mark. Sweetheart, this is Mark Lemon." Was that pride in his voice? she wondered. Surely not!

"Happy to meet you, Mrs. Templeton."

"Kelly. Call me Kelly." If the man noticed that her voice held more command than request, he didn't allow it to show.

The pilot handed out Kelly's small bag which Jonathan took from her. Mark picked up Jonathan's larger, heavier suitcase and led the way to a car parked just outside the hangar. It wasn't as big a car, or as expensive a model as the ones Jonathan used in Boston, but it was new and roomy. Somehow Kelly couldn't picture Jonathan in a small compact car. Mark stowed the luggage in the trunk.

"Can you catch a ride into town with Tom if we go on alone?" Jonathan asked.

"I'm sure I can." Mark turned to call to the pilot. "Going into town, Tom?"

"Sure thing."

Mark handed the car keys to Jonathan and opened the door for Kelly.

"There's a couple of urgent matters I'd like to discuss, sir," he said when Kelly was seated.

"They'll have to wait, Mark. I'll call the office tomorrow. Did you have any trouble making the arrangements I requested?" he asked sharply.

"No, sir. None at all, but . . ."

"Anything else can wait." Jonathan opened the door and folded his long length into the car. He glanced at Kelly briefly before starting the motor and following the arrows out of the parking ramp, then easing the car into the stream of traffic.

"Anything you especially want to do?" he asked, breaking the silence between them.

"There's a few friends I'd like to phone. You never did tell me how long we'll be here." She tried not to sound accusing, but it came out that way.

"I'd like to stay four days. It's the middle of the week and we're not needed at the resort."

"Four days! I can't possibly stay four days. I thought this was an overnight trip. I only brought one other outfit besides the one I'm wearing."

"Is that all that's bothering you? Don't they have clothing stores in Anchorage?" His hand left the wheel and caressed her knee. "We can get you outfitted without any bother at all."

"I don't want to be outfitted like an orphan dragged in out of the boonies! I prefer my own clothes, thank you!" She faced him angrily. "I thought I was coming here to see a gynecologist and to be fitted with a contraceptive shield. That's the *only* reason I'm here."

"Why are you so angry? What's so unusual about a man wanting to buy clothes for his wife?" He pushed down on the gas pedal and the car shot forward.

"We're not a normal married couple, and you know it. You have your life and I have mine."

"That's not true. We've been living together. Doesn't that count for something?"

"We've been sleeping together. There's a difference."

He muttered a curse and turned to her, his eyes glittering with suppressed anger. A van cut in front of them and he jammed on the brake, swearing mightily.

"Good grief, Kelly! Marriage is a two way street and if I'm willing to give a little, you should do the same."

"If you'll remember, Jonathan, I never asked you to 'give a little.' It was your idea to resume our . . . our married status. I was perfectly content with my life and ready to sign the divorce papers. I'll admit it was petty of me to not let you know where I was. But I had eight miserable months with you and I was just human enough to want someone to suffer for it."

He was silent for a long moment. "It was that bad?"

"Yes, Jonathan, it was." She felt no joy in telling him.

He looked at her briefly again. "I'm sorry I made you so unhappy," he said softly.

She felt drained of all emotion. "It wasn't all your fault. I shouldn't have married you until I knew what would be expected of me."

They arrived at a parking ramp when Jonathan rolled down the window and said, "Jonathan Templeton." Immediately the door opened into the underground parking area and they were escorted to a space near the elevator. Two uniformed attendants hastened to help them out while another spoke on the telephone.

"Mr. Templeton is here," he announced importantly.

Suddenly the whole situation struck Kelly as funny and she burst out laughing. Jonathan looked down at her with surprise and confusion.

"What's so funny?" His tone wiped the grin from her face.

"You wouldn't understand, Jonathan."

"Try me," he insisted.

She ignored him and followed the attendant into the elevator. Jonathan entered too and handed the man a bill.

"I'll take them from here."

As the elevator rose, long forgotten memories came rushing back to Kelly. The door opened, Jonathan picked up both bags, and, without looking at her, led the way down a short hallway. He set the bags down, and opened the door, and before Kelly could catch her breath, he had picked her up and carried her into the room. He set her on her feet and stood looking down at her.

"Hello," he said softly.

She looked at him with stricken eyes before turning away to hide her tears. The room was just like it had been before. Two dozen roses stood on a table beside the bed. A bottle of champagne rested in a bucket of ice. A filmy white nightdress was draped over the chair. Her eyes fastened on to the nightdress and she said the first thing that came to mind.

"I'm not a virgin this time."

Jonathan pulled her to him. "And I'm responsible for that, too." He kissed her gently, tenderly, and let her go when she moved to leave his arms. "You have an appointment with the doctor in . . ." he looked at his watch ". . . forty-five minutes. Would you like to shower? You can use all the hot water you want."

Watching various expressions flit across his face, Kelly thought of his arrogance, and the highhanded methods he had used to get what he wanted. But his persistence disarmed her.

"I wish I knew what was going on inside that head of yours," he murmured, almost as if to himself.

"I was thinking of the electric bill if they heat all the water used here with electricity."

"Liar!" The way he said the word made it more a caress than a censure. He took her coat from her and gave her a gentle push. "Time is fleeting, woman. Take your shower, or I'll be in there with you and we'll miss the appointment altogether."

Standing under the warm water, Kelly thought of the last time she had stood here—with Jack. They had soaped each other, frolicked and played like two kids, and finally come together as one under the sensuous spray. On that day she had never imagined life would be anything but beautiful. She stepped out of the shower, toweled herself dry, and slipped into clean underwear, willing herself not to think of anything but the present.

They went down in the elevator together and walked across the lobby past elegantly dressed matrons, tourists, and young executives hurrying by with expensive briefcases tucked under their arms. The weather was comparatively warm and Kelly walked beside Jonathan, her coat open and her head bare.

"Do you want to walk or take a taxi? It's only a couple of blocks."

"I'd rather walk. And I can go alone. You needn't come with me."

"I don't have anything else to do." He took her elbow and they stepped onto the sidewalk. Kelly lifted her face to the slight breeze blowing through her hair. She was glad she had come. She liked the city. This was where she'd live if she had to leave the resort. Her eyes took in the sights and her nose the smells, all familiar to her. They walked past the office building where she and Jack had first collided. If he noticed or remembered, he didn't give any indication of it. Minutes later Kelly left Jonathan sitting in the waiting room of the Medical Building and was ushered into the doctor's office.

When she came out again, Jonathan was talking to a small boy with a cast on his arm. They were deep in conversation and Kelly hesitated before interrupting.

"It was that dumb old Chad that did it. He dumped me off his bike. Shouldn't have been riding on the handlebars, my mom said." The small boy was standing between Jonathan's knees looking earnestly into his face.

"Your mom is right. It was a dumb thing to do. How long do you have to stay trussed up like that?"

"The doc said I'd get it off before Christmas."

"Good. Just in time to help Santa Claus deliver presents."

"There ain't no Santa Claus. That's what Chad said." The boy's bright eyes were fastened on Jonathan's face.

"I'm beginning to believe you're right, about Chad being dumb. You believe in the tooth fairy and goblins on Halloween, don't you?"

"Yeah. I got a quarter under my pillow when I lost this tooth." He opened his mouth wide. "Mom said the tooth fairy left it."

"Well, what do you know. I wasn't sure there was a tooth fairy."

"Yeah, there is. I put the quarter in my bank. I wanted to buy bubble gum, but mom said no."

Jonathan got up and put his hand on the boy's head. "We've settled that then, haven't we, scout?"

"Settled what? And my name is Amos."

"I thought we'd decided Chad was dumb, your mom right, and that there really is a Santa Claus."

The boy gave a toothless grin. "Yeah."

Jonathan lifted Kelly's coat from the hook, the boy following after him.

"You got any kids, mister?"

"No, but I've got a wife."

"Oh." The boy looked at Kelly and dismissed her. "I was gonna tell ya that if ya had kids to tell 'em not to ride on the handlebars."

"Well, if I had any, I'd be sure to tell them. Bye, scout. Take care of yourself."

"My name's Amos," the boy called as they went out the door.

"Some conversation," Kelly commented as they walked the narrow hallway.

"He was a dandy. All boy." His face was pensive for a moment, then he smiled down at her. "Everything okay with you? Did you get what you came for?" She nodded and he put an arm across her shoulders and squeezed. "I hope it's a good strong one. It's going to get a lot of use."

Kelly blushed to the roots of her hair and tried to look cross and failed. "You've got a one track mind."

"Two tracks. I'm hungry. How about pizza?"

"Sure."

They paused for the traffic light to change, then strode across the wide street.

"What about tonight?"

"What about it?"

"Where do you want to eat? What do you think I meant?"

"I didn't know what track you were on. I don't care where we eat as long as it isn't fancy."

"How about the room? We can have something sent up. Maybe there's a sexy movie on closed-circuit television." She laughed up at him, he grinned down at her, and they ran into a man carrying a large bundle. Jonathan apologized and they continued down the street.

The movie was a comedy. In spite of herself, Kelly found herself enjoying it. They had eaten a delicious meal, shared a bottle of wine, and thumbed through the current newspapers. Now curled up against the big fluffy pillows, Kelly watched television while Jonathan lounged on the end of the bed. Instead of the filmy white nightdress, she wore a nightshirt that came down to her knees. Always in her memory were the other nights she had spent in this room. Here she had reached boundless heights of ecstasy and lived her happiest moments.

She was so absorbed in her own thoughts that the movie ended and she continued to stare at the long list of credits. She was only half-aware of Jonathan reaching for the remote control button and stretching out a hand to stroke one finger down her cheek with a featherlight touch. Her thoughts shifted as he moved up close to her, disturbingly, tantalizingly handsome in his pajama bottoms, his chest bare, his freshly washed hair fluffy from the hair dryer.

"I don't think you realize how sweet an invitation you are, sitting there in your nightshirt . . . your eyes all dreamy . . . your mouth soft . . ."

She didn't move and he drew her against him, bending his head and hesitating for an unbearable moment before touching her lips. All the emotional bruising of the time spent in Boston and the months since flowed and melted away under the balm of his lips. Her mouth clung in a moment of incredible sweetness.

Very softly she said, "Jack."

He lifted his head and was perfectly still, letting his eyes, soft with love, drink in her face. Then, with a deep sigh, he took her in his arms and held her close, her head buried in his shoulder, while he gently stroked her hair. He didn't say a word, but turned her face to his and kissed her mouth, fiercely, passionately. Kelly closed her eyes and moved sensuously closer to him.

His lips left hers and he looked directly into her eyes, a faint smile softening his mouth.

"This is the woman I married," he murmured. "Soft, sweet, but spunky, willful . . ."

In a sort of fascination she watched his hands slide over her body and lift the nightshirt up and over her head. He moved her down until she lay across the bed. The soft light of the lamp shone on his hair as he bent his head. She felt the feathery touch of it against her skin, then the warm caress of his lips in the curve of her neck.

Sudden tears ached behind her eyes. She moved her hand to the back of his head and gently stroked his hair.

"It isn't the same, is it?" she whispered into the cheek pressed to her lips.

"No, darling," he said between kisses. "It's better. Much better." This was not the cold-eyed Boston businessman speaking. This was Jack, her lover: tender and affectionate, his eyes warm with love.

From then on nothing mattered except satisfying their desperate need for each other. They swirled in a mindless vortex of pleasure created by caressing fingertips, biting teeth, and closely entwined limbs. It was long and rapturous, that worshipping of bodies, and when they finally came together, it was forceful, but ecstatic and only momentarily satisfying. Time and again he drew her to him, seemingly tireless, murmuring softly of the hunger that gnawed at him and the thirst for the mouth she offered so willingly.

They made love deep into the night, until sheer exhaustion sent Jonathan into a deep sleep and Kelly into that void between sleep and awareness. As she lay molded to his body, her head resting on his chest, she finally accepted that Jonathan was Jack and she loved him. She wept silently.

CHAPTER TWELVE

"GOOD MORNING, SLEEPING BEAUTY." Jonathan's voice spoke softly in her ear. She opened one eye. Light filled the room, gilding the red roses on the bedside table. She opened the other eye and surveyed the pale yellow walls, rich mahogany furniture . . . and a gorgeous male body bending over hers. She ran her fingertips lightly over his chest, as if to make sure he was real. He was. She smiled, then yawned and stretched.

"I've been waiting half an hour. I thought you'd never wake up!" He sounded more like a small boy than a lover, and she laughed.

"I was tired." She smiled again and let her fingers move across his chest to a nipple. It had been a long, delicious night.

"Complaining?"

"Are you kidding me?"

He looked tenderly into her eyes, and there was something in his face she hadn't seen for a long while—a kind of unfettered love she had thought she would never see again.

"I love you, Kelly . . . love you . . ." His words melted on her lips and when she tried to speak, her words kept fading, swept away by his kisses.

"Jonathan . . ."

"Don't say anything." His lips covered hers before she could speak. "Are you sleepy, darling?" His voice was a whisper when they finally broke the kiss. She was curled up in his arms, one leg braided between his.

"Mm-hmm . . . Jonathan?"

"Yes, love?"

"What are we going to do?"

"We're going to take one day at a time, sweetheart." His voice was soft and his warm breath tickled her ear.

"But, Jonathan . . ."

"Shhh . . ."

"Jonathan . . ." This time she forgot what she was going to say as his body slid slowly over hers and she was swept away, adrift on a cloud of sensation as his whole being seemed to enter hers.

Two more hours passed as they made love, dozed, and made love again. Then they were standing beneath the stinging spray of the shower, laughing about the luxurious use of hot water, soaping each other, teasing. She lifted her face for his kiss and the stream of water hit her full in the face.

"I'll drown," she gasped.

He grasped her soap slick body and pulled it tight against him. "What a way to go!"

"You're obscene!" She giggled and leaned her forehead against his chest.

Kelly's happy glow lasted all through the breakfast brought to their room by a white-coated busboy. She ate as if she were starved, finishing off tiny sausages, fluffy eggs, and a Danish roll dripping with melted butter. They smiled into each other's eyes often and, when possible, Jonathan reached out to touch her thigh, her arm, or flutter fingertips across her cheek.

"Still want to go back to the resort today?" he asked. They were drinking coffee, the breakfast dishes having been removed.

"I can't wear these clothes for four days."

"You won't have to. Your clothes are here. I had them shipped out from Boston." He watched her anxiously.

"Why did you do that?" There was a shadow of concern in her eyes.

"I wanted you to have them. I lived in an apartment here in Anchorage for a month before coming out to the resort. I can't turn loose everything all at once, no matter how·much I want to. The apartment serves as a headquarters along with the office I established here. I brought all your things there. I wanted you to have them . . . no matter what."

The tender regard in his eyes made her hand tremble as she reached out to him. He took her hand silently. What could she say?

"What are you thinking?" His voice was strained.

"Okay."

"Okay, what?"

"Okay, I'll put on my glad-rags and we'll do up the town." She smiled wickedly at him and caressed him with her eyes. He looked as happy as a small boy and she wanted to throw her arms around him.

"Shall we go to the apartment? You can cook my breakfast tomorrow morning. Blueberry pancakes."

"Can I take the roses?"

"The hotel will send them over with the rest of our things. First I've got to go to the office and take care of a few urgent matters. At least Mark thinks they're urgent." He handed her a key from his pocket. "Take a cab and I'll meet you there in a couple of hours." He scribbled an address on a card. "Tell the doorman who you are and he'll take care of you."

After pausing beside the desk to leave instructions about the bill and their luggage, they left the hotel together. Jonathan put Kelly in a waiting taxi, handed the driver some money, and gave the address of the apartment building. He stood on the sidewalk and watched the cab drive away.

Kelly was in love again and gloriously happy. She smiled to herself, her blue eyes dancing, her face reflecting the warm glow of feeling loved. How had she allowed Jack and Jonathan to become two separate people in her mind? A little tremor trilled down her spine. Thank God he had forced her to make this trip. It would be hard to wait until she could be with him again.

A blast of horns brought her from her reverie. The taxi dodged into a lane of traffic, crossed a busy intersection, made its way down a tree-lined street of apartment buildings, and pulled into a circular drive. The building was ultra-modern and ultra-expensive, Kelly thought without cynicism. She had become a reverse snob, she admitted reluctantly. It wasn't Jonathan's fault he was born with a silver spoon in his mouth, any more than it was hers that she wasn't.

Kelly crossed to the large, glass door that opened automatically as she approached. The inside of the building fairly screamed the word "exclusive" and the man who came to meet her looked like the maître'd at some posh French restaurant.

"May I be of help?" His tone clearly implied that she had wandered into the wrong building. Kelly bristled.

"I'm Mrs. Jonathan Templeton. Will you direct me to our apartment? My husband will be along in a couple of hours."

"I'm afraid I'll need identification, madam." He stood in front of her as if guarding the Mint.

"My key." She showed it to him and dug into her purse. "My driver's license." Pure deviltry made her add, "Will you need to frisk me?"

His face turned a dull red and she was instantly sorry for her flip words.

"I'm sorry, Mrs. Templeton. Rules . . ."

"No. *I'm* sorry. I understand the need for such rules." She smiled so sweetly that the stern face almost relaxed.

He led the way down the thickly carpeted hallway, paused beside a table holding a beautiful potted plant and pushed a button. Paneled doors opened silently and Kelly stepped into the elevator.

"Insert your key in number five on the panel, ma'am. The elevator will take you to the fifth floor."

"And?"

"Yours is the only apartment on that floor."

"Oh . . . Thank you, very much."

The door closed. Kelly inserted her key and the cage moved. In mere seconds it slid to a gentle stop and the door opened. She faced another door with the name plate "Jonathan Templeton." She stood for a moment, her eyes riveted. Would she ever get used to what money could do?

The key turned silently in the lock and the door swung open to reveal a room right out of a decorating magazine. Nothing was out of place. The delicate green silk on the sofa was smoothed to perfection and the soft matching pillows were tilted at just the right angle. Louis XV chairs, tables on delicately carved legs, silk-shaded lamps all stood on a Persian carpet of muted greens, faded rose, and soft blue. The music coming from the intercom went so perfectly with the room that she scarcely noticed it.

Kelly closed the door and went to stand in the center of the room. It seemed a sacrilege to walk on the carpet. Jonathan must employ a live-in housekeeper. Everything was perfect. The plants, which were set in just the right places, would need constant care. She moved through a formal dining room toward swinging doors, then veered around the table toward an arched opening from which came the soft murmur of voices.

Her feet refused to carry her past the doorway. It was as if they were suddenly glued to the floor. Momentarily she could feel nothing and she stood as if the breath had been knocked out of her. Katherine and Nancy were seated at a small table, a coffee service between them.

"Oh!" Katherine looked up, startled. "Oh!" she said again and Nancy swung around to stare too. Katherine gained her composure first. "What do you want? What do you mean coming in here like that? You frightened me!" At first her voice was breathless, then accusing.

A wave of sickness rose into Kelly's throat. She fought

it down, knowing Jonathan had sent her here, alone, to face his hostile sister.

"What do you want? Can't you say anything?" Nancy's thin face showed bitter resentment.

"Hush, Nancy. I'll handle this." The rebuke was gentle, but failed to erase the belligerence from her stepdaughter's face. "Jonathan isn't here." Katherine stood up, moved to the back of her chair, and gripped it with ringed fingers. "He's out of town. He sent word yesterday that he won't be back for a week."

"How long have you been here?" Pride and anger were replacing sickness and betrayal.

"What do you mean, how long have we been here? We came as soon as Jonathan found a suitable apartment for us. In his position he needs social contacts, and Nancy and I are his family, in case you've forgotten." Her thin mouth quivered.

"I can hardly forget that gruesome fact," Kelly said drily, pleased that she could speak at all.

"Don't be vulgar." Kelly felt a small triumph at having upset Katherine's composure even a little but it vanished when her sister-in-law spoke again. "Are you still trying to get a large settlement out of Jonathan?"

"And . . . if I am?"

"He's prepared to be generous, although he has ways of reducing it. Jonathan does have his pride. It's hard for him to admit he made a mistake by marrying you." Katherine's contemptuous eyes never left Kelly's face.

The silence lengthened. Kelly refused to let Katherine see how coldly angry she was. She noted with satisfaction that Katherine's cheeks were flushed. She was nervous and frightened but Kelly intended to stay.

"Have you seen Jonathan?" Nancy faced Kelly like a spitting cat.

"Of course," Kelly replied flippantly, though her heart was breaking. "How do you think I got the key?" She dangled it from her fingers.

"Did you come to get your things? He said he brought them here. He didn't want you showing up in Boston to get them. You had created enough embarrassment for him."

"He needn't have worried."

"I'm glad you've finally realized you have no place in Jonathan's life. He and Nancy are going to be married as soon as the divorce is final. Probably before Christmas." Katherine looked directly into Kelly's eyes and spoke with deliberation. "We are all anxious to put this distasteful episode behind us. And if it means a large settlement, so be it."

"I understand completely."

"I thought you would." Katherine moved past her down a long hall to a door at the far end. As she opened the door, Kelly walked past her and shut and locked it in the woman's face. She leaned against it, closed her eyes, and breathed deeply. Anger put her feet in motion and she went to the large wardrobe at the end of the room and swung open the double doors. The clothes she had left in Boston were hanging on neat racks—blouses, slacks, daydresses, and evening clothes all grouped together with rows of shoes underneath.

Kelly grabbed an armload of dresses and carried them to the bed, then searched through the vanity for scissors. She began cutting the expensive garments in two pieces, separating them at the waist and dropping them to the floor. When the bed was empty, she returned to the closet for more clothes and kept cutting until her thumb throbbed. All at once she wanted to cry. She let the scissors fall to the floor and picked up her purse, ashamed of her childish act.

She left the room, locking the door behind her. Nancy and Katherine were standing in the living room. Katherine's face was pale and strained; Nancy's was still belligerent. Outwardly composed, Kelly managed a sardonic smile and dropped the apartment key in a glass dish on the coffee table, then walked directly to the door, forcing the older woman to step out of her way.

"Tell Jonathan he can keep the clothes for Nancy if he'll increase my settlement another twenty thousand." She closed the door softly behind her, and walked down the five flights of emergency stairs to the main lobby. She smiled brightly at the man at the desk and went out onto the street. She knew exactly what she was going to do. She was going home!

A taxi took her to the railway station. Before boarding the train, she placed a call to the station manager in Hurricane and asked him to contact Mike by radio and have him meet her. Thirty minutes later, she was on her way.

Retreating farther and farther into her thoughts, Kelly hardly noticed the landscape passing outside her window. Her heart ached for her lost love, but her pride was wounded as well. Jonathan had deliberately set about to win her back. Once he'd succeeded, he'd sent her to the apartment to collect his revenge. She hoped the taste was bitter in his mouth. It wasn't money he wanted. When she'd left him, his pride, too, had suffered a terrific blow that wouldn't allow him to rest until he had damaged hers.

Kelly's eyes were hot and dry, but she refused to close them for fear the tears would come. She refused to shed useless tears.

The train rolled on, passing station after station, the click of the wheels singing a familiar tune. But Kelly's thoughts were far away. Now she would have to tell Mike and Marty that Jonathan owned the resort. Eventually his agents would arrive to dispossess them. She calculated mentally. They should have until December to vacate the property. If Jonathan intended to marry Nancy by Christmas, he must have already started divorce proceedings.

The miles flew by and finally the train pulled into the station at Talkeetna. It was dark when Kelly stepped off, dark at only four o'clock in the afternoon. She pulled the fur collar of her jacket up around her face and walked toward Mike, who was waiting at the end of the platform. Her eyes were glued to his face as she approached. She walked into his arms and hid her face against his shoulder.

"Oh, Mike. I've been such a fool!"

"Yeah."

At last she pulled away from him and he took her hand. He led her to the waiting utility truck, whose running motor sent out a cloud of white fog. Kelly slipped into the passenger seat and Mike revved up the engine. Kelly didn't speak until they were on the highway.

"I have something to tell you. Mike. It isn't going to be easy for me to say, or for you to hear, but it's got to be said. When I married Jonathan, I signed papers allowing him to handle the probate of Daddy's will, and then I completely forgot about it until he reminded me of it when he first came to the resort. He also told me he'd paid six years of back taxes. Now the property is legally his." She waited for the explosion that was sure to follow.

Mike was silent for a long while. "That . . . bastard!" He hissed the words from between clenched teeth.

"I'm sorry, Mike. I'm so sorry. My stupidity has cheated you and Marty out of your share. I was so gullible!"

"Join the crowd," Mike said wearily. "I was even beginning to like the bastard."

"What are we going to do? How are we going to tell Marty?" She felt, rather than heard, the soft groan that came from her throat.

Mike glanced at her, then took her hand. "She's a big girl. She'll take her lumps along with the rest of us."

"But she and Tram gave up their jobs in Fairbanks. Oh, why didn't I stay in Portland?"

"Maybe we can raise the money to buy him out." Mike was grasping at straws and they both knew it.

"He'd never sell to us. He's out for revenge and he's got us in the palm of his hot little hand." Her words were bitter.

"What happened?"

She knew what he meant, but couldn't bring herself to tell him. "Nothing much. He led me down the primrose path, then pushed me into the icy slough."

"I knew something had happened when you called."

After that they were silent. Mike concentrated on the highway that was becoming slick with a freezing mist. Kelly buried her hands deep in the pockets of her coat and stared straight ahead. She felt better now that she had told Mike about the property, and she promised herself that somehow, someday, she would make it up to him and Marty.

"Drop me off at Marty's, Mike," she said when they turned into the driveway. "I've got to tell her and I'd better do it now."

Mike parked beside Marty's cabin. The air was crisp and the tangy, familiar scent of woodsmoke invaded Kelly's nostrils. This was home. She wished she'd never left it.

Marty opened the door before they reached it. "What in the world happened?"

Kelly stomped the snow from her street shoes and took off her coat before she answered. "Plenty!"

"I figured that. You look as if you've been through a wringer. Why in the world did you come back alone. Jonathan . . ."

"I never want to set eyes on him again!" Once again, tears burned in her eyes.

"Well I'm afraid you're going to see him, because he's here."

Kelly's head jerked around. "Here? I don't believe it!"

"Believe it. He flew in right after Mike left to pick you up. And he's raving mad!"

"That's too damn bad. So am I!" Kelly walked over to the warm, cheery fire and turned her back to it. Mike took off his coat and boots. Tram stood beside his chair and watched her with gentle eyes.

"Tell us what happened, for heaven's sake," Marty demanded. "I've been so worried since Jonathan came storming in here demanding to know if we'd heard from you." Her face was creased with concern.

"Jonathan and I have irreconcilable differences. I don't want to discuss them. But I've got something else to tell you." She told them that Jonathan now controlled the resort. "Marty, Tram, I'm so sorry. I don't know what else to say. I wanted you to know the worst right away so you could make plans."

Marty looked as if she would burst into tears. "You can't mean he'll boot us out of here? But . . . this is home!" She turned angrily to Mike. "Why didn't you take care of those taxes? We could have raked up the money somehow."

"I didn't know they were overdue. I thought they'd been taken out of the estate."

"Don't blame Mike. Blame me," Kelly said wearily. "There's one small bit of good news. Jonathan may own the property, but he doesn't own the business or the furnishings. Maybe he'll give you enough for them so you can get a new start somewhere else."

"It isn't that," Marty wailed. "I don't think I could bear it if I didn't know that home was here and I could come back to it when I wanted to." The anguish in her tone tore at Kelly's heart and she wished for words to comfort her. But before she could think of any, the door opened and Jonathan stepped into the room.

All the anger and humiliation she had felt in the apartment came boiling up. Her angry eyes locked with his across the room. He stood inside the door in his sheepskin coat, his bare head dusted with a sprinkling of snow. He acted as if there was no one else in the room. The silence lengthened and became heavy with tension.

"Am I being excluded from the conference?" He spoke to everyone, but his eyes remained on Kelly.

"Yes!" Kelly cried. "You most certainly are excluded!" She hadn't intended to speak so bitterly. She wanted to be calm, uncaring. "I've told them you own the resort."

"I see," he said quietly.

"No, you don't *see* anything. You're too stiff-necked to see down to our level, but if you could, you would realize that we'll survive together. We have each other. Who do you have, Jonathan? Katherine and Nancy?"

"I'd rather discuss our misunderstanding in private." He removed her coat from the hook and came toward her. She met him in the middle of the room and snatched it from his hand.

"We've said it! The next time I speak to you will be before the divorce judge. Or do you have the clout to divorce me without a hearing?" Her anger was intensified by the stricken look that crossed his face. What an actor he was! He started to follow her to the door but she turned on him like a spitting cat. "Stay away from me! I'm going home . . . to my house! If he tries to follow me, Mike, break his leg!" At the door, she turned with a parting remark. "I want you out of here tomorrow. All debtors are allowed thirty days to vacate and we're taking every day of that time." Her lungs felt as if they were about to explode, but she managed one more breath. "You come near my cabin and I'll . . . I'll fill you with buckshot!"

Kelly slammed the door and ran across the snow-packed yard to her own front door. The lamp was lit and a new log lay on the hot coals in the fireplace. Thank goodness her father had made a bar to go across the door. She went to the closet to get it, then placed a chair beneath the knob on the rear door. Only then did she take off her coat and slip out of her wet shoes.

CHAPTER THIRTEEN

THE NEXT FEW days were the longest and most unhappy Kelly had ever experienced.

The morning after she had locked herself in the cabin, she heard Jonathan's voice on the C.B. radio calling Hurricane. He requested they send for his plane. Then he called her.

"Kelly, are you on the channel?"

She turned off the set.

It was almost noon when she heard the plane land in the clearing. Still in her nightgown and robe, she went to the window. Tram took Jonathan to the clearing in the pickup and returned. Kelly stood by the window, tears streaming down her face. A part of her life was over. She cried for lost dreams, for the agony of disillusionment. She had to face the fact that her long-cherished idea of love was simply a myth, that the kind of love she wanted didn't exist except in the imagination of poets and novelists.

During the long day when she sat beside the fire or lay on the couch hoping for the sleep that eluded her, memories of the scene with Katherine and Nancy stayed doggedly in her brain. She relived each word they'd said over and over again and each time she asked herself how she had ever allowed herself to get involved in such a humiliating situation. When she finally dozed, a pounding on the door awakened her.

"Kelly . . . Kelly . . . open the door," came Marty's voice.

Kelly got up off the couch. The room was cold and she shivered as she lifted the bar and opened the door.

"Good heavens! You look like you died . . . days ago."

"I did."

Marty handed her a pan wrapped in a heavy towel and took off her coat and boots. "It's cold in here."

"I know. I was sleeping."

Marty took the pan into the kitchen. "You didn't even start the cookstove," she wailed.

Kelly almost smiled. Marty tended to over-dramatize. She built up the fire while Marty tackled the cookstove, muttering and complaining all the while.

"And I thought you'd welcome me and your supper with open arms. What do I find but you lying on your fanny and the fires almost out and . . ."

"Oh, Marty! Stop that and say what you came to say."

"Okay. Why didn't you come up to the lodge and eat with the rest of us? Your leg isn't broken!"

"I didn't want to!"

"Oh!" Marty seemed to relent. "In that case," she said with her impish grin, more relaxed now, "I'm glad I came."

Half an hour later, Kelly announced, "The stew was delicious." She set the empty bowl in the sink.

"Of course. It's my best recipe, and about the only thing I'm sure will turn out well. It's a good thing Tram isn't hard to please. He'll eat anything that doesn't bite him first." Marty settled down in a chair and pulled her feet up under her. "We've decided to get me pregnant." She giggled. "Tram says he'll work on the project day and night."

"You're lucky." Kelly handed Marty a cup of coffee.

"So are you."

"Oh, yeah? Sure I am!" She avoided Marty's eyes.

"I think he loves you," Marty said softly. When Kelly didn't answer, she added, "He didn't take the property from us."

Kelly turned huge, luminous blue eyes to Marty. "What do you mean?"

"After you left last night, I thought Mike was going to kill him . . . and I would have helped. It was Tram who calmed us all down. He's not a violent person. His motto is 'talk first, fight later.' Anyway, the crux of it is this . . . Jonathan paid up the taxes and settled the inheritance tax, or we would have had to sell some of the property to pay it. But the property still belongs to us. Jonathan said we could consider it a loan at low interest."

"Don't believe him. He doesn't do anything out of the goodness of his heart. He's lulled you into believing that, but he'll lower the boom on you if things don't go the way he wants them to go. I know him. He's devious. He's divorcing me so he can marry his sister's stepdaughter. Maybe he's going to give me our property as a settlement," Kelly added with a dry laugh.

"I think he loves you."

"Don't say that! You don't know what you're talking

about. I've lived with him. I know him better than you do."

"Okay, okay. You don't have to jump down my throat."

"I'm sorry. I feel so washed out. I feel as if everything has stopped but me, and I'm still whirling around in confusion, fear, and despair. Stay by me, Marty. Someday it'll be over and I'll look back on this time in my life as if it had happened to someone else. I just don't want you and Mike to build up false hopes about this place. I won't believe we still have it until the deed is in our hands."

Marty studied Kelly intently. "Time will tell," she said lightly and rose to her feet. "Meanwhile, we've got guests coming this weekend. Two wildlife photographers and a couple who want to ride on a dogsled. Tram will take care of the shutterbugs and Mike said his team is ready to supply the rides. You and I will have to cook and clean. You do the cooking."

"I hate to cook."

"So do I. But you're better at it than I am."

"I think you can do better than you let on. Aunt Mary taught us both at the same time."

"I didn't pay as much attention to the lessons as you did."

"Oh, get out of here!" Kelly's voice was warm with affection. "I'll be up in the morning to give you a hand."

Marty smiled tiredly and suppressed a yawn. "I'll need it."

Kelly worked furiously the next day, trying to tire herself out so she could sleep that night. She carried out ashes, scrubbed and cleaned, washed and ironed. When she could find nothing else to do, she started up the small chain saw and cut the small chunks of wood needed for the cookstove. Not once did she allow herself to think of Jonathan. Her arms grew so tired holding the chain saw that she dropped it and almost sawed into her leg. She was sensible enough to know it was dangerous to work, so she hitched Charlie to her old sled and they rode around the yard.

Charlie loved it, and Kelly began to doubt Mike's judgment that Charlie would never make a good sled dog. She told him so that evening during dinner.

"I hitched Charlie to my old sled, Mike, and he took to it like he was born to it."

"He was." Mike helped himself to another serving of potatoes.

"Well?" Kelly prompted when it became apparent he wasn't going to say more.

Marty groaned. "Mike hasn't outgrown his childish habits. You have to pull every word out of him."

Mike grinned at Kelly. "Humor me."

"Get out of here! I should take a club to you."

Tram looked at Marty questioningly. She laughed. "Don't worry, darling. They won't kill each other. This has been going on since they were ten years old."

"If I told them everything I know, Tram, they'd be as smart as me." Mike waved his fork at the girls.

"Oh, stop that and tell me." Kelly knew the twins were trying to raise her spirits, and she appreciated their concern.

"No sense of humor," Mike grumbled. "Charlie's sire

was the lead dog of a team that placed in the Iditarod Trail Race a few years back."

"You're kidding!" Marty cried. She turned to Tram. "You wouldn't know about this, honey. You haven't been in Alaska long enough to know about the World Championship Dogsled Races. If a dog has the stamina to even finish that thousand mile race, his value goes up, up, up." She turned puzzled eyes to her brother. "Hey! How in the world did you manage to get Charlie?"

"Charlie's got a flaw. He's not a fighter. If I let that team of mine loose, they'd make dog meat of him. He won't even fight on a one-to-one basis."

"How about stud service?" Kelly suggested.

"No good there either. He's sterile."

"I like him. He's my dog. You gave him to me," Kelly said defiantly.

"You can have him, but keep him away from my team when I have them hitched. They're hard enough to handle as it is."

The next morning Kelly played an extra long time with Charlie. He jumped, barked, chased the frisbee until his tongue was hanging out. Kelly knelt down in the snow and hugged his shaggy neck.

"You and I are alike, Charlie. We didn't fit into what was expected of us."

At noon a delivery van backed up to the door of the lodge. Kelly saw it pull away a few minutes later and dismissed it from her mind. Probably someone asking directions. An hour passed before she went up to the lodge with a bundle of laundry and noticed that tire tracks in the snow led right up to the door. She opened it to see a mountain of crates and boxes with Marty, Mike, and Tram standing in the middle of them.

"What's going on?" she gasped. Guilt was written all over Marty's face. "Marty! What's all this stuff?"

"Now don't get in a stew. Jonathan sent out a few things. It'll be added to what we owe him," she said quickly.

"A few things?" Kelly edged her way between the boxes. "Washer, dryer, dishwasher, vacuum cleaner, microwave oven, sheets, towels . . ." She stopped reading aloud, but continued making the rounds of the boxes that filled half the family room. "And an antenna. That's so you can pull in that Tulsa, Oklahoma station and hear the football games, isn't it," she said sarcastically. Her eyes followed a path of melted snow to the back rooms.

"Kelly . . ." Marty called before her husband hushed her.

Stacks of boxes lined one wall of the big dormitory room. They were uniform in size, and the name Jonathan Templeton was stamped on each one. Kelly stood numbly looking at them. He was moving in, invading her home. He wouldn't be satisfied until he'd taken everything from her. Returning to the family room to retrieve the bundle of laundry she'd dropped, she wondered vaguely if she looked like she felt—as if she'd been kicked in the throat.

"Don't look like that, Kelly! I can't bear it!" Marty cried.

Kelly waved a weak hand at the clutter of boxes. "Money talks. I can see where that leaves me."

"Don't you dare say that!" Marty broke away from

Tram and rushed over to her. "We needed things to make this place pay. It's a loan, Kelly. Just a loan."

"Then what're his things doing back there?" She jerked her head toward the bedrooms.

"We couldn't very well refuse to rent the dormitory. Be reasonable, Kelly," Marty pleaded.

"Did you agree to this, Mike?"

Mike remained silent and his sister prompted him angrily.

"Tell her! Tell her the three of us talked it over with Jonathan and agreed the place needed refurbishing."

"Oh, hush, Marty! Yes, I agreed, Kelly. Business is business." Mike didn't look at her.

"I thought I was a partner in this venture, too," Kelly whispered through stiff lips. "Don't I have say about something as important as this?"

"We knew what you'd say," Mike said stubbornly.

"I hope you enjoy all this." Kelly waved her hand at the boxes again and went out the door before they could see that she was trembling. "Oh, Tram!" she heard Marty wail.

Kelly forced her trembling legs to support her down the path and was grateful for the cold air she sucked into her lungs. She prayed the leaden weight in the pit of her stomach would dissolve.

Inside the sanctuary of her own home, she threw herself down on the couch. Great, shuddering sobs tore through her. It was a relief to let the misery flow out of her. She could cry here. There was no one to see her. The tears came in an overwhelming flood, pouring down her cheeks and seeping between her fingers.

At last the tears stopped and she lay on the couch staring into the fire. She was tired. She put another chunk of wood on the grate, went to her room, and changed into her long flannel gown. She took her pillow and down-filled comforter back to the couch, and fell asleep almost instantly.

Kelly woke early the next morning. The room was so cold she could see her breath. She got out from under the warm blankets, put more wood on the fire, turned on the electric water heater, and crawled back under the blankets. She felt rested and clearheaded. It was obvious to her now that Jonathan's strategy was to drive her away, but it wasn't going to work. He and his money would never separate her from this place and the two people she loved best. But deep inside, she wondered if she had the strength to stand up to him.

She showered and dressed, then, on impulse, put on fresh makeup. No sense in looking the martyr, she told herself, even if she did feel like one.

She let herself into the lodge kitchen where Mike sat at the table talking on the C.B. radio.

"Ten-four. I'll be coming your way this morning. Stand by and I'll give you a call. If you have time, we can have a bit of lunch together."

"Ten-four, Barefoot. I'll be on the by and listening." The girl's voice was soft and musical.

Mike gave Kelly a sheepish grin.

"Is that the new girlfriend?" she asked.

"Sort of."

"What do you mean . . . sort of? What's she like?"

"Well, she's not fat like Geraldine Jenkins!" he said gruffly.

Kelly laughed. "I see you've got all the loot laid out," she said lightly, glancing around the room at the shiny new appliances.

"Yeah. You still mad?"

"No. I don't think so, anyway. I can understand how you and Marty were tempted to take them."

"Oh, that's just great!" Mike got to his feet.

"Calm down," Kelly said quickly. "I said I understand and I do. And, in case you're wondering, I'm not going to let Jonathan Winslow Templeton the Third drive me away from here!"

Mike grinned. "Good girl! I was beginning to think you'd lost your spunk."

"Don't you believe it, buster. I'm as gutsy as ever!" They were brave words, but would she remember them when she faced her husband again?

The test came sooner than she expected.

In the middle of the morning, Marty was in the wash room trying out the new washer when Jonathan's voice came in on the radio.

"Break . . . Mountain View."

Kelly looked dubiously at the set. She desperately wanted to turn it off, but she didn't dare in case of an emergency. She pressed the button on the microphone and said, "Go ahead."

There was silence and then Jonathan's voice. "Will someone bring the truck out to the clearing?"

"Ten-four," Kelly said through stiff lips. She went to get her coat, then relayed the message to Marty, who went to find Tram.

On her way to her cabin, Kelly heard the plane circle to land, but she didn't look skyward. She hated herself for running away, but she needed time to prepare herself for the eventual meeting. Part of her had hoped that, despite the boxes piled in the dormitory, he wouldn't come back. She should have known better, she thought bitterly.

CHAPTER FOURTEEN

WHEN THE FRONT door of the cabin was flung open, Kelly moved away from the chest where she had put away her sweaters and went to stand in the bedroom door. Jonathan glanced at her, then, using the boot-jack beside the door, removed his boots.

"Don't bother taking off your coat and boots. You're not staying." When he didn't answer, she added, "I said you're not staying. This is my house and I don't want you here."

"Who said anything about staying? I came to get my things." He walked past her into her father's room.

"Good." She followed him to the doorway. "The sooner you're away from here, the better I'll like it. Be sure to give me the papers to sign before you leave."

"What papers?" He took his big suitcase from the closet, unzipped it, and spread it open on the bed.

"Don't play games. The divorce papers. You did it all for nothing, Jonathan. I didn't want a settlement when I left you and I don't want one now."

"It was a childish act of vandalism destroying all those clothes."

"They wouldn't have fit Nancy anyway. I didn't want them. All I want from you is the title to this property and I'll keep after you until I get it. I won't let you do Mike and Marty out of their share."

"Didn't they tell you—"

"They told me what you told them," she interrupted coolly. "But I didn't believe it."

He shrugged and dropped a stack of underwear into the bag. "Think any damn thing you please," he said, the words falling icily. "You will anyway. All you know how to do is to break and run."

"What did you expect me to do? Stay and play second fiddle to Nancy?" she almost shouted. "And have that creepy sister of yours look down her nose at me?"

"Watch it, Kelly. Katherine means well. If you'd stayed, you would have seen that I can handle Katherine. But you had to get back here, didn't you? You love this place and . . . Mike and Marty . . ."

"You're damn right I do and you're doing your best to buy them away from me. Can't you be satisfied with what you have? Why did you have to come here and mess up my life?"

"Why not? You sure as hell messed up mine." He stuffed the last garment in the bag and zipped it shut. "I'm staying here, Kelly. You're not going to ruin this vacation for me." He looked at her squarely and she saw new lines of weariness in his face. She was glad if she had pierced his consciousness just one little bit. "I intend to build that glider with Mike and Tram. While

I'm here you'd better pull in your horns and act civilized."

"I can't believe you want to stay here! What about the divorce? What about Nancy?"

"What about her? She knows better than to interfere with my plans." He picked up his suitcase and she moved out of the doorway. He pulled on his boots while her mind screamed, *Get out! Get out!* He turned and impaled her with his eyes. "You don't understand one thing about me, do you, Kelly?" His tone was soft, but his frustration was apparent.

Somewhere in a quiet, little corner of her heart she might have felt pity for the man who was so rich in material things and so lacking in what really mattered— love and compassion. But she couldn't close her mind to the memory of Katherine saying, "He didn't want you showing up in Boston."

"I understand enough. Don't come here again." There was a slight tremor when she spoke, but her eyes met his unwaveringly.

"You needn't worry." He picked up his suitcase again. "I brought Bonnie and Clyde back with me. The least you can do is go up there and welcome them back." He went out the door.

Kelly stood in the middle of the room for countless minutes, his words echoing in her mind, his ravaged face fixed in her memory. Was he ill? Stop! she told herself. Stop thinking.

Outside, she was met by an exuberant Charlie with a new red frisbee in his mouth. She took it from him and sent it sailing into the air. Charlie made great, bounding leaps to catch it. He tossed his head, let his toy fly out of his mouth, then pounced on it with his front paws before nuzzling it out of the snow and racing back to her. His big, shaggy body almost upset her when she grabbed the frisbee and held it away from him.

"Oh, Charlie," she laughed. "You're a lover, not a fighter, but that's all right with me."

Inside the kitchen door she stomped the snow from her boots before removing them. "Welcome back, you two."

Bonnie was seated in a wheelchair and Clyde was trying to make coffee in the new electric urn.

"Kelly! You don't know how glad I am to be back here," Bonnie exclaimed. "It's just like comin' home, honey. How y'all been? I worried about you, even if Clyde told me not to." Bonnie's bleached hair was piled high and her makeup was all in place. She looked well-rested and as perky as ever. Her encased leg rested on a prop attached to the chair.

"I missed you, Bonnie. How are you doing, Clyde? You trying to figure out how to operate that thing?"

"We missed you, too," Bonnie continued. "Every day I'd say to Clyde, 'I wonder how Kelly is doin' with the cookin', and he'd say, 'You just quit your worryin', honeybunch, that gal's been down the trail and she'll manage.' "

Kelly grinned at Clyde. "And I did, Bonnie. My cooking is not up to your standards, but we didn't starve."

"Well . . . ain't ya going to say anything a'tall about all the new stuff?" Bonnie's eyes glittered with excitement. "I tell you, Kelly, I ain't never had such a time in all my life. Clyde said that I ain't better get used to pointin' and sayin' that I'll take this or that. He said it was a once in a lifetime for me, and Clyde's right. It sure was fun."

Oblivious to Kelly's irritated expression, Bonnie continued. "Jack picked up me and Clyde and this here chair and took us down to the department store. Clyde pushed me around and Jack says for me to point out anything I needed out here and not to pay no attention to what it cost. He said it didn't make no difference if it was on sale or not, to get the best. I had those clerks a runnin' in circles! I'd point and they'd jump. I said it wasn't hardly fair for me to have all the fun, but he said you could go anytime you want to get more things." Bonnie paused and waited and Kelly realized she had to say something.

"Good for him," she said, but her sarcasm was lost on Bonnie, who was off on the description of how they'd picked out the radio antenna.

"Jack said to the man we wanted to listen to the ball games and the man said what we needed was a satellite and we could watch them on TV and Jack said . . ."

Kelly's mind tuned out Bonnie's chatter. Jonathan had won Bonnie over just as he had won Marty and Mike. Damn! Wasn't he going to leave her anything?

"Kelly. Kelly . . ." Bonnie's voice sounded far away.

"Oh, I'm sorry, Bonnie. I was wondering about lunch."

"That's what I said. What should I do about lunch?"

"Mike won't be here. The rest of us can have soup and sandwiches. I'll fix it."

"I'll do it. My arms ain't broke. Help me out of this thing, Clyde. Jack said if I sit all the time I'll lose my figure."

Kelly clenched her teeth. If she heard "Jack said" one more time, she would scream!

The afternoon was one of the longest Kelly had ever lived through. By evening she was so uptight she felt ill. Jonathan spent the day in the dormitory room. "Gettin' settled in," Clyde said as he passed through the kitchen carrying boxes to the shed. Bonnie's exuberance was dampened somewhat when she realized that Jonathan was not going to live in the cabin with Kelly. She continually gave Kelly inquiring looks that Kelly ignored, and after a while Bonnie settled into a gloomy silence.

Sheer willpower and the determination not to let Jonathan intimidate her forced Kelly to remain at the lodge for the evening meal. She was even able to smile occasionally, speak pleasantly when spoken to, and choke down a portion of the food on her plate. Not once did her expression reveal the panic that rose in her throat each time Jonathan looked at her.

The men talked about the glider they planned to assemble and the tower to hold the huge antenna. Jonathan talked easily, discussing ways to fly the machine when it was completed, asking advice, drawing each of the men into the conversation, never once becoming condescending. Marty and Bonnie listened eagerly but Kelly felt like an outsider, excluded.

When the meal was over, the men continued to sit at the table. Kelly and Marty loaded the new dishwasher and made fresh coffee. Kelly put on her coat to take food scraps out to Charlie, then continued down the path to her own cabin. She had never felt so alone or so miserable in her life.

That weekend the retired couple and the two wildlife photographers arrived, and Kelly worked with Bonnie preparing meals. The shed had been turned into a workshop and the big woodburning stove kept it warm enough for the men to work without gloves most of the time. Jonathan spent his days there, coming in with a red nose and, at times, frost on the beard he was growing. He never attempted to speak to Kelly alone and most of the time he ignored her. But it was obvious to Kelly that everyone else adored him.

"I don't understand why you're being so stubborn, Kelly," Marty finally commented. "Why don't you talk things out with Jonathan? I'm sure he'll meet you halfway. You're just making yourself miserable."

Kelly looked at her for a long time, biting back bitter words. Finally she said: "I love you dearly, Marty, but . . . please mind your own business." Tears came to Marty's eyes, but Kelly refused to say more.

The following weekend brought blessed diversion in the form of Andy Mullins, who arrived with another couple, and Kelly's spirits responded immediately to Andy's buoyant personality. He threw his arms wide when he saw her.

"There she is! Ladies and gentlemen, Miss Alaska!"

"Hello, Andy. I thought you were going back to the reservation." She held out her hand which he clasped in both of his.

"I called in sick. Told them I had terminal longing to see a pretty girl at Mountain View Lodge." He turned to the couple with him. "Kelly, meet Bob and Maggie."

The woman was a pretty, dimpled blonde with a flawless complexion, who looked at Kelly with disinterest.

The man with her was short and stocky and could scarcely keep his adoring eyes from his companion's face. Here was a couple they wouldn't need to entertain, Kelly thought with a twinge of envy. The couple followed Clyde to their room, but Andy lingered with Kelly.

"How are things going with you?" His eyes roamed over her face. "Don't lie."

"Okay. I'm . . . so-so, Doc."

"Did your husband go back to tea-town?"

"No. He's staying here at the lodge. In the dormitory."

"Separated?" He searched her eyes, and she nodded.

"I'm sorry you're so unhappy." His voice dropped to a whisper. "There's nothing I can say, except that the hurt will go away after a while."

"Promise?" Her lips quivered and she blinked to hold back tears.

"Cross my heart and hope to die."

Andy hung his parka on the rack beside the door. "You know something? I like it here. I really do."

"You sound surprised. I think it's Bonnie's cooking you like. Come see her. She's reigning supreme in the kitchen once again."

Kelly held the swinging door open. Andy posed in the doorway, his smiling eyes sweeping the kitchen. "Where's my queen of the cookstove?"

"Andy!"

Bonnie's chair rolled out of the storage room. Jonathan followed behind carrying several canisters. Kelly stood by the door, a fixed smile on her face. Jonathan glanced from her to Andy with a rigid expression and a tiny muscle jumped in his cheek.

"Beautiful as ever," Andy said, taking Bonnie's hands. "And I see you've still got the fellows trailing after you. How are you, Templeton?" He held a hand out to Jonathan. For a second Kelly thought Jonathan wasn't going to take it and the smile slipped from her face. Then, looking as if he detested both of them, he shook it.

"Doctor."

The sound of the deep voice touched something in Kelly's memory, making her heart jump.

"I never got to thank you for sending me that candy, Andy. Or for what you done that day." Bonnie held onto Andy's hand, patting the back of it.

"I'll tell you what," Andy said with a leering grin. "Since I missed out on wrapping up that sexy leg of yours, I'll take a blueberry pie and call it even."

"It's a deal! Push me over to the table, Jack, and I'll get started. Clyde fixed me this here table, Andy. I can get my leg under it and work just fine."

"Is that ugly old Clyde still hanging around?" Andy teased. "I might have to ship him yet to get you away from him."

"You're a flirt, Andy Mullins. A plain old flirt."

"Shhh . . . Don't tell Kelly. She's suspicious of me as it is."

Jonathan watched Kelly, his eyes shuttered. "I thought you were due back at the reservation," he commented without looking at Andy.

"I got an extension to attend another seminar and come back here to see my girls," he answered lightly. "How's Charlie doing?" he asked Kelly. "Suppose we can hitch him to the sled and go for a ride? I ride . . . you mush."

Kelly laughed. "Oh, no! This is a democracy! We take turns."

"I hate taking turns!"

"Tough! The policy at Mountain View Lodge is share and share alike."

"Not everything," Jonathan said stiffly, bitingly.

Andy seemed not to notice his tone. "I thought there was a catch somewhere," he said gloomily. "Oh, well, if I've got to mush, I'll mush."

Kelly was kept so busy fetching and carrying for Bonnie while she prepared the meal that she didn't have time to think of the conversation until later. When she did and remembered Jonathan's tense words, "Not everything," she saw in her mind's eye a hollow-cheeked figure. Jonathan had lost weight. She hadn't looked at him, really looked at him, for a while. She hadn't noticed before that the work he was doing in that cold shed was taking a toll on him physically. Soon the glider would be ready to fly and he would be leaving. Then she could finally begin to rebuild her life.

"I think that doctor has a crush on you." The meal was over and Marty and Kelly were cleaning up after having sent Bonnie off to her room to rest.

Kelly looked up from scraping food into Charlie's bowl. "Andy is like that with all the women. He just likes to flirt."

"Jonathan didn't like it," Marty said with a warning tone that pricked at Kelly's patience. "I think it bugs him to have men pay attention to you."

"That's too bad! He can shove off anytime he wants. No one's holding him here," Kelly retorted bitterly.

Marty stopped working to look at Kelly with puzzled

eyes. "Why do you get so angry? You used to be the most happy-go-lucky person I knew, but lately you're like a bear with a sore foot."

"I'm sorry. I didn't mean to snap."

"Oh, Kelly. Everything would be so wonderful if you and Jonathan could iron out your differences."

"Don't count on it, Marty, because it isn't going to happen."

"Are you interested in Andy?" Marty asked hesitantly.

The simple question sparked an idea in Kelly's mind and she thought a moment before saying, "He's very nice." She allowed her eyes to go dreamy for an instant. "He's nice, he's kind, and he's fun. I haven't had any fun in a long time and I admit I like to be with him."

"I hope that's me you're talking about." Kelly spun around, her eyes wide. "Mike! Stop sneaking up on me!" She moved to hit his arm but he grabbed her hand and twisted it behind her.

"Now, me proud beauty. I've got you in my power," he said in a villainous voice.

"Let go or I'll tell Marty about the girl you talk to on the radio, the one with the melodious voice."

"What girl?" Marty was quick to pick up.

"All right," Mike said, and let go of Kelly's arm. "But you're a killjoy."

"A girl's got to take every advantage she can," Kelly said haughtily, rubbing her wrist.

"Are you man-handling the pretty women, Mike?" Andy asked, coming through the door. "You want me to knock him on his can, Kelly?" he teased.

"Not this time, Andy. I'm afraid he might fight back

and I want you to come down to the cabin. I've got a bottle of wine just begging to be opened."

"That's the best offer I've had all day. Hold on till I get my coat and I'll be right with you." He went back through the swinging door and Mike went to speak with Clyde.

"Kelly!" Marty hissed. "Are you out of your mind? Jonathan saw you wrestling with Mike and heard what you said to Andy. He looked as if he could have killed you! He won't like it one bit if you take Andy down to your house."

"Marty, understand this. I don't care what Jonathan thinks. From now on I intend to please myself!"

Kelly and Andy stepped out into the cold night and walked down the path to the cabin. Kelly switched on a light and Andy whistled appreciatively.

"Mmmmm . . . nice! Cozy!"

"Cold, though. Hang your coat beside the door and I'll stoke up the fire."

"Let me do it," he offered and set the firescreen aside. He knelt down in front of the fire to prod the glowing embers with a fire tool. "I can think of better ways to keep warm," he grumbled.

"I just bet you can," Kelly laughed. "How about a hot buttered rum? That should warm you up."

"If that's the best offer I'm going to get, I'll take it."

"You're not nearly the wolf you pretend to be, Andy Mullins. If I said, come on, Andy, let's go to bed, it would shock you to death."

"Maybe, but I'd die happy."

Kelly felt laughter bubble up in her. "Poor, deprived Andy. I bet you have all the Indian maidens on the reservation coming to your clinic with every excuse from hangnail to heartburn." She set out mugs and put the kettle on to boil. "I'm sure I have a bottle of rum around here somewhere. There it is on the top shelf. Will you get it down, Andy?"

Andy came up behind her and reached for the bottle, his other hand resting on her shoulder. Kelly didn't hear the door open, but she felt the cold draft. Looking under Andy's arm, she saw Jonathan standing in the doorway. He stared at her in silence, then shut the door and took off his coat.

Andy's hand squeezed Kelly's shoulder in conspiratorial understanding. She knew she would have to say something.

"We're having a hot rum, Jonathan. Would you like one?"

He strolled toward them, a tall, taut figure, maddeningly in control of himself. "I'll have mine straight," he said, getting out a glass.

"There's whiskey, if you'd rather have it," Kelly murmured.

"This will do fine." He poured himself a drink, gulped it down, and poured another.

Kelly's heart sank as she saw how much he was drinking. He swallowed it rapidly, his fingers tight around the water glass. She mixed the hot drink for herself and Andy, handed the glass to him with a forced smile, then went to stand beside the fire. Andy followed.

"I'd like to be here when you take that glider up," Andy said. "Mike mentioned your plan to try her out next week."

"It'll depend on the weather," Jonathan replied and

the look he flashed at Kelly was as brief as lightning and just as searing. He stood beside the kitchen table, the rum bottle in one hand and the water glass in the other.

Andy made several more attempts to keep the conversation going which Jonathan answered as briefly as possible. Finally Andy set down his mug and went to get his coat.

"Thanks for the drink, Kelly. I'd better get back up to the lodge or Maggie and Bob will think I've deserted them."

"I'm glad you came down, Andy. We'll do it again, soon." The smile stayed on her face, although her muscles were aching from the strain.

As soon as the door closed behind Andy, Jonathan set his glass down on the table with a crash. "So, were you going to take him to bed?"

"And if I was? What business is it of yours?"

"I'll tell you what business it is of mine," he shouted. His hands closed roughly on her shoulders and his dark eyes burned into hers. His fingers moved to her long bare throat. "You're my wife, damn you! No man touches my wife, but me!"

He dragged her to him, his mouth bruising her lips, his arms hurting her. He seized her dark hair in his hand and pulled her head back, then kissed her hard and long, his lips forcing her own to part so his tongue could plunge and probe.

She fought him with all her strength. She would never respond to him in this mood. If only his lips would soften, if only he would show some tenderness. He flung her onto the couch and stood over her with clenched fists, his face contorted with fury.

"I could kill you, Kelly! I don't want to hurt you!"

She looked up at him, white and trembling. "Please go."

He nodded wearily, his eyes flashing with shame and self-contempt. "I'm sorry," he whispered.

In a few quick strides he had plucked his coat from the rack and disappeared into the cold, dark night.

CHAPTER FIFTEEN

THE MEN CARRIED the glider out of the shed, unfolded the brightly colored wings, and snapped them in place. Kelly had looked forward to, yet dreaded, this day. It was mid-morning. There were several hours of sunlight left in the clear, cloudless day. Clyde started and restarted the motor, while Tram buckled Jonathan into the folded canvas chair suspended from the aluminum frame.

Kelly stood beside Marty, silently watching Jonathan. An almost breathless feeling came over her, an urgency to beg him not to go up in the flimsy contraption. He didn't look at her and when he put a crash helmet on over the ski mask he was wearing, he looked like an astronaut preparing for blastoff. The men gathered around him, as excited as small boys, giving advice, wishing him luck, telling him not to damage their toy.

"Are you going to wish him luck?" Marty asked. When Kelly shook her head, she added, "Well, I am!" She ducked under the wing and placed her hand on Jonathan's arm to get his attention. "Good luck, Jonathan.

Be careful. Don't get to thinking you're a bird up there and land in the trees."

He lifted a mittened hand and waved. The sight sent new dread shooting through Kelly.

Then the roar of the snowmobile drowned out any other words. The chain link between the aircraft and the snowmobile tightened and the glider began to move. Mike would tow it out to the clearing, then pull it into the wind. When the plane was airborne, Jonathan would release the tow rope. He planned to circle the area several times, keeping the resort in sight.

In a matter of minutes the gilder and the snowmobile were out of sight. Kelly heard the roar of the engine as the machine picked up speed, then the orange, green, and yellow wings of the glider appeared like a giant butterfly above the trees. Jonathan was up there! The thought struck Kelly like a physical blow. She closed her eyes, not daring to look. When finally she opened them again, Jonathan and the giant wings looked like a large bird in the sky. He circled and passed over them and headed toward the mountains. Suddenly the small purr of the motor died and there was silence.

Everyone strained to hear the engine start again. "Start it, boy . . . start it," Clyde mumbled aloud.

The silence was deafening. "What's happening?" Kelly's voice was so loud it shocked her. "What's wrong?"

"The motor cut out on him, but he can ride on the current until he can get it started again," Tram said calmly.

"But if he can't get it started again . . . he'll crash!" Her plaintive voice and anguished eyes begged Tram to tell her it wasn't true.

"What do you care?" Marty said cruelly. "You wouldn't even wish him luck."

"Hush up!" Tram said sharply. Marty burst into tears and ran for the lodge.

Kelly scarcely knew when Marty left them. Her eyes were glued to the speck in the sky that was getting smaller and smaller. Mike roared away on the snowmobile, and as Kelly stood numbly, Clyde backed out the truck, paused long enough to pick up Tram, and drove away.

"What good is the truck?" Kelly shouted. "You can't go cross-country!" She ran toward the cabin. "Don't let him crash! Please don't let him crash!"

Minutes later she was loading the sled with blankets, a first aid kit, whiskey, a battery light, and survival supplies. She had often seen her father aid stranded motorists or hunt for a lost tourist and she knew what to take. She was wearing her down-filled snowmobile suit. "Always take more warm clothing than you think you'll need," she remembered him saying. She grabbed her fur parka and two sleeping bags, and called to Charlie.

"Come on, boy. It's up to you and me . . . or Mike. Those two greenhorns in the truck will never find him." She talked softly to the dog, who stood patiently while she fitted his harness. "We'll take your new frisbee along, Charlie. See, I'll put it here on the sled where you can turn and see it. Let's go, Charlie. Jonathan is somewhere out there and he could be hurt! Mush . . . mush!"

Charlie was delighted to be pulling the sled. He took off across the snow, past the kennel of yipping huskies, without giving them a glance. Kelly ran along behind, holding the handles. Once she'd been able to run several miles before hopping onto the sled runners, but after they passed the grove and were halfway across the clearing, she had to rest and let Charlie do the work. Keeping her eye on the spot on the horizon where she had last seen the glider, she kept Charlie moving, although she knew he was tiring. She strained for the sound of Mike's snowmobile, but there was only silence.

Kelly was reasonably sure Jonathan would try to come down before he reached the mountains. She remembered hearing him say, "Lean forward and the glider goes down, lean back and it goes up. It's the shifting of your weight that controls it."

The wind picked up, stinging her face, and she pulled the ski mask down over her cheeks and nose. Gray clouds came rolling in from the north and the sky that had been clear a few hours ago was suddenly dull. Kelly pulled Charlie to a stop to allow him to rest and decided to put on the cross-country skis attached to the back of the sled. After that, the going was easier, but she looked at the sky with worried eyes and tried not to think about Jonathan lying in the wreckage of the glider. Doggedly she kept going, every step taking her farther and farther from the resort. Several times she blundered into a snowdrift. Often she was tempted to stop and rest. But soon the first intermittent snowflakes began to fall, and within fifteen minutes huge, fluffy flakes were falling fast. Worried that she wouldn't be able to see the wreckage of the glider, Kelly began calling out a "Ha . . . looo," a long high shrill sound that she knew carried on the brisk wind.

She looked at her watch and was surprised that she and Charlie had been traveling for almost two hours. It would be dark soon. She was frightened, so frightened she thought she would be sick, but she kept moving and calling. Once her voice cracked and she thought she couldn't continue. Charlie howled.

A stabbing pain in her side forced her to stop for a moment. She thought she heard a faint sound, and lifted her cap from her ear to listen. Nothing. She let go with a long shrill "ha . . . looo," and waited anxiously. The sound that floated back to her was indistinguishable, but definitely human!

"Mush, Charlie. Mush . . ." she shouted, directing him to the right. "Ha . . . looo, ha . . . looo," she called into the near darkness. The answer became clearer, and she followed the sound, her heart beating a rapid tattoo of relief.

"Here . . . here . . ."

Charlie saw him first and barked his pleasure. Then Jonathan materialized out of the snowstorm, standing beside the glider, his helmet in his hand and his ski mask off. Snowflakes stuck to his dark beard. He grinned broadly at her and she threw herself into his arms, crying hysterically. The force of her weight knocked them both to the snow. Jonathan gave a surprised gasp:

"Kelly! For heaven's sake. Kelly!"

It hadn't occured to her that he wouldn't know the person calling was her. Now he lifted her ski mask and held her close against him.

"You fool girl! Whatever possessed Mike to let you come out in this storm?"

"Mike had nothing to do with it, you idiot! Whatever possessed you to go up in that awful thing? You scared the hell out of me! I wish you'd broken your neck!"

Jonathan's laugh rang out, and he nuzzled her warm

face with his cold one. "No, you don't! Shhh . . . Stop crying. . . . You were worried about me? You cared? You love me . . . that much?"

"I don't even like you!" she shouted against his neck, but she was hoarse from calling out to him and the words came out in a croak.

Jonathan sat up and pulled her up with him "Are you all right?"

"I'm hoarse, you . . . flying turkey!"

"Do you think if I kiss it, it will make it well?" he asked huskily.

As they sat in the snow, the heavy flakes threatening to cover them both, Jonathan pulled her onto his lap and cuddled her close. Warm, firm lips found hers and he kissed her softly, tenderly, lovingly. She didn't want to cry again, but she was so tired. They sat there for a long time, his arms tight around her, not speaking, merely needing the closeness and security of each other's bodies.

"What do we do now, my little Sherpa of the mountains?" he whispered. "If we sit here much longer, we'll be buried under the snow."

Kelly moved out of his arms and looked about. She could barely make out the shape of the glider.

"How did you get down?"

"I found a smooth spot and came down. Worked great!"

"Great, my fanny! If it worked so great, why didn't you bring it back home?" she said crossly.

"I tried, sweetheart. I really did, but the wind was all wrong."

"Come on, Charlie. We could set a match to the silly

thing, but Mike wouldn't be able to see a house afire in this storm," she grumbled.

"Kelly!"

"Just hush up, Jonathan! I'm so mad, I might just hit you! Fold up the wings on that thing and we'll use it for shelter. It's not good for anything else."

She unpacked the sled and unharnessed Charlie. "I'm sorry I didn't bring you anything to eat," she told the dog.

"What about me?" Jonathan said. "I'm starving."

"Then starve. I'm still mad!"

Kelly turned on the battery light and unfolded a thin nylon tarp which she spread over the wings of the plane.

"Scoop snow up on the ends and tramp it down," she instructed, then covered the snow beneath the tarp with a ground cover before throwing in the blankets, sleeping bags, and her fur-lined parka. After turning the sled up onto its side, she crawled into the shelter. "It isn't home, but it'll have to do until it stops snowing and we can shoot off a flare."

"A flare?" Jonathan asked, crawling in beside her. "What else do you have in that Girl Scout pack?"

"Chocolate, raisins, and whiskey."

"No TV dinners?" he teased.

"What did you expect? I didn't have time to pack a picnic lunch. I was scared out of ten years growth!" Her fingers were shaking as she tried to take the top off the whiskey flask. Jonathan laughed and she snapped, "You act as if you're on a holiday! You fool! Didn't you know you could have been killed out here?"

"I was almost at the point where I didn't care. Now, I'm grateful to be alive! Take a drink of that whiskey, darling. You're going to need it." He moved closer to her but she leaned back.

"Stay away from me, Jonathan!" She couldn't see his face in the darkness, but she knew he was smiling. "Stay away, or I'll make Charlie bite you!"

"Charlie wouldn't do that." The dog heard his name and tried to sneak into the shelter. Jonathan rubbed his nose. "Lie down, boy. See, he likes me," he said arrogantly.

"He wouldn't if he knew you like I do."

"What do you mean by that?" All teasing was gone from his voice.

"Just what I said. I'll be truthful and admit that when I thought you had crashed, my heart almost stopped beating. But that doesn't mean I'll live with you. Frankly, I don't like you, Jonathan."

"What have I done to deserve this dislike?" His voice came quietly out of the darkness.

"How can you even ask such a question?" she demanded wearily. Their body heat was warming the shelter and she took off her cap and mittens.

"We've got to have the truth before we can understand each other, Kelly." She was silent. "Let's start with . . . Boston. I was too possessive of you, wasn't I?"

She gave a groan of despair. "I don't want to talk about that."

"We must, darling. I've had plenty of time to think about it. I realize now that I acted out of jealousy. I was eaten up with it." The words came out reluctantly. "I wanted you to be so completely mine that I smothered you."

"Jonathan . . ."

"Let me say this because I may never have the courage again. As soon as I took you to Boston I knew it was a mistake. I forced you into a new environment before you had even gotten used to me. But I wanted you with me so badly I didn't care. I didn't want to share you with Katherine, or Nancy, or any of my friends. I didn't want you to have anyone in your life but me. I hated Mike and Marty because they had a piece of your love and I wanted it all. I was actually glad when you didn't like Nancy or Katherine."

"Your own sister?" She was aghast.

"It's contemptible, isn't it? Do you think I wanted to feel like that? I couldn't help it," he said harshly. "You'd fallen in love with me without knowing I was a Templeton of Boston. I was thrilled with the idea that you loved me and not the man with the name. I can't remember when I felt loved, or even liked, because I was me."

"How can you say that? Katherine loves you."

"Katherine loves the Templeton name, the Templeton traditions. I'm merely the vehicle for carrying on those traditions. She doesn't care about me as a man. It took me a while to figure that out, but now I know it's true." His voice was hoarse with emotion.

"Why didn't you tell me this before?"

"I have my pride," he spit out. "I didn't think you would understand. You had Mike and Marty. I had only you."

"But when we went to Anchorage . . ."

"I was in heaven . . . then hell when you came back here without me. Why didn't you wait for me at the apartment?"

"You set me up! Why did you send me there knowing Katherine and Nancy were there?"

"I didn't know they were there until I got to the office. They'd only arrived the day before and Mark tried to tell me at the airport, but I was so anxious to be alone with you I wouldn't listen."

"Katherine implied they had been there for a long time. She said you found the apartment for them so they could make . . . social contacts for you."

"She lied," he said flatly. "When I went to the apartment and found her there, I told her to butt out of my life and take Nancy with her."

"She said you were going to marry Nancy before Christmas."

"Never!"

"She said you didn't want me to come to Boston to get my things, that I had embarrassed you enough. She said . . . no implied . . . that you were making love to me in order to lower the settlement you feared you would have to pay to get a quick divorce. She offered to buy me off."

"Oh, I'm sorry, darling. No wonder you left as you did! I thought you wanted to get back to be with Mike. I was so jealous . . ." He put his arms around her and drew her to him. "Forgive me, darling. Please forgive me and . . . love me."

"I still love Mike and Marty, Jonathan. Not the way I love you, but you must understand I won't exclude them from my life." She rubbed his furry cheek with her fingertips.

"All right. Actually, lately I've had the feeling they

like me, that they would accept me into the family, in spite of the Templeton name."

He lowered his head to kiss her and Charlie let out a fierce growl. Startled, they broke apart. The dog stood in a taut stance, the hair on his back straight up. Guttural noises came from deep in his throat. Kelly reached for the light and shined the beam out into the darkness. Two red eyes gleamed back at them. Charlie lunged toward the animal and the red eyes disappeared. Kelly and Jonathan waited tensely and presently Charlie returned to stand in front of the shelter.

"What was it?" Jonathan whispered.

"A wolf." Kelly laughed softly and switched off the light. "Wait until I tell that smart-aleck Mike that the dog he gave away is a great sled dog and a fighter, too! Charlie would have tackled that wolf! Good boy, Charlie. Remind me to buy you a new ball."

"I bought him a new frisbee."

"Playing up to my dog! I ought to give you a black eye!"

Jonathan laughed. "If you're going to do it, get it over with so we can get into that sleeping bag. I've never slept in one before. Will it be warm enough without these suits?"

"We won't know if we don't try it, will we?"

They snuggled down in a single bedroll, the blankets and fur parka over them, their legs entwined as intimately as their arms.

"I feel as if we're in a cocoon. I'm as warm as toast."

Kelly giggled. "Why not? You've got all that whiskey inside you."

"And you on the outside. Mmmm . . . your mouth tastes like chocolate."

"There's some left. It's there beside the lamp."

Jonathan lifted his head. "Charlie's eating it. That's okay, Charlie," he called, "I've got all I need, right here." Soft arms wrapped around his neck and she rubbed her cheek against his. "Do you mind the beard, sweetheart," he asked against her lips.

"I love it. Kiss me, Jonathan."

His lips hovered. "Not Jack?"

"I've got Jack out of my system. It's Jonathan I love. For too long I loved two men. Now I've settled on one."

"I love you, sweetheart. Stick with me and help me learn to share you. It won't be easy for me. I never believed you cared for me the way I cared for you. From the day we met, I wanted to put you in my pocket and keep you all to myself. I know now that I was crushing you, killing that beautiful spirit that flows from you and touches everyone around you." He stroked her lips with a tenderness he had never shown before. "I'll make it up to you, darling."

"It wasn't all your fault, Jonathan. I had a dream of a prince sweeping me off my feet and our living happily ever after in his castle. I should have tried harder to understand you and convince you that I loved you. We'll have to work hard to stay together. Love alone isn't enough."

"We'll never go back to Boston, darling. I never want to see that sad, haunted look on your beautiful face again," he muttered thickly, his lips nipping at the smooth line of her jaw.

"We have to go back," she said firmly, her hand

against his cheek. "Don't you see, darling? We can't solve a problem by not facing it."

"I don't want to go back. I've never been so content in my life as I have been here in your home, even though my jealousy was eating me alive. I love it here. I've already taken steps to move my headquarters to Anchorage. We may have to go back to Boston for a month or two, but that's as long as I want to stay. We'll build our life here."

Kelly almost burst with joy at knowing how much he cared for her. She held him to her with all her strength and murmured soft words of love against his lips.

"I've missed you horribly, my only love. I never again want to spend a single minute away from you. Hold me and love me."

His mouth closed fiercely over hers, parting her soft lips, urgent in his need. Her body felt boneless as he fitted every inch of her against him. She could feel his powerful body tremble with desire, and she moved her stocking foot up and down his muscular calf.

"Damn, damn . . . underclothes," he muttered. "They should be banned." His hand fought its way under her shirt.

"In Boston?" she giggled.

"Everywhere! Darling, I've got to have you!" His mouth devoured her softly parted lips and her senses soared under the slow, sweet arousal of his caress. "I don't suppose you brought the . . ."

She pulled back. "Of course not!"

"Would you be terribly unhappy if we . . . if it happened?"

"No. Would you?"

"I'd love to have a baby with you. What better way to hold you to me than to keep you barefoot and pregnant?"

"Jonathan!"

"I'm kidding, sweetheart. Remember that boy we met in the doctor's office? The one who wanted me to tell my kids not to ride on the handlebars of the bike? Well I want one like him . . . but I'll take what I can get. A boy and four girls."

"Four girls?"

"Well . . . three?"

"Two! And that's my final offer!"

"I'll take it!"

MARRIAGE TO A STRANGER

CHAPTER ONE

THE SILENCE IN the cabin was deep indeed, deeper than the vast wilderness in which the cabin stood. The man's voice was quiet for a few minutes and the silence pounded against her eardrums. Molly stared at him and vaguely knew he was trying to make it easy for her, but there is no easy way to tell a girl her father is dead. Jim Robinson, bush pilot, and his wife, friends to both Molly and her father, had come to tell her the news before she heard it on the wireless radio. Fortunately the news hadn't reached the remote cabin thirty miles south of Fairbanks. Jim was thankful for that, but the girl was taking the news so calmly, he feared she was in shock.

"Molly?" he said anxiously. Then again, "Molly?"

She looked dully from Jim to his wife, her face blank, uncomprehending. She shifted her gaze, with anguished eyes, to the open doorway and to the lake beyond. Fragments of sunlight leaped and danced gracefully on the blue water and it seemed to Molly that she was suspended in time and space and if she closed her eyes, she could remain there, safe and secure in the life she and her father had made together. She hung in a nondescript void. The silence was as deep and as high as the blue of the sky and the depth of the lake. A memory floated through her mind. Suddenly she recalled her father telling her to be still and listen to the silence. She had not known what he was talking about. Now she knew.

Jim took her arms and tugged her toward him, forcing her head down onto his shoulder.

"We never know why these things happen, honey. Why it was Charlie and not one of the other members of the expedition." He realized suddenly that her unnatural calm hid acute bewilderment as well as grief.

The girl's stillness frightened him and he grasped her upper arms and forced her away from him so he could see her face.

"Let it go, Molly!" he said urgently. "Don't hold it inside. It has happened and we can't change it."

"I know. I want to cry, Jim, but it won't . . . come. I loved him so much. I . . . don't know what I'll do without him! No one knew that range like Da—d—Dad. I just can't believe he could fall in a crevice!" The tears came. Big racking sobs shook the small body that Jim held against him. She cried tears of despair. Her voice, sobbing and tremulous in anguish, called to her father over and over again. The big man could do nothing but hold her while his wife stood by helplessly, her own eyes swimming in tears.

After a while the sobbing ceased and Molly raised her wet, swollen eyes to Jim.

"Evelyn will stay with you," he said gently. "Her mother will take care of our boys."

"Thank you." Her voice held a queerly resigned note

which Jim found far more pathetic than her tears. "I'll be all right now, but if you will excuse me, I'd like to be alone for a while." Her unwavering glance held his. "I'm sorry, Jim, for making it so hard for you to tell me." He touched her head with clumsy tenderness.

They watched her leave the room; head bowed, shoulders slumped as though the weight of the world rested upon them. She had retreated once again into the deep recesses of her own reserve and Jim shook his head as he heard the door of her bedroom close softly.

Evelyn looked anxiously at her husband.

"What will she do, Jim?"

"I don't know, but as much as Charlie loved that girl, I'm sure he must have considered the possibility that she could be left alone. He knew these expeditions were dangerous, although he never let Molly know. He cautioned me more than once not to mention it to her."

He sighed and pulled his wife down beside him on the couch. They sat for a few minutes without speaking. Both turned their heads toward the bedroom door, but no sound came from beyond. If Molly insisted on wrapping herself away in that impenetrable reserve of hers, there was little they could do for her; they could only wait and hope that by staying near she was comforted.

Jim looked down at his wife and saw that although she had leaned her head back against the couch and closed her eyes, big tears were creeping down under her lashes and trickling unheeded down her cheeks.

"Evelyn!"

She opened her eyes and he saw mirrored there all the sorrow and compassion her generous heart felt for her friend. With an exclamation he leaned forward and gathered her up in his arms. They sat quietly together for a long while before Evelyn broke the silence.

"Do you think she'll go to Anchorage, Jim? She has never talked much about the time she spent with Charlie's sister, but I got the impression she wasn't happy there."

"I don't know if she will go to Anchorage or not. I do know she can't stay here alone. Good Lord! It's ten miles to the nearest neighbor. She may be twenty-five years old, but she's as innocent as a babe. Every single man within a hundred miles will be finding an excuse to come by here."

"And a few that are not single," Evelyn asserted dryly. "She's been here with Charlie for about six years, hasn't she?"

"Ever since she left the convent school, except for the few months she spent in the city with Charlie's sister. Charlie taught her a lot about how to take care of herself, or he wouldn't have left her here alone for a week or two at a time. Of course Tim-Two was here to look out for her while he was away."

"I forgot all about the Indian. You'll have to tell him."

"Yes, I know. He's been with Charlie for a long time. He came here one winter about half starved to death. Charlie took him in, and he's been here ever since. I haven't any idea how old he is, but I imagine he would be a pretty wicked enemy."

Evelyn laughed softly. "Just to look at him scares me. That one eye of his that goes off in the other direction gives me the willies!"

Jim stood up. "I'll go talk to him. Make some coffee, will you, honey? I think we should leave Molly alone for a while. She'll come out and talk when she's ready."

He went through the kitchen and out the back door toward a cabin that was set about a hundred feet behind the house. Tim-Two had built the cabin himself. It was small, tight, and really quite ugly, like the man himself.

Evelyn busied herself about the kitchen. She stoked up the big wood range and set the granite coffeepot on to perk. She looked around the neat room. Nicely built cabinets lined one wall, with a stainless steel sink set into the middle of the counter top. A hand water pump was perched on one end of the sink. The big cooking range dominated the opposite wall; shiny black, with touches of blue on the big oven door at the bottom and on the doors of the two warming ovens at the top. The hot water reservoir was on one side of the range and the woodbox on the other.

She sat down at the trestle table that divided the kitchen from the living room, and let her gaze wander over the cozily furnished room. A stone fireplace, big enough to accommodate a six-foot-long log, took up the entire end of the room. In this cold country heating was a main concern, and heat from the fireplace and the cooking range in the kitchen kept the rooms comfortably warm. Evelyn knew, too, about the potbellied stoves in each of the two bedrooms. There was a rocking chair on one side of the fireplace and a comfortable pillow-lined couch on the other side. In between the two was a bright braided rug. The pillows, curtains, Charlie's pipe on the table, all caught Evelyn's eye as she looked about the room. Molly had done a good job turning this old barn of a cabin into a home; not fancy by city standards, but very comfortable. The girl was a natural homemaker, no doubt about that. It was unfair that she would have to leave it all.

Molly lay on the bed in her room, arms under her head, dazed eyes focused on the ceiling. Dry eyed, now, thinking about the big, burly dark-haired man that was her father. When her mother died, the nature of her father's work had forced him to make arrangements for her to be cared for in a convent school. From the age of six her life had been regulated by the strict nuns. When she reached the age of eighteen, she had about decided to enter the cloister because she knew of no other kind of life. Disturbed about the step she was considering, Charlie took her out of the convent and brought her to Anchorage to live with his sister. He wanted her to have a taste of living in the outside world before she turned her back on it forever.

Molly endured the time she spent with Aunt Dora and her cousins like a prison sentence. Fashion and the social life of Anchorage was their life and from the beginning she had felt oddly out of place in their home. After two months she longed for the quiet of the convent and begged Charlie to let her go back there if he didn't want her to share his home in the bush. The happiest day of her life was when she packed her things and Charlie loaded them in his old pickup truck and headed north. That was almost six years ago and Molly could count on one hand the times she had been to the city since then.

Charlie had been afraid that the wild north country would be lonely for his only child, but she took to the life like a duck to water. Her natural instinct for making a home exerted itself and she plunged into the work with vigor. The first few months she scrubbed, cleaned, painted, and hung pictures. She made curtains and slip-covers for the couch and chairs. The delighted Charlie let her have full reign of the house and was constantly amazed at all she could do. The sisters at the school had trained her well in the art of cooking, as Charlie discovered to his pleasure, and he wondered how he had ever gotten along without her.

Lying there on the bed, Molly thought about the love her father had for his work and that now he would never finish the job he had started. He loved Alaska and spent many evenings discussing with her the potential of the country. He was the country's foremost authority on ice age mammals, and his research had taken him to every part of the great Alaskan tundra. What would happen to his work now that he was gone? He had colleagues, but Molly had met few of them. He mentioned their names from time to time, but she didn't think he worked closely with them because he preferred to work, for the most part, alone. She wondered if she should contact one of them and offer her father's files. Well—she would have to think about that for a while.

She gave a deep, dejected sigh and slipped off the bed. Many things would have to be decided, but not now. There would not be a funeral service for her father, but a memorial service would be held later on and she supposed she would have Aunt Dora to contend with and she wasn't looking forward to that.

Glancing about the room, Molly caught her reflection in the mirror and was surprised she looked no different than she had yesterday after all that had happened. The outside of her was still the same, but the inside was totally different. She wondered if anyone else in the world felt as empty as she did.

Having no exalted opinion of herself, Molly was completely unaware of her beauty, although she realized she was prettier than some girls. A few of the men that had come to call on her cousins had looked at her in a friendly way, but her shyness had prevented her from making friends with any of them. Her cousins hadn't seemed anxious for her to mix socially with the crowd they ran with. This hadn't bothered her for they all seemed to be quite frivolous.

Jim and Evelyn were sitting at the trestle table when Molly came out of the bedroom. *What a totally feminine girl she is,* thought Evelyn. Her small five-foot three-inch body was slim but softly rounded. She was an elfin-type girl who moved lightly on the ground as if her feet were skimming the surface. The honey-colored hair hung almost to her waist and she wore it now in one long, loose braid hanging down her back. Occasionally she wore it in a neat braid on top of her head and it made her look like a small girl playing dress-up. Violet eyes, rimmed with dark lashes, were set into a face that had known very little makeup. Her good health gave her the soft, clear skin and the slight rosiness to her cheeks. She had no vanity about her eyes or the soft mouth that was quick to tilt into a smile. Molly Develon was a very pretty girl; not only pretty on the outside but on the inside, as well. Being shy and sweet-natured, she would never knowingly offend anyone.

Evelyn jumped up and went to the range. "Sit down, Molly, I'll get you some coffee. Jim will be leaving in a few minutes."

She set the coffee cup in front of Molly and went around the table to sit on the long bench beside her husband. He put his arm around her and she snuggled close.

"Don't think you need to stay with me, Evelyn. I've been here alone many times." Molly's voice was soft but controlled.

"I'm staying and that's the end of it," Evelyn said firmly.

"Of course she's staying. I'll get all the more lovin' when she comes back to me." Jim's attempt at light banter brought a smile to his wife's face.

"Don't let him fool you, Molly. He gets his share of lovin'."

"Yes, I know, and I do appreciate you doing this for me."

Jim reached across and took Molly's hand. "Molly, there isn't a person south of Fairbanks who wouldn't have broken their necks to do something for you. You've endeared yourself to all of us. We all want to help, you have only to ask." Tears came to her eyes, she swallowed the lump in her throat, but said nothing. "If you agree," Jim continued, "I'll arrange a memorial service for Charlie day after tomorrow. Herb Belsile, Charlie's attorney, and I will take care of everything."

"That's kind of you," Molly murmured. "Perhaps you will notify Aunt Dora in Anchorage?"

"Sure. Now . . . there are a few things I would like to say before I go," Jim said kindly. "Herb will be out in about a week to see you. He knows Evelyn will be staying here with you and he seems to think he should come out here rather than you going into the city to see him. I don't have any idea what provisions Charlie made for you. Herb will have to tell you that. But Molly, honey, you can't stay out here alone this winter." He paused and Molly's heart gave a queer little jerk. "What I'm trying to say is this. In the next few days try and get yourself in the frame of mind to accept whatever Herb has to tell you. Charlie will have left you financially secure, but he wouldn't have wanted you to stay here alone."

Molly's breath caught and she stared at him. It hadn't occurred to her that she wouldn't stay here; this was her home.

She said, with a catch in her voice, "I love this place. I don't want to leave it. The happiest years of my life were spent here."

"You'll have to be practical, honey. It would be dangerous for you to spend the winter here alone."

"I'll have Tim-Two and if Dad left me money, I'll hire someone to come and stay with me. I have the citizen's band radio and the snowmobile."

"You're very capable, Molly, but think of this. A lovely young girl here alone, miles from anyone except an Indian of undetermined age. While Tim-Two is devoted to you, and would defend you with his life, it's still too great a risk for you to take. The ratio of men to girls in this area is about ten to one, and the ratio of pretty young girls to men is greater than that. Men from miles around will be dropping by when they learn you are here alone, and some of them could be pretty obnoxious. Think about it, Molly." He smiled at her and squeezed her hands. "Let's don't worry about it now. You know Evelyn and I would be happy to have you with us, that is, if you could stand two wild Indians ages four and six."

"Thank you, Jim. I know you're thinking of what is

best for me, but try to understand. This is the only home I've ever known and if I must leave it, it won't make the slightest difference where I go . . . Anchorage, Fairbanks, or New York City. My heart is here." Molly looked up, her violet eyes bright with unshed tears. "Until I came here, I had spent my life in a convent school except for the two months with Aunt Dora. I don't think I could bear to leave this place. I love the tall pines, the spring flowers, the snow, the wildlife, and my dog. I could never take Dog to the city, Jim. I'll do anything to stay here!"

Jim sighed and told her he understood how she felt. He didn't realize it at the time, but in the next few weeks he would remember those words: "I'll do anything to stay here."

After Jim took his leave, the women sat quietly, listening to the sound of the motor as the plane circled the house and headed back to Fairbanks.

Molly sat in the rocking chair by the fireplace, the chair she occupied most evenings. Evelyn found herself busy answering calls on the battery-powered radio. The news about Charlie was out and it seemed everyone within radio range wanted to offer their condolences. Molly heard Evelyn say over and over again, "Thank you so much, but . . . no, I don't think she needs anything. Yes, I will tell her. I'll be staying with her for a while. Jim will be getting in touch with you regarding the service. Thank you, I'll give her the message. No she hasn't made any plans."

How thankful she was for Evelyn. Molly sat and rocked. Her thoughts raced. *Dad . . . how I'll miss you. We had such a short time together. What will I ever do without you? I must not feel sorry for myself; I must think clearly and figure out a way to stay here in my home. If only I could find someone to stay with me, but not many people want to spend a winter in an isolated place such as this. It will be lonesome here without you, Dad, but not as lonesome as it would be if I were in the city . . .*

Hearing a faint scratching sound, Evelyn opened the kitchen door to admit a large shaggy dog. He walked across the room to where Molly sat in the rocking chair and laid his head in her lap. He looked up into her face with large adoring eyes. She reached out her hand and stroked his head.

"Hello, Dog," she said softly. "You'll miss him too, won't you, fellow?"

The back door opened once again and the Indian, Tim-Two, came noiselessly into the kitchen. He checked the water reservoir on the cooking range, then the big wood-box beside the stove. He placed several armloads of neatly cut logs by the fireplace, then knelt and built up the fire. The evenings in the north woods were cool. The Indian didn't look at Molly; he seldom did. As he passed her chair he placed a hand lightly on top of her head and she knew he had been told about her father. He had never touched her before. Tears came again to her eyes and at that moment she felt closer to that old Indian man than to anyone else in the world.

CHAPTER TWO

ALWAYS, IN THE Alaskan country, there is the wildlife. Virtually no day passed without a succession of wild creatures coming within viewing distance of the house. They had been a constant source of delight to Molly; the deer, elk, moose, sly fox, porcupines, and the black and grizzly bears that lived in the valley.

Molly's Siberian husky, fondly called Dog, never seemed to learn that he made the porcupines nervous and after more than one encounter came home bristling. Molly kept a pair of pliers handy for pulling out the quills. She liked to think Dog was smarter about frightening off the black or grizzly bears, a potential hazard in the summer. Usually, the bears were looking for food and probably wouldn't bother you, but Charlie had warned her of the danger and she would scurry into the house or take refuge in the woodshed when one came near. Dog would dash back and forth, keeping his distance, barking ferociously until the bear, tired of the racket, went on its way.

Their land, bordering a twenty-acre lake, lay alongside the right-of-way of a highway that came south out of Fairbanks. The highway was a mile beyond that. In the summer supplies were brought in on the floatplane that landed on the lake eighty yards from the house. During the winter months they came by rail or ski plane. Orders were mailed or sent via the wireless radio to Fairbanks or to Anchorage and when the store had filled the order and was ready to send it, they would broadcast the news over a daily radio program of personal messages for people living in the outlying areas. Listening to this program was also a good way to keep up with the local happenings. When they heard, "freight for Develons leaving tomorrow," Charlie, Tim-Two, and sometimes Molly would head for the rail line where the freight would be dropped. The trip was made by skis, snowshoes, dogsled, or snowmobile, whichever the load demanded. Charlie kept a four-wheel drive vehicle in a shed along the highway, but the uncertainty of getting the motor started and road conditions made that means of transportation unreliable.

Snow cover lasted from October until May or early June. Winter was a lonely time, especially during the coldest spells. The vast area around the cabin would seem lifeless except for the birds. The gray jays and the gay little chickadees would find their way to Molly's feeder and would scold noisily when it was empty. The small, furry animals kept out of sight, burrowed deep in the snow, coming out only when their empty stomachs demanded food.

In the evenings, when it was cold and dark and the wind was howling, Molly or her father would stoke up the fire in the huge fireplace and put a record on the battery-powered stereo and listen to Beethoven, Bach, or, occasionally, to a Nelson Eddy ballad about the frozen North. With the records and plenty of fresh reading material Molly and Charlie had been content.

In the winter the moose would move out of the hills into the woods about the cabin. During the hunting season Tim-Two would shoot a good sized one to be butchered for the winter supply of meat. Hanging the carcass in the woodshed, the below zero temperature would keep the meat, and from it Molly would cook delicious steaks, roasts, and stews.

In summer, with the snow gone, the long daylight hours would bring a frenzy of activity. Tim-Two would replenish the wood supply, and you could hear the ringing of the ax and the buzz of the chain saw for days. Molly would get the "berry picking fever" and collect blueberries, raspberries, cranberries, and currants. She would make fresh pies and cobblers as well as can countless jars of jams and jellies.

Being out in the woods in Alaska in the summer meant having to contend with the pesky mosquito, but they soon got used to covering themselves with insect repellent before leaving the house.

It was a lovely way of life and Molly wanted no other. She wanted to live the rest of her life here in this house in this valley. Like all girls she had dreamed of falling in love, but in her dreams the husband and children lived with her here in this place.

Jim came for Molly and Evelyn the day of the memorial service for Charlie. Landing the floatplane on the lake they boarded from the small dock Tim-Two had put in for that purpose and for Molly to use for fishing. The trip and the service were an ordeal for Molly. Not being used to meeting people she found it difficult to greet and respond to her father's many friends who came forward to speak to her. Knowing she was being observed, she kept her head down and her eyes dry, holding her grief until the time she would be alone.

Strangely Aunt Dora posed no problems, probably thinking Molly was of age and she would no longer need be concerned with her.

Jim suggested that Molly spend the night at their home in the city. Molly consented to this knowing how much Evelyn wanted to be with Jim and the boys. However, no amount of talking could persuade her from returning to the cabin in the bush.

For the next few days Molly tried to put Herb Belsile's visit out of her mind. Although she kept the house spotless most of the time, she and Evelyn went over it together and the task kept Molly's mind busy as well as her hands. They made repairs on Molly's limited wardrobe and sewed several shirts for Evelyn's boys.

When Molly thought about it, she chided herself for her lack of faith that her father would provide her with the means of staying in her home. Knowing how he loved her, she was sure he had made arrangements that would make it possible . . . and yet the anxiety struggled painfully in the back of her mind, and even that was partially blocked out by her overwhelming desire that, in spite of all the reasons Jim had given her for leaving, she would stay.

On the morning of the attorney's visit the house was filled with the delicious aroma of fresh baked bread and apple pie.

Evelyn laughingly said, "Jim will follow his nose right to the house."

With beef roast and potatoes in the oven, Molly took time to freshen up before their guest arrived. She bathed her face and slipped on a soft blue blouse and matching skirt. She wrapped her shining braids around her head and slipped her feet into slim heeled pumps. On an impulse she applied a touch of lipstick to her lips. "Dutch courage," she told herself. With that thought, she turned back to dab a small amount of perfume to the base of her throat. She wanted this meeting to be over as she had never wanted anything else since the whimsical desires of her childhood. It was ridiculous, of course, because her father would have planned what he thought was best for her. She could almost hear his reassuring voice saying, "It will be all right."

Jim's voice was coming in on the citizen's band radio. "KGF-1452 . . . calling KFK-1369 . . . come in, Evie baby. Your ever-lovin's callin' . . ."

Grinning, Evelyn picked up the microphone. "Jim, you idiot, everyone within fifty miles is listening!"

"Ten-four, Evie baby," Jim's voice came back. "What's wrong with them all knowing I'm your ever-lovin'?"

"Nothing at all, but the radio is supposed to be used for business and not for . . . horsin' around."

"Yes, I know. You are my business, Evie baby. See you in a few . . . KGF-1452 mobile down and clear."

Molly heard the plane go over the cabin and a few minutes later it landed on the lake. The girls threw light sweaters over their shoulders and went out onto the porch.

Jim was striding purposefully up the path. Molly was surprised to see two men following Jim. She knew the shorter, heavier man was Herb Belsile, her father's attorney. The other man was some distance away, but Molly was sure she didn't know him and guessed he was one of Herb's assistants.

Herb approached Molly, holding out his hand. "Hello, Molly. I'm sorry we are meeting under these circumstances. Please accept my deepest sympathy. Charlie was one of my best friends."

"Thank you, Herb." Molly gave him her hand. "Do you know, Mrs. Robinson, Jim's wife? She has been kind enough to spend a few days with me."

Evelyn was standing in Jim's embrace, but extended her hand to Herb.

"Nice meeting you, Mr. Belsile. Molly and I hope you men are hungry. We've been cooking up a storm."

The third man had not come forward to be introduced. He was standing back, feet braced apart, staring at Molly. He was casually dressed in tan twill pants and a tan and green ski sweater. Molly looked at him and thought him handsome. He was looking directly at her and she couldn't look away. His eyes were luminous black, and like his mouth were just there in his face, grave, quiet, and bitter. They remained on her and Molly found herself caught in a silent waiting game with him. Slowly those shining, bitter eyes looked over her from the crown of her head to the tips of her shoes, and back to her face. Her eyes flicked up warily and she looked straight in the dark fire of his eyes. His mouth went colder and he nodded his head in greeting, against his will, or so it seemed.

Molly held her breath until her chest hurt, then breathed deeply when his eyes left her. He had measured her with his eyes for some purpose known only to himself, had estimated her, and found her lacking. A tightness crept into her throat. She merely stood there, hands at her sides, endeavoring not to clench her fingers with nervousness. He was the type of man to judge one on first impressions, she decided, with a mental sigh. At least it seemed to her that was what he was doing, because his dark face was wearing a positively thundercloud look.

Herb was talking to Jim and Evelyn so Molly stole another look at the man. He was tall, very tall, with a broadness to go with it. He had dark hair that curled down on the collar of the turtleneck sweater he wore. He had a dark face, a tight jaw, and a bleak mouth. *He doesn't like me,* she thought suddenly, *and how foolish of me to care.* With that she turned back to Herb.

"Oh, Molly," he said, "this is Adam Reneau."

Molly glanced at the man and nodded, but did not offer her hand. She turned from him and led her guests into the house.

Jim kept up a lively conversation with Evelyn while they set the meal on the table. Occasionally Molly glanced at the man. She had a feeling his eyes missed nothing as he looked around the room. An uneasy feeling came over her that this stranger was assessing her home. Something akin to panic made her heart pound and she felt a compelling urgency to get this day behind her.

During the meal Molly made little contribution to the general conversation. She was content to listen as voices echoed around and above her. She kept her eyes on her plate and tried not to look at Adam. The one time she let herself look at him she found the dark eyes watching her intently without much expression in them. Her chin tilted slightly and she said with a cool dignity that surprised her:

"Would you like some pie, Mr. Reneau?"

She served him silently, determined not to speak to him again unless it was absolutely necessary.

"Very good pie, ladies," Herb said. "Very good. Don't you think so, Adam?"

"It's delicious, Mrs. Robinson." His voice was deep and soft, not at all the tone he had used with Molly.

"Oh, I can't take any of the credit." Evelyn gestured with her fork. "Molly baked the pies."

"Is that so," he said dryly, making it a statement and not a question.

"Oh, my, yes!" Evelyn rambled on. "Molly can cook circles around me any day. Charlie was proud as punch at the way Molly could cook. Why—" Suddenly she was aware she was embarrassing Molly when the color came up to flood her face.

"Is that so?" Adam Reneau said again flatly.

"Well, now . . ." Herb started to stand up.

"Sit right here," Evelyn insisted. "I'll clear off these dishes. You'll have plenty of room to spread out your papers and things. Jim and I have things to talk about. We'll take Mr. Reneau out and show him around."

"That's kind of you, Mrs. Robinson, but Adam will have to stay. What I have to tell Molly also concerns him."

Molly's eyes flew to Herb's face. Her future having

something to do with this cold man? *Impossible! And if Herb thinks he's going to turn my affairs over to this . . . man, I'll soon straighten him out about that.* She blinked, opened her mouth to say something, but thought better of it after one quick glance at that horrible man's disgusted expression. She compressed her lips and cleared the dishes from the table and carried them to the sink. When she returned, she sat down at the table opposite Herb. Adam Reneau took the chair at the end of the table between the two of them.

Herb got out his briefcase and piled papers on the table. He shuffled them around several times. It seemed to Molly he was ill at ease. He cleared his throat while going through the papers and beads of perspiration popped out on his brow. He was definitely uncomfortable and Molly's anxiety grew.

"Molly," he said at last. "Adam already knows the contents of your father's will and that is the reason he came here with me to explain it to you. But first, I want you to know, I did everything I could to talk Charlie out of this plan. When he first brought the idea to me six months ago, I told him then I thought it was an out and out harebrained scheme. Although, I can understand, to a certain extent, why he did it, even if you and Adam won't." His voice took on a pleading note. "He loved you more than anything else in the world, Molly. After you, he loved his work. I think he thought that by bringing you and Adam together he was doing his best for both you and his work."

"What does he want me to do?" It was strange and frightening to ask the question.

Her face was so full of anguish Herb's heart went out

to her. He placed his hands over hers on the table and said as kindly as he could: "Your father wants you to marry Adam."

The surprise of his statement took her so completely, she went white and stared at him in terrible silence. Her body went rigid, her face set. Her lips moved, shook, and fell apart.

"I don't believe it . . . Dad wouldn't!"

Her tortured eyes turned to Adam. Resentment. It was there in the grim line of his jaw and in the bitter unsmiling eyes. He leaned back in his chair, his grim face tight.

"It wasn't my idea, Miss Develon." The mockingly drawled words were like a slap in the face.

"Wait a minute, Adam," Herb said firmly. "Let me explain things to her."

"Explain away, Herb, but I want her to know, straight off, that I don't want to marry her. A year, six months, a woman never lets go once she gets a legal hold on you. You could figure a way out of this for me if you would set your mind to it."

"I tried, Adam. This will is ring tight and Charlie had the right to do as he wished with his property."

"Charlie knew how badly I wanted to work on this project or he would have never thought up this idiotic scheme."

"I know." Herb spoke as patiently as if he were speaking to a child. "But in all fairness to Molly, she didn't know of his plans."

"I'm not so sure. Women go to great lengths these days to get a rich husband."

"Adam, really! Why don't you leave us and let me talk to Molly alone?"

"Not on your life! I'm staying! This concerns me and I'm going to hear every bit of it." He turned his dark eyes on Molly. With the faintest suggestion of a sardonic smile on his face, he settled back and folded his arms, as if that was his final word.

This can't be happening to me, this can't be happening to me . . . the words ran through Molly's mind over and over again. *They are talking about me as if I'm not here, as if my opinion counts for nothing. Well, I can set that man's mind to rest. I wouldn't marry him if he were the last man on earth. He's the most annoying, hateful, egotistical person I've ever met.*

Herb looked at his old friend's daughter's flushed face. She was a beautiful girl, twenty-five years old with the youthful look of innocence. Adam was a lucky man. She could have been ugly and dull. Herb felt a pang of compassion for her. This unsophisticated girl was no mate for the hard, experienced man sitting beside her. Almost ten years her senior, with more money than he could spend, plus his good looks, he was a prime target for designing females out on the prowl for a husband. This could account for his bitter outlook on life. Everyone that came in contact with him wanted something. Charlie Develon must have known him well and had plenty of confidence in him to trust him with his lovely daughter. A lot could happen in a year. Herb sighed and turned to the girl. He had to try and make her understand that her father had done what he thought was best for her.

"Your father came to see me about a year ago, Molly.

He was disturbed about your future. His heart wasn't in the best condition, but that wasn't what troubled him. He desperately wanted to go on this expedition he had planned for so long. Knowing there was a certain amount of risk attached to the trip, added to the fact his heart wasn't as sound as it should be, he wanted to find a way to make your future secure." Herb paused and reshuffled his papers.

"The fortune he left you is considerable. Not a huge amount, but enough for you to live comfortably. What bothered him was the attachment you had formed for this house and this valley. I'm aware of your childhood and how you spent it and can understand the feeling you have for this house. Charlie was hoping he would live to see you married with children of your own." He paused and shifted around in his chair, watching Molly with worried eyes.

Her heart contracted painfully at the thought of her father carrying this burden of concern for her and she bit her lips to stop their trembling.

Herb continued, "Charlie realized that if anything should happen to him, you wouldn't be able to stay here alone. He didn't want you to stay here alone. He was clear in his instructions about that."

Molly started to protest, but Herb waved her silent and glanced at Adam.

"This is what Charlie wanted you to do, Molly." His voice became stronger and took on a professional tone. "Charlie wanted you to marry Adam and live here in this house with him for one year. At the end of that time you can divorce Adam if you wish, and I can turn your money over to you and you can do as you want. You can live here alone or you can hire someone to live with you. You may wish to build some cabins around the lake, and turn this beautiful area into a hunting and fishing lodge, or you may want to sell it and go to the city." Herb took a deep breath. "Let me finish. I need to tell you what to expect if you do not choose to marry Adam. In case you and Adam do not marry . . . ," he looked nervously at Adam, who was looking intently at the kitchen range, "your Aunt Dora will have the control of your money for five years."

The expression on Molly's face might have been amusing had the circumstances been otherwise. She looked positively stunned. She stared at Herb as if he were a man from outer space, and seemed totally incapable of speech.

"Why? Why did he do this to me?" She was surprised to hear that her voice was so calm and even . . . and then not surprised, because a kind of cold numbing chill was gripping her heart, killing all feeling. "Why, Herb? Why did he want me to marry this . . . stranger, and why does this stranger feel he is being forced to marry me?"

"In the first place, Molly," Herb said after a pause, "Adam was no stranger to Charlie, and Charlie didn't plan to leave you so soon. His intentions were to have Adam come out here to help him with his work and for you two to get acquainted. Now, in answer to your second question. Adam is a biologist and is working on the adaptation of living things to hostile environments and there are few environments as hostile as the Alaskan tundra. It would set Adam's research ahead five years if he had access to your father's files. Charlie knew this and planned to bring Adam in to work with him, but knowing his time might be cut short he made these . . . other arrangements. His plan was for you and Adam to marry and live here for a year. You would be in the home you love and Adam would have his files to carry on his studies."

Adam's chair scraped the floor and he let out a snort of disgust. Herb gave him a slightly displeased look.

"I want to finish, if you don't mind, Adam. You know the rest, but Molly does not, so please be patient a little longer. Molly, your father has arranged for me to have the files destroyed if Adam refuses to marry you."

The words fell like a bombshell against Molly's ears. It was incredible to her that her father would consider destroying his files, his life's work. He always said his files were his contribution to society.

Herb was talking again and Molly brought herself back with an effort to hear what he was saying.

"I'm going to leave you two alone so you can decide what to do. You know the alternatives. Keep in mind the fact that Charlie knew you both very well and spent many hours carefully planning each detail of his will. I have a personal letter from him to give each of you. Think about what you want and what you have to lose if you decide to refuse the terms of the will. When you've made your decision, call me. I'll be on the porch." He took two sealed envelopes from his briefcase and handed the first one to Molly, the second to Adam. Then he left them.

Molly looked at the letter in her hand. Tears flooded her eyes so she could hardly see her name on the envelope. She stood up, but kept her face averted from Adam. With trembling lips and with as much dignity as she could muster, she said, "Excuse me for a few minutes."

He got to his feet. "Certainly."

With head up and back straight she walked to her bedroom door on shaky legs. In the privacy of her room she allowed the tears to course down her cheeks unchecked. She cried softly, as a deer cries when wounded, or a very small animal when caught in a trap. Her tears splashed down on the envelope she still held tightly in her hand. The awareness of the loss of her father was more acute now than any time since the accident. Horrified at her lack of control, she took a tissue from her bedside table and wiped her eyes and blew her nose. After a few minutes she was composed enough to open the envelope. With trembling fingers she unfolded the single sheet and began to read.

My Darling Molly,

Herb will have told you of my plan for you before he gave you this letter. I hope, with all my heart, that you will marry Adam. He is a good man. He needs a girl like you and you need a strong man like him. I know him well and trust him. He is the type of man who will appreciate a home such as you and I have enjoyed these past years. He will take care of you for a year and at the end of that time you will be able to decide for yourself the direction your life will take. Don't be angry with me, my Molly. Trust me. I am trying to grab some happiness for you.

Your loving Dad

Molly reread the letter several times, returned it to the envelope, and slipped it into the drawer of her nightstand. She didn't understand the last sentence. "Grab some happiness" . . . Did he think she would be happy with that man out there? Poor Dad. He didn't leave her much choice. She had never known her father to make a hasty judgment or an uncalculated decision. In spite of her dislike for the man she would marry him, if he agreed. A year wasn't really so long, considering the alternative.

CHAPTER THREE

A CALM AND composed girl went back into the living room. Adam had moved from the chair by the table to the couch by the fireplace and lounged there, his head resting against the back, seemingly lost in thought. He stood up when Molly came into the room. She didn't see any sign of the letter Herb had given him from her father. Somehow she had expected to see it in his hand. He waited for her to sit down and indicated the chair opposite the couch, but Molly wanted to be standing on her feet when she told him what she had to say. She tilted her head so she could look him straight in the eye.

"Mr. Reneau." Her voice was calm and controlled. "I'm sorry you've been put in this uncomfortable position. If I had the authority, I would turn my father's files over to you so you could finish your research, but as you know, I can't do that. It would break my heart to see his life's work destroyed. I'm willing to marry you, for a year, if it's agreeable with you."

By the time she had finished her speech she was almost breathless from the effort of trying to maintain her calm, and her last words almost faded away as they left her trembling lips.

"It didn't take you long to decide. Are you sure you are willing to marry this . . . stranger? Can it be you have discovered I am a wealthy man and that's the reason for your change of mind?" His voice was edged with a sneer and his hard black eyes probed hers.

"Think what you like. It may be hard for you to believe this, but there are some things more important than money . . . and if you are suggesting—"

"Hadn't it occurred to you?" he broke in rudely.

"No, it had not occurred to me." Her anger made her voice louder and sharper than she had intended. "And—and I'll tell you one thing, Mr. Reneau. If we agree to this . . . er . . . arrangement, I'll ask Herb to draw up a contract to the effect you'll have no financial responsibility for me . . . ever! I'll insist on this!"

She was amazed at her temerity to say such a thing, but she was glad. It might be just as well to show him from the beginning that she had no intention of allowing him to bully her, especially since this marriage was just as advantageous to him as it was to her.

Adam raised his dark brows. "Shall we sit down, Miss Develon?"

Molly sat in the rocking chair and Adam returned to the couch. There was a brief pause of silence before he spoke.

"You realize, of course, if we agree to this contract, it will be an impersonal relationship and at the end of the year we will get the marriage annulled, which is much simpler than a divorce. It will only hinge on the results of a doctor's examination . . . of you. You are a virgin?"

He felt a sharp stab of pleasure as the color came up and flooded her face, then a tinge of regret, for he knew this girl had not the cosmopolitan veneer of the women he usually associated with. The thought crossed his mind that it had been quite a while since he had seen a woman blush.

Determined not to let him put her down, Molly tilted her head and looked straight into his amused eyes.

"Of course," she said matter-of-factly, then added; "I wouldn't even consider anything but an impersonal relationship . . . with you, Mr. Reneau."

Adam laughed out loud as the blush burned brightly in her cheeks. "You think not?" he said softly, perfectly aware of the fury that was making her speechless. He lounged back against the couch, his arms crossed over his chest, a speculative gleam in his dark eyes.

Unable to continue staring at his mocking face without losing her temper, Molly dropped her gaze and watched her fingers intently for a moment as they aimlessly pleated the material of her skirt. The silence became heavy. The only sounds being the voices coming faintly from the porch as Jim talked with Herb. Adam continued to observe her, quietly and openly.

Molly squirmed inwardly. She felt a desperate desire to get this business over and settled. She hesitated, biting her lips in spite of her self-control.

"Well . . . have you decided . . . ?"

"Have I decided to marry you?" He finally spoke, although he waited so long Molly was not sure he was going to answer. "Yes, I decided to marry you as soon as I read Charlie's will." His dark eyes raked her face searchingly, while remaining inscrutable themselves. "If you had been fat, bald, and with a mustache, I still would marry you. The fact that you're young, beautiful, and obviously a good cook, is a bonus I didn't expect."

Molly was conscious of that dark, unreadable scrutiny and an icy chill crept through her body.

"You are that desperate to use my father's files." It was a stated fact.

"Yes," he said, not taking his eyes from hers.

"I see." Molly resisted the absurd desire to giggle childishly. "People will have to know that this marriage between us is a business arrangement."

"I have no wish, myself, that it should become public knowledge. At the present only Herb and myself are aware of the conditions of the will—besides yourself, of course. The Robinsons will guess, and have to be told, but we can trust their discretion, I'm sure."

Molly stiffened. The idea of any kind of pretended marriage affinity between herself and Adam Reneau was ridiculous. Surely he wasn't suggesting such a thing.

"What do you propose we do?" Carefully she controlled her voice so that it sounded cool and businesslike. She found herself looking at him with personal eyes, feeling a shock at discovering that he was so very attractive, that she could like him if only he were not so cold and withdrawn.

"After our marriage I'll take you to meet my father. This marriage will make two fathers happy, yours and mine. My father is eighty-four years old. I am the result of his one and only love affair. He married late in life and he wants to see me happily married before I reach middle age. This is very important to him and I insist he be made to believe my marriage is as happy and fulfilling for me as his was for him. We will spend a few days with him after the wedding and give him the impression that we enjoy a normal, loving marriage. Afterwards, when the time comes for the annulment, if my father is still living, we will simply tell him the marriage didn't work out. I don't believe he will ever have to be told since at present his health is so poor."

Adam leaned back on the couch watching her all the time. His expression was as unreadable as ever. His thoughts raced ahead to the time he would present his wife to his father. She would be perfect for the part. The inscrutable mask of his expression broke slightly, one dark brow lifted, and his dark eyes glinted with amusement.

"Do you think you can comply with the terms?"

"Terms?" She gave him a startled look.

"Can you pretend to be in love with me?"

Surprise made the color come quickly back to her face. She didn't dare look at him. Instead she stared down at her hands clenched in her lap. Inwardly she quaked and shrank from the thought of deceiving an old man—but so much was at stake!

"Would it be so hard to do?" There was a tight smile on his mouth, and Molly thought she could hear a trace of a challenge in his voice.

There was a shocking little silence, and it seemed to drag on for hours before she could say anything. Finally, the violet eyes looked directly into the pitless dark ones and she said in a low voice:

"The terms are . . . acceptable."

"Good." He got to his feet. "Now, I'd like to see your

father's study and look over the place where I'll spend the next year of my life."

Molly said nothing, but led the way to her father's combination study and bedroom.

The house had originally been built of rough logs, but in later years insulation and an inner wall had been added. One side of the square cabin was taken up with living room and kitchen; the two bedrooms and bath were in the other half. The elimination of a hall was due to difficulty in heating. Charlie's bedroom door opened off the living room and Molly's from the kitchen. The doors were left open most of the time to allow the heat to circulate. The bath between the two bedrooms had doors opening into each. Later a small room had been added in connection with her father's to accommodate a guest that came from time to time to help him with some phase of his work.

Adam looked around the room. It was large; desk, files, and bookshelves on one side, the bed, chest, and closets on the other. The room had been carpeted for extra warmth, but still had a fur rug by the bed, which Adam was glad to see was rather large. A round, potbellied stove sat in one corner of the room. He looked at it and grimaced, thinking about his centrally heated apartment in Anchorage.

"It keeps the room quite warm," Molly said rather stiffly. "You'll be glad it's here when it gets down to twenty-five degrees below zero."

She opened the door to show him the guest room. It was furnished with a single bed and chest. "We keep the door closed when it's not in use."

Opening the door to the bathroom, she went in and closed the door going into her bedroom.

"The bathroom is modern except for running hot water. We carry the hot water from the reservoir in the kitchen range. This room stays warm enough if we leave the bedroom doors open part of the time." She led the way out, not offering to show him her room.

In the living room she went to stand before the fireplace. "Tim-Two, my father's employee and friend, lives in the cabin behind the house. He's lived here longer than I have and he'll stay. I'll pay his wages out of the allowance Herb will give me for living expenses."

Adam smiled at this show of independence.

"Very well. What does Tim-Two do around here to earn wages?"

"He keeps the stoves and the fireplace supplied with wood, and the reservoir full. He plants a garden in the summer and furnishes us with fresh meat and fish. I would trust him with my life and I intend to keep him here with me . . . always." She looked at him defiantly, as if daring him to challenge her authority where Tim-Two was concerned.

Adam, reading her mind more accurately than she realized, elevated that black brow again.

"You think you'll need protection from me?"

"Of course not," she denied hastily.

"Let me assure you that I have no intention of raping you. I've never taken an unwilling woman to bed; not even a willing one that didn't know the score. Your virginity is safe with me until the time you wish to give it freely."

For one heart-stopping moment Molly stood there, her

face scarlet. The violet eyes were bright with humiliation—but even as he watched, she bit her lips viciously and answered in the type of voice he had become used to hearing from her. Her rigid control, for the first time, began to intrigue him.

"I never, for one minute, considered myself in any danger from you, Mr. Reneau."

"In that case shall we consider the matter settled . . . Molly?" He said her name hesitantly and it sounded strange coming from his lips. "It'll seem rather strange if we keep up this formal mode of addressing each other after we are married."

She nodded.

The dark brows jerked upward in obvious mocking amusement and one hand came out, his fingers lifting her chin. He looked, laughingly, into her eyes.

"Say, 'yes Adam.'"

Molly looked into the dark eyes. They were friendly. The face was not quite so dark and forbidding, and the grim mouth tilted into a smile. Before she could help herself she said, "Yes, Adam."

He turned from her, putting his hands in his pockets, all business once more.

"We'll be married a week from today, spend some time with my dad, and come back here. I'll make the arrangements in town."

With that short pronouncement he went to the door and called Herb.

When the men left an hour later, the plans for the wedding had been made. Evelyn was staying the week with Molly, and Jim would come for them the day before the ceremony to give them time to do some shopping. Herb furnished Molly with an allowance check and assured her that he would take care of the legal documents. Molly insisted that a contract be drawn up between herself and Adam relieving him of any financial obligation to her. When Herb commenced to argue the legality of such a contract, Adam silently shook his head, and he let the matter drop.

The Robinsons had been sworn to secrecy. To all appearances, Molly and Adam had met a year ago and fell in love. The ceremony, which would have taken place at Christmas, had been moved ahead due to Charlie's death.

Everything had moved so quickly that Molly found herself too tired to think about all that had happened to her in the last few days. Her brain was crowded with a jumble of thoughts and impressions. Finally she concentrated on only one of the thoughts. She was not going to have to leave her home and for that she was thankful.

CHAPTER FOUR

A WEEK LATER they were married in a small church in Anchorage. Adam insisted on the church service, saying his father would frown on a civil ceremony in a public building. There was no long white dress and no virginal white veil to trail Molly as she walked down the aisle toward the dark-browed man who was her father's choice for her husband. She wore a simple gray suit and a small matching hat and carried a single white rose that Evelyn thrust into her hand at the last moment. As she walked down the narrow aisle she noticed the church was decorated with vases of sweet-smelling flowers. She smiled as she recognized Evelyn's touch. This was her only act of unspoken rebellion against the unwanted marriage that had been forced upon her friend.

Molly was deeply grateful to her for her unquestioning cooperation and for the way she had strived to hide her deep misgivings.

The ceremony was short and simple and seemed like a dream to Molly. Firmly she had refused the minister's plans for having the church vocalist sing the traditional songs, which she felt would be meaningless for this occasion. Adam stood by the altar waiting for her as she walked toward him on the arm of Herb Belsile. She made her responses in a low voice, not daring to look at Adam, whose responses were strong and steady. When he slid the ring on her finger, her heart gave a sudden jolt at the contact of his firm fingers. She tried to draw her hand away, but he held it firmly and refused to let it go. He was still holding it when they walked out of the church.

Molly sat looking at the brand new wedding ring on her finger. A band of gold with diamonds encircling it. The beauty of it filled her with panic. This was the tie that bound her to Adam Reneau. She stole a side glance at him as he sat at the wheel of the big car, his face composed, concentrating on weaving in and out of the heavy traffic of Anchorage. He was so still, so withdrawn. Panic rose up in her, and she felt as if she were going to faint. She opened the window of the car and let the cool breeze hit her face, taking deep gulps of the air trying to alleviate the suffocating sensation that clutched her throat. With determined effort she pushed all unpleasant thoughts out of her mind. She would take one thing at a time. First, she must get through the reception and the meeting with Aunt Dora and her cousins. She would think of nothing else.

Adam said nothing on the short drive. As he turned the car into the hotel parking lot, he glanced at her and noticed her slight pallor.

"You're tired." His low voice was mixed with surprise and concern. "You're tired and frightened. Is it the reception or the meeting with my father that's bothering you?"

His nearness and the sudden unaccustomed tenderness

in his soft voice was nearly her undoing. Her breath caught in her throat. She admitted to herself the knowledge that she had been fighting. She had felt a strange physical attraction for him. She closed her eyes. He must never suspect that she felt any warming toward him. That would be fatal.

"It's Aunt Dora and my cousins, Dee and Donna," she blurted out suddenly. She twisted the white rose she still held in her hands and refused to look at him.

"Dee and Donna Ballintine are your cousins?"

She nodded.

He raised her hand and looked at the ring on her finger. "Do you like the ring?"

Again she nodded her head.

"Are you never going to talk to your husband?" Gentle fingers brought her chin around and she looked into laughing dark eyes. She smiled back into them and started to shake her head. They both laughed.

"That's better." He still had a firm hold on her chin. "Let me worry about the Ballintine girls and Aunt Dora . . . okay?"

The dark eyes so close to hers were looking intently at her face; the golden hair, the creamy skin, the soft mouth. She felt a trembling in him where her shoulder rested against his chest. His fingers caressed her cheek and he said in a voice not quite so firm and controlled: "Do you think the groom could kiss the bride on her wedding day?" He touched her cheek coaxingly, and drew his finger to the corner of her mouth. It was a truly lovely mouth.

"You shouldn't . . . !" The breath was leaving her.

"I'm going to." He laughed softly and deeply.

He seemed to hesitate, then leaned nearer and laid his lips very gently against hers. It was a light kiss, but Molly's heart stopped for a moment and then raced ahead furiously. He released her and she looked into his dark eyes. They were no longer laughing.

It was in something of a daze that Molly got out of the car and walked with him across the parking lot toward the hotel. She wore only a light coat over her wedding suit and she shivered in the brisk late September wind that blew into Anchorage from the mountains. She was glad to leave the car, to get away from the destructive intimacy she had shared with her new husband. *Husband?* she thought desperately. *A man who was forced to marry me, who kissed me because he thought I wanted him to, and God help me, I did want him to. Husband ... in name only, and I must not forget it. I won't forget it!*

It was a small reception, arranged by Adam, and catered by the hotel. A number of guests were standing by the buffet tables drinking champagne and talking. A toast was made to the bride and groom. Adam introduced her to some of his friends and she suffered through such remarks as, "Your bride is beautiful, Adam ... where did you find such a lovely creature? ... You sly dog, you, where've you been hiding her?" It went on and on. Herb, Jim, and Evelyn were the only people in the room Molly knew. Adam stayed by her side and after several gulps of champagne she began to feel a little light-headed and was glad for the supporting hand under her arm.

"Your aunt, Mrs. Ballintine, has arrived."

"Aunt Dora?" she said nervously.

Molly cast Adam a startled glance before looking toward the door and her aunt. Dora Ballintine drew her mink stole around her thin shoulders as she came across the room to greet her niece. A large, expensive hat sat atop her blue-tinted gray hair. Her ankle-length matching dress was flattering to her still girlish figure. Everything about Aunt Dora had to be perfect and it usually was. She swooped forward and kissed Molly on her cheek.

"Well, Molly! So you are married," she exclaimed so everyone in the room couldn't possibly help but hear her. "It must have been sudden. You didn't mention it at the service for poor Charlie."

"Hello, Aunt Dora," Molly said calmly. "I'd like you to meet Adam."

"I know Adam. I certainly do." She turned accusing eyes on him. "We didn't know you knew our little country relative, Adam. I must say, Donna was terribly . . . surprised."

"Was she, Mrs. Ballintine? I can't understand why," Adam said politely, black brows raised.

"You disappeared so suddenly, dear boy. Donna was most upset—parties and things you were both invited to, you know."

"I'm sure a beautiful girl like Donna didn't lack for an escort, Mrs. Ballintine," he challenged coolly.

"Well, of course not," she said, turning back and looking Molly over from head to feet. "Why, Molly, you look quite . . . pretty, but we are going to have to do something about your hair. I do wish I could have taken you to my hairdresser before the wedding. A good cut and styling would do wonders for you." Her voice was warm and kind, but to Molly's sensitive ears it was belittling.

Hurt pride lifted her chin. She opened her mouth and closed it again. She was no match for Aunt Dora.

For an instant a caustic look came over Adam's face, then it softened as his arm went around the slender girl beside him and he drew her close.

"I think my wife is enchanting," he said softly, smiling down at her. "This lovely hair will stay just as it is as long as I have anything to say about it."

Molly tilted her head to meet his gaze, her heart soared. How wonderful to have someone defend her, if only out of duty.

"I didn't mean . . . oh, here's Donna. Dee was unable to make it, but Donna canceled everything to come."

Aunt Dora's eyes brightened as she saw her daughter framed in the doorway, as if posed for a picture, waiting to catch every eye before she made her entrance. No doubt about it, she was beautiful. Tall, slim, vivid blue eyes, silver hair, and beautifully dressed. Crossing the room with a studied grace, she came forward with hands outstretched; she had eyes only for Adam.

"Adam!" The soft husky voice breathed his name. "I couldn't imagine what had happened to you." Big blue eyes misty with emotion looked pleadingly at him.

"I've been busy, Donna. Busy getting married to your cousin," Adam said evenly. "Are you going to congratulate me and my bride?"

The girl's lips tightened ever so slightly and she stood still for a moment and stared at him.

"Congratulations, Molly."

The blue eyes that turned on Molly told her that she was in love with Adam and she hated her with every fiber of her being. Molly glanced at Aunt Dora and was surprised to see her looking back at her with actual dislike on her face. *Wouldn't they be pleased if they knew the truth about this marriage,* Molly mused. *They'll never, never know, if I can possibly help it.*

A passionate protest was building inside her. It was impossible not to grasp the implications of the relationship between her cousin and her new husband. He looked so handsome, tall, and sophisticated. It was almost disheartening to see him and her lovely cousin standing side by side. They looked so right together; so worldly, so polished. She felt dowdy, small, and insignificant beside them. Donna leaned forward and kissed Adam on the lips.

"Darling, do excuse Mother and me," she said huskily and swirled away from them in a sea of chiffon, only a trace of her perfume lingering.

The meeting with Aunt Dora and Donna almost completely unnerved Molly and the next half hour was spent in an agony of self-consciousness. Someone handed her another glass of champagne which she drank too fast, and when they were ready to leave the reception, her head was really in a whirl.

"My father is anxious to meet his new daughter-in-law," Adam said as they were leaving. "We're staying with him for a few days before we go north to the cabin. Come and see us. But wait a few weeks!" They left amid laughter and good wishes.

"Lord have mercy!" Adam exclaimed as they made their way to the parked car. "I'm glad to get out of there."

Molly was grateful for the strong arm that hurried her along. He glanced at her only briefly as he slid under the wheel and eased the car into the stream of traffic.

She leaned her head back against the soft cushions of the seat and let her mind wander over the events of the day. Oh, to be back in the house by the lake! How much longer would she have to keep up this nerve-racking pretense? The reception was over, and she had one more obstacle to face before the blessed quiet of the country. She must meet Adam's father and convince him she was in love with his son. She owed Adam that after the way he stood by her through the meeting with Aunt Dora and Donna. Somehow she knew that her aunt and her cousin would never forgive her for marrying Adam. Their opinion wasn't important to her, but Adam's was. They would be spending a lot of time together this year and it was only sensible not to antagonize each other. She had learned a lot about the man she had married. *No wonder he didn't want to marry me,* she thought. *I'm not his type at all. It must have been a bitter pill for him to swallow to have to introduce me to his friends. When this year is over, we'll go our separate ways. I'll not depend on him too much—I'll stand on my own feet. It's the way it'll be from now on.*

Adam looked down at the girl beside him. *No confidence in herself,* he thought. *Fresh and beautiful, unaffected and untouched. God, how many men do I know that would like to get their hands on her? I'll have to be careful and not get involved. Family life isn't for me. At the end of the year I'm taking off as planned. I shouldn't have kissed her.* He didn't know why he did it except she was so . . . sweet . . .

"Shall we drive around a bit before we go to meet my father?"

She sat up straight in the seat and looked at him earnestly.

"I'll not let you down, Adam. I appreciate you standing by me when I met Aunt Dora."

With a twinkle in his dark eyes he said, "I see now that marrying me was the lesser of two evils."

"Believe it or not, I could have stood for Aunt Dora having control of my money, but I couldn't stand by and see my father's files destroyed," she said with spirit.

"Neither will happen now. We'll get through this year together and try not to get involved in each other's private life. When we break, a year from today, it will be as friends." He smiled at her. "Don't worry about Dad," he continued. "He's going to be in seventh heaven when he meets you. You're the answer to his prayers for me. Just be yourself and he'll love you. Try and make him believe you love me just a little and he'll be happy."

"I'll try." She smiled at him as if they were sharing some huge joke.

He drove into an underground parking area, angled the car into the area marked Reneau, and turned off the motor.

"My father lives on the top floor of this building," he said as they left the car. "He has a heart condition and never leaves the apartment. His sister, my Aunt Flo, lives with him. This has been a very exciting day for them, knowing I was getting married and bringing my wife to meet them."

"We'll be spending the night?"

"No. I've an apartment on the floor below. We'll stay there."

The color flooded her cheeks and she despised herself for being so self-conscious.

"You'll have to get used to being alone with me," he murmured consolingly.

She took a deep steadying breath. "I know."

Adam unlocked a door and they stepped into a private elevator. Pushing one of the two buttons, he said by way of explanation: "This elevator stops only on Dad's floor and mine."

The car slid smoothly to a halt and the door opened. A wave of apprehension passed over Molly. She looked up at Adam and he smiled reassuringly. They stepped out into a room that was surprisingly quaint and homey. A small birdlike figure hurried toward them. The lined face beneath the iron gray hair was wreathed in smiles. She looked as Molly always pictured a storybook grandmother would look. Even before she spoke the tension went out of Molly and she met her outstretched hands.

"Molly, my dear." She was obviously almost moved to tears.

Molly reacted instantly to the warm greeting from this gentle lady and kissed her on the cheek.

"Hello, Aunt Flo." Adam's amused voice was low and gentle. "Have you no greeting for me?"

"Oh, Adam, you bad boy! Why have you waited so long to bring her to us?" She reached up to kiss his cheek and he leaned down and gave her an affectionate hug.

"I told you she was worth waiting for, Aunt Flo. Now wasn't I right?"

"Yes, you were right for once, you rascal. But come, Robert is waiting and anxious to meet your bride." She led the way to a door at the end of the room and moved aside to allow them to enter.

"This is one of his better days, Adam. Take her in." She smiled at Molly and squeezed her hand.

Adam's father was in a rolling chair by the window. His penetrating gaze looked her over. How like Adam;

the same dark, forbidding countenance and piercing black eyes. His hair was wispy and gray, and the lines in his face showed age and suffering. There was no evidence in his expression of the anxiety Aunt Flo had spoken about, but his frail hands worked nervously with the blanket that covered his knees. Adam urged her forward, slipping an arm around her shoulders.

"Father," he said in a low voice and there was an almost miraculous change in his expression as he looked down at the lined face. "This is Molly."

The silence that followed could be felt, tense and profound. Two large tears rolled down the old man's cheeks and fell on the blanket. His lips moved, but no sound came out. Suddenly he seemed to be very weary. The sight moved Molly deeply, her violet eyes went to Adam imploringly, then she dropped on her knees beside the chair.

"You're not pleased?" she asked with trembling lips, her eyes swimming with tears.

The old man raised a hand and drew her head down on his lap. His thin hand stroked the blond hair. Molly was vaguely aware that Adam had produced a handkerchief and wiped his father's eyes.

"Is it true, Adam," the shaky voice asked, "you and this girl are married?"

"Quite true, Father. Molly and I were married this afternoon." The positive voice had an effect on the old man. He gave the blond head a final pat and sighed deeply.

Molly raised her head.

"You have my blessing." The black eyes gazed into Molly's and she met them unflinchingly. "Give me your hand, daughter." She obeyed, feeling strangely close to this frail old man who was so like Adam.

"My son is a lucky man, but you are lucky too. Don't forget that. He is the best of his mother and me." He looked fondly at Adam. "There is no finer man than my son."

Molly took the old man's hand and held it to her cheek. The depth of devotion between these two men was incredible, and it was wonderful to see. He had accepted her as a mate for his son. A feeling of complete tranquility settled over her. She sank down on the floor by his knee.

Adam pulled up a chair. Molly could tell that he was pleased with the way his father had warmed to her.

"Now tell me, Adam, how did this come about? How did you persuade this lovely child to marry you?" Molly noted, with satisfaction, the strength that came back in the old man's voice.

Adam told his father the story about the wedding being brought forward due to Charlie's death. Molly was fascinated at his expert handling of the affair. The most amazing thing was that he had not told his father a lie.

What followed was a very pleasant half hour. Molly smiled easily, her eyes going from one man to the other. They included her in their conversation and for the first time since her father's death she had a feeling of belonging. She had an odd premonition, that whatever difficulties lay ahead, she would be glad she had brought peace to this gentle old man who had so little time to live.

After a while Adam excused himself, saying he would see if Molly's cases had been brought over from the hotel, but he would be back, because they were dining with his father and Aunt Flo. He took Molly's hand, pulled her to her feet, and folded her in his arms. Tenderly, he kissed the corner of her mouth. Molly felt a heady sensation coursing through her body. It was exhilarating, yet disturbing too. Unaware that her eyes were following him as he walked to the door, he left the room.

Molly looked down at Mr. Reneau who was watching her intently.

"You love him, girl?" he asked softly.

Without hesitation, Molly nodded her head. "Yes, I do, very much." Her lips trembled as the words came out.

"Ah . . . ," the old man sighed and settled back in his chair, his face serene.

They talked of many things. It was relaxing here in this room high above the busy street. She told him about the house in the bush and her dog named Dog. He laughed with her about that. She told him of Tim-Two and the moose he hunted each year, of the jars of jam and jellies she canned, and promised on the next trip she would bring him a jar of each along with a loaf of homemade bread to spread them on.

He told her about Adam as a small boy. His determination to win each contest he was in, his stubbornness when he thought he was in the right, his deep desire to be accepted for himself alone and not for his money. He also told her of his grief following the death of his mother when he was a lad of twelve. The old man's eyes glowed when he talked of his son.

Molly felt a small nagging guilt at the deception of their marriage. She was glad she had told the old man she loved Adam. It had come out of her so suddenly and it seemed so right to say it. Adam would never know; she and the old man would share the secret.

The elderly man took his place at the head of the table that evening; Molly on his right, his son on the left. The delicious meal was served by the white-coated man called Ganson. It was obvious servant and master were equally fond of each other. Her eyes misted and the lump in her throat almost choked her when her new father-in-law invited the household help into the dining room to toast his "lovely new daughter." Adam was pleased, his dark eyes going from her to his father.

Later he whispered they should depart, because they would be expected to want to be alone. Molly took her leave of Aunt Flo, then went to the old man's chair. Leaning down, she placed her young cheek against the wrinkled one and whispered in his ear that she was pleased he had accepted her. He turned his head and placed a kiss on her smooth brow and squeezed her hand.

Feeling almost lighthearted, Molly went with Adam to the elevator. Once inside he turned to her with serious concern on his face.

"Don't get too fond of him, Molly. It'll be tough losing two fathers in one year."

"No! Not so soon?"

"I'm afraid so. And, thank you," he said almost humbly. "You played your part well."

Molly was too emotionally shattered to answer.

They stepped out of the elevator and into a carpeted hallway. Adam opened the door and waited for her to enter.

"Go in," he directed, his voice noticeably cooler now, as if trying to get back to the business relationship again.

She walked slowly into the room, her heels sinking into the soft carpet. The room was large, but lacked the homey atmosphere of his father's apartment. Comfortable couches and chairs were placed at random around the room and the walls as well as the various tables were decorated with objects he had collected on his trips abroad. Molly was impressed, in spite of herself, and smiled as she noted a priceless vase of Peking jade sitting alongside a hand-carved miniature canoe from his native state.

Adam grinned sheepishly.

"Not exactly *Better Homes and Gardens,* but it's home."

"It's interesting. I've never seen things like these." Molly looked curiously around the room.

"Go ahead and look," Adam said wearily. "But if you don't mind, I'll have a drink."

She wandered about the room looking at the different objects of his collection. The room was large and although it was filled with a profusion of paintings, porcelains, carvings, minutely patterned tapestries, and a richly colored Persian carpet before the fireplace, it didn't appear to be cluttered.

Presently Adam was beside her, a glass in his hand. She looked from the glass to his face, questioningly.

"It's very weak. You need it after today." He put the drink in her hand, then with his hands in the small of her back urged her over to the couch.

"Sit down and enjoy it." He sank down in the chair opposite, stretched out his long legs, leaned his head back, and closed his eyes.

Molly watched him, her senses stirring in spite of herself. He was handsome; his dark features were more re-laxed than she had ever seen them. Just looking at him lounging there, his shirt collar open, revealing the smooth brown skin of his throat rising up from the broad muscu-lar chest, the muscles of his thighs firm against the mate-rial of his trousers, she felt a warm weakness flooding her system, and the desire to touch him made itself known to her.

She gave herself a mental shake and took a gulp of the drink in her hand. When she looked at him again, the black eyes were open and he was gazing at her. His eyes, narrowed and unreadable behind the heavy lashes, were staring into her violet ones, then dropped to her mouth, then to the rise and fall of her breasts. He sat up suddenly, his eyes darkened. He gulped the rest of his drink and got up to get another.

He returned to his chair.

"This is the first time we've been alone so we can talk." He ran his hand through dark hair in a gesture of resignation. "I meant what I said in the elevator, Molly. Dad won't be with us long."

"I couldn't help but like him. At first I was ashamed of the deception. It was like we were playing a cruel joke, but when I saw how happy he was, well . . . I was glad." She paused, then asked anxiously, "If he has just a . . . short time, don't you think you should stay here near him?"

"That's one of the things I want to tell you. Dad knows about my research and how much it means to me. He thinks the reason I'm going north is so I can use some of your father's specialized equipment. He has devoted peo-ple to care for him here. They've been with him for years and I might add, it's a two-way street. He's devoted to them and looks out for their welfare." He whirled the drink around in his glass and smiled to himself. "My father is a very wealthy man. He pursued his interest, which was manufacturing a pipe that can be used in the polar region. It just happened that he made a lot of money at it. He understands that I'm interested in another field, and I'm lucky because his money makes it possible for me to do the things I want to do without financial pressures." He looked directly at Molly. "If I can be half the man my father is, I'll die happy."

"You love him very much."

"Yes, I do, and I wouldn't insult him by giving up my work and waiting around for him to die." His voice had become husky, and he raked his hand through his thick hair again. "I'll come back once a week to see him. I'll get someone to come stay with you, if it should become necessary to be away overnight. Occasionally you may want to come with me. Dad would enjoy that. But we must be very careful to comply with the terms of Charlie's will. I've the feeling that if your Aunt Dora could get her foot in the door, she would be happy to give us some trouble."

"I'm sure she would," Molly agreed, then asked, "Will Jim take us back?"

"We'll take my plane when we go up this time. I'll have boxes to take and I imagine you'll want to do some shopping."

"The only shopping I want to do is at a yarn shop."

"Knit, do you? Good, you can make me a sweater. Husbands should have top priority." His voice was teasing.

Molly warmed at his use of the word "husband" and teased back, "If I can find the time."

"If the weather gets too bad for the ski plane, I'll have the helicopter come up once a week. It can also come for us anytime Aunt Flo or Ganson thinks it necessary." He stood and stretched his long frame. "Are you tired?" He reached down to grasp her hand and pulled her to her feet. She had kicked off her shoes; he looked down in surprise. "You are a little thing," he said, touching the golden hair coiled on the top of her head. "You don't even come up to my chin."

"Yes, I'm rather short," she said, and added before she thought, "but good things come in small packages."

He threw back his head and laughed. It was the first time she had heard him laugh aloud and the sound was so pleasant that she laughed with him.

"Come on. I'll show you to your room." He led the way into a rather long hallway. "This is my room," he said as they passed the first door. "You use this next one. There are two more bedrooms; my friend, Pat, uses one and my housekeeper the other. She's away now, but when she's here, she helps Aunt Flo while I'm away. Oh, yes, Ganson will come down and fix breakfast for us in the morning. After that, you can do it if you want to. We've got a well-stocked pantry."

"I'd like that. I love to cook."

"I'm glad to hear it. It's going to be a long winter."

They walked into a white and gold bedroom with white carpet and white and gold French provincial furniture. It was beautiful.

"This room isn't used very often."

Molly went to the large bouquet of white roses on the

dressing table. She bent her head to smell the sweet fragrance, then raised her violet eyes to Adam.

"Every bride needs a few flowers," he said.

"Thank you. They're beautiful."

"And so were you, Molly. No bride was ever prettier. Someday you'll have a real wedding and all the trappings that go with it." His smile crinkled the corners of his eyes and his lips. He turned to go. "Your cases are here. There's a bath through that door. Get a good sleep and I'll see you in the morning."

He went out and closed the door. Molly remained still for a moment. A feeling of disbelief came over her. Here she was . . . married, and alone on her wedding night. *My husband treats me like a little sister,* she thought, *and it's just as well, for after all, he didn't want to marry me.*

She was more exhausted than she realized. She slid into the big bed between the silken sheets, but before she went to sleep, his words came back to her. "It's going to be a long winter." She sighed. It may be a long winter for him, but she had the feeling it would be all too short for her.

CHAPTER FIVE

MOLLY SLEPT SOUNDLY that night. She had no dreams. When she awoke, she lay on her stomach with her eyes closed and listened for any sound coming from the apartment. After a while she opened her eyes cautiously and looked at her watch. If she got up, now, she would have time for a bath before breakfast. She rolled over and sat up.

Her bare feet loved the feel of the soft carpet as she made her way to the bathroom. The bathtub was a marvel to her; big, square, it would take gallons of water to fill it. She smiled as she thought of the tub at home and the hot water she carried from the reservoir. She bathed, dressed quickly, and left the sanctuary of the bedroom.

In the hall she heard the unmistakable rattle of pots and pans. Cautiously she pushed open the swinging door. Ganson was at the stove and the delicious aroma of frying bacon reached her nostrils.

"Good morning, Mrs. Reneau."

"Mrs. Reneau? You're the first to call me that."

"Yes, ma'am, but that's your name, now."

She had expected to be tongue-tied and had worried

about her shyness, hoping she would be able to overcome it enough to keep from making a fool of herself for the few days she was here. But it was easier to talk than she thought it would be. She climbed upon a stool near the table where Ganson was working.

"What do you call Adam?"

"Why, I call Adam, Adam." He grinned at her. "What else would I call that boy? I smacked his butt many times when he was a tadpole. Only one Mr. Reneau in this house and that's Robert."

He set two places at the kitchen table.

"If you call Adam, Adam," Molly said, "you'll have to call me, Molly."

"Well, now, that makes sense, Molly. I'll do just that, but you better go get that lazy husband of yours before the eggs get cold."

Molly got off the stool. She didn't want to go to Adam's room and hesitated before going to the door. It swung open and Adam strolled in. Relief flooded her and the smile she greeted him with was warmer than usual. In cream cotton trousers that clung to his muscular legs and a dark blue shirt laced up the front with cream cords, he looked different from the man who stood with her before the minister yesterday. Her gaze was drawn like a magnet to his face.

"Are you showing her how I like my eggs, Ganson?" he asked with a devilish glitter in his eyes, dropping a light kiss on the top of Molly's head.

"Too late, they're ready." Ganson set two plates on the table and slid two slices of bread in the toaster. "I'll be back to clean up, or I'll send one of the girls down. You don't want me hanging around." He winked at Adam. "Coffee is ready, Molly." He left them.

"Molly . . . already! You must have made a hit with Ganson. He can be terribly formal unless he takes a liking to you."

"He's nice. Everyone here is. I was afraid I'd be shy and tongue-tied, but they're all so friendly I forget to be shy." She poured the coffee and placed the buttered toast on his plate.

"Almost everyone responds to a nice person. Ever think of that?"

"Yes," she said slowly, thinking of Aunt Dora and her cousins. "But it doesn't always apply," and added almost absently, "I liked your father very much."

"How about his son?"

"I'll have to think about that!" She was acutely conscious that his dark eyes were on her and her heart began to flutter erratically.

He grinned and Molly wished they could be friends. If she was congenial, if she could be a pleasant companion, he might not resent so much having to spend the year with her.

Adam told her he would be away part of the day. He explained he had arrangements to make due to his coming absence from the city.

"By the way," he said as if suddenly remembering, "I put some of my things in your room. Ganson would notice right away that we hadn't spent the night together and think it strange."

Molly could feel the color coming up into her cheeks, and poured coffee to cover her embarrassment.

Later in the morning when she entered the apartment

above, Adam's father was waiting for her. They had a short time to visit before Ganson came to tell them lunch was ready.

"Shall I push your chair, Mr. Reneau?"

"What did you call Charlie, girl?" he asked rather gruffly.

"I called him . . . Dad."

"Then call me Papa," he said firmly.

She smiled down into a wrinkled face with gentle, almost pleading eyes. "Very well, Papa, but let's have lunch, I'm starved." She pushed his chair to the dining room.

Adam returned in the middle of the afternoon. Standing in the doorway of the sitting room, he watched Molly, his father, and Aunt Flo laughing together over an old picture album. His father was talking and suddenly Molly let out a peal of laughter. The old man could hardly keep his eyes from her young face and Adam felt a surge of gratitude. He came across to them and squatted down beside Molly. Her eyes sparkled; her high spirits had brought a flush to her cheeks. She had blossomed astonishingly in the last few days. To her surprise and his, he leaned over and kissed her on her still smiling lips.

"What tales are you telling my wife?" He spoke to his father while still looking at Molly. "It must have been funny."

"Oh, it was," Molly said quickly. "I'm surprised you managed to grow up."

"I wasn't all that bad."

"Papa told me some of the good things about you, too."

He adores her, Adam thought gratefully. *Bless you, Charlie!*

The days in Anchorage passed quickly and it was time to go. They went to Mr. Reneau's apartment to say good-bye. They found the old man sitting much as they had found him on Molly's first visit. He brightened notice-ably when they came in.

"We'll be leaving soon, Dad." Adam reached down his hand and the frail hand rose up to meet it. "I'll be back a week from today. Molly will come with me later."

"I'll look forward to it, son." The old man turned his attention to Molly. "Bring her with you when you come. She's promised to bring me some raspberry jam." His eyes twinkled.

Molly bent to kiss his wrinkled cheek. "Wild horses couldn't keep me away," she whispered in his ear.

"Take care of her, Adam. You done good, boy. Real good." His eyes went from one to the other. "You two will have plenty of time up there in the north country to make me a grandson. See that you get the job done."

Molly's face turned scarlet and she dared not look at Adam, but she could hear him chuckle.

"You'd like that, wouldn't you?" Glancing at Molly's flushed face, he added, "You've made Molly blush."

A silence hung while the two men watched her with amusement.

"You're wicked. Both of you!" she sputtered.

"Listen to that, Dad. Accusations already." Adam held out his hand.

"Good-bye, Papa. We'll see you soon." Molly kissed the old man's cheek again and the last glimpse she had of him, he was still smiling.

It seemed strange to Molly to be sitting in the plane with Adam at the controls. He continued to surprise her with the various facets of his personality. By far the nicest thing she had discovered about him was the close friendship between him and his father. She stole a look at him. His lean and shapely hands on the controls of the plane were well cared for, but definitely masculine. His dark hair gleamed in the sunlight, his mouth firm, his chin obstinate. She knew the black eyes could be bitter or sparkle with amusement. He could change his face in an instant from a frown of disapproval to boyish handsomeness. He confused her, yet excited her. They had so little in common, and yet here they were married and on their way home, to her home. How had it happened?

"The trip shouldn't take over an hour," Adam was saying. As he spoke his eyes flicked her face and hair, framed by the fur collar of her coat. The wind had ruffled her hair and little wisps of it lay around her face. Her eyes were large and faintly apprehensive.

She looked down at the green landscape of forest and plains. This rugged, beautiful country was her country. She loved it passionately.

"It takes my breath away," she exclaimed, her eyes bright with excitement. "It's so beautiful . . ." She trembled suddenly, with an unbelievable happiness, and impulsively said, "Don't hate it too much, Adam. The time will go quickly and you can take Dad's files, specimens, and anything else connected with your work away with you at the end of the year." Her voice held an apologetic note.

"I won't hate it," he said with an earnest frown. "I'll get a lot of work done this winter. Besides, if I back out now, my dad would skin me alive." Again she caught a side glimpse of the warm smile that altered his features so much. "I'd like to invite a friend and coworker out to stay for a few weeks, Molly. He's in Australia at the present time working on an expedition we plan to make. He'll be back soon and we'll work together on the new information we get from your father's files." He was looking straight ahead while he spoke. "It will make more work for you, so if you'd rather he didn't come, say so."

"I can cook for three as easily as for two," she replied quietly.

"You'll like Patrick. He's companionable, easygoing, but rather a wolf where women are concerned. I'll have to tell him the circumstances of our marriage. If you agree to have him stay with us, he can use the little room off my room. We can add a table to the one in the study so we'll both have a place to work."

It was apparent to Molly he had given this some thought. She glanced at him through her lowered lashes. He was looking straight ahead with calm indifference. The thought of a stranger living with them in the close confines of the small cabin wasn't pleasant, but she didn't know how she could refuse the request.

Adam landed the plane on the lake and taxied to the dock. Tim-Two was there waiting to catch the rope and lashed the plane securely. When it was safe for Molly to disembark, Adam held his arms up to lift her down. The warmth of his breath slid across her face as he set her on her feet. It was exciting to feel the strength of his hands on her waist, and she surrendered momentarily to the sensation of being held so close to him. It would be so easy to clasp her arms around his neck and hold him close. The thought surprised her. She gave a nervous little laugh.

"Thank you, sir."

Her life had changed so much in the past few weeks that it was hard for her to comprehend. She had been married, gained a new father, and come back to her home with a husband who thought of her as he might a younger sister, if he had one. She was determined to make it a pleasant year, one she could look back on with fond memories. One, Adam, too, might fondly recall years from now.

Leaving the men to struggle with the crates and boxes, Molly ran up the path toward the house. Dog came bounding out to meet her. Knowing better than to jump on her, as his great weight would knock her down, he wiggled and twisted and his tail wagged as fast as he could make it go in his pleasure at seeing her. She fell down on her knees and hugged the shaggy head.

"Did you miss me, Dog?" She buried her face in the thick fur. Dog tried to lick her face, but she held him off, got to her feet, and the two of them raced to the house.

Before going to Anchorage for the wedding, Molly and Evelyn had removed all of Charlie's personal belongings from his bedroom and packed them in boxes which Tim-Two stored in the attic. Molly went to her father's room. All traces of Charlie were gone. The large pieces of furniture had been rearranged to give more work space. She was glad, now, that they had done this. It was no longer Charlie's room—it was Adam's. She went through the bath into her own bedroom, closing the door behind her. It was going to be strange having Adam in the house, sharing the intimacy of the bathroom.

She hurried out of her suit and quickly changed into jeans and shirt. She let her hair down, brushed it vigorously, and formed two thick braids that hung down over her breasts. Looking as young and fresh as a colt, she hurried to the kitchen to put away the supplies being brought from the plane.

Tim-Two brought the grocery boxes and she busied herself arranging the supplies on the shelves. After many weary trips, all the crates were brought up as far as the porch. Adam came into the house wiping the perspiration from his face.

Molly was standing on tiptoes on a kitchen step stool reaching for a top shelf. He came to stand beside her.

"What are you trying to do? Break your neck?" He put his arm around her legs to steady her.

Molly hadn't heard him come in and was so startled she lost her balance and sat down on his shoulder, her hands grabbing frantically for his head for support.

"You scared me! Adam, put me down, I'm too heavy." Her squeals and laughter filled the room.

"Too heavy?" He twirled her around the room. "You're not as heavy as any one of those boxes I just lugged up from the plane."

"Please! Adam . . . please!"

He went from the kitchen to the living area with her still perched on his shoulder.

"I'll let you down if you find me a good cold beer," he bargained.

"Yes, yes, I will!"

He raised his hands to her waist and let her slide down the length of him until her feet touched the floor. Turning her around, he took her two braids in his hands. Then, holding her captive, he looked down into her flushed, laughing face.

"Just thought I'd let you know who's boss," he teased.

Laughter bubbled as she looked at him. Adam, in this lighthearted mood, was a man to grab the heart right out of her. Pulses in her body were leaping at his warm, masculine closeness. Her hands were resting against his chest and she forced herself away from him.

"We'll just see about that." She danced away from him, trying desperately to keep him from knowing she was trembling from the contact with him.

The rest of the afternoon was spent unpacking boxes and putting things away. Adam worked in his room and Molly in the kitchen. Long before dinner time the gaslamps were lit. The daylight hours were getting short this time of year. It was completely dark when they sat down to dinner. Molly had prepared a meal of homemade noodles and beef, biscuits, homemade jam, and cobbler made from canned peaches. Adam was hungry and ate heartily.

"Is there anything you especially like or dislike in the way of food, Adam? As long as I'm cooking, it may as well be something you like."

The black brows raised and he thought for a moment.

"I like most things. In some parts of the world I've shut my eyes to eat the food." He met her probing eyes and grinned. "I especially like chocolate cake," he admitted.

They cleared away the dinner things together, then sat for a while before the fireplace. The autumn nights were cold. Adam stretched his arms above his head and yawned.

"I'm bushed. How about you?"

Across from him Molly yawned, too, and catching his glance, smiled apologetically. "Yawning is contagious."

"You're tired. Go to bed, Molly. I'll turn out the lights and bank the fire."

Molly went to the kitchen range, took the large teakettle of hot water to the bathroom, and poured it into the washbowl. Going back to the kitchen she refilled it with hot water from the reservoir and set it on the range.

"Hot water, if you want it, Adam," she said, indicating the kettle. "Good night."

"Good night," he answered absently.

Molly made sure all her personal garments were out of the bathroom before leaving it and closed the door behind her when she returned to her bedroom. Turning out the lamp, she slipped under the covers of her bed. She lay for a while and was almost lulled to sleep when she heard Adam moving about. Presently she heard him carry the teakettle to the bathroom. *All very homey sounds,* she thought as she drifted off to sleep.

CHAPTER SIX

THERE IS NO lovelier place than the Alaskan wilderness in the autumn. The dark, drooping evergreens shadow the tranquil waters of the lakes. The beauty of the wilderness does much to inspire an even greater confidence in the people who live in the rugged country without all the customary trappings of modern living.

Soon the first snows of autumn would fall. Inside the spruce log cabin, set on the shores of the quiet lake, Molly felt, if not exactly happy, content. She and Adam had been living together in the cabin for almost a week. A pattern for their days had been formed. After breakfast he went to his room to work and she went about her usual household chores, always listening with half an ear to the citizen's band radio. Occasionally she would get a call from Jim going over in his plane or from a neighbor who just wanted to hear the sound of another human voice. Most of the calls were due to curiosity about her wedding and perfectly understandable to Molly. A wedding, a death, or a birth in the district was always news.

Every afternoon Adam spent a couple of hours out-of-doors. He was fascinated with Tim-Two's proficiency with an ax and practiced the use of the tool each day. The exercise was good and he thought it fun to see the chips fly. Some afternoons Molly would sit on a log and watch him. Occasionally she would take her fishing pole, sit on the dock, and tempt a fat fish to take the wiggling worm on the hook she dropped in the lake.

They always listened to the personal message program that came on the radio while they were having their noon meal. The people who lived in the sparsely populated wilderness received messages running the gauntlet from doctor's advice to shipping notices via this method. However, this meant the entire district knew about the medication Mrs. Jackson was taking, about the new snowmobile ordered by the Martins, and that the Petersons had a grocery order and the O'Roarks a guest coming up on the morning train. In case of an emergency concerning his father, Adam would hear the news during this time and Molly was always relieved when his name wasn't called.

The days slid by reasonably fast. Both Molly and Adam were involved in their own activities, their own thoughts. Adam kept the reservoir connected to the big cook stove filled with water and the evenings Molly took her bath he carried the steaming water to the tub for her. He was friendly, helpful, but not since the first day when he perched her on his shoulder had he been teasing or in any way familiar. He seemed to have settled down to the business of work, all serious and withdrawn.

He didn't ask her to accompany him on the first trip he made back to Anchorage. After breakfast one morning he merely announced he was going.

"I'd like to send a few things to your father," Molly said, "if you have time for me to pack a box."

"Sure. I have time, but hurry along. I don't want to be away but a few hours." He gave her a troubled glance. "You'll be all right here?" She nodded and reached for paper to wrap the small jars. "Keep the radio tuned in. I'd like to know you're in touch." She nodded again and wrapped a loaf of fresh bread in a cloth and tucked it into the box.

She looked rather apologetic. "I suppose this looks like a trite offering to you, but I did promise him I would send it and I wouldn't want him to think I made the promise casually."

"Of course not. He'll enjoy it. I'll tell him you'll come with me next time." His voice was brisk and impersonal. He went out the door and down the path to the lake.

Presently Molly heard the sound of the motor as he taxied the plane out onto the lake, then the soft purr as the plane circled the house and headed south.

Alone in the house she decided it would be a good time to clean Adam's room. She changed the bedclothes, swept and dusted, being careful not to disturb anything on his desk or work table. She knew this was important from all the times she had cleaned while her father was alive. She did allow herself the luxury of looking in his closet at the neat row of clothes hanging there. Her hands lingered on the rough jacket he used for outside work, and impulsively she lifted the sleeve to her cheek and the smell of his maleness caused unfamiliar sensations.

An awareness of the absurdity of her action caused her to leave the room abruptly. A man of Adam's years and experience could never be interested in her. He had married her and he intended to make the best of the situation. That's all she meant to him. Molly hadn't the faintest notion of what the future held for her. She only knew that since she had met him she had lost the last vestiges of her girlhood.

The house was lonely without him. In just one short week he had become an important part of her life. She missed him. Angry at herself for daring to think foolish thoughts she threw herself into a frenzy of housecleaning. When the house was immaculate, she set loaves of bread to rise in the warming oven and on a sudden impulse stirred up a chocolate cake.

She tried to keep her thoughts from Adam, from what he was doing in Anchorage. Would he visit a woman friend? Would he get in touch with her cousin, Donna, while he was there? She deliberately turned down the volume on the CB radio so she wouldn't be listening for the sound of his voice. In spite of all this, her ear was tuned to catch the first sound of his plane as it passed over the house.

Long before she expected him she freshened herself and put on a blue dress with a pencil slim skirt that made her look inches taller. Then she sat down on the couch to knit on the sweater she was making for one of Evelyn's boys. The rhythmic movement of her fingers was soothing to her nerves.

When the plane went over the house and began its descent to land on the lake, Molly's heart began to beat erratically, but she forced herself to remain seated. She was curled comfortably on the couch when she heard his steps on the porch. Their eyes met for a brief moment as he hesitated in the doorway and in that instant she was conscious of every detail about him. He looked big, masculine, and angry. It was difficult to comprehend what he was saying when he spoke to her.

"Why in the devil didn't you answer me when I called on the CB?" He walked over to the radio and saw the volume had been turned down. "What do you think went through my mind when ten miles out I couldn't raise you on this damn thing?" To her astonishment he was very angry. "One of the last things I told you was to keep the radio tuned." He came to stand in front of her with his black eyes blazing and his hands on his hips. Molly was too stunned to say anything. "Molly!" He practically shouted her name.

She sought about wildly for something to say. Then she lifted her head in sudden defiance, angry with him because he was treating her like a child. *Was that it? Was this the way it was going to be?* She would not stand for it! She was an adult and would be treated like one.

"You're pretty bossy all of a sudden, Adam. I don't have to account to you for everything I do. I can look after myself without any help from you." She sputtered recklessly because he was watching her with those hard black eyes and she didn't like the way he was doing it.

"Like hell!" he sneered. "I won't leave you here alone and have you deliberately disobey my instructions. I couldn't imagine what had happened to you or why you didn't answer. You answer every other Tom, Dick, and Harry that calls you." Her eyes were abnormally bright and his lips narrowed. "Well?" He said the word with sardonic emphasis.

"Why are you so angry?" Molly blurted. "Why am I, suddenly, so unreliable I can't be trusted to spend a few hours alone? I've spent many days and nights alone here with Dog and Tim-Two while my father was away."

Adam shook his head. "Listen to me, Molly—"

"You listen!" she flung, flushed and excited. "You think I've no brains at all! I'm an encumbrance to you! Something you have to put up with in order to take advantage of my father's work. Well, I'm sorry I've intruded into your life. I didn't want to, you know!" She knew she was being unreasonable, but couldn't help herself. Her eyes flared bitterly at him.

Adam reached out and with a cruel and painful grip on her forearms, jerked her to him.

"Now, you listen to me!" he grated between clinched teeth. "You've got to understand—"

Molly tried vainly to free herself. "I understand very well, mister," she exclaimed fiercely.

With a muffled curse, he pulled her up against him, his muscled strength holding her there, stilling her struggles. He pressed her head against his shirt. At close quarters his masculine strength had a hypnotic effect on her. She wanted to lean forward and let her whole weight rest on his chest. She felt a sense of unreality at what was happening. His maleness made her legs feel weak. She melted against him. In the circle of his arms and hearing the heavy beat of his heart, she was conscious of a change in his breathing. It quickened.

He must have sensed her sudden, abject surrender. From somewhere far away she heard him say,

"Molly . . . Molly . . . ," the words sounded like a groan.

She felt his hand in her hair tugging her head back and before she could speak or move his mouth came down over hers in a hard, angry kiss that took her breath away. There was no gentleness, no tenderness. He kissed her savagely and thoroughly. She struggled and a little whimper came from the back of her throat. Then she arched against him, not yet understanding the strange new emotions that he had awakened in her body. She was only conscious of the pressure of his mouth and his long legs as his hands pulled the entire length of her body tight against his. Without knowing why, or what she was doing, her arms went up and around his neck and clung there.

Somewhere in the deep recesses of her mind she thought, *so this is how it feels?* This need, spreading through her loins, was making her incapable of feeling anything but this intense desire, and not understanding this sensation, she knew only that what she needed was him.

He pulled his mouth away from hers and looked down at her.

"Oh, Christ," he said in self-disgust. He looked at her lips beginning to swell from his kiss, and at her eyes wide and questioning. He hadn't meant to touch her, much less kiss her. He turned on his heel and went to his room, closing the door behind him with more force than was necessary.

Molly stood where he had left her. Her breath was still catching in her throat and her hands went up to touch her burning, flushed cheeks. She sank back down on the couch. She couldn't believe this had happened to her. The memory of the way she had clung to him brought waves of hot color to her cheeks and she wondered, unhappily, what he must have thought of her wanton behavior. She dreaded the moment when she must face him again.

The moment she dreaded came sooner than she expected. Adam came out of his room and stood looking down at her, his face considerably softer. Her body tensed and her heart began to beat erratically again as she withstood his dark gaze.

"I'm sorry I frightened you, Molly, but you did provoke me!" He took a small package from his pocket and tossed it into her lap. "A gift from Dad. He remembered he hadn't given you a wedding present."

Molly's troubled gaze went from him to the package in her lap and realizing he was waiting for her to open it, untied the wrappings with shaking fingers. Lifting the lid of a small jewelry box, she saw, nestling on a bed of dark velvet, a pair of exquisite diamond earrings. She gave a small cry of surprise.

"I couldn't possibly accept these. They are far too valuable." She closed the lid on the box and thrust it toward him.

"Dad wants you to have them." He hesitated. "They were my mother's."

"Your mother's?" She flushed to her hairline.

"Yes," he answered brusquely.

She couldn't help herself. Her eyes were swimming with tears.

"Your father has paid me a great compliment and for his sake I'll be honored to wear your mother's earrings. But only for the year we're together. After that I'll insist you take them back."

"You're to keep them. They're not a loan."

"I couldn't do that, Adam, they should belong to your

permanent wife," she whispered huskily with a sinking feeling in the pit of her stomach.

"I'll probably not marry again and Dad gave them to you," he said stubbornly.

"I wish we didn't have this shadow of deceit hanging over us," she said softly. "Your father is too sweet to be deceived this way."

"It's rather late to think of that now," he said dryly. "In any case, what's done is done." Then, as his eyes mocked her, "Is that a chocolate cake on the table?"

"It's for you and Tim-Two. He likes cake, too, and any flavor will do."

Not knowing what else to do, she took the earrings from the box and attempted to attach them to her ears. Adam watched her.

"Here let me do it." He reached down his hand to pull her to her feet.

She felt a tremor in her throat as his warm breath fell on her face. He fastened first one earring and then the other to her ears, before taking her by the forearms and holding her away from him. He tilted his head first one way and then the other as he gave her careful scrutiny. Her pulse was beating very fast. She was sure he had noticed, because he looked from her ears to her eyes, to the mouth he had so recently kissed, and to her throat where the pulse was beating.

"Very nice," he said, smiling, "very, very nice." She smiled back at him, and he added softly, "Am I forgiven?"

Silently she nodded her head. "Then let's have dinner . . . hmmm? I want to tie into that cake."

Molly caught him looking at her often during dinner.

For the first time he helped her clear off the table when they were finished. Afterward he put records on the player and turned down the gaslight. When Molly went to sit in front of the fireplace, he went to his room, then returned with a pipe and a sack of tobacco before sinking down on the couch and filling the pipe. Using tongs, he lifted a coal from the fire bed, held it to the tobacco, and sucked on the pipe. When he sat down again, he was puffing gently.

"You're full of surprises," Molly said and breathed in the good tobacco smell. "I didn't know you smoked."

He looked at the pipe in his hand. "I seldom do, but sometimes I like one after dinner, if you don't mind."

"I rather like it. Dad always smoked a pipe after supper."

The familiar scratching on the back door sent Molly to let Dog in. He followed her to her chair and laid his big head in her lap. She caressed the soft fur on top of his head and scratched his ears, all the time aware Adam was watching. Soon Dog returned to a far corner of the room, away from the heat of the fire. He sprawled in the corner, his neck stretched out, his heavy jowls flat on the floor.

"How long have you had him?" Adam asked.

"About four years. Jim brought him to me. He was just a bounding puppy then, all ears and feet."

"Is he the only dog you have here?"

"Yes. He's been a faithful friend," she said wistfully. "You know a dog responds to kindness, regardless if the person that gives it is rich or poor, skinny or fat, pretty or ugly, dumb or smart, I could go on and on . . ." she said with a laugh.

"Yes, that's true," Adam said, as the clock on the mantel sounded the hour. He got up to wind the clock. "Are you about ready to call it a day?" He was still facing the mantel.

Molly looked at the clock, it was half past ten! Embarrassment drew her to her feet. He wanted her to leave the room so he could go to his, but was too polite to say so! That was the reason for the small talk, biding his time until she went to bed. How stupid of her not to realize that. She went to the kitchen and turned down the lamp. Looking back, she saw him rubbing his eyes and his temples. He showed no sign he knew she had left the room. Calling Dog to her, she put him out the back door.

"Do you have a headache, Adam?" she asked in a calm voice which gave away nothing of what she was feeling. "I can get an aspirin for you."

"I would appreciate it," he said, going back to the couch.

She took two tablets from the bottle on the shelf and drew a glass of water from the hand pump. She carried them to him and waited for him to drink.

"Thanks." He put the glass on the table, took her hand, and pulled her down beside him on the couch. She was so taken by surprise that she offered no protest, even when he put his arm around her and drew her close against him. She was terribly conscious of the hard muscles in his arm as he cuddled her, turning her so that her breasts were against the side of his chest and her head on his shoulder. He stretched his long legs out to the fire and leaned his head back.

"Each night when we sit here, I've wondered what it would feel like to hold you like this," he said tiredly.

She was stunned into silence. She felt his fingers at the

nape of her neck and at the top of her head feeling for the pins as he pulled them out of her hair. Heavy, silken, and bright as gold it cascaded down over her shoulders. He brought a big handful forward over her breast.

"I've been wanting to do this, too," he said huskily, twisting a large rope of it around his hand.

Molly turned her face into his shoulder and nuzzled his warm flesh. The crackle of the fire and the ticking of the clock were the only sounds she heard above the beating of his heart. Her arm went around his waist and she held him, feeling the tension of the muscles in his long back.

He turned and buried his face in her neck, pushing back her hair and letting his free hand travel over her as if he were blind and trying to know her through his fingertips; over her arms, down over her breast, lingering there, then to the narrow waist and on to her rounded hips where he molded her full length to his.

"Molly . . ." he whispered, "I don't know if I'll be able to keep my bargain not to touch you."

He raised his head to look at her. He was so close she could see every little detail of his face: the dark, smoldering eyes; the strong nose; the sensual curve of his mouth; the darkened cheekbones; the brown column of his throat. She could smell the warm smell of his body and the tobacco smell of his breath. She had never been in such an intimate position before and an aching stirred inside her.

She saw his mouth, the firm lips slightly parted, then it was against hers, rough and demanding with an insistence that sent her blood thundering through her ears. His hands were moving everywhere, touching her hungrily, fondling, an urgency in their movements. Naked desire mounted in her head leaving her trembling in his arms. She slid her fingers inside his shirt so she could touch his skin, some inner femininity giving her the knowledge of how to caress him.

Adam was breathing heavily. He tore his mouth from hers and his lips traveled over her face and then, as if compelled, back to her mouth. Unskilled as she was and although she clung to him with her hand on his bare chest feeling the trembling of his body, she sensed he was not getting satisfaction from her inexperienced lips. He drew back and kissed the violet eyes closed, smoothed the damp hair from her forehead, fondled the small ears, and gazed at her upturned face.

"Oh, Molly," he whispered, "I'm going to despise myself tomorrow. You're so sweet!" He kissed the corner of her trembling mouth.

"Tell me what to do," she breathed against his lips.

"No," he muttered and continued dragging his lips over her face.

"Tell me." She brought her hand up to his face and turned his lips toward hers.

His hands slid down her back and as if the feel of her shocked his senses, she felt his body shudder.

"I want you. I want to make love to you," he said, and then urgently, against her cheek, "open your mouth for me!" She parted her lips and his mouth covered hers.

The hungry demand of Adam's mouth was a whirlpool into which she thought she would drown. Now she knew why her earlier kisses had been so unfulfilling. His mouth was conveying his tortured need of her more powerfully than any words could say. He had aroused her and now she was no longer in control of her emotions. His hands stroked down her body with an eagerness he didn't try to disguise, which made her flame into receptive response.

He wanted her so much it was agony, but he knew so much better than she what this kind of lovemaking would lead to. A stab of remorse tore through him, and he pulled himself out of her arms and got to his feet.

"Molly, are you aware of what this is leading to? I want no regrets!" he said harshly. He took a long deep breath and looked at her as she lay where he had left her, her face hidden in the cushions of the couch.

A frightening awareness of the seriousness of what had happened came over her. She felt hot, shamed blushes covering her face and neck. Flushing with humiliation and self-disgust, she kept her face turned from him.

"Molly," he said softly. "You're young and beautiful. I'm alone here with you. I'm a man, Molly; a man with a man's desires. I've been used to having a woman and it's going to be a long winter."

The callous words struck Molly like a cold dash of water. "It's going to be a long winter"; he had used the words before. Tempestuous feelings were threatening to overpower her. *Love and hate,* she thought. She ran her tongue along the inside of her lower lip where his had been moments before. The cold fingers that had touched her heart on hearing his callous words had turned into a firebrand that was a burning anger.

Adam was still talking softly; whispering, persuading. "You've a lot to learn, my little innocent," he whispered, "but I guarantee it won't be against your will."

At that Molly raised her head. Her voice, when it came, was shaking.

"Oh, damn you, damn you," she said with trembling lips, her eyes dry and blazing with fury. "It's going to be a long winter and you think you'll amuse yourself with a new experience, a stupid, foolish, willing virgin!" The words tumbled from her mouth. "And to think I was beginning to think you as wonderful as your father said you were. You're nothing but an opportunist. You married me to get my father's files and while you're about it, you'll sleep with his daughter because it's going to be a long winter. Let me tell you this Adam Reneau, I'm a stupid innocent, but I'm no man's plaything. If it's a whore you want—"

Adam grabbed her and shook her hard, his hands biting into her arms.

"Stop it! Don't use that word! You're my wife and what I suggested was for our mutual pleasure." His hard dark eyes were fastened onto her flushed, angry face.

"Your pleasure, not mine!" She glared at him, her face stiff with rebellion.

"Your pleasure too, Molly, I'd have seen to that." The irony of that ate into her. The anger had gone out of his voice and he tried to draw her close. "I'm not the kind of man to take a woman against her will."

Molly wrenched herself away from him. "I don't know what kind of man you are." She looked him in the eye, her mouth firm now with determination. "You're leaving in a year. You want no ties or emotional entanglements. You made that clear before we made the . . . agreement."

"You're right, I don't. I'm leaving at the end of the year. My plans have been made for a long time." His voice was level and controlled, but his dark eyes were bright with an emotion which she was not quite certain she recognized. "But that has nothing to do with now."

"Then there's no more to be said. Thank you for the valuable lesson I learned tonight." She flipped her hair back behind her ears and walked calmly from the room.

In spite of himself, Adam grinned.

When she closed the door on him, she leaned against it and wished she was far away, anywhere away from him. The thought of Aunt Dora's house was not as awesome as before, but this was her house and she would not leave it! Her frantic mind tried to think of ways to get him out of her house, out of her life. She could fake an illness and insist on staying in town. She could say she wanted to visit a friend in Portland. She could go back to the convent. She didn't want to do any of those things. What a fool she had been! The year to her now seemed endless. How could her father have been so wrong about a man's character?

She shut the door leading to the bathroom. With slow movements she undressed and slipped into her nightdress. She looked at her reflection in the mirror and pulled the tangled hair out from under the neck of her nightdress. Divided in the back it fell down the front of her, almost to her waist. She looked at it and hated it. In a sudden fit of rebellion at all that had happened to her, she grabbed the hand shears from her dressing table and began to cut. She cut off handfuls of hair and cried, her eyes so blinded with tears she could hardly see what she was doing. Doggedly, she sawed with the shears and threw the hair on the floor. When none was left to cover her breasts, she stopped, turned off her battery light, lay down in her bed, and buried her head in the pillow. Misery and humiliation flowed over her. She had acted like a recalcitrant child.

She slept fitfully during the first part of the night, chased by nightmares, then in the small hours of the morning fell into a deep sleep to awaken with a pounding headache, a hangover of the emotional evening before.

She got out of bed, dressed herself in jeans and shirt, and kept her eyes averted from her dressing table mirror. After making her bed and picking up the strands of hair from the floor, she turned to look at the results of last night's ravages. She brushed the tangled hair that came now in uneven lengths to her shoulders. Her face was pale and her eyes were rimmed with deep, dark circles. Her mouth was slightly swollen as if it had been kissed many times, but it was set, now, in a grim line. She noticed, with a surge of humiliation, a small blue spot Adam's lips had made on her neck and drew up the collar of her shirt and buttoned it to hide the brand he had left on her.

Before her humiliation reached an intolerable level and she would be unable to face him, she picked up a ribbon, flung her hair back and gathered it in at the nape of her neck, and tied the ribbon around it.

A strange kind of calm had come over her by the time she was ready to leave the bedroom. She went into the kitchen as she did every morning. Tim-Two had already been there and the range was ready for breakfast. She put the granite coffeepot on to boil and set the table with one place setting. While placing the slices of bacon in the skillet she heard Adam's door open and turned to face him.

He stood in the doorway with his hands in his pockets

with the same black thundercloud expression on his face that he had the first day they met. Under the slanting brows his eyes were blazing black between the narrowed lids. Not at all unnerved by his mood she looked straight at him.

"Good morning." She said it calmly. "You did wish to have breakfast?"

He lifted his shoulders and his frown deepened, if that was possible.

"Why did you do it?"

She turned back to the stove. "Why did I do what?" She was still calm and proud of it.

"You know what I'm talking about." His voice was louder. "Why did you cut your hair?"

"It's no business of yours what I do."

"It was a foolish, juvenile thing to do," he grated between clutched teeth.

Her silence showed her regard for his opinion. She set his breakfast on the table. The coffeepot was on a pad near at hand. Still not looking his way, she lifted her parka from the peg by the door. After putting on the coat she took the remainder of the chocolate cake from the shelf and went out the back door toward Tim-Two's cabin.

The first snow will be coming any time now, she thought as she walked along the lakeshore. Tim-Two had been away from his cabin, and she had left the cake on his table. She and Dog walked the path toward the lake. The sky was a gray blanket and the dreariness of the day weighed on her. Tim-Two would be taking out the dock now that the lake would be freezing over. The crush of the ice would split the boards and break the posts. Always she had loved the coming of the winter. The evergreens would bow down under the heavy load. The whole world would be bright, clean, and shining. The small animals would scurry around leaving tracks in the snow. She would get out her cross country skis. She and Dog would take long hikes when the weather permitted.

How could she have been so wrong? she asked herself for the thousandth time. How could she have ever thought she might love him or that he was capable of love? He loved his father, but she didn't think he was capable of loving a woman, only using them. His father must have known that and that was why he was so pleased by their marriage. The thought came to her that Adam was a cruel man. You could tell by the cold way he had treated Donna at the reception. Not that she hadn't deserved it. Well, she was cured! It had come about the hard way, but she was cured. She would abide by her father's wishes, but at the end of the year she hoped she would never again set eyes on Adam Reneau.

Molly trudged back to the house. The cool wind had cleared her head. She made the firm resolve to take one day at a time until she was free of him.

The kitchen was empty when she came in. Adam was working in his room. She could hear his typewriter going. She shivered. It was colder and she would have to build a fire in the small potbellied stove in her bedroom.

Halfway through the morning she heard Jim Robinson's welcome voice come in on the radio.

"KGF 1452 calling KFK 1369. Come in, Molly, darlin'. Big Bird is flying over and he'll set down on your lake if you have the coffeepot on."

She lifted the microphone and pressed the button.

"That's a big ten-four, Big Bird. I've got the fastest cof-feepot in the North."

"Well get it perkin', pretty girl. I'll be there in a few." His voice came back and added because regulations de-manded it, "KGF 1452 mobile clear and will soon be land bound."

Molly put fresh water and coffee in the pot and wished she hadn't taken all the chocolate cake to Tim-Two. She got out coconut bars she had baked several days ago, set out two cups and saucers, put on her parka, and went to the porch to wait for Jim.

Her eyes misted a little when she saw the familiar fig-ure come swinging up the path, the usual friendly grin on his face. She ran down the steps and onto the path to meet him. His arms went across her shoulders and he en-veloped her in a bear hug.

"I'm glad to see you." She fought back the tears.

"How's my Molly girl?"

"Oh, fine, fine," she said and the desire to cry left her.

They walked arm in arm up onto the porch and into the house. Jim hung his coat on a peg near the front door, while Molly was removing hers. He turned to look at her and the surprise showed on his face.

"You've cut your hair?"

"It's much easier to keep this way, Jim."

"Evelyn always envied your beautiful hair. She—"

"It's much easier to dry this way," she broke in. "Sorry I don't have your favorite cake. Will coconut bars do?"

"Is everything all right with you, Molly girl?" he asked quietly.

"Why wouldn't it be, Robinson?" Adam's voice came from the doorway of his room.

"Hello, Adam. How's the work going?"

"Fine." Adam came into the kitchen and got a third cup from the shelf. "I'll pour the coffee, Molly."

Molly sat across from Jim. Adam pulled his chair up to the end. The two men made small talk about the weather and compared the two floatplanes, now at anchor on the lake. Molly sat quietly, looking mostly at Jim, and entered the conversation only when necessary. Finally Jim rose to go.

"Anything you need, Molly?"

Before she could answer, Adam said, "Nothing, thanks, Robinson. I go to Anchorage each week and I get what we need."

"Well, anytime . . ." He spoke directly to Molly.

"There is something you can get for me, Jim. You know the lamp I use in my bedroom? Will you get a supply of batteries for it? The next time you go over, you can drop them."

"Sure, Molly. I know the ones you need."

"Charge them to my account at the hardware in Fairbanks, Jim. The one where Dad and I always trade." The stubborn, determined look on her face was disturbing to Jim.

"Sure thing," he said, putting his big fist beside her chin. "I'll have them for you in a day or two." He shrugged into his coat.

"Oh, Jim," Molly said, reluctant to let him go, "tell Evelyn I've almost finished the sweaters for the boys and I have yarn left for mittens if she'll send me the size."

"Will do, Molly. So long, Adam. Take care of my little sweetheart here."

Adam nodded.

Molly went to the porch and watched Jim go down the path. It was cold and she hadn't put on her coat, yet she dreaded going back into the house to face Adam. He was still sitting at the trestle table when she went in. She picked up the coat she had left on the chair and walked past him to hang it on the peg, then went to her room and closed the door.

She was standing beside her dressing table when the door crashed open. Adam stood there filling the doorway. His face was stiff with anger, his dark eyes spitting at her.

"Are you going to pout like a silly, sulky child all winter?"

"Get out of my room. I have a right to my privacy." Her nerves screamed, but her voice was cool and calm.

"You made me look a fool in front of Robinson." The words thumped at her like small blows.

"I didn't invite you to join us."

"That's what I mean! It was obvious to him and to me that I wasn't to be included." For a few seconds he stood glaring at her, breathing heavily, his nostrils curiously flared. "And . . . as for that"—he nodded at the pile of cut hair on her dresser—"I should spank you!"

She looked unflinchingly back at him. "I entered into this arrangement with you against the advice of my friends and I have only myself to blame if I now have regrets. My only excuse is that I wanted to stay in my home. This is my home and you may share any part of it except my bedroom. I'll cook your meals, but I don't want your company. Do you understand?"

"And if I don't," he drawled insolently.

"If you don't, I'll call Jim and ask him to take me to

Herb Belsile. I'll work in town. Tim-Two will take care of the place until I can come back home."

"You're stubborn and foolish enough to do just that! You would have your father's work destroyed," he said ironically.

"If it was that or my self-respect, Dad would want me to." Her voice shook as she said the last.

Tall and taunting, he continued to lean against the door, his grin mocking her as he sensed her agitation.

"Don't worry, little virgin," he jeered. "I won't seduce you! God . . . I can't believe you! You're twenty-five years old and know no more about life than a ten-year-old."

Their eyes met for moments. The calm violet ones and the mocking black ones. She turned her back on him and stood silently looking out her window. She didn't hear him leave, but she heard the door to his room close and knew he was gone.

CHAPTER SEVEN

FOUR NIGHTS LATER the first snow fell. By morning the ground was covered with a foot of the fluffy white stuff. Molly stood by the kitchen window watching Tim-Two come toward the house to stoke up the morning fires. She was up earlier than usual. Worn and disturbed, she had slept fitfully, waking repeatedly, her mind refusing to rest. She had been awake for some time before she dressed in her dark room, relieved that another day had come.

Tim-Two came into the kitchen after stamping the snow from his feet. Silent, as always, he checked the range, the stove in Molly's room, the big fireplace. Without a word to her he went out again.

She was sipping her second cup of coffee when she heard Adam's door open. This interrupted the quiet of the room so much that she looked at him in dismay. She had become so nervous and jumpy that she felt a sudden springing up of tears which she could not shed. His eyes were on the window and she sat quivering in relief because they were not on her.

"We must have a foot of snow," he said matter-of-factly.

"At least that," she answered.

"Are you not having breakfast?" He eyed the coffee cup in her hand.

"Not now. I'll have some later."

He took a mug from the shelf and poured his coffee. He brought it to the table, sat opposite her, and looked at her pale face. The shadows beneath her eyes made them appear more violet than ever.

She averted her eyes and refused to look at him. She was not sulking or even unfriendly, rather utterly and deliberately indifferent to him. This was harder for him to bear than either rage or enduring anger.

"I'll make your breakfast," she said quietly, getting to her feet.

"Don't bother. I'll have some later, too."

She shrugged her shoulders. "I think I'll go out then."

"Wait and I'll go with you," he said, but she was heading for her room as if she hadn't heard.

Dressed in her warm parka and snow boots Molly walked through the snow. The air was fresh and invigorating, and she couldn't help but feel better just being out in it. Before she realized it she was walking the letters of her name, stamping out the letters as she used to do for Jim to see as he flew over. Laughing to herself as she jumped from one letter to another, she failed to see Adam standing on the porch watching her. He came toward her and as she turned she saw him.

"Stop," she shouted, "you'll ruin my message to Jim."

"I want to help," he called back.

He jumped to a position under the letters Molly was

stamping out and laughingly asked what message she was writing.

"Just my name," she told him.

"Okay," he said cheerfully. "I'll add my name to yours."

He started stamping out the word "AND" under Molly's name. She had finished the "Y" and stood watching him.

"I'll lift you over and you can start my name." Before he finished speaking he had reached for her and swung her over. "You'll have to write my name backwards— you're on the wrong end."

He finished the word he was stamping out and jumped to the letters she was making, then on to start the next word. Molly watched him with somber eyes.

They had written "Molly and Adam," and he was adding the word "ARE."

Now he looked at her with a questioning smile. "Molly and Adam are . . . ?"

Molly felt the heaviness that had been in her heart for days suddenly lift.

"Are fine," she added. He smiled and jumped to make the final word.

The strain of the last few days was eased, if not completely, enough so they could be comfortable in each other's company. The next hour they walked in the snow stopping at the lake so Adam could check the plane before they turned toward the house. Dog spotted them and came out of the woods where he had been pestering small animals in their burrows. The three of them frolicked and played in the snow until Molly was flushed and out of breath.

The morning set a new tone to their relationship. The tension of the last few days had been broken and a tolerance toward each other was adopted. It was not the friendly companionship of the first week, but an acceptance of the fact they were living in close proximity in the house, and relaxed atmosphere was preferable to a tense one.

Molly was hungry when they came in out of the cold and set about making eggs and hotcakes. Adam sat at the table with the small transistor radio turned to the weather broadcast.

"How many pancakes?" she asked him.

"Do I have to commit myself now?" he answered with a grin. "I'm pretty hungry. Neither of us has enjoyed our meals for the last few days."

She nodded in acknowledgment, but didn't look at him.

"I think I should get the floatplane out of the lake today," he said later between mouthfuls of hotcakes. "Sounds as if it's going to be colder and the lake will freeze any time."

"Maybe you should." She looked at him for the first time since they sat down. "The temperature can drop fast this time of year."

He stopped eating and looked at her intently. "Will you go with me, Molly?" he surprised her by asking.

"No . . . no." She shook her head.

He reached over and laid his hand on hers as it rested on the table and as badly as she wanted to jerk her hand away, to do so would be childish so she let him hold it. It was cold and trembling. His fingers were warm and firm.

"Can we talk about it, Molly?" he asked softly. His words fell into a pool of silence.

Any minute I'm going to cry, she thought, *and I'd rather die than have him see me. What is the matter with me anyway? Last night I knew I hated him and now I'm not so sure.*

"Things are never quite so bad if they're talked about," he persisted gently.

She raised her head and looked into the warm black eyes. She was surprised at the kindness and sympathy that she saw there and her heart settled peacefully as she felt his fingers increase the pressure on her hand. *He wants to make things right between us,* she thought. The relief that she felt showed itself in the small smile she exchanged with him.

"Okay." Rapidly her brain rehearsed what she wanted to say to him.

"First may I say that the last four days haven't been very pleasant ones for me and I'm sure not for you either." Then he added with a grin, "If we can't be lovers, we can be friends, can't we?"

"I'd like to be friends." She looked him directly in the eye, which was her way when she was serious, and said firmly, "I won't be used, you know. It's insulting . . . humiliating."

"Molly, we're married! I meant no insult to you!" He said it earnestly. "I know you wanted me as much as I wanted you. It's nothing to be ashamed about."

The red flush that came up from her neck and flooded her face caused her to turn her face away until she could regain her composure. Her thoughts were so distasteful, she let an exclamation escape her.

"Don't look so distressed. It's a perfectly natural urge."

"But," she whispered, "I want to be loved before . . ."

"There are many different kinds of love, Molly." He searched her anguished face, his brows drawing together.

"The true, deep love between a man and a woman can be very painful. Seldom do they love equally. My father was a slave to the love he had for my mother. He stood back and worshiped her from afar and when she died, a part of him died, too. I don't want that, Molly. I want to own my own soul."

"Is that why you were never going to marry?"

"That's part of it. The other part is that I want to be free to go when and where I please." Then taking her other hand, he shook them gently. "What about you, Molly? What do you want?"

She gave a shaky laugh. "To keep from going to Aunt Dora!"

He grinned. "Molly, I swear that you'll never have to go to Aunt Dora." Still holding her hands, he said seriously, "Let me say one more thing. You're sweet, beautiful, and charmingly innocent. Many men will desire you for these traits and the one you give yourself to will be a very lucky man."

"Thank you." She had never thought she would hear him say such things after their angry exchange of words.

"I'll take the plane into Anchorage and have the helicopter bring me back. After the lake freezes we can mount the skis on the plane."

"Will you see your father while you're there?"

"Yes, I'll see him. Sure you don't want to go?"

"Not this time. I think I'll wash my hair. I'll have the bathroom all to myself."

"You've got a spanking coming, my girl, for that haircut. Don't you forget it!" he told her sternly.

"It will grow. And it's a relief not having all that hair

to dry each week." Her heart gave a frightened little leap at the thought of the threat.

His eyes traveled over her face and came to rest on the small blue spot on her throat. Her cheeks turned slowly pink and she looked away from the knowing glint in his eyes.

Suddenly he exploded in laughter and grabbed her hands to pull her to her feet.

"Molly, you're priceless!"

Her back stiffened and her chin went up in resentment of his ridicule.

"You adorable little kitten, don't get your back up." He gathered her into his arms in a big bear hug. He looked down at her, his black eyes full of devilry and his usually grim mouth tilted in a wide grin. Molly smiled reluctantly and put her finger over his lips.

"Kittens can scratch, you know." It was difficult to believe she was standing here this close to him.

He laughed again. Lowering his head, he kissed her parted lips.

"I was going to spank you, but you're too big to spank. I'll kiss you instead!"

He looked down into her startled, resentful face and put both his hands on each side of her head. He shook it gently.

"You're a very kissable girl, Molly Reneau!" His black eyes danced with amusement. "I could learn to like your kisses too much!"

Molly laughed in spite of herself and turned to cross to the window. She looked out without really seeing the view. Her whole body yearned to go back to him, but her pride kept her voice light when she finally spoke.

"Where will the helicopter set down when it brings you back?"

"I think the best place is over to the north. I'll bring my snowmobile back so we'll both have one. Do you like to ride?" He was getting out his big parka and heavy boots.

"Yes, I love to ride. Dad got all the equipment for me. We had great times on the snowmobile."

"And so will we!" he said firmly.

Molly felt immeasurably older as she stood by the window while Adam was preparing to leave. She welcomed the time she would be alone so she could sort out her jumbled feelings.

"Don't forget about the radio," he was saying, "and don't be attempting to lift those heavy logs. Tim-Two will be in. I'll tell him I'm leaving for a few hours. And another thing, leave the bedroom doors open so the heat can circulate and cook something good for my dinner. I'll be starving."

Molly turned, her eyes sparkling and her laughter ringing out. "Anything else, boss?" she asked in a little girl voice.

Coming close to her, he looked down, an exaggerated stern look on his face.

"Yes, there is something else," he said softly. "Leave the volume up on that radio and don't you forget it!"

After he was gone Molly mulled over everything that was said between them from the first words that morning until he went out the door. He was a man of changing moods. So fierce and cruel when he was mad, but so sweet and gentle when he was pleased. She loved him. Her anger was the result of disappointment that he would want to take her to bed without any words of love or permanent commitment. She had to admit that he was honest with her. He was leaving at the end of the year. He could have had his pleasure of her and left her as he had planned. *We're married,* she thought, *but I don't feel married. Oh, God, what misery have I let myself in for?*

She spent more than two hours in a frenzy of cleaning. First the bedrooms, then on through the house until it was spotless. She had a dull throbbing headache by the time she was finished, and a splitting one when she had finished preparing a pot of stew for their dinner.

Although she didn't feel well she was determined to wash and dry her hair before Adam came back. She washed it in the bathroom and came back to the big fireplace with a towel to rub it dry. Her muscles were sore and her head throbbed viciously. Lord, how she ached! Her head felt thick and full. She rubbed her hand over her forehead and felt uneasy at the warmness of her skin. Wobbling a little in her pain, she went to the kitchen for aspirins, then came back to sink down on the couch. *I'll not be sick! I'll feel better if I lay down for a while,* she reasoned. She covered herself with the afghan from the back of the couch and drifted off to sleep only to waken shaking with chills.

She got to her feet, swaying dizzily. It was so cold! The temperature must have dropped. She managed to get two small logs on the fire before almost crawling back to the couch to fall into a deep, feverish sleep.

CHAPTER EIGHT

MOLLY OPENED HER eyes and gazed into Adam's dark ones. "I didn't hear you call," her voice quavered.

He nodded his head, his black brows drawn together, as they were when he wore his grim face. Her eyes felt as though there were lead weights tied to the lids; to open them would take all the strength she possessed. Something deep in her mind told her he wasn't angry because she didn't answer the radio call. She drifted off to sleep again.

"Her fever is high," Adam said irritably to Tim-Two. "I'm getting a doctor out here."

Molly could hear his voice coming from a far distance. Loud and commanding, he talked on the radio, then in softer tones to Tim-Two; the doctor would come in the morning and for him to bring in more fuel for the stoves. She felt gentle hands lifting her. Two tablets had been placed in her mouth and she was commanded to drink by that soft, gentle voice she loved.

"I'll be all—right," she said weakly. Two weak tears

started at the corner of her eyes. She shivered and uncon-sciously snuggled closer to him. "Please . . ."

"Please, what, Molly?"

"I'm so cold . . ."

A sudden feeling of comfort engulfed her as arms went around her and she was drawn close against him. The heat of his body burned into hers, enveloping her in deli-cious inertia. She heard him ask, in a queer, uneven tone, "Are you still cold?" She nodded weakly. *I'll be all right,* she thought, *if I can sleep for a minute.*

When she opened her feverish eyes again, she was in her own bed and a big man was sitting in the chair watch-ing her. It seemed so odd to see a man in her room and before her eyes could focus she was gone again. She mumbled occasionally in her delirium and cried one time. Her father dried her tears. *Dad,* she sobbed, *where did you go?* Her hands were taken in his big ones.

"Sleep now," he said softly.

Several hours later she awoke and appeared to be more coherent. She looked at Adam sitting in the chair beside her bed.

"How sick am I?" she asked hoarsely.

"You've got a good case of the flu." He smoothed her hair back from her face.

"You'll be cold sitting there, Adam. Are we having a blizzard?" She closed her eyes and drifted back to sleep.

When she awoke again, she was lying in a cocoon of warmth. She felt drowsy and far away, but safe and warm. She reached out to bring the warmth closer to her and snuggled against it. Arms held her tightly. She felt oddly at peace and didn't want to move out of this warm, hard nest. She lifted her head and looked at the man who held her. He bent his head, kissed her brow, and pulled her closer. The only sound Molly heard was the beat of his heart under her cheek, and his murmured words.

"Go to sleep."

She slept fitfully the next hour, then fell into a deep sleep dreaming she was in Adam's arms, kissing and being kissed in return. She awoke to find him sitting on the bed beside her.

"Hello," he said, "who are you?"

"I don't really know," she said drowsily. "Who are you?"

"I'm the man who held you in his arms last night. Remember?"

"I thought that was Adam."

He laughed softly and gazed down at her tenderly. "Feeling better?"

"My bones ache and my head throbs like a drum," she said weakly. She looked faintly puzzled; her memory returning in snatches. She realized she was in her nightdress. Embarrassment made weak tears come to her eyes.

"Don't think about it, love." Fingertips turned her head back and wiped away her tears.

She flushed under his gaze. "You didn't get much sleep last night," she said shakily.

"I slept fine. Don't you remember?"

"Yes, but—"

"No buts! The doctor will be here this morning. Go back to sleep. When I hear the plane, I'll have to take the snowmobile down to the clearing to pick him up. You won't be frightened if you wake up and I'm not here?"

She shook her head, her eyes already drooping. He sat there until she was asleep.

Molly slept off and on all that day. The doctor came and went, leaving medication for Adam to give her. He woke her regularly with the tablets and a glass of water, tenderly holding her up so she could drink. She heard Tim-Two come in and put fuel in her stove, and heard Adam talking in the kitchen. Adam cooked food on the range and from her room, she was able to hear him curse once in a while as well as smell what he was cooking.

Late in the evening she awoke, aware she needed to use the bathroom. She lay dreading to make the move. Finally she could wait no longer and got out of bed on trembling limbs and stood for a while holding onto the end of the bed until her fuzzy head cleared. She staggered to the bathroom and closed the door louder than usual in her anxiety to hurry. She was making her way back to the door while holding onto the wash basin when Adam knocked, then opened the door.

"Are you all right, love?" He picked her up in his arms and hurried her back to bed. Lowering her gently, he tucked the covers around her. She was shivering uncontrollably, her teeth chattering.

He went to the kitchen and returned with a bundle that he thrust under the covers at her feet.

"Tim-Two and I have been heating stones on the range. I've wrapped them in a towel." Kneeling down, he put his arms around her blanket-wrapped form and hugged her close, trying to warm her. Gradually her shaking ceased and he sat on the side of the bed.

"I'm making some broth. Tim-Two says you've got to drink it. He's been worried about you. He's keeping the house so warm he's about to roast me out!" he said teasingly.

"I don't know what I would have done without you," she said in a weak and trembling voice.

"It's about time for your medicine again and I must take your temperature. If it isn't down by morning, the doctor is coming back."

"No, Adam," she protested, "I'm better now. It must have been terribly expensive to bring the doctor out here."

"Expensive, be damned," he fumed. "I'll have him come five times a day if we need him."

Tears brightened her eyes. She quickly closed her lids so he would not see. He squeezed her hand, kissed her brow, and went back to the kitchen.

Later he brought a warm wet cloth and washed her face and hands. Then to her amazement he turned her gently so he could brush her hair. A feeling of sheer pleasure passed through her sore and aching body. When he had finished to his satisfaction, he put an extra pillow under her head.

"Now, you've got to eat something." He came back minutes later with a tray he had already prepared, set it on her nightstand, and handed her a mug of warm broth.

"Can you hold this?" he asked. "If not, I can hold it for you."

She reached for the cup with shaky fingers. The broth was amazingly good. When she thought she had all she could hold, she extended the cup back to him, but he shook his head.

"All of it," he commanded, and she obeyed.

When he left again and she settled down in the bed, her confused mind wouldn't rest until she tried to analyze his unusual behavior toward her; his kindness and compassion, his willingness to minister to her. Could it be he felt sorry for her? *Oh, God,* she thought, *not that.* She didn't want his pity. *It's a brotherly feeling he has for me. That's it. I'm his little sister again and I don't want that either!*

She could hear him swearing in the kitchen. *He's all man,* she thought. Tim-Two came in the back door and Dog came padding into the bedroom. He laid his big head on the bed and little whimpers came from his throat. Molly reached out her hand and rubbed his head. Finally he stretched out on the floor and twitched his ears as if trying to understand why she was in bed this time of night.

Lulled to sleep by the murmur of voices and the warmth of the bed, Molly awakened when Adam came into the room carrying the transistor radio and the gaslamp. It was late. She thought she had only dozed.

"What time is it?"

"About midnight. I've been waiting to give you your medicine."

"I'm sorry you had to wait."

"Don't be. I've been listening to the radio. We've had a very big snowfall." He put his arm under her and lifted her shoulders so she could drink. "How do you feel?"

"Better, I think." Her voice was weak and she was shaking again. "But I get so cold."

"We'll remedy that." He took off his robe and flung it over the chair.

Molly's startled eyes took in the broad bare shoulders, the wide chest with dark hair going down to his pajama bottoms, the strong brown throat, and the muscled arms.

He looked so different, so masculine, and ... athletic. Her frightened eyes must have conveyed her feelings.

He laughed softly, turned out the gaslight, and lifted the cover as he slid into bed beside her.

"Don't be frightened, love. I can feel your heart pounding like a little rabbit caught in a trap."

He turned her so her back was toward him and wrapped himself around her spoon fashion, her head pillowed on his arm. He tucked the covers around them and enfolded her in his arms.

"Isn't this better than being alone?" he whispered in her ear. Then teasingly, "I'm not going to seduce you, kitten. I'll wait until you're spitting and scratching!"

It was difficult for Molly to think coherently. The nearness of the warm body pressing against hers with nothing between them but the thin material of her nightdress and his pajama pants was both comforting and disturbing. Questions lay like a coiled snake inside of her, the residue of past hurts. Then uncaring for anything but the moment, she relaxed against him conscious of the rhythmic thumping of his heart against her back.

His probing fingers smoothed the hair from around her ear. His lips nuzzled her neck. "Go to sleep. I'll wake you for your medicine."

Her hand moved to his and her fingers interlaced with his fingers. She knew no more, drifting deeply into her first natural sleep of several days.

She lay motionless, her body aching, but aware she was alone in the bed. She shifted her position and opened her mouth to call, but the words didn't come. Was she alone? Had she dreamed someone was with her? Weak tears ran down her cheeks. Then he appeared in the door, flashlight in one hand and a glass in the other. Relief flooded over her.

"Time for this stuff again," he said when he saw she was awake. "I've put more fuel on the fire, I think it's getting colder."

When he put out his light and got into bed beside her, he lay on his back and cuddled her against his side. Feeling the wetness of her cheek where it lay on his shoulder, he tilted her face and kissed her tearstained eyes.

"What's the matter? Head aching again?"

She said nothing, but stretched her arm across his bare chest and pressed closer to him.

"Want me to rub your back?"

"You don't need to."

"But I want to," he persisted, and rolled her so she lay almost on top of him. His hand went up and down her back, rubbing and massaging the sore muscles. It felt so good! Being so intimately close to him was wonderful. A small sigh escaped her. He chuckled softly and kissed her forehead.

"Having a husband isn't all bad, is it, love? Go to sleep. It'll be morning soon."

The next morning the ground was covered with deep new snow. The day began when Adam came into her room and sat down on the side of the bed. Laying his hand on her forehead, then his palm to her cheek, he pronounced her fever broken and said the doctor would not have to come back out after all.

Molly, a little fuzzy in the head from the fever and the medication Adam had given her the night before, lay motionless. She was too weak to do anything else.

"Hungry?"

She nodded.

"Good," he said. "You're going to have breakfast."

He was no sooner out the door than Molly reached for the comb on her nightstand and flicked it through her hair, and then, making sure Adam was still in the kitchen, reached for the cold cream jar, and quickly dug her fingers into the cream and smeared it on her face. Seconds later she had wiped it off on a tissue that she concealed beneath her pillow.

Adam didn't knock at the door. He came into the room as if it was his own. He carried a small round tray with a bowl of something steaming on it. He put the tray on the nightstand and sat down on the bed again.

He smiled. It was a beautiful smile and it wrung Molly's heart.

"Good morning!" he said as if he hadn't seen her minutes before.

"Good morning." The intimacy of last night was making her self-conscious and she hesitated to meet his eyes.

He leaned forward and put his hands on either side of her pillow and, resting on them, looked down at her face. Quickly he bent forward and kissed her on the lips. It wasn't a loving kiss; it was a kiss, however, and Molly loved it. When he lifted his head, she wished he would do it again. Her dark-lashed violet eyes looked into his dark ones.

"You smell nice," he said thoughtfully. "It must be the cold cream." His eyes flicked over her face, taking in everything. "And you've combed your hair," he added.

Molly flushed and looked away from him. Even if he noticed, why did he have to mention it? He was smiling and the only thing she could do was to smile back.

"I've made oatmeal," he announced.

Once again he leaned forward and once again he kissed her . . . very gently.

He stood and placed the tray on her lap. "Eat," he commanded, and went out.

Molly didn't realize how much better she felt until after she had eaten. The meal had been simple, but delicious; cooked oatmeal with a generous sprinkling of brown sugar, buttered toast, and hot cocoa. She wondered when Adam had learned to cook. She must remember to ask him. Moving the empty tray from her lap to the nearby chair she slid out of bed and looked around for her robe. Her eyes fell on the neatly folded clothes she had worn the day she became ill. An unexpected thrill passed through her at the thought of Adam undressing her. The nightdress he had chosen for her that night was flannel and revealed little, but nonetheless, he had seen all of her. A helpless feeling of discomfiture came over her. She found her robe and wrapped it tightly around her.

During that day and the days that followed, Adam was kindness itself. He poured warm bath water for her and while she was bathing he changed her bed. He wrapped her in a blanket and laid her on the couch, tuned the radio for her, or fetched magazines. He cooked good meals and insisted she eat to gain her strength back. He never came back to her bed after she was up and around. At the end of the week Molly was well enough to take over her household chores and Adam went back to his work on her father's files in the bedroom.

CHAPTER NINE

AFTER A WEEK of below-zero weather Adam was sure the ice on the lake was sufficient to support the ski plane. He needed to bring in a large amount of supplies and it was much easier to get them to the house from the lake than from the clearing where the helicopter had to land.

He called for the helicopter to come for him after making sure Tim-Two would be around to check on Molly.

"You'll go my next trip. Dad is getting anxious to see you again. Pat will be coming out in a week or two so we'll be needing extra supplies. Make a list. It will give you something to do while I'm gone." He grinned at her. "And don't take a notion to clean the house from top to bottom. You're not strong enough yet."

"I won't," she assured him. "I've got my knitting. I'll sit by the fire like Mother Hubbard!"

He tugged at a strand of her hair, a crooked little grin on his face, and Molly felt her heart thudding. When they heard the plane overhead, he went out the door. She watched until he was out of sight beyond the timber.

Molly leaned her head back and gazed into the fire.

She found herself obsessed with the memory of Adam's face—the narrowed dark eyes that carried such varied emotions when they looked at her. She had seen those eyes in so many different moods. They had laughed, teased, smiled, grown fierce with anger. She found she could not bear to think of them looking into hers with icy coolness in their depths. She wondered if she would be able to bear the loneliness when he went away for good. *It's lonely now, knowing he's coming back,* she told herself, *but how will it be when I know he'll never . . .* she shook herself. She didn't want to think about it.

Adam's voice came in on the radio, calling from the helicopter.

"How about it, Molly? Got a copy?"

She picked up the mike and pressed the button. Her heart was pounding.

"Ten-four, Adam," she said breathlessly. "I have a good copy."

"I'll be back in a few hours with the ski plane. Stay tuned in and I'll call as soon as I'm in range. Ten-four?"

"Ten-four, Adam. I'll be listening."

The day went rather fast. Molly had several calls on the radio from neighbors going over in their planes. She would chat easily with them until they were out of range. Tim-Two came in to check on the stoves. Later in the afternoon she became tired of knitting and made a chocolate cake. She decided to divide it this time and she iced one-half on two separate plates and sent a plate back with Tim-Two when he came again to check the stoves.

It was getting dusk when Adam's voice boomed into the quiet house.

"Break, break, Molly. Do you have a copy?" He repeated the call anxiously before she could pick up the mike.

"I'm here, Adam. How far out are you?"

"So you finally answered." He had a chill in his voice. Molly's heart sank, then lurched when he added, "I was getting worried." Her throat was so tight she could hardly answer.

"I just picked up your call. Do you have us in view?"

"I can see you down there." Then with a teasing note in his voice, "Is my dinner ready?"

"Now I hear the plane," Molly said. "And, no, I don't have your dinner ready, I thought you were taking me out tonight." There was a faint giggle in her voice.

"I'll take you out all right. I'll take you out to the woodshed."

Then before she could answer he cleared off the channel.

Molly was happy. He was back again! He came into the house stamping fresh snow from his boots, his arms full of packages, his eyes sweeping the house as if he was glad to be back.

"Come, wife, and kiss me."

Molly's face reddened. She looked at his black eyes that were dancing merrily at her discomfort.

"Come," he repeated, and she went to him and placed warm lips on his cold ones for a brief instant.

"Hum . . ." he said. "I got a better kiss from Dog when he came to meet me."

Her eyes twinkled up at him. She took his packages and put them on the chair beside the door, so he could take off his coat.

"You're getting snow all over," she fussed to hide her happiness at having him home again.

"Did you miss me?" he persisted.

"Of course, it was nice and quiet all day!"

He hung up his coat, put away his boots, then in his stocking feet brought his bundles to the table. Opening one, he produced several bottles of liquor.

"If I'd had this the other night, I would have made you a hot toddy," he said. "And in way of a celebration, I've brought home some barbequed ribs!"

Molly wondered if he realized he had said, "brought home." Could a man like Adam ever consider this small cabin his home?

"I baked a chocolate cake!" she announced.

". . . and I brought you a present."

"You didn't . . . ?"

"I did."

He handed her the largest of his packages and stood with a grin on his face while she opened it.

Her hands were shaking and her fingers felt all thumbs, but she managed to tear away the paper and remove the lid from the box. She lifted out a soft, fluffy, violet-colored robe, and under the robe, were matching woolly slippers.

She looked up and met his eyes; her own were enormous in her flushed face. She couldn't move or speak.

"I knew it," he was saying. "I knew the minute I saw this robe it was the color of your eyes." He took it from her and held it open. "Try it on."

"Thank . . . you," Molly stammered. "I . . . don't know what to say."

"Well, just don't say: 'oh, Adam, you shouldn't!' " His voice was high and funny and she giggled.

"Well?" She turned so he could see her from all angles.

"Just fits," he said. "I knew it would. I told the girl you came up to here on me." He held his hand up to under his chin. "And I told her you were about this big around." He made a small circle with his hands.

She grinned broadly, her eyes bright, her face radiant. "I love it," she told him.

It was a meal to remember. Adam heated the ribs in the hot oven and Molly made a salad. In the warm, cozy atmosphere of the kitchen they ate the ribs with their fingers before finishing off the cake. Afterward Adam helped with cleaning up, but told her he wasn't making a habit of doing so. Later, they sat before the fireplace and planned next week's trip to Anchorage.

"We should leave early," Adam said, "and spend about four hours there."

"How was your father?" Molly asked.

"Doing well, considering. He always asks about you." He was sitting on the floor, his back to the couch. Dog had come to him and placed his head on his thigh to be petted. Adam scratched his big ears.

Molly bowed her head over the sweater she had started for Adam. She had bought the Australian wool last year on an impulse, not really knowing what she was going to make out of it. Just this afternoon it had occurred to her that the off-white color would go well with Adam's dark good looks. She hadn't told him what she was working on and he hadn't asked.

Now that the weather had turned cold all the doors inside the cabin were left open because they needed the extra heat in the bedrooms. The bathroom doors were left open at night when the room wasn't in use. Adam, being the last each night to use the room, opened both the door to Molly's room and his own before he went to bed.

Molly, now, lay in her bed and listened to the sounds coming from the other bedroom. She thought of the two nights he had spent in her bed. How sweet and gentle he had been! *Would it be so wrong,* she thought, *to let him make love to me? We're married! Could I bear for him to leave me after knowing what it feels like to be possessed by him?*

She lay on her back, eyes closed, remembering how he had rubbed her back, caressed her, and folded her in his arms to keep her warm. She could feel the stubble on his chin that morning as he slept with it resting against her forehead. Her heart began to beat rapidly and a hunger for him like a pain went through her; through her lips, her breasts, and into her loins. The pain grew and the blood rushed to her face. Disgusted at her thoughts she flopped over on her stomach and buried her head in the pillow. *What's the matter with me?* she thought. *I'm like a bitch in heat.* Of one thing she was almost sure: Adam would keep their relationship on the present level. If it should ever change, she would have to be the one to make the first move.

Molly kept herself busy during the days that followed. The weather was cold, always hovering around the zero mark. She spent an hour each day out of the house. Tim-Two brought out the sled and harness. She hitched up Dog, who loved every minute of pulling the sled. They went with Tim-Two on short runs to his trap lines. This wasn't Molly's favorite thing to do, and she was always relieved when they found them empty.

The moose were coming down out of the hills and into the timber now. Soon the hunting season would be here and Tim-Two would shoot one for the meat it would supply. Molly never stayed around to watch the slaughter or the butchering of the meat. When Tim-Two brought in the neatly wrapped packages from the woodshed, where they were frozen, she would pretend they had come from the meat market in town.

One afternoon she took the snowmobile out alone and enjoyed a ride down the path to the lake and through the timber to the clearing where the helicopter landed. Believing that she had been gone only an hour, she was surprised when she returned to find Adam preparing to go look for her.

"Where in the hell have you been?" he demanded, with the thundercloud look on his face.

"Only down through . . . the timber," she stammered, surprised at his anger. "Why?"

"Why?" he repeated. "You've been gone an hour, that's why!"

She couldn't understand why he was so angry, and the questioning look in her violet eyes told him she didn't understand.

"I saw fresh wolf tracks around the lake yesterday. You're not to go out of sight of this house without me or Tim-Two. Is that understood?"

"This is the first time I've been out by myself." Her eyes looked squarely into his.

"And it will be the last time, my girl!" he said firmly. "Tim-Two thinks there's a wolverine about. He saw the sign in his trap lines."

"But—" she started to explain she had lived here for

five years and wasn't exactly a greenhorn, but he wouldn't let her say it.

"Don't argue, Molly. I've told you what you cannot do and that's the end of it." He took off his parka. As far as he was concerned the matter was closed.

At first Molly was angry at his high-handed method of telling her about the danger, but after thinking about it she understood his concern. Although it was early winter and there was still plenty of small game for the wolves, they were a dangerous lot and not to be trusted. The unpredictable wolverine was another matter altogether. They attacked when and where they wanted, if they were hungry or not, just for the sheer pleasure of the kill. Molly had seen the results of a wolverine kill and it was not a pleasant sight.

The next day Molly hitched Dog to the sled for a ride around the yard. Adam came out to go with her and they headed for the frozen lake. She rode on the sled and Adam on the runners behind. Dog was in rare form. He had two playmates and for more than an hour they played like two children on the ice. When they came back to the house, they sat before the fire and drank hot cocoa. It felt as though they'd been together forever, there was such ease and companionship between them.

The day before the trip to Anchorage, Adam asked if there was any reason why they couldn't stay overnight in the apartment. He would like to stay two nights, he said, as he had some business he should attend to. They were eating their evening meal at the trestle table and Molly looked across at him in her questioning way.

"It's perfectly legal as far as the will is concerned, Molly. Charlie didn't mean for us to spend every day here. And I'm sure your aunt would think twice before she tackled me and my father."

"I wasn't thinking of that," she said. "I was thinking I wouldn't go this time and you could take care of your business. I'll go with you when you go again for the day."

"No, for two reasons. First and foremost, I'll not leave you here alone overnight, and second, I promised Dad I'd bring you the next time I came in."

"Then it's settled," she conceded.

"I'll take you out to dinner," he promised. "We'll do a night on the town."

"No," she said quickly, "that won't be necessary. I'm not taking suitable evening clothes." Not that she had suitable clothes to take, she thought dryly.

"That's no problem. We'll buy something."

"No . . . no, I'd rather not."

"Is that all you can say—'no, no!'" He laughed at her. "Well, we'll see." He was in one of his teasing moods and Molly couldn't help but laugh with him.

That night she looked over her simple wardrobe. She didn't have much to choose from. Finally, she picked out two simple dresses to wear during the day, and a pair of wool slacks with matching sweater to wear to and from the city. She laid out toilet articles, a nightie, and the robe and slippers Adam had given her. As an afterthought she tucked in the diamond earrings, the gift from his father.

CHAPTER TEN

THEY WALKED DOWN the snow-packed path to the plane. Adam tucked her in the seat and wrapped her with a blanket before fastening her seat belt. She never tired of watching him. He was so confident, so capable. She had dreaded the trip to town, but now that she was actually on her way, she felt a little thrill of excitement and looked forward to seeing Adam's father and his Aunt Flo again. The one thing she was sure of was a welcome there. She felt none of the apprehension of the first visit.

Once the plane was in the air Adam told her something about Anchorage. She and her father did all their business in Fairbanks and she admitted she knew little about Alaska's largest city. Nearly every second Alaskan lives in Anchorage, he told her. It was a sprawling modern city of almost two hundred thousand, located between Cook Inlet and the Chugach mountains. There was considerable damage to the city during the 1964 earthquake, but the rebuilding had been completed, and the city had become a headquarters for large corporations and government agencies. Adam's father's company was headquartered there. He said he had little to do with the company, but owned voting stock and attended board meetings.

Adam expressed regret that his native state was fast becoming a "get-rich-quick" oil boom state. Being a strict conservationist, he'd rather the state stayed poor and they kept what they had. He was "between the devil and the deep blue sea," he explained, wanting to keep Alaska as it was and owning stock in a company manufacturing pipe to lay it to waste.

Adam set the plane down on a runway set aside for the landing of ski planes and they were towed into the hangar by a small vehicle. Adam's car was in a nearby garage and they were soon on the way to his apartment building. They passed the famous Captain Cook Hotel, and he teasingly told her if she was a "good" girl, he would take her there for dinner.

Molly said nothing, but the thought of going out with him brought terror to her heart. Her confidence was fast leaving her. In the city he appeared different from what he was with her in the cabin. She was frightened that she would do something ridiculous and embarrass him.

As they were going up in the elevator of the apartment building Adam suggested they stop at his apartment and freshen up before going up to see his father. He opened the door and Molly went in and looked around. She was not as astonished at his collection of things as she had been the first time she visited here. Somehow after knowing him better she understood his desire to keep these pleasant mementos of his travels.

He carried her case to the bedroom she had used before.

"Shall we have a good bath and use all the hot water we want to?" Amusement brightened his dark eyes.

"Why, not," she answered. "What time does your father expect us?"

"I'll call and tell Ganson we'll be up in about an hour. Okay?"

"Okay," she echoed. "Are you glad to be back in civilization?"

"I don't know if you would call this civilization. It's pretty much of a jungle, but I'll admit I enjoy the hot shower!"

Molly hung her two dresses and the robe in the closet, and opened the drawer of the dressing table to put away her toilet articles. A lipstick rolled to the front of the drawer when she opened it. She picked it up and looked at it. It wasn't one of hers and she was sure it hadn't been in the drawer when she was here before. A queer, tight little feeling closed in around her heart. Had Adam brought a girl here on one of his visits to see his father? He said he was accustomed to being with a woman. No! She wouldn't think about it! She had no right to feel disappointed. He was perfectly free to do as he pleased as long as he abided by the terms of her father's will. She put the offending tube out of her sight in another drawer and went into the bathroom to take her bath.

Wallowing in the deep tub filled with the sweet-scented water, Molly forced her mind to dwell on how she could dress her hair. Not being used to the shorter length, she had been letting it hang, held back by a band, but that wouldn't do here. She didn't want to look like a teen-ager. She decided to try and roll it into a flat bun on top of her head, somewhat as she used to coil her braids.

If that wouldn't do, she would try a bun at the nape of her neck. Either way would make her look a little more sophisticated.

She chose to wear the plum-colored wool dress. It had simple lines and a flared skirt that swayed gently as she walked. She slipped her feet into the black pumps and sat for a long while brushing her hair, trying to decide on a style. After several attempts to make a bun on top of her head she had to settle for one at the nape of her neck. She was applying plum-colored lipstick to match her dress when Adam knocked on the door, then opened it and came in. She looked at him through the dressing table mirror. A lump rose up in her throat so that she could hardly swallow.

He had just come from his shower. His hair was damp and curling. He had on a light tan knit shirt tucked snugly into navy blue trousers. The long-sleeve shirt was opened at the neck and she caught a glimpse of the curly black hair on his chest where she had once laid her cheek. His eyes held hers for a long moment. The pulse at the base of her throat beat madly, and she saw him lower his eyes to look at it. She remembered the spot his mouth had made on her neck and she desperately wanted to look to see if it was still there, but she didn't dare take her eyes from his. He broke the silence.

"Why did you pin up your hair for God's sake?" He came to where she sat facing the mirror. "What's the matter with the way you wear it at home?"

"Because this makes me look my age," she replied, her voice quite matter-of-fact.

"It makes you look ridiculous!" His fingers went to her neck and he started to remove the pins.

"Adam!" She tried to twist away from him. "It took me a long time to get it pinned up."

"I like it the other way," he insisted. "Beautiful things should not be pinned up or tied down." He continued taking out the pins. "Now give me the brush." He held out his hand.

She slapped the brush down into his hand with emphasis. He stood behind her and brushed her hair with long, even strokes. He brushed it straight back over her forehead and behind her ears. He brushed it from under the nape of her neck. At last he was satisfied and handed the brush back to her.

"Where's one of those ribbon things?"

"I didn't bring one," she said sulkily.

"I'll send Ganson to get one."

"No . . . no . . . , I've got a white one here in the drawer."

"I thought you did." He grinned. "I saw it this morning."

She handed it to him and he slipped it under her hair and across the top of her head.

"Now you look like Molly again." He took her hand and pulled her up from the seat. "You look very, very pretty!" he said, and kissed her on the nose. "Let's go. Dad is waiting for us."

Molly received the same welcome as the first time she came to the apartment. Adam's Aunt Flo met her in the hall as soon as the elevator door opened and came forward with open arms. She embraced her enthusiastically, then held her away and looked at her.

"Such beautiful golden hair, such lovely skin and innocent eyes. Adam, I was afraid I had dreamed her," she exclaimed.

"She's real all right, Aunt Flo." He looked down proudly as his aunt turned her toward the sitting room. He caught Molly's eye and lifted his eyebrows with questionable humor. A feeling of guilt flooded over her. The deceit they were practicing was abhorrent to her. This dear little lady was so ready and willing to accept her. Molly knew she could grow to love her as well as Adam's father.

They entered the sitting room and found the old man in a chair by the fireplace. His eyes were on the door as they came through it, and as they came forward he had eyes only for Molly. To her he looked much the same as he did the last time they were there and she went to him immediately, genuinely glad to see him again. She forgot Adam and the part she was supposed to play. She took his frail hand and bent to kiss his wrinkled cheek.

"Hello, Papa," she said softly. She was surprised at the strength of the hand that held hers.

"Hello, daughter," the weak voice replied. "I was beginning to think you weren't coming back to see me."

"Oh, yes, I was coming," she said archly, "but I had a bout with the flu and didn't want to bring you my bugs."

He chuckled and looked at Adam. "Hello, son." The dimmed eyes which took in the tall, dark-haired figure that bent over him were filled with love and admiration.

"How are you, Dad?" Adam's face held the look Molly had seen before when he greeted his father.

She looked from father to son and felt a warm glow as if she were witness to a rare and wonderful thing. The love and admiration they each had for each other were obvious. *There must be some fifty-odd years between their ages,* she thought, *but there is no generation gap here.*

"Sit down, sit down," the old man was saying.

Adam pulled a footstool up close to his father's chair for Molly because the old man had not released her hand. He sat opposite them and stretched out his long legs. Molly flushed when she met his eyes and looked away. She wished he would leave. She sincerely liked his father and didn't want him thinking she was play-acting. He settled himself to stay so she decided she would have to try and forget he was there.

"So you're going to stay two nights." The father was addressing the son.

"We'll be staying tonight and tomorrow night. Tomorrow night I'm taking Molly out on the town."

Oh, no, not that again, she thought. She didn't dare look at him lest he see the fright in her eyes.

"Good, good." Mr. Reneau looked at Molly affectionately. "Adam told me you had cut your hair, daughter. I was a little disappointed until he explained how hard it was to take care of, up there in the woods. Now, I think I like it. You're young and there's plenty of time for you to do it up like an old woman!" This was quite a long speech for the old man.

Molly gave an exasperated sigh. It was irritating to know they had discussed something as personal as her hair. At least Adam hadn't told him she cut it in a fit of temper.

"Thank you for the earrings, Papa," she said. "I would have worn them tonight, but I didn't think diamond earrings were appropriate with a street dress." She smiled at him mischievously.

"Adam's mother was young like you when I gave them to her. she wore them almost every day." His face creased even more in a gentle smile.

Molly talked on and on. The old man hardly took his eyes from her face. She told him about the snow and the fun they had hitching Dog to the sled, about going to check Tim-Two's trap lines, and the moose hunt in another week or so. She explained that they only took one moose a season and that was for the supply of meat. She also told him that she couldn't stand to watch the butchering because if she did, she couldn't eat a bite of the meat. He smiled and nodded his head and told her Adam's mother was like that. She told him about the wolf tracks Adam found down by the lake. Glancing at Adam, she saw the amusement in his eyes and she turned her face stubbornly, and refused to look at him. She was sure she heard him chuckle and almost turned to glare at him. Just in time she controlled the desire and went on to tell about the wolverine sign Tim-Two had found, and also how fast their wood supply was going down due to the cold.

Adam sat quietly, never uttering a word. Molly was embarrassed that she had talked so much. He was lazing back in his chair, his eyes between the dark lashes were mere slits, but he had an impish grin on his face.

"Adam," she said, exasperated at his silence. "Aren't you going to say anything?"

"I couldn't get a word in if I wanted to. Your mouth has been going ninety miles an hour." That devilish look was in his eyes again, the one that was always there when he knew he was getting under her skin.

"Don't mind him. You should be used to his teasing way, by now." Mr. Reneau gently shook the hand that was still in his.

"I could . . . hit him, when he gets in that devilish mood," she said heatedly.

The old man laughed so hard Molly was afraid for him. He laughed until the tears came. She looked at Adam; he was laughing too, so she guessed there was no danger to the old man.

"Good for you," Mr. Reneau said finally. "Why don't you try it sometime?"

"I just might do that!" Molly said with spirit.

"If you're going to be here with my dad, I'll make some phone calls." Adam went to the door still grinning.

"I'll be here," she said, ignoring his retreating back.

There was little sleep for Molly that night. All through the long dark hours she tossed restlessly. In spite of the pleasant afternoon and evening in his father's apartment, Adam's announcement that they were going "out on the town" the next night filled Molly's heart with dread. What would she wear? She had never been "out on the town," whatever that was. She only knew that she didn't want to go, and desperately wished that she was back home in the bush. *This time I'll really make a fool of myself,* she thought desperately. The thoughts whirled around in her head, but one stayed with her. She would phone Herb Belsile and ask for money to buy a suitable dress and wrap. She drifted off to sleep with that idea in mind.

When morning came, she waited impatiently until it was time for Herb to be in his office, then waited until she could use the telephone privately. The time came, finally.

The housekeeper was in the kitchen and Adam went into his bedroom and closed the door. She hastened to the phone, looked up Herb's number, and dialed.

It was a blessed relief when she heard the familiar voice on the line! He wasted valuable time making pleasantries, and after assuring him she was well, she told him she needed money to buy clothes.

"How much do you need, Molly? You have a balance in your bank in Fairbanks."

"I know, Herb, but that's only a small balance. I'd like to have several months' allowance deposited here in Anchorage that I can use today." She kept her voice low.

"I'll arrange it for you." He told her the bank he would use and advised her to sign the checks with her married name, Molly Reneau. Then he asked if there was anything else she would like to discuss with him.

"No, Herb, I'm doing fine, and I appreciate the money. I won't be needing an allowance, now, for several months." After a few more pleasantries were exchanged, she rang off.

When she turned, Adam was barring her way.

She gasped! "I didn't know you were there."

"I'll bet you didn't. What was that all about?"

She took a deep breath and turned her face up to meet his accusing stare.

"I was talking to Herb Belsile."

"I know who you were talking to. I was going to use the phone in the bedroom, and I heard you."

"You listened!" she said accusingly.

"Not on the phone. I came out here and listened."

Pride, and then anger came to her defense. "I was talking to my attorney about money. Is there anything else you'd like to know?" After the sleepless night her nerves were on edge and she wanted to get away from him before she disgraced herself and cried.

"Why do you need several months' allowance?" he asked bluntly.

"You've no right to know about my financial affairs any more than I have the right to know about yours, Adam Reneau."

"You think not, Molly Reneau?" he said sharply. "You're my wife. You know what that means? It means that I'm responsible for you whether you like it or not."

Her mouth compressed. Before she could give a suitable retort, his voice softened, he let his hands go up and down her arms in a caressing motion, and he continued:

"You're worried about going out tonight and want to buy new clothes."

The amazement showed in her eyes before her glance fell. "Now you know all my little secrets."

He made a kind of growling noise in his throat and tried to pull her toward him, but she resisted. "It isn't so important what you wear, Molly."

"It is to me," she replied.

He pulled her to him and hugged her. "We'll go out and buy you the best-looking outfit in town, if that's what you want."

She pushed herself away from him. "It isn't what I want, Adam! I'll buy my own clothes, thank you."

He gave a sharp exclamation and his black brows drew together. "Not with me, you won't! I'd look like a fool."

"You don't need to go alone." She knew she shouldn't have said it. She saw the determination flash in his eyes and knew her case was lost.

"I'm going! I'm paying! If you're such a square about your husband buying your clothes, you can pay me back."

For a long moment she didn't move. The expression on her features was easy to read; the doubt, indecision, and then resignation as she came to a decision.

"All right, but only if I pay back every cent. I'm not a charity case. My father left me provided for."

She was standing determinedly, trying so hard to be independent. A sudden desire came over Adam to cherish her. He looked at the trembling mouth and wanted to kiss it. Not the brotherly kisses he had been giving it, but the passionate kisses of a man who wants to make love to a woman. He knew he dared not, so he casually said, "You win. We'll do it your way this time." He could see the apprehension on Molly's face and was surprised at himself for trying so desperately to put her at ease.

CHAPTER ELEVEN

MOLLY'S APPREHENSION ESCALATED the moment they stepped into the fashionable dress shop where they had come to buy her clothes.

The room they entered was pale green with touches of white. The deep carpet, white sofas, long glass tables, and potted plants gave the impression of an elegant sitting room. A tall, slender, fashionably dressed woman came to meet them.

"Adam!" She gave him an electric smile and held out her hands. "How nice to see you." He took her outstretched hands.

"And nice to see you, Jaclyn." His voice was cool, and he dropped her hands after only a brief contact.

The woman stood there smiling, seemingly unaware of the rebuff, which was apparent to Molly. She sensed, immediately, the aloofness that had come over Adam. She wished desperately he hadn't come with her and fidgeted nervously. She felt gawky and uncomfortable standing beside him looking up at this tall, chic woman.

"This is my wife." Adam turned to her and took her hand.

Jaclyn turned astonished eyes to Molly. "Your wife? You? Married?" There was no mistaking the amusement and disbelief in her voice.

Her eyes swung to Molly and surveyed her with unsmiling curiosity. She took her time assessing her, missing nothing. The scrutiny went on for so long that Molly felt acutely embarrassed. Adam seemed to be amused.

"Well," Jaclyn said at last, "her figure is good, although she's rather short."

Molly's blood was boiling; her anger was directed at Adam as well as the woman. How dare he bring her here to be looked at, judged, and have her imperfections pointed out to him. Her mouth opened, but before she could frame a suitable retort, he squeezed her hand to silence her.

"The reason we're here is to select a wardrobe for my beautiful wife. I don't wish to spoil her natural beauty. I know exactly how she should be dressed—with very little sophistication, do you agree?" His tone was cool and oddly patronizing.

"Of course you're right, Adam. You've always had excellent taste . . . in clothes," she said grudgingly.

"Take us to one of your rooms and show us evening dresses and wraps."

When they were seated in a small mirrored room and Jaclyn had left them alone, Molly turned on him.

"I don't like any part of this," she fumed. "I'll not be looked over like I was a . . . horse!"

Adam smiled down into her angry face. The violet

eyes sparkled with indignation. He chuckled softly and put his arm around her.

"She's a professional, Molly, that's why we came here. Whether you like her or not she knows clothes and, remember, you're the one that wanted to be suitably dressed."

"I don't care," she sputtered, "I still don't—"

"If you don't shut up, I'm going to kiss you." He tried to appear very stern. Molly got only so far as to open her mouth when his came down on it and stopped the words and all thoughts of words. He kissed her long and hard, not the little kisses he had been giving her, but the same kisses he gave her on that night she almost lost her head. Her heart was beating wildly when he finally raised his head. His eyes had narrowed and his breath was coming a little faster. A wild thought came to Molly. *He enjoyed kissing me as much as I enjoyed being kissed!*

They both looked up to see the woman, Jaclyn, watching them with a look of annoyance on her face. Molly felt a wave of pure exultation. *The woman was jealous! Well,* she thought spitefully, *that paid her back for the snippy remark about my height.*

"If you're ready, Adam," she said, in what Molly believed to be her professional tone, "we'll show you what I think would be suitable for your . . ."—there was a short meaningful pause—". . . wife."

Models began to appear as if from nowhere in response to the command from Jaclyn. They displayed one gorgeous creation after the other. Molly's head began to swim in her efforts to choose from the collection of clothes that were paraded before her. Without objection she accepted Adam's choice and went with Jaclyn to the fitting rooms.

The dress she, or rather Adam, chose was cut from white velvet. The bodice folded itself lovingly around her young breasts. It, as well as the tiny stand-up collar, was studded with rhinestones. The skirt fell quite straight and simple to her feet. She loved it and thought it must cost the earth, but three months' allowance should cover the cost of the dress and the long white wool coat. The seamstress took her measurements while she was undressed. The evening dress would be shortened and she assured Molly she would be able to wear it that evening.

The shopping had not been the ordeal Molly feared. Coming back to the small room where Adam was waiting, she found him standing with Jaclyn viewing clothing brought in by models, who after holding up the garment for his inspection, would wait until he shook his head either up and down or sideways. Jaclyn was busy with a pad and pencil. The clothing ran from skirts and sweaters to day dresses to slack suits and loungewear.

Desperation made Molly's voice sharper than she intended it to be.

"Adam!" She clutched his sleeve. "Adam, what—"

"Just a minute, darling," he cut her off.

"What . . ." The agitation in her voice caused him to turn and whisper in her ear.

"Shut up, or I'll kiss you again."

"I can't afford this stuff!" she hissed.

Adam turned back to Jaclyn as if she hadn't spoken.

"Deliver these things to my apartment, Jaclyn, and add a supply of underthings." Then to Molly's utter consternation he added, "And see to it there are some negligees and nighties included and . . . ah . . . be sure one is black lace."

He squeezed her hand so tightly she thought he would break the bones. She was mortified! She had been stripped naked here in front of this woman as if she were a store window mannequin! All her instincts urged her to tell them both off; instead, she walked sedately beside Adam to the door. There, Jaclyn spoke the only words she had said to her since they had entered the shop.

"I hope you enjoy your new wardrobe . . . Mrs. Reneau."

Molly's head went up and with it a shrewishness she didn't know she possessed.

"It will do . . . for now, Jaclyn. Thank you for showing us your collection." With all the dignity of a queen she marched ahead of Adam and out the door.

When they reached the street, it was a different matter. In no uncertain terms she let him know that she was not having all those clothes.

"I can't afford them. The dress and wrap will take my allowance for three months!" She ended on a pleading note: "And another thing, that woman didn't believe we were married. She thought you had picked me up and was . . ."

"Was . . . what?" he laughed. "She thought you were my mistress! Wouldn't she be surprised if she knew the truth?"

"You let her think . . . it," she snapped bitterly.

"I don't care what she thinks, Molly mine." He tucked her hand into his and put both their hands in his coat pocket.

"I'll call Herb and tell him I'll need more money," Molly said dejectedly.

"No, you won't. You can pay me back when the year ends. Now let's hear no more about it." He was walking so fast she was almost trotting to keep up with him.

In the late afternoon Molly lay down on the big wide bed in her room and tried to doze off, but her mind was too active. Her eyes wandered around the room, her room, temporarily. She wondered who had used the room and left the lipstick. She shied away from thoughts of Adam being with a woman. The quiet of the room began to have its effect and her eyes became heavy with sleep. The sleepless night and the shopping tour had taken a toll of the strength she had gained after her bout with the flu. She turned over on her side, tucked her hands under her cheek, and slept.

She awoke an hour later feeling amazingly refreshed and went into the bathroom to run her bath. From the array of toiletries assembled on the shelf beneath the large mirror she selected the liquid bubble bath and generously doused her bath water. The result delighted her. The tub filled with soft bubbles emitting a haunting fragrance. She luxuriated in the big square tub, loath to get out. The steam from the bath had allowed a few tendrils of her hair to escape the hairpins she had used to pin it up. She was raising up out of the tub to reach more pins when she heard her bedroom door open.

Through her half-open bathroom door she saw Adam walk into her bedroom with his arms piled with boxes which he dumped on the bed. She gasped in dismay. His laughing dark eyes met her startled ones, traveled down over her bare shoulders, then deliberately lower. He walked into the bathroom and seated himself on a stool. Molly was shocked speechless.

"Want me to wash your back?" he asked Molly. She tried to sink lower into the bubbles.

"You're being a smartass, Adam! Get out of here!"

He reached for a washcloth, dipped it in the water, and let it trail across the back of her neck.

"Nasty words! I'll have to wash your mouth out with soap." He whispered in her ear, then nipped the lobe gently with his teeth.

She grabbed the cloth and was about to swing with it when he jumped out of the way.

"Go ahead with your bath, kitten. I'll unpack your dress."

Molly sank lower in the tub and prayed the bubbles would last until he left the room. She could see him unpacking the white dress and hanging it on a hanger. To her chagrin he unpacked everything. The lacy underthings, the nightgowns. He laid out high-heeled silver sandals she had not seen before. He rummaged in the boxes and came toward the bathroom with an infuriating devilish grin on his face. He was holding up for her inspection a sheer black lace negligee.

"Here's something for you to put on when you get out of the tub," he drawled.

"Get out of here, Adam Reneau!" she said crossly, and threw the wet cloth at him. He dodged it easily and came to kneel down beside the tub.

"You shouldn't throw things at your husband," he scolded.

She could feel his breath on her cheek. His hand went out to cradle the back of her head. She was looking into his eyes when his lips came down on hers. His kiss was light until her lips parted voluntarily, then it deepened, his breath quickened, and he pulled her to him, lifting her wet arm out of the water to guide it around his neck. His hand caressed her bare back and coming around cupped and squeezed her small pointed breasts that were half concealed by the bubbles. She felt an electric current going through her. He tore his mouth from hers and buried his face in the damp, fragrant skin of her neck.

"Do you know what you're doing to me?" he demanded huskily, and not waiting for an answer, he gently pulled down her lower lip with his thumb and forefinger and fastened his lean mouth to hers again.

Molly had never been kissed by any other man and even he had never kissed her in this savage, passionate way before. She arched toward him, pliant in his arms. Only a small part of her consciousness urged her to try and stop him.

His dark eyes were glazed with emotion when he lifted his head. Aroused as she was, Molly hardly knew when his lips had left hers. He kissed her on the nose, then gently drew her arm from around his neck. Scooping up a handful of bubbles, he covered her pink-tipped breasts where they rose out of the water.

"Am I the only man to have kissed you?"

She nodded, not taking her eyes from his. She felt as if she was mesmerized. He placed little nibbly kisses on her face and neck.

"You are precious, Molly mine." He got to his feet and without looking at her went out and closed the door.

Molly sat perfectly still for some minutes after he left, showing no trace of the emotion chasing through her veins. Why didn't she feel any shame for allowing him to caress her as he had? The way her body responded to his caresses frightened her. She shook her wandering thoughts together and got out of the tub.

Toweling herself dry and generously dusting herself with talcum powder, she picked up the black lace garment Adam had dropped on the floor. It was lovely and she couldn't resist trying it on. She opened the door and peeked into the bedroom before going in. She was sure he wouldn't be there, but she was taking no chances. She shed the sheer robe for a more practical one and gave herself up to the pleasure of looking over her new wardrobe.

Molly dressed slowly for her evening out with Adam. She needed the self-confidence of knowing she looked her best. The new gown and coat would certainly help. She had no idea of what Adam's mood would be. She was nervous at the thought of meeting him after the scene in the bathroom.

She stood back from the mirror to judge the finished effect and wondered at the miracle fashionable clothes could achieve. The sleeveless bodice, with the small mandarin collar, the straight skirt, and the high-heeled sandals were a perfect foil for her slender young figure. Makeup was minimal—a touch of blue eye shadow to highlight her eyes, a smear of coral lipstick to outline a mouth made vulnerable by the fullness of the lower lip, and a dusting of powder gave a matte appearance to the small straight nose. She had brushed her hair until it shone and, knowing Adam's aversion to having it pinned, had left it to hang to her shoulders, the ends slightly turning up. She was gazing unbelievingly into the mirror at the elegant stranger when, after a rap on the door, Adam walked in.

Molly's pulse began to race as he looked her over from the top of her head to the tips of her silver shoes peeking out from under the white dress. Twin fires lit his dark, exciting eyes and Molly waited breathlessly for him to speak.

He came to stand behind her, his eyes holding hers in the reflection of the mirror. He put his hands on her bare arms.

"So beautiful, and so damned unaware of it!" He turned her around to face him and fondled the diamond earrings she had fastened to her ears.

He looked particularly handsome in the dark suit; the whiteness of his shirt contrasted with the darkness of his skin. His black hair had been brushed into place, but was already rebelling against the direction it had been forced to go. His brilliant dark eyes never moved from her face while he stood strangely silent. Molly felt her pulses warm her body as his appreciative gaze wandered over her. The force of her emotions deepened the color of her eyes, the most piquant feature of her beauty.

"You have lovely eyes, Molly mine," he murmured, his eyes lingering on her face.

Molly, obeying a totally reckless impulse, held up her face to him. Her lips tilted slightly as he bent his dark head and kissed her on the nose.

"I've promised Dad he could see his lovely daughter before we go." His beautiful voice turned her heart over. He picked up her white coat and laid it over his arm and they left the apartment.

Adam stopped the car outside a tall gray building. A

private club, he told her as he hurried her into the warmth of the building. After tossing his car keys to a warmly dressed doorman they removed their wraps and entered the dining room. It seemed all eyes were focused upon them as they paused in the doorway. The men looked appreciatively at the lovely girl, and the women openly eyed the handsome man beside her.

Adam was evidently well known here. The headwaiter called him by name when he showed them to a table. As they seated themselves, the orchestra began to play. The music was soft and romantic and one or two couples got up to dance on the small dance floor.

"I hope you like salmon," Adam said. "I took the liberty of ordering our meal in advance."

Molly nodded, trying desperately not to be nervous. She looked around the room at the fashionably dressed, sophisticated women who were perfectly comfortable in these surroundings. This was Adam's world. He was at ease here. A little wave of depression hit her.

Adam ordered a bottle of champagne with their meal, and as they waited for their first course to arrive, she sipped it cautiously, remembering the effect it had had on her when she had first drunk it at their wedding reception. He laughed at her and smiled a sweet, almost loving smile.

When she had almost finished what was in her glass, he filled it up again. She began to feel wonderfully gay and chattered to him all through their meal. He responded with a mood to match hers and she thought she had never been so happy.

To the curious onlookers they presented a picture of two people completely engrossed in each other. Adam's eyes never left her face and it was plain to see the lovely girl adored him.

Charlie had taught Molly to dance when she first went to the bush to live, but she had danced only with him and a few times with Jim Robinson at a club in Fairbanks. Adam asked her to dance and was pleasantly surprised when she got to her feet. The dance floor was small and dimly lit and when they began to dance, he was glad that she melted into his arms without a trace of nervousness. Their steps matched perfectly as they moved slowly around the floor to the romantic music the orchestra was playing. He rested his cheek on the top of her head. Molly was so enchanted by the magic of it all that she was afraid to speak in case the spell would be broken. She relaxed against him, oblivious of everyone. They lost themselves in the enchantment of their first dance together.

The music stopped and Adam smiled down at her. With his arm still around her waist they made their way back to their table. Couples from the nearby tables watched them leave the dance floor. Some called out greetings to Adam as they passed. He nodded coolly to each one who spoke, but declined to stop and they proceeded on to the alcove and their table.

He had seated Molly and was about to seat himself when a voice from behind him spoke his name. Molly looked up to see a girl so incredibly beautiful that she blinked. She was as dark haired as Adam, but her skin was a soft matte whiteness. Bright red lipstick covered her pouting lips and her voluptuously rounded figure was dressed to perfection in a revealing black gown that showed a large expanse of her body.

"Hello, Wanita," Adam said, nodding to her escort

who stood several paces behind her. The girl moved up close to Adam and linked her arm with his.

Molly looked from the girl to Adam. He was wearing his reticent expression, and his lips had a sardonic twist.

"I've missed you, Adam." The voice was soft, seductive.

"I find that hard to believe, Wanita," Adam said sarcastically, disengaging his arm from her hold. "If you'll excuse me, my wife and I are enjoying a twosome this evening."

Wanita stared at him, not bothering to hide her anger. As the silence lengthened she swung her large blue eyes around at Molly and her lips curled. She looked back at Adam, venom in her eyes.

"You married *her*?" There was no mistaking the sardonic emphasis she put on her words. Molly cringed. Adam didn't even bother to answer and the angry eyes swung back to Molly.

"Get you pregnant, did he?" she sneered. "An old pro like you should never have let that happen, Adam." Her fiery gaze turned on him.

"Good-bye, Wanita." Adam pulled out his chair and sat down. Neither said anything for a while after the girl left. Molly's arm was resting on the table and Adam laid his hand on it as they sat in silence.

"I'm sorry, Molly," he said finally.

She tried to smile naturally, but the smile never reached her eyes as she thought of Wanita's cruel insinuation. She found herself replying, saying it didn't matter in the least, trying to hide her pain. His hand on her arm moved back and forth in a caressing motion. He looked at her smiling lips and pleading eyes and his grin came back. His hand slid down her arm and his fingers interlaced with hers.

"Molly mine, you're precious! Shall we go back to the apartment and have a private party all our own?"

She nodded eagerly, trying to quell the deep sorrow welling inside her. "I might even get tipsy!" she said brightly. He chuckled at the thought.

When they left the dining room, his arm was around her.

The gay mood stayed with them all the way back to the apartment. While she was hanging up her coat Adam brought out a bottle of champagne and encased it in a bucket of ice. He was selecting records for the stereo when she came back into the room. He looked up, saw her, and held out his hand. She went to him. He was in a strange mood tonight. He seemed to want to touch her, and she wanted him to.

She was feeling relaxed and a lot happier now. The soft glow of the lamps and the sensuous music added to the feeling of time suspended. Adam's dark eyes had developed a mild look of teasing and at the same time she was sure he felt desire for her. She was grateful he found her desirable enough to want to make love to her. *This was enough for now,* she thought. If the fates were kind, maybe love would come later.

"May I have this dance?" he asked formally, taking the glass from her hand. They had toasted each other with two glasses of champagne and it had begun to lend its own particular magic to the evening.

She went into his arms. "Just this one. I'm booked up for the rest of the evening."

"Lucky man." They were moving slowly. He lifted

first one of her arms and then the other up onto his shoulders. She needed no other encouragement to clasp them around his neck. He wrapped both arms around her and they swayed together.

"I've never danced like this," she murmured, pressing her face to his shoulder.

He moved his hand down to her hips and pulled her even closer. "Well, I should hope not!"

"I think I'm a little bit tipsy, Adam."

"Hmmmm . . . I think so."

"Do you mind?"

"Not as long as you're with me."

"Would you mind if I was a little bit tipsy with someone else?" Her voice was taking on a dreamy quality.

"I would mind like hell if you were with anyone else."

"You would?" she said wonderingly. "Oh!"

"Oh, what?"

"Oh, I didn't know you would care if I got a little bit tipsy with someone else . . . Adam?"

"Hmmm . . ."

"Have you made love to a lot of women?"

"A few."

"Did you love them?"

"No. I made love to them, but I didn't love them."

"That wasn't very nice. I'd never do that."

"Do what?"

"Let men make love to me. I want just one man and I want him to want just me. I want him to love me."

He didn't answer. He encircled her neck with one large hand and tilted her chin up with his thumb. Her eyes were tightly closed, and as he looked at her, two crystal tears squeezed themselves out from under the dark lashes. Her mouth trembled and she tried to bury her face in his shoulder again.

"Darling? Molly," he said huskily, his hand going to the nape of her neck and pressing her head to him.

"I've had a little too much to drink!" Her voice was muffled against him.

He caught her up into his arms, carried her across to the couch, sat down, and cuddled her against him.

"Don't cry, love." His lips tasted the salty tears on her face. He rocked her back and forth and crooned to her. "Darling, don't cry!" He kissed her, not with passionate kisses, but with loving tender ones, from her eyes to her lips to her throat.

"I've had a little too much to drink." She said it again and even to her own intoxicated self it was a lame-sounding excuse. But it was so wonderful being here with him!

They sat silently. He rested his cheek against her forehead and she snuggled her face against his throat. Her arm was around his shoulders and her fingers gently stroked the nape of his neck. The music played on and he caressed her and soothed her, content just to hold her.

Molly stirred and tilted her head back so she could look up. "Adam . . . ?"

"Yes, love?"

"May I kiss you?" she whispered as her hand came around to the side of his face.

"I'd like that, love."

She pulled his face to hers and gently kissed his lips. He kept perfectly still and she kissed his face, the corner of his mouth, his cheeks, his chin, any part of his face she could reach. Then sighing, she turned her face again to his throat. She could feel him trembling now and his heart, against her breast, was beating rapidly.

"Adam, . . . will you ever sleep with me again?" In her intoxicated state the question seemed to be a reasonable one.

"That would be up to you."

"Do you want to?" she persisted.

"You know I do," he whispered huskily.

"Would you tonight, if I asked?"

"No, love, not tonight. The champagne's talking, not you."

"Yes, you're right, Adam." The muffled voice drifted off.

Adam sat for a while longer and held the sleeping girl. He smoothed the hair back from her forehead and removed the diamond earrings. Reaching down, he slipped the silver sandals from her feet. He gazed at her face and his life, up to now, raced before his eyes. *How many women out there were worth the trouble to run after? Wanita was a good example of what there was to choose from,* he thought bitterly. He kissed the parted lips once more, resisting the urge to crush her to him. Slowly and carefully he got to his feet and carried her down the hall to her room.

CHAPTER TWELVE

MOLLY AWAKENED NEXT morning and lay for a moment wondering where she was, surprised by the silence. She turned her head and looked at the clock and remembered.

A flood of memories came rushing in, tumbling over each other. Memories of dancing with Adam, of kidding him and wanting more. *Oh, God!* What had she done and said? Not wanting to dwell on these memories that made her feel guilty for desiring a man who didn't want her, she swung out of bed and stood looking down at herself. She had on a violet chiffon nightie and that was all! She gave a despairing little cry! As the heat of her embarrassment flooded her, she took a deep breath and looked about the room. Her dress of last evening lay over a chair, her undergarments tossed nearby. She faintly remembered asking Adam if she could kiss him. How could she have done such a thing? She would never drink another intoxicating drink as long as she lived, she vowed.

The new clothes were hanging in the wardrobe. The housekeeper must have put them away while they were out last evening. She quickly chose a pair of light green wool

pants and fluffy sweater to match and slid into them, surprised at the perfect fit. She brushed her hair and looked
closely at her face in the mirror. Gazing at herself, she
wondered how she could have been so naive to think a man
like Adam could desire that reflection in the mirror. She
sighed deeply and swept her hair back and secured it with
a ribbon, scolding herself silently for indulging in fantasy.

She started for the kitchen, then remembered the diamond earrings. Turning back to the dressing table, she
looked under and around everything on the table. They
were not there. *Oh, God!* Had she lost them? She went to
the living room and searched the floor near where the silver sandals lay. Desperately she went to the kitchen to
find the housekeeper. Ganson was there packing boxes.

"Hello. So you finally got up, did you?"

"Good morning. I'm so worried, Ganson, I can't find
the earrings Mr. Reneau gave me. I've looked everywhere!" Her voice rose in desperation.

At that moment Adam came through the swinging
door. "Looked everywhere for what?"

"I've lost the earrings!" she blurted out.

"You haven't lost them. I have them in my pocket."

Relief flowed through her. She went to him and leaned
her forehead against his chest. "Thank you. I was so afraid."

"I took them off when you went to sleep last night."
The color came into her cheeks as the memory of the pile
of clothes flashed through her mind. "Eat your breakfast.
We'll be leaving soon."

Adam set the plane down on the frozen lake. He had been
silent on the trip back. Molly glanced at him with anxious

eyes hoping to see some sign that he was glad to be back, but his face was expressionless.

The weather was changing; there was tension in the air; heavy clouds formed in the east. The sun was already low by the time the plane was anchored, and a circle of silvery light sprang around it. Within this large loop, four shining circles appeared. In each circle, a small, unreal but gleaming image of the sun shone. Looking up at the five tangent suns gave Molly a weird and alien feeling. The silver circles became hazy, the mock suns flashed evilly, the daylight seemed to flicker, and the vision vanished. The true sun sank into the dark clouds.

"You've seen the sun dogs," Adam said, helping her out of the plane. An icy blast of air hit her and his words were almost lost in the wind. "Ten to one we'll have a blizzard by morning."

Molly knew that to be true. The Indians were afraid of the sun dogs, thinking they were evil stars trying to kill the sun. They would beat pans and raise an awful racket trying to scare them away.

It was almost totally dark by the time they trudged through the snow to the house. Tim-Two had shoveled a path, but it was filling fast with drifting snow. Adam went to the shed for the snowmobile and sled so he could bring the supplies from the plane. Molly wanted to help, but he hustled her into the house and firmly closed the door.

She was glad to be home again. This is where she belonged. She let her hands run lovingly over the fireplace mantel, opened the glass door of the clock, and started winding the spring. The rhythmic ticking of the clock gave her the feeling of continuance and peace. After lighting the lamps she set about the chore of putting her city things away.

It was snowing heavily by the time Adam returned with the last load of supplies. He was tired, cold, and very hungry. Molly handed him a cup of coffee and quietly went about cooking their supper. When it was ready, he came to the table and ate automatically.

Abruptly he said, in a strangely husky voice, "It's going to be a long winter, Molly."

She stiffened at the sound of those familiar words, dropped her eyes, and stared at her plate attempting to hide her feeling of depression.

"Yes," she said slowly, and pushed herself away from the table to walk to the fireplace, her hands clasped fearfully in front of her.

Adam finished his supper and carried the dishes to the sink, then filled his cup with coffee and sat down in the big chair, studying her rigid back. When he spoke again, it was in a more normal tone.

"You can't stand up all winter, Molly, so sit down and relax."

Her shoulders drooped suddenly as she acknowledged the truth of his words. She relaxed even more and turned to him.

"If I did anything to offend you last evening, I'm sorry." Her voice was defensive. "Not being used to drinking much, I—"

"You did nothing to be embarrassed about, Molly." After hesitating a moment he added, "Do you have regrets?"

The evening was not as companionable as other evenings had been. Adam sat quietly in his chair. Molly rocked in hers and listened to the howl of the wind around the cabin.

Adam interrupted the silence by saying, "I better get to bed, there'll be a lot of snow to shovel in the morning."

Molly nodded, and got to her feet. "Good night."

"Good night, Molly."

Adam went out after breakfast the next morning to check on the ski plane. The wind had subsided some, but the snow was still falling. The atmosphere inside the cabin was easier this morning, and Molly went about her duties with an air of acceptance. She chided herself time and again for her illusive dreams. Although his dark eyes had followed her as she prepared breakfast, she sensed a tightness in him that had not been there before.

She was washing dishes when Adam came dashing through the kitchen door.

"I need the gun, Molly!" He snatched it from the wall over the fireplace. Checking its load, he made again for the door.

Molly ran after him. "What is it? What's the matter?"

"Wolverine. He's been in Tim-Two's traps and we can smell him near the shed." Molly lingered beside the door. Adam stopped in front of her. "I want you to shut this door and stay inside. Do you understand?"

She nodded, shut the door, and went to the window. Dog was running about, barking excitedly. *Dear God, don't let Adam be hurt. Please, please, please!* "I love him." She said the words aloud, unaware of doing so. Without a thought of Adam's orders she slipped into her parka, stepped into her snow boots, and went out the door.

Taking big frosty breaths of the chilling air, she knew

the foul-smelling beast was close by as soon as she stepped out the door. Rounding the corner of the house, she could see Dog holding the small wolverine at bay between the shed and the board fence. She heard the savage growling as the snarling beast lunged at Dog. Molly knew Dog didn't have a chance and screamed at him. He backed off as the undaunted wolverine charged him. Adam dropped to one knee in the snow, aimed the gun, and squeezed the trigger.

The shot hit the wolverine dead center and he dropped into a convulsing heap. Dog charged in, but was reluctant to touch the foul-smelling body. Molly called him and he obediently came to her.

Adam rose and swung around to face her. "I told you to stay in the cabin!" he shouted harshly.

"I know you did, but I was worried for Dog . . . and you." Her voice quavered in her relief that he was safe.

"You risked your life!" He yelled at her in his anger.

"I didn't think I was risking my life," she said in a way of defense.

"The odds were not in your favor with the wolverine. If he'd got past me, he would have been at your throat in a second." He was so angry now his face had turned red.

Her lips quivered as she realized the danger to Adam as well as to herself. If he had been distracted for even one second by her appearance . . . she shivered and dropped her eyes, abandoning her defense.

"Get inside!" he commanded.

She hurried into the cabin, shut the door, and leaned against it, weak at the thought of what she had done. She could hear Adam and Tim-Two discussing the wolverine.

"By damn, by damn!" Tim-Two was saying. "What a devil! Him would come right to the cabin, no?"

Adam stayed away from the cabin most of the day. He and Tim-Two tried to rid the place of the smell of the beast. He helped the Indian disinfect his traps; otherwise he would have no winter catch. All animals shy away from the smell of the wolverine. Molly suspected he was staying away so his temper would cool before confronting her again.

Darkness set in before he returned. The cabin was filled with the tantalizing odor of cooking meat and vegetables. He sniffed approvingly.

"Something smells good," he said.

She gave a pleased little smile, but avoided meeting his eyes. She knew that he knew his favorite dish was a peace offering.

She served him the stew and hot biscuits. After being out in the cold most of the day he was hungry and had several helpings. His mood had softened, but she kept her eyes down, not wanting to give him an opening to speak about what had happened. Adam realized this and kept silent.

He was restless and wandered around the room while she was at the sink. She was frantically trying to plan something to do when she finished the dishes. It would be unbearable to sit across from him tonight if they didn't talk. She finished and was hanging away the towel when he came up close behind her. He put his hands on her forearms and pulled her back against him. She could feel the thud of his heart—or was it her heart—she couldn't tell which. Leaning his head down, he nuzzled her ear.

"You do understand why I was so angry?" She nodded. "I was terrified at what could have happened to you!"

She didn't say anything. She wanted to say she was sorry, but she couldn't get the words out.

Still holding her, he let his mouth rest on the side of her neck. "You'll not disobey me again, when I tell you to do something for your own good?"

"No. And I'm sorry," she whispered, her voice breaking.

He let out a long breath and squeezed her arms tightly. "Let's put on some music and sit by the fire, okay?" He took her hand and led her into the living area.

Molly sat in her rocker and watched him while he loaded the stereo with the music he had selected. She filled her eyes with him, the broad shoulders, the narrow waist, the lean hips. *I'll always love him,* she thought. *How could I possibly love another man after knowing him?* She picked up her knitting, so she would have something to do with her hands and have an excuse for not looking at him.

He came to his big chair, sat down, and stretched out his long legs. He was so still Molly thought he had fallen asleep, so she dared a look at him. His black eyes were openly staring at her. She held his gaze for a moment, then dropped her eyes, the color coming up into her cheeks. She saw the long legs draw up out of her line of vision. He got up and came toward her, took the knitting out of her hands, and put it on the floor by her chair. Taking her hand in his, he drew her to her feet, and drawing her along with him went back to his chair and sat down.

He tugged at her hand, but she resisted him. He tugged harder and pulled her down onto his lap.

He settled himself comfortably after swinging her legs across the arm of the chair and pressing her head down on his shoulder. Molly attempted to raise her head and look at him, but he pressed her head firmly down again.

"Be still," he said, "I just want to hold you."

They listened to the music, much the same as they did the night in Adam's apartment. Molly snuggled closer in his arms and gave herself up to the joy of being close to him. He was in a strangely quiet mood. He stroked her hair and ran his fingers down the smooth flesh of her arm. She timidly lifted her fingers to his neck, then to his ear, coming to his cheek to find his mouth and trace it lightly. She felt his lips open and nibble at her fingers. She smiled a secret smile against his throat. She loved him, she wanted him, and he wasn't indifferent to her. The knowledge gave her the courage to allow her fingers to stray to the buttons on his shirt and slip her hand inside the opening to touch his skin. The hair on his chest was slightly rough against her fingers and she felt a shudder go through him as she gently tugged at it.

His lips descended to hers where they teased lightly, sending curious sensations along Molly's spine, and coherent thought slid into oblivion. She gave a convulsive shudder and put her arms about his neck signaling her complete submission with parted lips. His mouth crushed down on hers, demanding, hurting, and pleasing her. She felt the warmth of his body and the beat of his heart beneath her palms. He forced back her head and deepened the kiss to hot, insistent possession. She made no move to stop him when he unbuttoned her blouse, and his fingers teased the stiff nipples, caressing them so that they hardened even more. Every part of her body ached with the need of him. The little sounds she made seemed to arouse him more and he trembled violently and slid his lips from her mouth to her cheek, then down to her neck.

"Darling . . ." His voice was husky and almost inaudible. He buried his face in her neck. She could feel his lips and tongue. Her body was on fire for him and she felt as if she were suspended in outer space.

Adam lifted his head and his half-closed eyes flashed over her face. His was strangely pale.

"I thought I could hold you and not make love to you, but I can't," he said hoarsely. He lifted her from his lap and got to his feet. "Go to bed, Molly."

She looked at him dazedly, her trembling fingers working at the buttons on her blouse. With bowed head and on shaking legs, she went to her room. She was on the point of tears, tired and drained.

Molly stood in the darkened room for a few minutes before turning up the light and making ready for bed. There was an ache in the pit of her stomach. In her innocence she didn't realize aroused desire was a tortuous thing. It was twisting inside her now like a small trapped animal, clawing for its freedom. Automatically she put several pieces of hardwood in the round stove and went into the bathroom where she brushed her teeth and washed her face. The cool cloth felt good on her burning skin. When leaving, she did as she did every night, opened the door to Adam's room, and closed the door to her own. She slipped on her nightgown. Sitting on the side of her bed, she brushed her hair and words that had been etched into her subconscious filled her thoughts. Someday, Charlie had told her, a man will come into your life who will fill it with his presence. He will love and cherish you and give you children. When that time comes, it will be the beginning of an extension of yourself. Molly sat very still. The tension left her. She had reached a decision. After turning out the light, she opened the kitchen door and slipped into bed.

The wind had gone down and the reflection of the white snow coming in the windows gave the room a soft glow. There were stirrings now in the other room. Adam had put the big log on the fire, checked the doors, and let Dog out into the cold night. She heard him moving about in his room and then he came through the bathroom and closed the connecting door. She lay tense and waiting.

The moment came! He opened the door to her room so the heat could circulate.

"Adam . . . ?"

"You called me?" He came into the room, his flashlight beaming a path on the floor.

"Yes." She was trembling with unbelievable tension.

He sat on the edge of the bed. "Something wrong, Molly?"

"Adam . . ." she started again bravely. "I've been thinking about what you said. Although we both know this marriage isn't permanent, it's a marriage. There's no reason why it shouldn't be a real one. I'm—I'm willing to be a wife to you, if you want me." Her voice vibrated with emotion. He turned out the light. "I'll not hold onto you . . . you'll always be free to go." All her barriers were down; her pride was gone.

He saw that she was both desperate and uncertain, and also near tears.

"Are you sure?" he asked hoarsely.

She answered with only the slightest hesitation. "Yes, I'm sure."

Adam stood, took off his robe, and raised the blankets to slip in beside her. He could see the gleaming whiteness of her shoulders and breasts. He put his arms around her and held her tightly to him, one hand moving down her back, fingers lightly caressing. She went to him willingly and snuggled against him. She was trembling with relief and unbelievable happiness. She heard him catch his breath sharply as her bare breasts came in contact with his chest. Her arms went around him and she nibbled at his neck with her teeth, uncertain of what was expected of her.

"I don't know what to do," she said in shaking tones.

"What do you want to do, love?" His lips were against her forehead.

"I want to kiss you!"

"Well . . ." he said laughing softly, happily.

"Adam . . . Adam."

She whispered the words against his mouth. He caressed her with his lips, soothing her body with his hands. A wild, sweet enchantment rippled through her veins as his mouth moved over her cheek, down her throat, and onto her breast. The knowledge that he was not trying to rush her, holding his own passion in check, filled her heart with love for him.

"Molly, sweetheart . . . !" he murmured in her ear.

When it was over, she was filled with indescribable joy and contentment. He stroked her hair and kissed her. With all the honesty of her young heart she reached up to whisper against his cheek: "I love you. Have I made you happy?"

His mouth moved in search of her own. "Very happy!"

She cradled his dark head against her breasts, enjoying this new and wondrous sensation. She felt him in every pore of her body and in every beat of her heart. She was silent for a long while, then whispered in a voice filled with awe.

"I could never imagine how it would be. I'm glad it was you who showed me."

He propped himself up on one elbow. The pale oval of her face was framed in the golden hair strewn across the pillow.

"There is more, sweetheart, and for you it will only get better."

The words were said against her mouth as the warm urgency of his lips claimed hers, and he took her again to that heavenly oblivion where she was aware of only his warm body and urgent demands.

"Go to sleep now." His voice broke into her drowsy conscience. He kissed her shoulder and neck and heard her sigh of contentment. He ran his hand lovingly down the full length of her body and she took it in hers and held it tightly to her breast.

Molly awoke first and lay on her side watching him sleep. The strong, finely chiseled lines and contours of his face were relaxed. His mouth was firm and beautifully molded. How gentle he had been with her! She had never thought that the consummation of marriage could be such a glorious thing. She had been carried away on a passionate tide of love for him, out of her depth and into a new and completely uncharted sea that contained only Adam and the overpowering love she had for him.

Not once, but many times during the night she had confessed her love for him. He seemed to like hearing her say it. He called her "love," but never one time said he loved her. Not even when he reached out for her the second time, then a third, and made ardent love to her all over again.

The desire to touch him was irresistible to her now, and she pushed her fingers gently through his hair. So thick and soft it was! He stirred and she withdrew her hand and hid it beneath the covers, but it was caught and held tightly. Black eyes, just inches away from her own, were open and laughing into hers.

"What were you thinking, while you were looking at me?"

"You were awake?"

"I was watching you even before you awakened. What were you thinking?"

"I . . . was thinking that you must be hungry!"

He laughed and pressed his body down on hers. "In the position you're in, you couldn't have been thinking about food!"

She slid her arms around his neck, her hand coming around to stroke his cheek. "Your face is rough," she said with uninhibited frankness.

"It usually is the first thing in the morning. You'll just have to get used to it." He kissed her soundly before burying his face between her shoulder and neck. She jumped as his teeth nipped her. "Get up and fix my breakfast, woman!"

"In my position you want me to think about food?"

"Well . . . on second thought . . ." his words were shut off as his lips found hers.

Everything was bright and beautiful. It had stopped snowing and the world was crisp and white. The trees hung heavy with new snow and Dog scurried around making tracks as he chased the birds foraging for food. Tim-Two was preparing to reset his trap lines and Dog was excited at the prospect of a trip into the woods. Adam brought a fresh supply of wood into the house from the woodpile. His feet made snowy tracks on the kitchen floor, and he laughed at the scolding Molly gave him.

She was radiant with happiness, her sparkling eyes seeking Adam's at every opportunity. She was full of contentment, and her voice carried an extra trill when she spoke to Jim on the radio later that morning.

"How about it, Molly girl? How about that, pretty Molly girl? Do you have a copy this morning?" Jim's voice came in loud and clear.

Molly picked up the microphone. "Of course I have a copy! How are you on this lovely day?"

"Lovely day? It must be about thirty below!" He gave a burr sound.

"I'm baking fresh cookies, Big Bird. Do you have time to drop in?"

"No time for a tea party today unless you need me."

"I don't need a thing, Jim," she said gaily. She looked up to see Adam standing in the doorway, and gave him her brightest smile.

"You're sure now?" Jim insisted.

"Things are just fine with us, Jim. Tell Evelyn and the boys hello. Adam and I are sorry you can't stop this trip. Try and make time on your next run."

"Will do. I'm about out of range, so will clear with you until the next time." His voice faded as he flew out of range. Molly didn't answer, she knew her voice wouldn't reach him.

CHAPTER THIRTEEN

THE DAYS THAT followed were wonderful and the nights more so. Molly was walking on a bright cloud of happiness. She wanted to be with Adam every minute of the day; to see him and touch him. He seemed to feel the same. Whenever she was near, his arms reached out for her, and their smiling eyes would catch and hold. Some days didn't have enough hours for them to say all they wanted to say to each other. Other days they were content just to be near and to touch. No words were necessary.

Molly never let her mind wander to the months ahead. She looked back once and thought about her father. She hoped he knew how happy she was and wondered if this was, indeed, his plan for her. They never spoke about the forced marriage, or the separation at the end of the year. In the evenings she would curl up in his lap and they would listen to the radio or just stare into the fire, until their desire for one another became so great, Adam would dump her off his lap and growl: "Get to bed, woman!"

They had been living in their new happiness for a

week when their name was called on the "personal message" program during the noon broadcast.

"Attention, Adam Reneau," the announcer said, "you have visitors coming up on the morning train. Suggest you be at the track eleven A.M."

"That will be Patrick. I didn't expect him for a while yet."

Molly tried not to show her disappointment and dampen Adam's enthusiasm. But somehow she felt the end had come to her dream world. Another person to share her honeymoon? Her year with Adam? A feeling of jealousy toward this unknown Patrick flooded her.

Later that night in bed, after the hunger for each other had been appeased and she lay contentedly in his arms, he asked her if she was sorry that his friend was coming. What could she say? That she was terrified she was going to lose this precious closeness they shared? She couldn't tell him that, so she lied and said she didn't mind at all and his friend was welcome.

Adam took the snowmobile and the sled down to the tracks to meet the train. He and Patrick would ride it back. The sled was for the luggage. Before he left the cabin, he locked Molly in his arms and kissed her soundly. She wrapped her arms about his neck, reluctant to let him go.

He nipped her playfully on the chin. "Just a taste of you to take with me!"

Molly watched until he was beyond the big timber and out of sight. It was the end of her time alone with him. Before depression could set in she started preparations for lunch. Work was the therapy she needed. With lunch started she changed from her jeans and shirt to the light green slacks and sweater Adam had bought for her in Anchorage.

She was busy at the range and flushed from the heat of the oven when she heard voices on the porch. *Damn!* she thought. She had wanted to fix her face and hair before meeting Patrick. But when her startled eyes saw who was coming through the door, all thoughts of her appearance left her mind.

Dressed in a black snowmobile suit, her silver hair glistening as she removed the warm headgear, her blue eyes wide and innocent, her pink mouth twisted in a cheerful smile, was her cousin Donna.

"Molly! I've accepted your invitation. Mama said you wanted me to come out and since Patrick was coming on the train, I decided to come along with him. Won't this be fun? The four of us here together!" The voice coming from the beautifully shaped mouth was so friendly!

The silence that followed beat in Molly's ears while she stared at her cousin as if she had returned from the dead. She tried to ignore her pumping heart and steady her voice.

"Hello, Donna." Behind Donna was a man whose friendly eyes were staring at her. "You're Patrick." Her voice was calm even to her own ears.

"My wife, Molly." Adam came from behind the stranger.

Molly extended her hand and it was enveloped after he hastily removed his mitten. Patrick had a twinkle in his blue eyes, and a deeply tanned face under a thatch of sandy hair bleached by the Australian sun. He was not as tall or as heavy as Adam. Molly knew she would like him.

"I'm glad to meet you, Patrick." She wanted to smile at Adam's friend, but was afraid her face would crack with the effort. Desperately trying to stay calm, she said to Adam, "Did you have room for the luggage?"

His expression was unreadable. "Yes. Pat had to ride the sled, but we made it. I'll bring it in."

"I'll help." Patrick went out the door behind him.

Molly's fingers curled into her palms and she turned to face Donna. There was a moment of fierce glaring between them.

"Why have you come?" she asked bluntly.

Donna unzipped her suit. The snow from her boots was melting and making puddles on the floor.

"I think you know." All the sweetness was gone from her voice.

"I didn't invite you. I don't want you here."

"I know you don't, but Adam does."

"I don't believe it."

Donna looked disinterested. "Ask him. Ask him when I was in his apartment last."

"I don't believe it!" Molly repeated, her cheeks scarlet.

Donna smiled cruelly. "Poor little Molly!" she mocked. "Don't tell me you've fallen for him!"

"I think you're here to cause trouble!" Molly was shaking now.

"What you think doesn't interest me in the least, Cousin Molly," Donna snapped, then quickly turned to smile as Patrick came in the door carrying a large piece of luggage. Adam came in behind him carrying a heavier load.

Molly's burning cheeks welcomed the icy blast from

the open door. Adam looked at her with a slightly puzzled expression on his face, but before he could speak, Donna came quickly forward and grasped his arm.

"Put my things in Molly's room, Adam. She says she has oodles of closet space." Her voice carried the purring tone again and her big blue eyes gazed up at him adoringly.

Adam hesitated only a moment before taking the cases to Molly's room.

Molly stood, uncertain and confused, then went into the kitchen on the pretext of checking the bread baking in the oven. Her mind was whirling. How dare Donna say she had been invited to come here! She had never invited any of Aunt Dora's family to come visit, much less Donna, whose contempt for her was most obvious of all. She doubted she had exchanged a dozen words with her cousin in the last five years. Donna wanted Adam. She had made that plain enough. A cold, icy dread started forming around Molly's heart as she remembered the lipstick she found in the bedroom of his apartment. *Had he been meeting Donna while on his trips to the city? Had he asked her to come here?*

Donna was entertaining the men with a story about mutual acquaintances in the city. She was cheerful and witty, and Adam seemed to be enjoying her company. She had slipped off the bulky snowmobile suit, looking slim and beautiful leaning against the mantel, her tight-fitting coral knit slacks and sweater a perfect foil for her figure and silver hair.

Molly grabbed up a cloth and went to wipe up the puddle of water made by Donna's boots.

"Here, let me do that." Adam tried to take the cloth from her hand.

"I'll do it." Her voice was tighter than she intended, and she kept the cloth in her hand, refusing to relinquish it. Almost glaring at him, she added, "Lunch is almost ready."

He frowned, then shrugged his shoulders and joined the others. *He didn't even kiss me when he came in*, Molly thought angrily.

She poured the coffee for lunch and reluctantly admitted her cousin had an unfailing gift for monopolizing male attention. Her husky overtones, her tinkling laughter, the men's lower voices, all joined together. Molly was silent during the meal, speaking only when necessary.

"Your wife's a good cook, Adam. Pretty and a good cook. You can't beat that combination." Patrick was a diplomat, Molly decided.

"She is pretty, isn't she?" Adam's face creased with a smile. He tried to hold her eyes with his, but Molly looked away.

"Molly is a good cook," Donna chimed in. "She used to live with us, you know. Mama always said if Molly opened a restaurant in Anchorage, she would make a mint!"

"It would be a terrible waste to hide all that beauty in the kitchen." Patrick's voice had a slightly critical tone.

"I didn't mean to hide her. You know that, Pat, darling. I just meant she is such a good cook it's a shame to waste all that talent."

Molly got up from the table to serve the dessert and thought her churning stomach was going to betray her, but her self-discipline and pride came to her rescue.

Seating herself again, she looked directly at Patrick. "Tell us about your trip to Australia." Her voice didn't betray her, thank God, and she had, at least, got the attention away from Donna.

The remainder of the dinner conversation was lost to Molly as her mind turned over the possibility that Adam hadn't wanted to be alone with her. That thought was only a step away from the speculation that Donna was the woman he loved and he would not have insisted on consummating their marriage without her invitation.

If the two large cases Donna had brought with her were any indication, she had come prepared for a long stay. Her clothes took up more than half of Molly's wardrobe. The perfumes and cosmetics that she used to retain her clear, soft skin dominated Molly's dressing table. Her belongings were strewn around the room which had literally taken on her personality.

In the afternoon she changed from slacks to a long, plaid wool skirt which she paired with a long-sleeved, high-necked sweater. Looking elegant and sensual, she curled herself up in the big chair with a magazine and Adam's transistor radio after the men went to Adam's room to look over his work.

Molly stayed in the kitchen. She wanted to stay as far away from her cousin as possible. She cleaned shelves and rearranged the supply cabinet. The work absorbed a couple of hours and her jumbled thoughts were no closer together when she stopped than when she started.

Donna sauntered in to lean against the counter and

watch her. Molly knew she had something to say and braced for the ridicule that was sure to come.

"Adam said he would do anything to get his hands on Uncle Charlie's files." Molly glanced at her cousin and saw malice in her eyes. "Guess Uncle Charlie thought that would be the only way he could get a husband for you."

"What do you mean?" Molly's hands stopped their movement. Her cousin's blue eyes stared at her arrogantly, and the corners of her pink lips tilted.

"Adam told all of us, the gang at the club that is, that he would have to marry you, but he said he was going to get more out of it than just the files. We made some bets, and if you know Adam like I do, you know he can't resist a dare. He bet our friends at the club that he would have you in bed in less than a month." She paused, then added a contemptuous little laugh. "He intends to collect six thousand dollars on that bet." Her voice took on a confidential tone. "I wanted to warn you, Molly. I don't like you very much, but after all, you are my cousin. I think it was kind of stinking of Adam. After all, you're not wise in the ways of a man like him."

Molly stared at her disbelievingly. She felt sickened. Humiliation made her stomach heave. She could feel the betraying tears prickling at her eyes and turned away.

"Who told you about the will, Donna?" She used every effort she possessed to keep her voice calm.

"Adam—who else? He said if he didn't marry you, the files would be destroyed, and Mama would have control of your money and have to look after you for five years." Her voice took on a dreamy quality. "He knew I'd wait for him." She looked at Molly's drawn white face and pressed on. "He told me it was only for a year and if I loved him, I should be willing to wait that long."

Molly was shaken to the core. Along with her anguish, she felt a white hot fury. She wanted to strike that mocking mouth, but not even that satisfaction would have wiped out the pain Donna had caused her, or the truth of her statements for that matter. If ever she wished herself dead, it was at this moment.

Satisfied that she had accomplished what she had come here to do, Donna sauntered back to her chair by the fire and picked up her magazine.

Stunned by the obvious truth of her cousin's words, and the betrayal of the man to whom she had given her heart and body, Molly numbly went to the bedroom. After closing the door softly behind her and making sure the connecting bathroom door was firmly closed, she collapsed on the bed. A noise like pounding surf was reverberating through her head. Her limbs shook as if with a fever as reaction set in. Her tortured senses were unable to believe Adam would play such a cruel trick. She choked on a thousand unanswered questions. The humiliation came up in the form of a lump in her throat which she thought she would never be able to swallow. The shame of remembering how she had asked him, had almost begged him to come to bed with her, drew her to her feet, and a wave of weakness set her swaying against the bedpost. She looked at herself in the mirror.

"You fool!" she said aloud. "You dumb, stupid fool!"

She drew on all the courage she had and refused to give in to a storm of weeping. It may have been an inherited pride which decreed that humiliation must be borne with head held high. Whichever it was, her courage or her pride, she looked far from downcast when she opened the door and went out of the room.

Holding herself aloof from all that Donna had said, she spent the next few hours in the kitchen. The first hour or so was taken up with cleaning. She washed the cabinets and counter, scrubbed the wall behind the big range, washed all the globes on the gaslamps, and polished them until they shone. When the kitchen was spotlessly clean, she started baking. She made cookies and cake, the kind Jim liked best, rolled out a half a dozen pie crusts and put them in the freezer, then started a meat pie baking in the range oven. With the kitchen neat once again she put on her parka and went out into the cold, crisp air to bring in more wood for the range. It was totally dark now. The short winter days brought the darkness long before dinner time.

Dog was in the yard and ran to meet her, wagging his tail and making a circle of tracks in the snow. She almost broke her stony composure at his show of affection. Keeping her mind in the safe chamber of suspension, she threw a few sticks for him to chase, patted his head, and returned to the house.

After dumping her armload of wood in the box by the range, she took off her heavy parka and was hanging it on the hook, when Patrick and Adam came into the kitchen. She turned to face them.

"What's the matter?" Adam stopped short. "Aren't you feeling well?"

"I'm all right." Beyond his shoulder she could see Donna approaching and for an instant closed her eyes. Then she turned her head and forced her stiff lips to stretch into a smile. "Why wouldn't I be?"

Adam got out glasses and bottles and mixed drinks. *Entertaining is easy for him,* Molly thought resentfully. Donna kept up a flow of amusing chatter. Molly was able to maintain her composure; the shock of the betrayal had blocked out every emotion and she felt herself in perfect control. She was determined to be the master of her own actions.

Afterward, she didn't know how she got through the rest of the evening. Only her strength of character kept the inner misery from surging up and boiling out of her.

When Adam came to her, she looked at him with vacant eyes.

"Would you like a drink, Molly mine?" he asked softly, intimately.

She shook her head. *Deceit comes to him as naturally as breathing,* she thought. A mask of politeness moved over her face.

"Excuse me. I'll get the dinner on."

For a long while she didn't have to speak or look at any of them. Donna was at the end of the room. The "personal message" program was being broadcast for the second time that day and she was listening and laughing with the two men about the advice given Mrs. Watson regarding her lumbago and the report of the Johnsons' groceries being left at the wrong stop.

"I can't believe it!" she exclaimed. "Imagine, having everyone in the North knowing about your lumbago!"

"That's how Adam knew to meet us at the tracks," Patrick told her. "He heard it on this program."

"Is that true, Adam?" Donna turned the full force of her blue eyes on him. "You knew I'd be there with Patrick?"

"No. They just said visitors were coming."

The murmur of their voices surged over and around Molly, although she was near enough to join in the conversation if she had wished to; but the words they spoke were inaudible to her numbed senses. An air of unreality settled over her. With the perfectly groomed table prepared, and the food on it, she approached the others and told them that dinner was ready.

She served the meal calmly and efficiently, exchanging pleasantries with Patrick, asking him about the food in Australia. Her glance passed indifferently over Adam. He and Donna talked together about some person unknown to her. One time Donna's voice directed a question to her. She looked in her direction, and her face suddenly blurred, so she turned away and ignored her.

Patrick helped with the cleanup. She would never know what they talked about. The time seemed to go terribly fast and they were finished.

"You've worked enough for today, Molly. Come sit by me." Adam beckoned to her.

She shook her head, not bothering to answer. A frown came over his face and he came toward her.

"What's the matter with you? What's wrong?"

"Nothing's wrong, I'm going to bed." She started toward her room. He grabbed her arm and turned her around.

"You're not going to bed!" he grated. "We have guests."

She stood still, looking down at the hand holding her arm. A shudder of repulsion shook her.

"Your guests. Not mine."

"You said you didn't mind Pat coming and Donna is your cousin," he hissed at her.

"I'll prepare their food, but that's all. Let me go!" Her voice was deadly quiet.

He released her arm. "I don't understand you."

"No," she said, "I guess you don't." She left him looking after her with a look of astonishment on his face.

In her room she fumbled in the dark until her fingers felt the familiar lamp and turned it on. Her dazed eyes took in the articles on her table and the clothing strung around the room. She clicked off the lamp, not wanting to see these things, and undressed in the dark. She found her gown under her pillow, slipped into it, and crawled into bed. Her body was weary and her head throbbed. Her troubled mind whirled and she sought the sweet oblivion of sleep. Worn out by the emotional upheaval she had been through she immediately sank into a deep sleep.

She awoke and sat up in bed. The illuminated dial on her watch told her morning was several hours away. The events of the day before were clear in her mind. Knowing who was sleeping beside her, and not wanting to look at her, she kept her eyes averted and slipped out from under the covers. The air in the dark room was icy cold. Hastily she reached for her flashlight, then donned jeans and a flannel shirt. She brushed her hair back, secured it with a rubber band, and left the room. The fire had burned down in the cooking range and the big log in the fireplace was almost used up. She shivered as she tugged the fire screen aside to poke at the coals on the grate. After selecting several small logs from the woodbox she carefully piled them on the burning coals and replaced the screen.

The house was unnaturally quiet. She cocked her head

to one side and listened. Suddenly it occurred to her: the clock on the mantel was still. Aiming the beam of her light on the clock, she found the glass door of the clock case was open and the pendulum had been removed. She replaced the pendulum, wound the clock, and started the pendulum swaying. The familiar ticking was comforting in the quiet room.

She stoked up the fire in the kitchen range and made coffee in the granite pot. Cupping her cold hands around the steaming cup, she sat in the chair close to the fire and leaned forward to soak in the heat. The flickering flames cast a cozy glow around the dark room. The clock on the mantel struck five times. It would be a while yet before the unwanted people in her home would be up and around.

She began to tremble and picked up the afghan from the couch and wrapped it around her shoulders. She rocked gently. The firelight threw her shadow on the wall and she watched it, not thinking or feeling, just rocking. The kindling snapped and popped and the flames spread to the larger logs and flared.

She got up, walking carefully, like someone in great pain, and refilled her coffee cup. *They could keep love,* she thought as she sat down again. *It wasn't worth the price.*

She tried to think of her father, tried to remember how happy he had made her when he brought her here to this house, but her thoughts kept straying. With a jerk she would drag them back from the forbidden territory, but back they would go as soon as she relaxed her restraint.

It was very odd to be sitting here, making plans to leave. From the very first moment she had known she would be leaving. Her pride warred endlessly with common sense even as pain stirred in her stomach. It hurt her. *Oh, God, how it hurt!* She would have done anything in the world for him . . . anything. It didn't seem that all this had really happened to her. How could her father have made such a ghastly mistake in judging a man's character? He would understand that she was doing what she had to do. She would go to Herb Belsile and tell him she couldn't accept the terms of the will. Tim-Two would look after the house until she could return.

She leaned forward and looked out the window. The light was definite now and the old Indian was coming toward the house. He made no sign that he was surprised to see her up, but stoically went about his chores of refueling the range and the fireplace. She poured him a cup of coffee. He sat at the trestle table. When he was finished, he nodded and went out.

At the first stirrings from the bedroom Molly rose and started breakfast; first setting the table and then slicing the bacon. She was deep in thought when a hand descended on her shoulder and swung her around. Adam stood there.

His eyes searched her face and his black brows drew together, but his expression held no terror for her. Suddenly his face changed and his eyes smiled into hers.

"Did you miss me last night as much as I missed you?"

She raised one hand, then let it fall despairingly. She shrugged her shoulders and looked at him with dull eyes.

He seemed startled as though he had expected her to say or do something.

"Molly?" The silence lengthened after his voice died away. He made a grimace of displeasure.

She shrugged her shoulders again wearily and attempted to turn away. He yanked her arm and pulled her up close against him. She stood passive in his embrace. A wave of anger hit him and his mouth came down hard on hers, parting her lips and forcing her head back. His hands roamed over her, cupping her hips and holding them tightly against him. She made no protest and no response. When he lifted his head to look at her, she unhurriedly pushed herself away from him, and at that moment Patrick came into the room.

"Morning, Molly. Sleep the headache away?"

She nodded and gave him a half smile. "How many eggs, Patrick?" she asked quietly.

"However many you fix old Adam. I'm not as big as he is, but I eat as much." If he noticed any tension between them, he was ignoring it.

Adam sat at the table and Molly poured coffee. Patrick kept up a constant chain of chatter for a while, then fell silent because he wasn't getting much response from either of them. After serving the breakfast, Molly sat in her chair by the hearth and picked up her knitting.

Unconsciously she started to knit, then it dawned on her . . . she was knitting the sweater for Adam. Slowly she removed the needles and placed them on the table beside the chair and started unraveling the almost finished garment, rolling the yarn into a ball. She rocked as she pulled the soft wool, her fingers carefully winding the yarn. Adam came and stood over her, watching, then turned on his heel and went into his room.

Patrick brought his coffee cup and sat in the chair opposite her. She glanced at him and went on with her work. The thought drifted across her mind that this friend of

Adam's was nice and she could like him if things had been different. *I'll never get the chance to know him now, and he'll despise me when he can no longer use the files.*

Donna came out of Molly's room. She was wearing a white woolly robe and big fluffy lamb's wool slippers. Her silver hair was brushed back and held with a blue ribbon. She was plainly in a bad mood.

"I've never been so cold in all my life," she said crossly, coming to stand close to the fire. "Well . . . do you serve coffee or not?" Her question was directed to Molly.

She sat as if she hadn't heard.

"I'll get it, and don't be such a grouch, Donna." Patrick got up.

As he was speaking, the clock on the mantel started striking the hour. Donna turned, her face a mask of fury.

"I hate striking clocks," she grated. "I stopped that damn thing last night and I meant for it to stay stopped!" She yanked open the glass door of the clock case, jerked off the swaying pendulum, and threw it into the blazing fire.

Molly let out a cry and rushed to get the iron poker. Frantically she raked the burning coals until she had pulled the small disc and stem out of the flames. She raked it out onto the stone hearth and looked at it, her head bent.

"That was a rotten thing to do, Donna!" Patrick was angry and it showed in his voice.

"I hate clocks and she knows it. She just started it again to spite me," she said hatefully, not one bit put off by Patrick's anger.

"That's no excuse! You're a guest here."

"Guest? Adam's guest, not hers. She'd poison me if she could!"

Patrick knelt down beside Molly. "I don't know as I would blame her," he muttered. He took the poker from Molly's hand, returned it to the rack, and picked up the piece of metal, shifting it from one hand to the other as it cooled. "It isn't damaged, Molly," he said reassuringly.

Her face was white and the violet eyes, surrounded with dark circles, were bright with tears. She took the disc from him and put it in her pocket.

"Thank you," she whispered, and sat back down in the rocker.

"I don't know how Adam can stand this godforsaken place!" Donna hugged herself with her arms. "That bathroom is positively primitive."

Patrick stood looking from one to the other; Molly rocking and winding the yarn, Donna prancing around the room in a temper. He had seen Molly smile only once or twice since they had been here and the relationship between her and Adam certainly wasn't as he had been led to believe it was. As for Donna, he had seen dozens like that bitch and would never have brought her, but for her being Molly's cousin. After seeing the difference between the two of them, it seemed strange Molly would invite her. Suddenly it hit him! *How stupid can I be? The blond bombshell is still after Adam and she thinks the country cousin is no competition! But if I'm any judge of old Adam . . .*

"I suggest you get your own coffee and sit down, Donna," he said coolly.

"You don't have to be so nasty about it, Patrick. You may be used to living like a peasant, but I'm not!" She flounced into the kitchen and looked disgustedly at the big granite coffeepot.

Patrick stood uncertainly. He didn't want to leave Molly at the mercy of this cat. He wasn't sure, but something was very wrong here. Molly seemed to be in a sort of daze. She couldn't be like this all the time—an emotionless shell of a girl! She wasn't at all the picture he got from Robert and Aunt Flo. He wondered if he should talk to Adam about it.

Tim-Two came in the back door. Donna gave a shudder of revulsion when she saw him. He looked about the room, then walked to Adam's door, opened it and went in, closing it behind him.

Molly could hear the murmur of voices, then what appeared to be a curse word in Adam's voice. Tim-Two came out of the room and toward Molly, stopped in front of her, and said one word.

"Dog."

Molly understood the urgency in the one word. Alarm filled her and she got to her feet.

"What's the matter with Dog?" she asked shrilly.

Adam came out of the bedroom putting on his parka. He went to the gun rack, lifted out the rifle, and checked the load. Biting her lip to keep back hysteria, Molly ran after Tim-Two, grabbing her coat from the peg as she fled out the kitchen door.

Adam was shouting at her. "Stay in the house, Molly!"

Paying him no mind, she ran on and caught up with Tim-Two as he rounded the shed. She took one swift look and her steps faltered. Dog was lying in the snow behind the shed. She ran to him and dropped to her knees beside him. The impact of what had happened began to hammer in her brain. The snow was red with Dog's blood. His eyes were rolled back in his head and he was gasping for breath.

"Dog! Dog!" Dimly Molly heard her own anguished voice.

At the sound of her voice Dog tried to lift his head and focus his eyes, but the effort was too much for him and his big head sank down on the snow.

"Don't die. Please don't die!" Dog opened his eyes and tried to see the owner of the dear and familiar voice.

"Don't die, Dog," she pleaded. "I'll have no one!" Hiding her face in the soft fur of his neck, she talked to him beseechingly.

"Molly!" Hands were lifting her up. "You'll always have someone. You'll have me." There was an agonizing note in Adam's voice.

A great roaring noise was in her ears; she swayed and would have collapsed if the hands had not held her. About to cross the thin line into hysteria, she turned on him and jerked herself away.

"Get away from me," she gasped, and then, with rising hysteria, "Oh, God! You're going to kill him!"

"I've got to, Molly, can't you see that?" His hands were reaching for her, trying to hold her.

A thin, shrill scream tore itself from her throat. She brought her hand up and tried to claw him. His hands held her arms pinioned to her sides.

"You've taken everything," she screamed at him. "Still you're not satisfied! You'd kill my dog! My dog, the only thing left in the world that I love and the only thing that loves me!"

Adam knew he couldn't reach her and reason with her

through her hysteria. He stood helplessly for a moment and looked at her. Her face was deathly white and the dark-rimmed eyes were bright and darted wildly about. He shoved her toward Patrick who had come up beside him.

"Get her in the house and keep her there," he said harshly.

She burst into tearing, retching sobs and flung herself into Patrick's arms. He scooped her up and carried her to the house. It seemed as if the dam had finally burst. The emotional stress of the last day and night was finding release in the rush of tears that spilled out of her eyes and flooded down over her cheeks.

He had just sat her down in the house and closed the door when the sound of the rifle shot reached them. Molly clutched him and he held her tightly until the hard sobs ceased shaking her.

"Molly," he whispered in her ear. "Adam did the only humane thing to do. He put the poor beast out of his misery. He'd been in a fight with a bear, or maybe a wolf, and only managed to drag himself home. He would have been dead before night. You wouldn't want him to lie there all day and suffer." He tried to look into her face. "Surely you understand."

"Well, I'll say one thing for her," Donna's grating voice broke the silence of the room. "She sure knows how to play up a good scene. Good riddance, if you ask me. That dog smelled like a pigsty!"

"Shut up, Donna!" Patrick's patience with Donna was almost at an end.

Quiet now, Molly wanted desperately to be alone. She

lifted her head and wiped her eyes with the back of her hand.

"Thank you, Patrick." Her voice barely reached him.

She left him and walked slowly to the door of her room. She closed it behind her and leaned her weight against it as though to keep all of them out. Her disjointed thoughts whirled around in her brain. She must leave! She must get away from these people. A sudden sense of purpose sent her limbs into action, but how could she go and where could she go? She looked at her watch—if she were to leave at once . . . but . . . supposing he saw her and tried to stop her? Supposing he . . .

Adam had come into the house. She could hear his voice and the soft purring voice of her cousin. She never wanted to see either of them again as long as she lived! It had been a cruel, bitter lesson she had learned. She would never, no never, love anything again, she vowed. She had loved her mother, she had loved her father, she had loved this house, and she had loved Dog. She had loved . . . him. They all had been taken away from her!

When Adam and Patrick were settled into their work in the study, she would leave the house. It shouldn't be too difficult to slip out the kitchen door and walk away toward the rail lines. If she could make it to the tracks by the time the train for Anchorage passed, she would be on her way to Herb Belsile. Now that her mind was made up, there were things to be done. She changed from her jeans to heavy wool slacks and pulled on a sweater over her shirt. She lay out her fur mittens and thermal socks. She put what cash money she had and her checkbook in the pocket of her snowmobile suit and zipped it shut. She wished she dared take the snowmobile, but the noise when she started it would alert Adam.

Molly looked about the room she had always kept so tidy, and made a grimace at the disorder. Her cousin's belongings were everywhere. Suddenly the entire weight of her wretchedness hit her and she could hardly wait to leave this room, this house, where she had been so happy and where she had felt the blackest despair.

She heard Adam and Patrick go to her father's room, then the familiar sounds as they began their work. Hurriedly she dressed in the warm clothing she had selected and put on her snow boots. With wool stocking cap and mittens in hand, she went to the door and listened for sounds of her cousin moving about in the kitchen. She could hear music. She hoped Donna was curled up in the chair with the transistor radio. Cautiously she opened the door. With relief she saw Donna sitting in the chair with her back to the kitchen.

Molly walked softly to the back door and let herself out into the cold winter day.

CHAPTER FOURTEEN

WALKING STRAIGHT INTO the woods from the back door Molly circled the house, and headed in the general direction of the railroad tracks. She figured she had an hour and a half to walk the two miles. There was plenty of time to reach the tracks before the train came through. She hadn't gone far, however, until she wished she had brought her snowshoes, but they had been on the porch and she hadn't wanted to take the risk of being seen to get them. She walked as fast as she could in the deep snow, trying to pick the places where the snow was hard enough to hold her light weight.

She passed the clearing where the helicopter landed and noticed the first small intermittent snowflakes. She looked around with worried eyes and tried to walk faster. Within fifteen minutes flakes were falling—huge, fluffy, and thick. Several times she blundered into deep drifts and floundering through them came near to exhausting herself. She dared not stop to rest and consoled herself by thinking she would rest when she got to the tracks.

Doggedly she kept going, putting one foot in front of

the other. Every step was taking her farther away from the sneering face of her cousin Donna and the deceitful opportunist she had married. She had been blind, stupid, and gullible to allow him to arouse her unmanageable emotions to the point where she had asked him ... she had actually asked him to come to bed with her! She had not thought it possible to experience such humiliation and despair as she had felt when Donna told her he had actually made bets with his friends about getting her to bed! How he would enjoy telling them that she had asked him! She would never forgive him for that or for telling Donna about her father's will.

She looked at her watch and was surprised to see she had been walking for over an hour. She should be coming to the tracks any time now. The new snow was getting deep and it was harder to stay out of the drifts. She was tired and hoped it wouldn't be much farther. She staggered and scrambled out of snowdrift after snowdrift. She had a stabbing pain in her side, but she dared not stop. The time for the train to pass was getting short.

Looking around her, she began to feel a little afraid. She tried to reason out where she was, to recall how far she had to go. A frightening thought came to her. When she had crawled out of one of the drifts, had she veered off in a slanting direction? Could she be lost? She was frightened now, so frightened that for a moment she thought she was going to be sick from the fear that cramped her stomach.

Wanting to look at her watch and yet afraid to, she hurried on. Coming to where a large tree was uprooted and turned on its side, she sat down on the big trunk to get her breath. She knew for sure, now, she was lost. She had been walking for more than two hours. There would not be more than an hour of daylight left. A pain of terror shot through her. She could very well die out here!

Should she try and follow her own tracks back to the house? The new snow had probably filled them by now. Common sense told her she had missed the train and should turn back. Even if she could find her way back . . . to go back in defeat, to have Donna sneer, and . . . him know she was a prisoner in her own home? Again pride warred with common sense, with all her father had taught her about survival in the wilderness. She wouldn't go back! She got to her feet and pressed on, her eyes straining ahead to catch a glimpse of just anything but snow and trees. Thinking of nothing, she put one foot ahead of the other and trudged onward.

It was colder. The snow whipped about her and she thought of calling out. But she didn't call out, the thought went out of her mind as another pushed its way in. Did it matter so much if she did die out here? Would anyone care? Really, who would care besides Jim and Evelyn? Tim-Two would miss her, but he would still stay on in his cabin. It wouldn't change his life. She would never deliberately let it happen she thought, but if it did . . .

Coming to another large overturned tree, she sat down to rest, and let the large trunk shelter her from the wind. She was so tired. She was sure she had never been this tired before. She lifted up one mittened hand and let it fall. All her strength was gone. Her mind wandered to the good things; to her father and to Jim, who loved Evelyn and his boys. It was too late for her to find someone like Jim. She sat there for a long time and let the sweet numbness drift over her.

Did she hear her father calling? He always called her like that.

"Mol . . . ly." He must be coming for her, but she would like to stay here and sleep. It was nice and warm here.

"Mol . . . ly!" He called again. She opened her eyes and saw him coming toward her. She tried to get up, but he was running and she didn't have time to get to her feet.

"Dad! Oh, Dad!"

"Molly, darling! Oh, my love, are you all right?" He grabbed her roughly into his arms and pressed his warm cheek against her cold one. "Oh, Molly," he groaned unsteadily. "Thank God, we found you!"

"Dad . . ." Her voice was barely audible.

Adam's frantic, questioning eyes sought those of the Indian beside him.

"She thinks I'm her father!"

"Mind wanders, when lost," the Indian replied.

"We've got to get her back to the snowmobile." Adam swung her up in his arms and staggered through the snow.

It was completely dark, now, and Adam, carrying his precious load, followed the Indian. The terror that they would find her too late was replaced with a feeling of thankfulness and a promise . . .

In her semiconscious state Molly knew her father was taking her to a warm, safe place and she wanted to talk to him, she had to tell him . . . she had to tell someone!

"I can't go back there. Donna is there . . . and she told me about . . . him."

Adam caught his breath and shifted her in his arms so her lips were closer to his ear.

"You didn't know him like you thought you did, Dad."

Her soft voice quavered and tears squeezed out from under the tightly closed lids. "He made bets with his friends about me! About going . . . going to bed with me . . . and I loved him and asked him . . . to . . ." Her lips trembled and her face contorted into a mask of utter despair.

"Oh, my God!" Adam's eyes misted over and he dropped down on his knees in the snow and rocked her in his arms.

"Darling, darling, don't cry!" Her face against his was cold and wet. He kissed her tears and tried to warm her cold face with his lips. He unzipped the neck of his suit and pressed her face against his neck and looked up at the Indian who had stopped and stood with his back to them.

He got clumsily to his feet with the girl in his arms. Sudden rage at what had been done to her filled and consumed him. He barely felt her weight as he plowed through the snowdrifts to the snowmobile.

The beam from the Indian's light found the machine where they had left it on the high ground when his native instinct had told him she had turned off in the direction where they found her. The Indian got into the back of the machine and held out his arms for the girl. Adam wrapped her securely in a blanket and reluctantly handed her over to him.

The big light on the machine picked out a path through the timber. Adam's temper cooled as the wind hit his face. What a blind, stupid fool he had been not to have seen the change that came over her immediately after her cousin arrived. He'd been so engrossed in discussing the work with Patrick that he hadn't noticed anything was wrong until she announced she was going to bed just after dinner. Was it only last night? It seemed he had lived a lifetime in the few hours he and the Indian had been searching for her.

God, how he had hated to shoot that dog! He could understand now her unreasonable attitude and why she had lashed out at him with such hate and venom. He didn't think he had ever had anything depress him as much as the sight of her kneeling there in the snow begging the dog not to die! At that moment he had made up his mind to get Patrick and Donna back to Anchorage as soon as he could so he could be alone with her again. He had gone to the study to prepare some work for Patrick to take back to the apartment. She was gone when they came out of the bedroom, but thinking she had gone to the cabin to talk to Tim-Two, he hadn't been alarmed. Later, when the Indian came in and said he hadn't seen her, the knot that tied itself up in his stomach at the thought of her being out there alone was still painful to him. Thank God for the Indian and his knowledge of the woods!

They came out of the timber and into the yard. He stopped the machine beside the porch and climbed out.

"Thank you, my friend, thank you," he said as he lifted Molly from Tim-Two's arms. The Indian got out and silently walked toward his cabin.

The door opened and the light from the house splayed out onto the porch. Adam carried Molly into the house and gently lowered her down on the couch.

"You found her." Donna lazily got up from the chair, tossing her magazine aside. "I knew you would. She intended for you to find her."

Adam straightened and his dark eyes found her face. She almost recoiled from the look he gave her.

"Get your things out of my wife's room." His voice was deadly quiet and his lips barely moved as he spoke.

Donna looked dumbfounded.

"Now!" he said. "Pack them up. You're leaving in the morning and you'll sleep in the other room tonight."

"What has she said to you?" Donna stammered. "She's lying if she said anything . . ."

The murderous look he turned on her shut off her words and she closed her mouth.

"When you've packed, go into the other room and close the door. I don't want to see your face again tonight, or I won't be responsible . . ."

A look of pure fright came into Donna's face and she hurriedly left the room.

Adam looked toward the other person standing quietly by.

"If the weather clears, can you fly her out of here in the morning?"

"I sure can, old man. I'll get her out of here if I have to take her out on her broomstick."

"I'll appreciate it. Would you mind taking the snow-mobile to the shed?"

"Not at all." Patrick plucked his coat from the peg on the wall.

Adam knelt and removed Molly's wool cap. He smoothed back the hair from the tear-streaked face. His heart filled with such an overpowering protectiveness that he just sat looking at her for a moment before taking off her snow boots. He held her bare foot in his hand. It was warm to his touch, a good sign. He was thankful for the full-length zipper on her suit that allowed him to lift her out of it easily. She would have died out there if it hadn't been for this warm suit. He wrapped her in the afghan from the back of the couch and covered her with the blanket from the snowmobile.

Patrick came in and stoked up the fire in the range. He put the coffeepot on and got out the makings for sandwiches. Adam sat beside Molly and Patrick grinned to himself. Donna was slamming things around in Molly's room as she packed the expensive wardrobe she had brought to impress Adam. Hearing this, Patrick's grin turned to soft laughter. He wouldn't have missed hearing Adam tell her off for anything! He took a sandwich and a mug of coffee and put them on the table beside Adam.

Adam glanced up as if reluctant to take his eyes from Molly.

"Thanks. Do you think I should wake her? She hasn't had a thing to eat all day."

"I'd let her sleep until you can get her in her own bed."

"I guess you're right." Adam picked up the coffee and sipped it slowly, his clouded black eyes still on his wife's face.

"You've finally got it, haven't you, old man?" Patrick put his hand on Adam's shoulder. Adam didn't answer and he said quite seriously, "I don't blame you, old buddy. I only wish I'd seen her first." Adam looked at him then. He grinned and went back to the kitchen.

Later, when Donna left Molly's room, Adam went there. He turned up the light and went over the room, making sure every sign that her cousin had been there was removed. He remade the bed with clean sheet blankets and rearranged Molly's few simple toilet articles on the dressing table. He took out the warm nightgown he had dressed her in once before and thought about how open and honest she was. How unaffected! *God, how lucky I am, or how lucky I was. Is it too late? Has the feeling she had for me been killed by my stupidity and her cousin's vindictiveness? How many years lay ahead? Years without her! My life was only an empty shell; a man without love, without a meaningful life, until I met her.*

Molly slept for hours. The emotional strain, the long hike in the deep snow, and the fact she had very little food in the last forty-eight hours had taken a toll of her strength. She was exhausted and slept on, unaware of the gaunt-faced man who kept vigil beside her bed.

When she awoke, she lay for a minute with her eyes closed. She was warm and she knew she was in her own bed. Finally she lifted her lids. Her eyes swung around to the man sitting in the chair beside the bed. He sat up and leaned forward when he became aware she was awake.

"Oh no, not . . . you!" she gasped, and turned her head away. Weak tears filled her eyes and ran down her cheeks. Her lips trembled helplessly.

Adam got down onto his knees beside the bed and tried to turn her face toward him.

"Don't turn away from me, darling. I've waited all night for you to wake up." His voice was pleading, but the shame and humiliation she had felt came surging back and she resisted the hand on her cheek. "Darling, she's gone. Donna is gone. Patrick took her back in the plane this morning . . . please, look at me!"

A soft cloth wiped the tears from her eyes and she turned her head and looked into his face. She didn't know what she expected to see, but what she did see was pleading eyes that were slightly bloodshot from lack of sleep and a gaunt, worried face with cheeks that were dark with a day's growth of beard.

"Darling, she's gone," he repeated. "I wanted to tell you the moment you woke up that the things she told you were not true. Please believe me, love! You told me last night what she had said to you, why you took such a risk to get away from me."

Molly's tearful eyes focused on his face. He seemed so sincere, but she wouldn't trust him a second time! He would break her heart again! She closed her eyes tightly to shut out the picture of his face so close to hers. She felt him draw her close and she was too weak to resist. He buried his face in the curve of her neck and his whispered words went on.

"Let me talk to you, Molly. Don't shut me out." His voice was emotional, not at all like his usual voice. "Once, years ago, when I was young and thought of myself as something special, I made bets with some of the other fellows at the club. But not for years, and certainly not about you! I've never mentioned you to anyone at the club. I'll swear to it! You can't believe I would do something like that, Molly. Look at me and tell me!"

He shook her gently and she opened her eyes. She wanted to believe him. Oh, how she wanted to believe him! Her eyes filled again and her mouth trembled as the doubts came back to her mind.

"You told her about the . . . will. Asked her to . . . wait for you."

"Sweetheart." He kissed the tear wet eyes. "I never told her anything. Her mother was entitled to read the will and probably did. I expected that. I haven't talked to your cousin but one time since I knew about Charlie's will."

"She . . . she was in your apartment." Molly persisted.

"Our apartment," he corrected gently. "Yes, the last time I went to Anchorage she saw me at the airport and she knew I was at the apartment. She came up and inquired about you. She didn't stay five minutes. I went up to see Dad and she asked to freshen up before she left because she had an important date. Ganson was with us the whole time, love."

Molly's mind was still troubled. He had explained everything so beautifully, yet he hadn't said the words she so much wanted to hear. He read the doubt still in her eyes and put his arms under and around her and hugged her desperately to him.

"Sweetheart." His voice was ragged in her ear. "I don't know what I'll do if you don't believe me! Remember our first night together? I was coming to you that night when you called out to me. That was the happiest night of my life, darling. You told me over and over that you loved me. Have I lost you, Molly mine? Have I?"

The words rang in Molly's ears. He had been coming to her! Her heart sang out and her arms went up and around his neck, giving him the answer he hoped for. He kissed her desperately and lovingly, going from her mouth to her eyes, to the curve of her neck, forgetting the day's growth of beard was scratching the soft skin of her face. Molly gloried in the hurt of his rough face against hers, and sought his mouth with her own trembling lips.

"Darling, I love you. I love you so." He murmured the

magic words that set her heart aflame. "I knew I loved you even before that perfect night when you gave me the most precious thing a woman has to give a man. But now that I almost lost you . . ."

The happiness in Molly's heart cried out . . . *he loves me! Can it really be true?* Her desperate heart wanted to believe it was true. The black eyes were staring adoringly into hers. He was gentle now, the relief plain on his face, and she put her palms up to his rough cheeks and he turned his lips into them.

"I love you, Adam. Through it all I loved you. That was why I was so desperate."

The black eyes that could be so hard and cold were now warm and glowing and misted over as he hid his face against her breast. She felt him tremble as if with a chill and she pressed his dark head against her. His trembling ceased and he raised his dark head, trailing his lips across her cheek to her mouth. He rubbed her lips gently with his until he got just the degree of opening he desired and then he kissed her, earnestly and hungrily.

"I've something else I want to tell you, my darling."

"What could you tell me that's more important than this?" She held up her lips for another kiss.

He laughed softly and kissed her again, running his hand under the bedclothes and down over her breasts to her flat, sunken, empty stomach that was growling in protest.

"I'm going to have to get some food into you." He gently caressed the empty spot. "But, first, I want no secrets between us, so I'm going to tell you something."

She looked at him searchingly, suddenly frightened

that what he had to tell her would snatch away her happiness.

"You remember the first day I came here and Herb told you about your father's will?" She nodded. "Herb gave each of us a letter from your father. You took yours to the bedroom to read and I opened mine in the living room. My letter was a second will. It was dated after the one Herb probated and it was the valid legal will." Molly's face reflected her astonishment. "In the final will your father left all his files and charts, his notes and any other material connected with his work, to me. He left the money to you with no strings attached. There was a letter attached to the will. In it he told me that if I found it impossible to abide by the conditions of the will Herb had read to us, or if either you or I found the other to be physically repulsive, I was to show the later will to Herb and have it probated. I thought about it, love, and I was tempted, but what Charlie counted on, happened. I had seen you! You came out of the bedroom and stood with so much pride in front of me and gave me your decision, I thought you were adorable and meant to have you for my own."

Molly eyed him disbelievingly. "You . . . didn't have to marry me to get the files?"

"No, pretty baby," he said with a laugh. "I didn't marry you to get the files. I married you because I wanted to. Because I didn't want you to get away from me before I had the chance to know you. To . . . find out if you could love me. I was pretty sure I would come to love you."

"You did?"

"Yes, I did." He kissed her.

"Remember the first time I tried to make love to you?"

The color that came up in her cheeks told him she did. "After I had time to cool off I was glad you turned me down. I knew when you gave yourself to me it would be because you loved me. I haven't had much love, Molly. Only from Dad, and now from you. The only true friend I have is Patrick, and now he is going to have to go on another expedition alone." He laughed joyously at the look on her face and hugged her close. "You're not going to get away from me, Molly mine. I'm staying with you or taking you with me from now on. Patrick can do the field work and I'll stay at home with my wife and kids and take care of the paper work."

Molly couldn't believe she heard correctly. "You'll not be leaving at the end of the year?"

"No," he said emphatically. He rubbed her stomach gently. "Besides, you'll be pregnant by then and I'll have to stay home and rub your stomach and feel my son grow."

He watched the color come up her cheeks and flood her face. His eyes danced with devilry. He loved making her blush. She was adorable and she was . . . his!

Molly's arms reached out to him and wound around his neck, inviting his possession of her.

"Molly?" His voice questioned when he raised his lips from her clinging ones.

Her eyes told him the answer and he stood up, fingers working at the buttons on his shirt. Her eyes never left him as he hastily shed his clothing and lifted the blankets to slip in beside her. Her soft, white, bare body against his said she wanted him.

The old Indian slipped in the back door. Keeping his eyes away from the bedroom, he stoked up the kitchen stove, put a big log on the already glowing coals of the fireplace, and silently went out again.

A week later Patrick came in the ski plane to take them to Anchorage to see Adam's father. A radiant Molly met him at the door. Her eyes sparkled with happiness. This was the girl he had expected to see the first time he came.

"Patrick, will you ever forgive me for the way I acted when you were here before?"

"I don't ever remember being here before, Mrs. Reneau." His blue eyes were merry with teasing. "You have a lovely wife, Mr. Reneau," he said to Adam. "May I kiss her?"

"You may not!" Adam firmly pulled Molly back against him, folded his arms around her, and planted a quick kiss beneath her ear. "Her kisses are spoken for— for the next forty years."

Later that day Molly and Adam walked hand in hand into the sitting room of his father's apartment. The old man was sitting in his same chair and watched them come toward him.

"Hello, Papa," Molly said and bent down to kiss his cheek.

"Hello, daughter, son." His eyes went to their interlaced fingers, then twinkled up to their eyes. "Sit down, sit down."

Adam pulled the big footstool up close to his father's chair as he always did for Molly, but today he sat down on it and pulled her down onto his lap.

"She loves me, Dad," Adam said with a kind of wonder in his voice.

"Well . . . ?"

"I love her," Adam said simply.

The old man laughed loudly. "So Charlie's plan worked, did it? I told him it would." He grinned broadly, his faded old eyes lighting up at the news he had sprung on them.

"You knew about the will?" Molly gasped.

"Sure did. Charlie and I talked about it."

A glance told Molly that Adam was as surprised as she was by this news.

"We—we came today to tell you," she stammered.

Robert Reneau settled back, enjoying the situation he had created. "Charlie came to see me before he made out the will. I've known Charlie Develon for thirty years. The doctors had given him about six months on the outside and he was worried about his girl. Of all the men he knew, son, he chose you to take care of his most precious possession. He wanted to get the two of you together and was planning to have you come and work with him when he returned from the expedition. He was sure you'd want her and love her once you met her." He paused to see what impact his words had made on them and smiled to see his son's arms tighten about his young wife. "He told me the plan and I thought it was a good one, but . . . I knew my son. Put the screws on him to force him to do something and he'll rebel, Charlie, I told him. So I persuaded him to make a second will giving my son a choice."

"Why, you old rascal!" Adam exclaimed. "I didn't know you even knew Charlie."

"How could you plan our lives like that? Why . . . we might not have even liked one another. Think of what the year would have been like for us if . . . you had been wrong!"

"But we weren't wrong. We were right." The old man interrupted Molly gleefully. "The plan worked."

"Yes, it sure did!" Molly said, and slipped her arms around her husband's neck.

More
Dorothy Garlock!

Please turn this page
for a preview of

*Train from
Marietta*

Available in March 2006.

Prologue

1933

THE DOOR OPENED SUDDENLY. Startled, Eddy reared up out of the chair, a glass of brandy in his hand. "Oh, it's you. Come in, Uncle William."

"Drinking alone?" The portly silver-haired man was dressed in gray, from his ten-dollar hat to the custom-made shoes on his feet. He surveyed the cluttered room. Little light penetrated the blinds that covered the large windows. Empty bottles littered the tabletops, and clothes were strewn over the backs of the chairs. The lingering smell of cigarettes and alcohol filled the air.

"Occasionally I drink alone, don't you?" Eddy took another swallow from his glass as he settled back into his seat. "What brings you out this time of night?"

William Jacobs closed the door, then carefully removed his hat and hung it on the rack. "I wanted to catch you when you didn't have a woman here."

Eddy set his glass down on the table by the chair. "I'm

not the womanizer you think I am," he said with indignation in his voice.

"No. I think you're just an easy mark for the little gold-digging flappers who hang out at your favorite speakeasy."

"You'd know a thing or two about flappers, wouldn't you?"

"You'd do well to remember, Edwin, which side of the bread your butter is on," William said menacingly, one thick finger pointed at his nephew.

"Why don't you remind me, dear Uncle," Eddy said, his voice dripping with sarcasm.

"Don't get smart with me, you little bastard!"

"Don't call me that!"

"You are one, you know."

"How could I forget when you remind me day in and day out?" Eddy glared at his uncle.

"Well, I know that my sister slept with every Tom, Dick, and Harry that came along. You could be nothing else."

"And don't talk about my mother like that either."

"I took care of her all her life. I'll talk about her any way I want to."

At this, the two men stared at one another in silence. They'd had this argument many times before; neither one was ever willing to back down.

"What's on your mind?" Eddy finally growled. "I'm sure something is or you'd be with your lady love."

"You know damn well what's on my mind and you'd better listen. If you know what's good for you, you'll forget about my lady love." William paused, then made his way through the clutter to where his nephew sat. "We're in deep trouble, and you're in it just as deep as I am. We've got to get some ready cash and soon. You're going to help me."

"I'll do what I can, short of robbing a bank." Eddy chuckled.

"What I've got in mind is easier than that and at no risk to you—"

"What do you mean, 'no risk to you'? Who do you want me to kill?"

"I wouldn't trust you to kill a grasshopper. You'd be sure to mess it up."

"Then what do you want me to do?"

For the next several minutes, Eddy listened with increasing shock as his uncle laid out his plan. He could scarcely believe what he was hearing! Finally, he shot to his feet. "I will not do it!"

"You will do it, or you'll be out of this fancy apartment on your ass and not get another dime from me. Look at the easy life you've had all these years. You owe me. Don't forget that I'm the one who pays for this apartment and the clothes on your back. I'm responsible for you being accepted by the Tylers to court their daughter, Susie. If you had half the sense you were born with, you'd get her pregnant and marry her. Then you'd have it made, even if she's not her father's favorite daughter. If we don't get one hundred thousand dollars soon, we could both land in prison."

Eddy looked at his uncle as if he had never seen him before. "I just can't do what you're asking. I like her."

"That's got nothing to do with it. If you do what I tell you, no one will get hurt. And you don't have to do it alone. Squirrelly's going with you."

"Squirrelly! You can't be serious."

"He's going. At least he's loyal and I can trust him."

"You can't trust me?" Eddy yelled.

"Keep your voice down, you fool. I've contacted a man in Texas who's put me in touch with someone who knows every stick and stone in the territory. He'll be a big help."

"You know that Squirrelly has about as many brains as a bedbug."

"He may not be very smart but he'll stay in line. I'll give him his orders."

Eddy looked down at the floor as he pushed a hand through his curly blond hair. "I haven't said I was going to do it. I've got to think about it."

His anger boiling over, William snatched the brandy glass from the table and hurled it against the wall behind Eddy. Broken glass and brandy flew in all directions.

"Here's something for you to think about, you ungrateful little whelp. Neither one of us will go to prison if we pay the money back. Which do you prefer? Who do you think will take the brunt of an investigation? A young whippersnapper like you or a respected businessman like me?"

"But—"

"No buts. It's time for you to pay me back for all I've done for you. Well? Yes or no?"

Eddy's shoulders slumped before he quietly said, "I'll do it."

"I thought you would."

Eddy hated the gloating look on his uncle's face. "Does your lady love know about this?"

"She knows."

William walked to the door, picked up his hat, and put it on. He took a cigar from his coat pocket, bit off the end, and spit it out on the oriental carpet.

"I'll be back tomorrow night to give you all the details. Get ready to leave by Sunday, Edwin."

William went out and slammed the door.

All was quiet in the room. Eddy stood up, walked over to the bureau, and pulled a bottle of brandy from the cupboard, pouring himself another drink. He carried it across the room and dropped back into his chair. As he took his first gulp, only one thing filled his mind.

How was he going to do this terrible thing?

chapter one

T.C. DIDN'T KNOW MUCH about style, but he knew the woman in the small depot was fashionably dressed. She was obviously from the city and as out of place as a rose in a cactus patch. She wore a small blue felt hat over light blond hair, which fell to her shoulders. Her princess coat came down over slim hips. The flared blue skirt that floated around her calves was edged with a blue satin ribbon. Her matching shoes, with slender heels, were planted firmly beside an expensive leather valise.

What a silly hat, T.C. thought, chuckling to himself. *It'd offer no shade at all. Within ten minutes, her face would be cooked in the West Texas sun.*

T.C. had glanced at her when he left the ticket counter and had wondered what she was doing in this rugged Texas town.

Worried about her trunk, Kate had gotten off the train to make sure it was in the baggage car. When the rail agent told her it had been left at the last stop and was being picked up by the train from Marietta, she had decided to wait and go on to California on the same train as her belongings. She wondered now at the wisdom of her decision. Shortly after she'd spoken with him, the agent had locked up and left. Now, all that remained on the platform with her were a lone cowboy and the button salesman who had been on the train ever since New Orleans.

The sun was setting in the western sky. Purple shadows were coming down from the hills. It would be dark soon. A slight chill had entered the air with the disappearance of the hot summer sun. The depot was far from town; all she could see of it was a handful of lights from the houses. The train from Marietta wasn't due for another hour. It would be pitch dark by then.

She was glad for the presence of the cowboy at the end of the platform. She'd first glanced at him when he'd left the ticket counter; her gaze had met his even though she'd known that she shouldn't make eye contact with strangers, particularly one as rough as the cowboy. Dusty boots and well-worn jeans made him look like he'd just come in off the range. He was wearing a battered hat that covered black hair. His mouth was set in a thin line as if he somehow disapproved of her. What was he doing here at this time of night? Regardless of his appearance, she didn't want to be alone with the other man.

The salesman, dressed in a stripped suit with a derby hat, paced back and forth near his sample case. She'd had the misfortune of taking the same route to California with him. When they'd first gotten on the train in New Orleans, he'd prattled on and on about buttons and snaps for hours. His twitchy, talkative nature had given her the creeps.

As the three stood waiting for the train, it seemed to her that they were the only people in all this vast and desolate land.

A door in the side of the depot opened on squeaky hinges. An old man pushed a trolley down to the end of the platform, leaving it so its bundles could be loaded into the baggage car when the train arrived. He then disappeared around the corner of the depot.

The button salesman coughed and took a step toward her. She turned to see the cowboy was looking in their direction. She pushed herself away from the rough board wall and quickly walked over to him.

"Is this train usually on time?"

"Sometimes," he said. "This isn't Grand Central Station, you know."

"Well, what do you know? I thought it was." She smiled up at him. But he didn't smile back.

What did she expect? He clearly couldn't take a joke. He'd probably just heard of Grand Central Station and had never been there.

"Thanks for that valuable information." She turned and walked back to take her place against the wall. At least the salesman had taken the hint and had moved back to his case. She looked at her watch but couldn't see the time in the dim light. She nudged the leather valise at her feet and thought that if her trunk never arrived, at least she had clean underwear and her cosmetics.

Then, in the distance, she heard the familiar sounds of a train approaching. Could the thing be earlier than the agent predicted or had an hour passed already? She looked at the cowboy and saw that he was peering down the track toward the east. Her eyes followed his, and soon she saw the billows of smoke rising up above the huge engine. The piercing whistle was loud enough to wake everybody for miles. The engineer was making a grand entrance into the station. Too bad there was only her, the cowboy, and the button salesman to appreciate the effort.

The train rolled slowly past her before finally coming to a stop. Two cars were brightly lit and filled with passengers, most of whom already appeared to be sleeping. Katherine picked up her valise, walked to the edge of the platform, and waited for the conductor to step down from the train. The older man smiled, took her elbow, and helped her up the steps into the car.

The cowboy was right behind her and edged past the conductor, who tipped his hat politely. Katherine turned to the right and entered the car. Halfway down she saw what she thought was an empty seat. Carrying her valise, she made her way along the aisle, but then realized a man sleeping in the seat. Frowning, she continued on until she finally found a vacant seat. She set the heavy valise down on the floor.

When she turned, the cowboy was still right behind her. With a grunt, she attempted to lift the heavy bag up and put it in the rack above the seat. Quick as a whistle, the cowboy snatched it out of her hand, and, as he slung it upward, the latch opened and her personal belongings spilled out over the seat and onto the floor. She looked down in horror to see a pair of her lace panties covering a pair of dusty cowboy boots.

"Sorry," he said.

Katherine was more embarrassed than she'd ever been

in her entire life. All she could think to say was, "I bet you are."

The cowboy pulled her valise from the rack and set it down in the seat beside her. He gathered a handful of lavender lace panties, silk slips, and lacy bras, stuffing all of them back into the valise. When he did, a jar of face cream fell onto his foot and opened. White cream ran down over the cowboy's boot. The smell of gardenias filled the air in the passenger car. All around the car, people were stretching their necks to look.

She thought the cowboy said something under his breath. It sounded like "Oh, hell!" but she wasn't sure.

Fearing that he would wipe the face cream off his boot with her lavender panties, she pulled a big handkerchief out of her pocket and handed it to him. He jerked it out of her hand with a disgusted look on his face and proceeded to wipe the cream off his boot. After glancing up and down the aisle to make sure he had picked up everything that had fallen from her bag, he tipped his hat toward Katherine and moved on to the front of the train in search of an empty seat of his own.

Fuming as the man walked away, Katherine sat down and moved over next to the window. He'd made her look stupid in front of everyone! She was certain that her face was beet red with embarrassment. *What a grouch,* she thought. It wasn't her fault he was so clumsy. Were all the men in the west clods like him?

A cough that came from the aisle caused her to turn. The button salesman stood with his hand stretched out toward her. There, clutched between his fingers, was one of her bras. She snatched it from his hand, pushed it into the pocket of her coat, and looked back out the window. The salesman chuckled before walking on.

Until now, the first part of the trip had been a pleasure. What more could possibly happen before she reached California?

Tate Castle, better known as T.C., moved on to the next car in the train in search of an empty seat. Finding one, he threw himself into it.

He never wanted to see that city woman again! All he was trying to do was help her lift that damned bag. How was he supposed to know that it was going to fly apart? *Did women actually wear those kinds of undergarments? Holding a handful of them was like holding a handful of air!*

Regardless, he was glad to be finally heading home. It seemed like forever had passed since he'd seen his ranch, his friends, and, most important, his daughter. He'd missed her something terrible and knew that she'd missed him too.

It was still a couple of hours to Muddy Creek where he would get off the train. He was bone tired. Tipping his hat down over his eyes, T.C. tried to sleep. The smell of flowers drifted up from his boot.

The train began to slow, the sound of the steel wheels screeching against the tracks waking Katherine. The train came to a stop at the next depot in a little town called Los Rios. A new group of passengers came on board. A very heavy-set woman, carrying bundles of clothing under her arms, came down the aisle and plunked herself in the seat beside Katherine. She looked over at her and grinned, showing snuff-stained teeth. Katherine smiled, then quickly turned away; it was obvious the woman had not bathed in quite a while.

"Hello, dearie, where are you goin'?"

Katherine acted as if she hadn't heard, and kept her face turned toward the window.

"I'm going to Saint Elena to see my brother and sister. I've not seen them in two years."

Katherine turned briefly and said, "How nice for you." The woman's odor was sickening.

"My brother's been sick," the woman continued, "and my sister lost her husband not long ago, no great loss as far as I can see. He wasn't worth diddly squat! Too lazy to come in out of the rain, you know?"

"Too bad."

The train lurched, and then rode smoothly down the track. The smelly woman kept talking, not seeming to care that her audience wasn't listening.

Katherine leaned her head against the window, her thoughts wandering.

A year ago, she had received her nursing degree, fulfilling a life-long dream. After working in a clinic in New York City, her uncle had made an offer that she couldn't refuse. He was a doctor in a large hospital in San Francisco and wanted for her to assist him. Practically jumping at the chance, Katherine had packed up her belongings and headed west. She was looking forward to seeing new things and meeting new people.

The leave-taking from her father had been painful. They had always been close and he had supported his daughter's dreams. She was sure there had been tears in his eyes when he told her good-bye on the platform.

In contrast, her stepmother, who had married her father when Katherine was very young, had merely waved good-bye and said that she wouldn't be surprised to see Katherine back at home within a matter of weeks.

Susie, her half-sister, had thought Katherine had lost her mind to even want to go out to an uncivilized place like California when there was so much to do right there in New York City. All that was out there were filthy miners and bawdy houses. Kate knew that Susie was glad to get her out of the way so she would have a better chance with Edwin, the handsome nephew of her father's partner, William Jacobs. Susie needn't have worried; while Edwin was a handsome man, Kate had never had any interest in him as a beau.

The woman's voice broke into her thoughts. "My nephew done fell down a well and drowned. Wasn't too bright, that boy."

Katherine's thoughts traveled back over the past year. Her stepmother, Lila, had become more distant from the family. She was so involved in all her social activities that she was seldom at home. And when she was, she harassed Katherine for her devotion to nursing and her lack of interest in finding a suitable husband: a man who could support her in style.

Susie was like her mother. She loved the social life. The only things that seemed to matter to her were the latest fashions, dinner parties, and who was seeing whom. Katherine was her father's daughter. Both of them enjoyed reading, talking business, and playing an occasional game of bridge. Since she had been a small child, they had been devoted to each other. While he also cared deeply for Susie, Katherine knew that she was his favorite.

She looked out into the lightening morning. The sun had begun to poke up over the hilltops. Telegraph poles whizzed by and occasionally the train passed a cluster of houses.

Katherine had hoped that the woman would take the hint, but she kept right on talking. She talked about her dog, her assorted aches and pains, and her lazy husband, who was mad that she was making the trip. Katherine wanted to jump up and move, but there was no place to move to. To top it all off, someone behind her had lit a cheap cigar, filling the cramped car with smoke. At least it helped mask the stink of the woman!

The conductor came through. "We will be stopping in a few minutes to take on water. Everyone, please stay on the train."

Katherine thought about how wonderful it would be to get a few breaths of fresh air. She hated the cramped feeling of the railway cars. When the train finally came to a stop, she excused herself and managed to squeeze out in front of the fat lady and into the aisle.

As she moved toward the front of the car, Katherine noticed that the button salesman had slouched down in his seat, his derby hat pulled down over his face. Light snores came from his open mouth. Katherine moved on past him. *I hope he sleeps all the way to San Francisco.*

The conductor had opened the door and was standing out on the platform. After checking the watch that hung from a chain on his vest, he moved into the next car. As soon as he walked away, Katherine quickly stepped down and moved to the side of the steps, out of the light that came from the car. Crushed rock sounded beneath her feet.

Oh, it was great to breathe the fresh air.

She looked out into the darkness and saw the long trough swing down from the water tank. Then came the rush of water pouring into the engine's tank.

Suddenly, something hard was jammed into her back and a hand grabbed hold of her shoulder. The sound of a revolver cocking startled her.

"Hello, Kate."